# Matilda's Last Waltz

# Matilda's Last Waltz

*Tamara McKinley*

St. Martin's Press
*New York*

www.stmartins.com

ISBN 0-312-26202-7

First published in Great Britain by
Judy Piatkus (Publishers) Ltd

First U.S. Edition: August 2000

10  9  8  7  6  5  4  3  2  1

# Dedication

I dedicate this book to my sons Brett and Wayne who finally understand why I love Australia. And to my daughter Nina, who searched for and found the hero inside herself – I'm so proud of you. Thanks to Marcus for his computer tuition, his drilling and guitar serenades, and to his sister Gemma for her support. My love to Ollie who has to put up with me when I'm writing, and last, but never least, thank you to my step-father, Eric Ivory, for his love, his humour and his ability to smell snakes. He is a true Tasmanian.

*'And his ghost may be heard as you pass by that billabong,*
*You'll come a-waltzing, Matilda with me'* –

Andrew Barton 'The Banjo' Paterson, 1917

# Prologue

Churinga. The sigh of the warm wind in the pepper trees seemed to whisper its name. Churinga. A place of magic, of sacred mystery, carved from the bush and scrub by her grandparents. It broke hearts and backs but until now Matilda had been willing to pay the price. For this was all she had known, all she had ever wanted.

Her throat constricted as she looked beyond the family graveyard and out into the wilderness. She must not cry, no matter how deep the pain, no matter how sharp the loss – for the memory of her strong, seemingly invincible mother forbade it. Yet in all her thirteen years, there had been nothing to compare to this sense of abandonment, this feeling that childhood was over and she was destined to follow a lonely trail in this great, beautiful, dreaming place that was home.

The horizon shimmered, diffusing the bright ochre of the earth with the impossible blue of the enormous sky, and all around her were the sounds to which she had been born. For this vast, seemingly empty land was alive with a voice of its own, and she took comfort from it.

The fretting of the sheep in the pens, the quarrelling of the galahs and sulphur-crested cockatoos, the distant cackle of the kookaburra and the soft jingle of harness, were as familiar as the rhythm of her pulse. Even now, in her darkest moment, Churinga's magic had not deserted her.

'You wanna say a few words, Merv?'

The shearer's voice broke the silence of the graveyard, jolting her back to the present and reality. She looked up at her father, willing him to speak, to show some kind of emotion.

1

'You do it, mate. Me and God ain't what you might call on speaking terms.'

Mervyn Thomas was a giant of a man, a stranger who'd returned five years ago from Gallipoli, scarred in mind and body from the things he'd seen – things he never spoke of except in the night when his dreams betrayed him, or when the drink loosened his tongue and his temper. Now he stood sombre in dusty black, leaning heavily on the makeshift walking stick he'd carved from a tree branch. His face was in shadow, the brim of his hat pulled low, but Matilda knew his eyes were bloodshot and that the trembling of his hands had nothing to do with remorse, merely the need for another drink.

'I'll do it,' she said softly into the awkward silence. Stepping out of the small circle of mourners, she clutched her tattered prayer book and approached the mound of earth that would soon cover the rough timber of her mother's coffin. There'd been little time to mourn. Death had come swiftly at the end and the heat made it impossible to wait for neighbours and friends who would have had to travel hundreds of miles to be here.

The sense of isolation grew as she felt her father's animosity. To give herself a moment to regain her courage, Matilda trawled the familiar faces of the drovers, shearers and jackaroos who worked Churinga.

The Aborigines were clustered outside the gunyahs they'd built near the creek, and watched curiously from a distance. Death to them was not something to mourn, merely a return to the dust from which they'd come.

Her gaze finally came to rest on the crooked headstones that marked the history of this tiny corner of New South Wales. She fingered the locket her mother had given her and, with courage restored, faced the mourners.

'Mum came to Churinga when she was just a few months old, wedged in a saddle-bag on my grandfather's horse. It was a long journey from the old country, but my grandparents were hungry for land and the freedom to work it.' Matilda saw the nods and smiles of agreement on the sunbaked faces around her. They knew the story – it echoed their own.

'Patrick O'Connor would have been proud of his Mary. She

loved this land as much as he did, and it's because of her that Churinga is what it is today.'

Mervyn Thomas shifted restlessly, his belligerent glare making her falter. 'Get on with it,' he growled.

She lifted her chin. Mum deserved a decent send-off, and Matilda was determined she would have it.

'When Dad went to war some people said Mum would never manage, but they didn't know how stubborn the O'Connors can be. That's why Churinga's one of the best properties around, and me and Dad intend to keep it that way.'

She looked at Mervyn for confirmation and received a resentful glower in return. It didn't surprise her. His pride had never recovered from returning from the Great War to find his wife independent and the property flourishing. He'd found consolation in the bottom of a glass soon after that, and she doubted the death of his wife would change him.

The pages of the prayer book were well thumbed and brittle. Matilda blinked away tears as she read the words Father Ryan would have said if there had been time to fetch him. Mum had worked so hard. Had buried her own parents and four children in this little cemetery before she was twenty-five. Now the earth could claim her, make her a part of the Dreaming. She was finally at rest.

Matilda closed the book in the ensuing silence and bent to gather a handful of soil. It trickled between her fingers and gently scattered on to the wooden box. 'Sleep well, Mum,' she whispered. 'I'll look after Churinga for you.'

Mervyn was feeling the heat and the effect of the whisky in his belly as the horse plodded towards Kurrajong. His shattered leg throbbed, and his boots felt too tight. This did not improve his temper. Mary had been put in the ground two weeks ago but he could still feel her presence, her disapproval, everywhere.

It had even manifested itself in Matilda, and despite his giving her a touch of his belt after that embarrassing performance at the funeral, still she eyed him with her mother's customary contempt. Two days of frosty silence had passed before he'd slammed out of Churinga and headed for Wallaby Flats and the pub. A man could drink in peace with his mates there. Could shoot the breeze and garner sympathy and free whisky as well as a tumble with the barmaid.

Not that she's much to look at, he conceded. In fact she was just a ripe old tart, but then he wasn't particularly fussy when the urge took him, and he didn't have to look at her while he did it.

He leaned precariously from the saddle to fasten the last of the four gates to his neighbour's property. The sun beat down, the whisky churned, and his own sour smell drifted up from his clothes. The horse shifted restlessly, jarring Mervyn's bad leg against the fence post, and with a yelp of pain, he almost lost his balance as well as his breakfast.

'Keep still, you mongrel,' he growled, jerking the reins. He leaned on the pommel and wiped his mouth on his sleeve as he waited for the pain to ease. His head was a little clearer now he'd thrown up, and after straightening his hat, he slapped Lady's flank and urged her forward. The homestead was visible on the horizon and he had business to discuss.

Kurrajong stood proudly on the crest of a low hill, sheltered from the sun by a stand of tea trees, its verandah cool and welcoming beneath the corrugated iron roof. It was a quiet oasis amongst the bustle and noise of a busy station. Horses cropped the lush grass in the home paddock which was watered by the bore hole Ethan had dug a couple of years back. Mervyn could hear the ring of the blacksmith's hammer coming from the forge. The shearing shed was still busy if the noise was anything to go by, and the sheep in the pens were kicking up a racket as they were herded and bunched by the dogs towards the ramps.

He took it all in as he rode up the long drive to the hitching post, and nothing he saw made him feel any better. Churinga's land might be good but the house was a dump compared to this place. God knows why Mary and Matilda thought so much of it, but then that was typical of the bloody O'Connors. They thought themselves better than anybody else because they had come from pioneer stock, which in these parts was considered almost royal.

Well, he thought grimly, we'll see about that. Women should know their place. I've had enough. They don't own me.

His belligerence stoked by alcohol, he slid from the ornate Spanish saddle. Grasping his crude walking stick, he made his erratic way up the steps to the front porch. The door opened as he was about to knock.

'G'day, Merv. We were expecting you.' Ethan Squires looked immaculate as usual, his moleskins gleaming white against the polish of his black riding boots, open-necked shirt crisp over broad shoulders and flat stomach. There was very little grey in his dark hair. The hand he offered Mervyn was brown and calloused but the nails were clean and the ring on his finger sparked fire in the morning sun.

Mervyn felt overweight and old by comparison, and yet there was only a few months' difference in their age. He was also aware he was in dire need of a bath and wished he'd taken up the offer before leaving the hotel.

But it was too late for regrets. To hide his discomfort he gave a bark of laughter and pumped Ethan's hand rather too jovially. 'How're ya goin', mate?'

'Busy as always, Merv. You know how it is.'

Mervyn waited for Ethan to sit down, then followed suit. Ethan's greeting had thrown him. He hadn't announced any intention of calling so why had the other man been expecting him?

The two men remained silent as the young Aboriginal housemaid served drinks. The breeze on the verandah was cooling Mervyn off and now he wasn't on the back of a horse his stomach was more settled. He stretched out his bad leg and rested his boot on the verandah railings. No point in worrying over Ethan's welcome, he always had talked in riddles. Probably thought it was clever.

The beer was cold and slid easily down his throat, but it didn't quite shake the bitterness he could taste at the thought of how lucky Ethan was. Not for him the carnage of Gallipoli but an officer's billet miles from the fighting. No shattered leg, no nightmares, no memory of mates without faces and limbs, no screams of agony to haunt him day and night.

But then Ethan Squires had always led a charmed life. Born and raised on Kurrajong, he'd married Abigail Harmer, who was not only the best-looking widow around but also one of the richest. She'd brought her son Andrew with her and given

5

Ethan three more before she died in that riding accident. Three living, healthy sons. Mary could only manage one scrawny girl – she'd lost the others.

Mervyn had once dreamed of having a woman like Abigail for himself, but being only a station manager was not considered good enough. Money always went to money, and when Patrick O'Connor had come to him with his extraordinary offer, he'd jumped at the chance. How was he to know Mary was land rich but cash poor – and that Patrick's promises had been empty?

'Sorry about Mary.'

Mervyn was startled from his dark thoughts. It was as if Ethan could read his mind.

'Still, I reckon she suffered enough. Not good to have so much pain.' Ethan was staring off into the distance, his cheroot clenched between even, white teeth.

Mervyn grunted. Mary had taken a long time to die, but had never once complained or let that steely determination slip. He supposed he should have admired her but somehow her strength had merely weakened him. Her courage shattering his own feeble attempt to blot out the horrors of war and the pain in his leg. He'd felt cheated by the bargain he and Patrick had struck, trapped in a loveless marriage which denied him the respect he craved. No wonder he spent most of the time in Wallaby Flats.

'How's Matilda taking it, Mervyn?'

Ethan's bright blue gaze rested on him for a moment then slid away, but Mervyn wondered if he'd caught a glimpse of disdain in that fleeting look or whether it was just his imagination. 'She'll be right. Like her ma, that one.'

Ethan must have heard the acid note in his reply for he turned and looked at Mervyn more deliberately. 'I don't reckon you came all this way to talk about Mary and Matilda.'

That was typical of him. Never wasted time on trivialities when he could outmanoeuvre another man. Mervyn would have preferred to sit on the verandah for an hour or two, drinking beer as he watched the work go on around him and wait for his moment before broaching the reason for his visit. He drained his glass and dropped his foot from the railing. Might as well get it over and done with now Ethan had taken charge.

6

'Things are a bit crook, mate. I don't feel the same about Churinga since I got back and I reckon, now Mary's gone, it's time to shoot through.'

Ethan chewed his cheroot, gaze drifting with the smoke. When he finally spoke, his tone was thoughtful. 'The land's all you know, Mervyn. You're too old a dog to learn new tricks and Churinga's a nice little station after all the work Mary put in.'

There it was again. Praise for Mary. Didn't his years of labour count for anything? Mervyn clenched his fists and dug them into his lap. He needed another beer but his glass was empty and Ethan wasn't offering more.

'Not compared to Kurrajong, it isn't. We need a new bore dug, the roof's falling in, termites are making a meal of the bunkhouse and the drought's killed off most of the lambs. The wool cheque won't barely cover the bills.'

Ethan stubbed out his cheroot, lifted his glass and drained it. 'So what is it you want from me, Mervyn?'

Impatience welled in him. Ethan knew perfectly well what he wanted. Did he have to rub salt into the wound and make Mervyn grovel? 'I want you to buy Churinga.' His tone was deliberately flat. No point in letting the other man know how desperate he was.

'Ah.' Ethan smiled. It was a smirk of satisfaction, and knowing how Ethan had always looked down on him, Mervyn hated him for it.

'Well?'

'I'd have to think about it, of course. But perhaps we could come to an arrangement . . .'

Mervyn sat forward, eager to wind up negotiations. 'You've always liked the land around Churinga, and with your property bordering mine, it would make you the biggest station in New South Wales.'

'It would indeed.' Ethan raised one eyebrow, blue gaze steady beneath dark brows. 'But haven't you forgotten one tiny detail?'

Mervyn swallowed. 'What detail?' he asked nervously, avoiding Ethan's penetrating stare as he moistened his lips.

'Matilda of course. Surely you hadn't forgotten your daughter's passion for Churinga?'

Relief drenched him and hastily he gathered his wits. It was all right, Ethan didn't know about the will after all. 'Matilda's too young to meddle in men's business. She'll do as I say.'

Ethan stood and leaned against the ornamental railings. The sun was at his back, his expression inscrutable. 'You're right, Mervyn. She is young, but she has a feel for the land that's as natural to her as breathing. I've seen her work, watched her ride as fast and as well as any jackaroo when she follows the mob at round-up. To lose that land would kill her spirit.'

Mervyn's patience snapped. He rose from his chair and towered over Ethan. 'Look, mate, I've got a property you've been eyeing for years. I've also got debts. Whether Matilda loves the land is neither here nor there. I'm selling, and if you ain't buying there's others who'd be only too pleased to take it off my hands.'

'How exactly do you plan to sell the land when it doesn't belong to you, Mervyn?'

The wind of Mervyn's temper blew itself out. He knew! The bastard had known all the time. 'No one need find out,' he croaked. 'We could do the deal now and I'll be gone. I ain't gonna tell no one.'

'But I'll know, Mervyn.' Ethan's tone was arctic, his pause just long enough to make Mervyn itch to hit him. 'Mary came to me several months ago, just after the doctor told her she didn't have much time. She was worried you might try and sell Churinga and leave Matilda with nothing. I advised her on how best to protect the girl's inheritance. She left that land in trust for Matilda. The bank has all the papers until she reaches twenty-five. So you see, Mervyn, there's no way you can sell it to pay off your gambling debts.'

Mervyn's gut rolled. He'd heard the rumours and hadn't wanted to believe them – until now.

'The law says a wife's property belongs to her husband. Patrick promised it to me when I married her, and it's my right to sell it now. And anyway,' he blustered, 'what was my missus doin' calling on you for advice?'

'I was merely doing the neighbourly thing by lending her the services of my solicitor.' Ethan's face was stony as he picked up Mervyn's hat and held it out to him. 'I might want Churinga but not enough to break my word to someone I respected. And I think you'll find that goes for most of the other squatters around here. G'day Mervyn.'

Ethan dug his hands into his pockets and leaned against the white verandah post as he watched Mervyn limp down the steps to his horse. The man's tug on the rein was vicious as he led it across the hard-baked dirt of the front approach to the cookhouse, and Ethan wondered if that temper had ever been loosed on Mary – or, God forbid, Matilda.

He glanced at the shearing shed before going back into the house. The season was almost over and the wool cheque would be welcome. Lack of rain meant expensive, bought-in feed, and if the sky was anything to go by, the drought would be with them for some time yet.

'What did Merv Thomas want?'

Ethan eyed his twenty-year-old step-son and gave a humourless smile. 'What do you think?'

Andrew's boots rang on the polished floor as they went into the study. 'It's Matilda I feel sorry for. Fancy having to live with that mongrel.'

Andrew flopped into a leather chair and slung one leg over the arm. Ethan eyed him fondly. He might almost be twenty-one, but his strong, wiry figure and dark mop of auburn hair made him look younger. Although the boy had turned his back on the land, Ethan was as proud of him as if he'd been his own. Andrew's English education had been worth every penny. Now he was doing well at university and would afterwards take up a partnership in a prestigious law firm in Melbourne when he qualified.

'I don't suppose there's much we can do, is there, Dad?'

'Not our business, son.'

Andrew's blue eyes were thoughtful. 'You didn't say that when Mary Thomas showed up here.'

Ethan swivelled his chair to face the window. Mervyn was heading down the track towards the first gate. It would take at least another day and night for him to reach Churinga. 'That was different,' he muttered.

Silence filled the room, broken only by the ticking of the grandfather clock Abigail had brought with her from Melbourne. Ethan's mind drifted as he stared out over his land. Yes, Mary had been different. Tough, indomitable little woman that she was, she'd had no armour against the terrible thing that had slowly eaten away at her insides. He could see her so clearly, it was as if she stood before him again.

Unlike Abigail's cool, fair beauty and striking height, Mary was small and angular with an abundance of red hair which she squashed beneath a disreputable felt hat. Freckles dusted her nose, and wide blue eyes and dark lashes stared back at him as she wrestled to still the black gelding dancing beneath her. She'd been furious, that first time they'd faced one another after her return to Churinga. The fences were down and her mob had got mixed in with his.

He smiled as he remembered the Irish temper of her. The way her eyes flashed and she tossed her head as she yelled into his face. It had taken the best part of a week to sort the mobs out and repair the fences, and by that time they had called an uneasy truce that hadn't quite become a friendship.

'What's so funny, Dad?'

Andrew's voice dispelled the memories and Ethan dragged himself back to the present. 'I don't think we need worry too much about Matilda. If she's anything like her mother, then it's Merv we should feel sorry for.'

'You liked Mary, didn't you? How come you never . . .?'

'She was another man's wife,' he snapped.

Andrew whistled. 'Strewth! I did touch a nerve, didn't I?'

Ethan sighed as he remembered the time he'd had his chance and lost it. 'If things had been different, then who's to say what might have been? If Mervyn hadn't come back so crippled from Gallipoli then . . .'

He let the unfinished sentence hang between them as the sights and sounds of war intruded into his mind. They still gave him nightmares, even after six years, but he was one of the lucky ones. Mervyn had finally been released from hospital almost two years after the war was over but was a different man from the one who'd eagerly caught the train in 1916. Gone was the lazy smile and careless charm and in their place was a shambling wreck who, after a long convalescence, found relief only in a bottle.

It was a poor substitute so far as his wife was concerned, Ethan thought. And I'm to blame, lord help me. He pulled his

10

thoughts together. At least all the time Merv was bed-ridden she could keep an eye on her husband's drinking. But once he was up and back on a horse, he would disappear for weeks on end, leaving Mary to cope with the running of the station. She'd been tougher than he'd thought, and although his plans had come to nothing, Ethan couldn't help but respect her strength.

'I admired her, yes. She did the best she could in a tough situation. Although she rarely asked for help, I tried to ease things the best I could for her.' He lit a cheroot and opened up the wool accounts book. There was work to be done and half the day had already been wasted.

Andrew unhooked his leg from the arm of the chair and sat forward. 'If Merv runs up many more debts, Matilda won't have an inheritance. We could always make her an offer in a couple of years' time and get the land cheap.'

Ethan smiled around his cigar. 'I plan on getting it free, son. No point in paying for something when you don't have to.'

Andrew cocked his head, a smile tugging at the corners of his mouth. 'How? Matilda's trust is hard won. She's not going to just give it away.'

Ethan tapped the side of his nose. 'I've got plans, son. But patience is called for, and I don't want you shooting your mouth off.'

Andrew was about to speak when his father interrupted. 'You leave it to me and I guarantee Churinga will be ours within the next five years.'

Matilda was restless. The silence in the house was heavy and she knew her father would soon return. He never disappeared for more than a couple of weeks at a time, and he'd been gone that long already.

The heat was intense, even inside, and the red dust she'd swept from the floor was beginning to settle again. Her ankle-length cotton dress clung to her as sweat rolled down her back. She unfastened the sacking apron and folded it over the back of a chair. The aroma of rabbit stew came from the oven and several flies buzzed around the ceiling. The fly papers she'd stuck to the kerosene lamp were black with bodies, despite the shutters and screen doors Mum had fixed a couple of years ago.

Dragging her hair from her sweaty face, she pinned it in an unruly coil on the top of her head. She hated her hair. There was too much of it and it wouldn't be tamed. And to add insult to injury, it was a pale imitation of her mother's Irish auburn.

Matilda pushed her way through the screen door and stood on the verandah. The heat was a furnace blast, bouncing off the impacted earth of the front yard fire break and shimmering on the horizon. The pepper trees in the home paddock drooped in it and the weeping willows by the creek looked exhausted, their fronds dipping uselessly towards the runnel of green sludge that still remained. 'Rain,' she muttered. 'We must have rain.'

The three steps leading down to the hitching post and front yard needed mending and she made a mental note to get it done. The house itself could have done with a bit of paint, and Dad's repair to the roof was already coming apart. But if she stood in the centre of the yard and half closed her eyes, she could see how Churinga would look if they had the money to do the repairs.

The lines of the house weren't grand, but the single-storey Queenslander was sturdily built on brick pilings, and sheltered on the south side by young pepper trees. The roof swooped down over the verandah which ran around three sides of the house and was finished off with ornate iron lattice work. A rugged stone chimney stood tall on the north wall, and the shutters and screens had been painted green.

Underground springs kept the home pastures green. Close by several horses cropped contentedly, seemingly undisturbed by the clouds of flies swarming around their heads. The shearing shed and wool barn were quiet now the season was over, the wool on its way to market. The mob would be kept in the pastures nearest to water until the rains, but if the drought lasted much longer they would lose even more.

As Matilda walked across the yard she whistled and from under the house came an answering yelp. A shaggy dark head appeared, followed by a wriggling body and wagging tail. 'Come on, Blue. Here, boy.'

She mussed his head and pulled his ragged ears. The

Queensland Blue was almost seven and the best sheep herder in the business. Her father refused to let him in the house. He was a working dog like all the others, but so far as Matilda was concerned, she couldn't have had a better friend.

Blue trotted beside her as she passed the chicken runs and stock pens. The wood pile was stacked behind the storage shed and the clear, bell-like ring of an axe told her one of the black jackaroos was working hard to make it bigger.

'Hello, luv. Hot, ain't it?' Peg Riley mopped her scarlet face and grinned. 'What I wouldn't do for a long cold dip in the creek.'

Matilda laughed. 'You're welcome, Peg. But there's not much water in it, and what there is is green. Why don't you drive up to the water hole under the mountain? The water's cold up there.'

The Sundowner shook her head. 'Reckon I'll give it a miss. Me and Bert gotta get to Windulla by tomorrow, and if he hangs about for too long, he'll lose his wages on the two-up game goin' on at the back of the bunkhouse.'

Bert Riley worked hard and travelled in his wagon all over central Australia, but when it came to gambling he was a loser. Matilda felt sorry for Peg. Year after year she came to Churinga to work in the cook house whilst Bert bent his back shearing. Yet only a fraction of their earnings went with them to the next job.

'Don't you get tired of moving around, Peg? I can't imagine ever leaving Churinga.'

Peggy folded her arms beneath her pendulous bosom and looked thoughtful for a moment. 'It can be hard leaving a place, but you soon forget and look forward to the next one. Course, if me and Bert could have had kids it would be different, but we can't so I suppose we'll just keep going until one of us drops dead.'

Laughter rippled through her ample body, making it dance beneath the cotton dress. She must have noticed Matilda's concerned expression, for she reached out and swamped her in an affectionate hug. 'Don't mind me, luv. You take care of yourself and we'll see you next year.' She backed away, then turned to the horse and wagon and mounted up. Grasping the reins, she let out a mighty yell.

'Bert Riley, I'm leavin', and if you ain't here in one second flat, I'm going without yer.'

Snapping the whip between the horse's ears, she headed for the first gate.

Bert came shambling out from behind the bunkhouse with the peculiar gait synonymous with all shearers and hurried after her. 'See yous next year,' he yelled over his shoulder as he climbed on to the wagon.

Churinga seemed deserted suddenly. As Matilda watched the wagon disappear in a cloud of dust, she stroked Blue's ears and received a lick of comfort in return. After checking the wool shed and shutting down the ancient generator, she turned her attention to the cook house, which Peg had left spotless, then the bunkhouse. The termite damage was worse, but there wasn't much she could do about it, so after a quick sweep round and a minor repair to one of the beds, she closed the door and stepped back into the heat.

The Aboriginal men were lounging around outside their gunyahs as usual, swatting flies, chattering listlessly amongst themselves as their women stirred something in the black pot over the fire. They were of the Bitjarra tribe and as much a part of Churinga as she was – but she wished they'd earn their bread and tobacco instead of sitting around or going walk-about.

She eyed Gabriel, their leader. A semi-literate, wily old man who'd been brought up by the missionaries, he sat cross-legged by the fire, whittling a piece of wood.

'G'day, missus,' he said solemnly.

'Gabriel, there's work needs doing. I told you to see to those fences in the south paddock.'

'Later, missus, eh? Got to have tucker first.' He grinned, showing five yellow teeth, of which he was very proud.

Matilda eyed him for a moment and knew it was pointless to argue. He would simply ignore her and do the job in his own good time. She walked back to the house and climbed the steps to the verandah. The sun was high, the heat intense. She would rest for a couple of hours, then check the accounts. She'd let things slide during Mum's illness.

Matilda hauled the great copper boiler off the range and poured water into the wash tub. The steam rose in the torpid

14

heat of the kitchen, and sweat ran into her eyes as she struggled with the copper's weight, yet she barely noticed. Her mind was on the accounts, the figures that wouldn't add up no matter how many times she tried. She'd had little sleep the night before, and after a morning spent in the saddle overseeing Gabriel's repair to the fences was bone weary.

The account books lay open on the table behind her. She'd hoped morning would bring a solution – but all she'd got for her troubles was a headache and the knowledge the wool cheque wouldn't be large enough to pay off their debts and see them through to next season.

Her anger rose as she prodded Mervyn's moleskins down into the water with a stick. 'I should have kept an eye on his spending like Mum told me,' she muttered. 'Should have hidden the money properly.'

His moleskins floated in ghostly swirls as she jabbed them, eyes misted over with the injustice of it all. She and Mum had managed all right, even made a small profit during the war years, but Dad's coming back had spoiled everything. Grasping the heavy working clothes, she began to scrub them with an energy that released her temper and frustration.

She remembered his homecoming as if it were yesterday. She supposed she should have felt sorry for him, but how could she when he'd done nothing to earn either her respect or pity? There had been few letters during his years away, and only a brief note from the hospital describing his injuries. He'd been brought home in a wagon almost two years later, and she and her mother had not really known what to expect. She'd remembered him vaguely as a big man who smelled of lanolin and tobacco, whose bristles scratched her face when he'd kissed her goodbye. But she'd been only five years old then, and more interested in the brass band that played so loudly on the platform than in the men in dull brown who boarded the train. She hadn't understood about war, and what it could mean to her and Mum.

Matilda's hands stilled as she thought of those two years he'd been bed-ridden. Remembered her mother's worn face as she fetched and carried and got nothing but abuse and a sharp slap if his bandages were too tight or he wanted a drink. His home-coming had changed the mood of Churinga. From

15

magic to misery. From light to dark. It had been almost a relief to see him climb on to his horse and head for Wallaby Flats, and even her mother had seemed less weary in the days that followed.

But of course he came back, and the pattern of their lives was changed forever.

Matilda leaned on the wash tub and stared out of the window at the deserted yard and sheep pens. The three drovers were herding the mob towards Wilga, where there was still water and grass. Gabriel and the others were nowhere to be seen, and she suspected they'd gone walkabout now the shearing was over. It was peaceful, despite the parakeets squabbling over the insects in the red gums and the constant sawing of the crickets in the dry grass. She wished it would stay that way. Yet, as the days had passed with still no sign of Mervyn, she knew it couldn't last.

With the washing finished, she hauled the basket around to the back of the house and pegged it out. It was cooler out here in the shadows of the trees, and she had a clear view over the home paddock and the graveyard. The white picket fence that surrounded it needed painting, and the kangaroo paw and wild ivy had taken over several of the headstones. Purple bougainvillaea entwined itself around a tree trunk, alive with the hum of bees and the flutter of glorious butterflies. A bell bird chimed somewhere in the distance and a goanna stared back at her from a fallen log where he'd been sun-baking. Then, with a scrabble of his lethal claws, he disappeared into the dappled undergrowth.

Matilda sank on to the top step of the verandah, elbows on knees, chin cupped in her hand. Her eyelids drooped as the hypnotic scent of hot earth and dry grass lulled her to sleep.

Despite the heat, Mervyn felt chilled. The fury of his humiliation at the hands of Ethan Squires, and the duplicity of his own wife, no longer burned in his gut but had settled within him, cold and malignant, as he rode towards Churinga.

The night had been spent in a bedroll under the stars, his saddle for a pillow, a meagre fire his only warmth in the freezing darkness of the outback. He'd lain there, staring at the Southern Cross and the great sweep of the Milky Way which touched the earth with lunar light, frosting the red landscape, enhancing the grey of the giant ghost gums – and seen no beauty in any of it. This was not how he'd envisioned his future during those years in the trenches. Not the way heroes should be treated. He was damned if he was going to let a slip of a kid steal what Patrick had promised would be his.

He'd risen at first light, boiled the billy and eaten the last of the mutton and damper bread the cook at Kurrajong had given him. Now it was late afternoon, the sun blinding him as it sank towards the distant mountain that had given Churinga its name.

He hawked phlegm and spat on to the corrugated earth. The Abos called it the charmed place, the protective amulet of stone which had dreamtime power – a Tjuringa. Well, he thought sourly, it held no charm for him, not any more. And the sooner he was rid of it, the better.

His spurs dug into the mare's sides as the first of the barred gates came into view. It was time to assert his rights.

The homestead was visible as he closed the last gate behind him. A wisp of smoke drifted from the chimney and deep shadows bled across the yard as the sun dipped behind the trees. It looked deserted. No ring of an axe, no fussing of sheep or dogs, no black faces peeking from the gunyahs. The shearing must be over, the Sundowners and shearers gone on to the next station.

He breathed a sigh of relief. Matilda must have had enough money hidden away to pay them. He wondered where her new hiding place could be, he'd thought he'd known them all, but after tonight it wouldn't matter. It was time she learned her place and stopped meddling in things which didn't damn well concern her. He would make her tell him. Make her finally accept that he was in charge – and then find a way to take Churinga away from her.

He unsaddled the horse and led it into the home paddock. Hoisting the saddle-bags over his shoulder, he stomped up the steps to the verandah and crashed through the screen door. Rabbit stew simmered on the range, its pungent aroma filling the little house, making his belly grumble.

The silence was oppressive. The shadows almost impenetrable where the light of the kerosene lamp couldn't reach.

17

'Where are you, girl? Get out here and help with these bags.'

An almost imperceptible shifting of shadows caught his eye. There she was. Standing by the door to her room – staring at him. Her blue eyes glistened in the meagre light and the halo of hair was burnished in the dying rays of the afternoon sun that trickled through the shutters. It was as if she was made of stone – mute and all-seeing in her condemnation of him.

A ripple of apprehension ran through him. For a moment there, he'd thought it was Mary come to haunt him. But as the girl came into the light, he realised it was only his imagination. 'What you creeping about for?' His voice was loud in the silence, harsher than he'd intended as he strove to recover from his fright.

Matilda took the saddle-bags in silence and dragged them across the kitchen floor. She unpacked the calico sack of flour and the parcel of sugar and put them in the larder. The candles and matches were stacked above the range and the can of tea placed next to the smoke-stained billy.

Mervyn slapped his slouch hat against his thigh before throwing it in the vague direction of the hooks by the door. He drew the chair from the table, deliberately scraping it across the floor because he could see she'd recently scrubbed it.

There was no reaction, and as he watched her move around the little kitchen, he was once again reminded of her mother. Mary had been a good-looking woman before the illness took her. A bit skinny for his liking, but what she lacked in height and breadth, she made up for in spirit. If she hadn't been so damned arrogant, she'd have made a good wife – and Matilda had all the makings of just such a woman. Perhaps not so forceful, but just as self-assured. Damned O'Connors, he thought. Arrogance was in their blood.

'Stop messing with that,' he rasped. 'I want my dinner.'

He felt a squirm of pleasure as she fumbled and almost dropped the precious bag of salt she'd been so carefully tucking into an old tea tin. He slammed a fist on the table for added effect, then laughed as she scurried to ladle the stew into a chipped bowl and spilled some of it on the floor.

'Now you'll have to clean it again, won't you?' he said nastily.

Matilda brought the bowl of stew to the table and placed it

in front of him. Her chin was high and there was colour in her cheeks, but he noticed her self-possession hadn't given her strength enough to look him in the eye.

Mervyn grasped her skinny wrist as he saw Bluey skulk across the kitchen floor and lap at the spilled dinner. 'What's that bloody animal doing in here? I told you not to let it into the house.'

Matilda looked at him finally. She couldn't quite hide the fear in her eyes. 'He must have followed you in. He wasn't here before.' Her voice was calm, but there was an underlying tremor that betrayed that calm for the sham it really was.

Mervyn kept hold of her as he kicked out, missing the dog by inches as it scurried away. 'Good thing you ain't a dog, Matilda. Or you'd have a boot up yer arse as well,' he murmured, releasing her. He was tired of the game, and the smell of the stew was giving his hunger an edge.

He dug a spoon into the mixture and ladled it into his mouth. Fresh damper bread mopped up the gravy. He'd been eating for a while when he noticed she had not joined him at the table.

'I'm not hungry,' she said quietly. 'I ate earlier.'

Mervyn mopped up the last of the gravy, then leaned back in his chair and jingled the coins in his pocket as he studied his daughter. Her figure was slender but had lost the coltish awkwardness of childhood, and where once there had been a soft roundness to the chin and cheeks, there was now a firmness in the adult planes. The sun had darkened her skin, bringing out the freckles and the blue of her eyes, and her long, wild hair had been partially tamed and fastened on top of her head. He noticed how strands of it had escaped and were coiled around her face, caressing her neck.

He was jolted by what he saw. This was no weak, malleable child he could bully into submission but a woman. A woman with the same implacable presence as her mother. He would have to change tactics and fast. If she found herself a husband then Churinga would be lost to him forever.

'Exactly how old are you?' he asked finally.

Matilda's gaze was direct and challenging. 'I'm fourteen today.'

Mervyn let his gaze drift over her. 'Almost a woman,' he murmured appreciatively.

'I grew up a long time ago,' she said acidly as she approached the table. 'The chooks need feeding and I haven't seen to the dogs yet. If you're finished, I'll clear away.'

He caught her hand as she reached for his bowl. 'Why don't you and me have a drink to celebrate your birthday? It's about time we got to know each other better. 'Specially now yer ma ain't here.'

Matilda pulled away and hurried to the door. 'I've work to do.'

The screen door slammed behind her and he listened to her light tread across the verandah and down the steps. Deep in thought as he reached for the whisky bottle.

Matilda's pulse raced as she crossed the yard with the swill bucket. There was a change in Dad that scared her far more than his temper, and yet she couldn't put that change into words. It was something in his eyes and in his manner. Nothing tangible but there all the same, and she had the feeling this new threat was far more dangerous than anything he could do with his fists.

She reached the dog pens and fumbled with the catch on the gate, but for once she didn't stop to pet the puppies before feeding them. The bark and bustle of the pens filled the void of silence that surrounded Churinga, but it couldn't penetrate the deep unease that consumed her.

She moved automatically as she emptied the bucket into the low troughs, then raked out the dog run. The sun had set behind Tjuringa mountain, now there was only an orange glow in the sky. Night came swiftly out here and she usually welcomed it for the stillness it brought. Yet tonight she dreaded it. For she couldn't shake off the feeling that things had changed. And not for the better.

The chickens squabbled as she scattered their feed, and checked the wire netting for breaks. Nothing a dingo loved more than a nice fat chook. They'd been losing quite a few lately. Snakes were another problem, but there wasn't much she could do about them.

Turning reluctantly towards the house, she gripped the bucket and tried to control the shiver of apprehension that made her heart thud. Dad was watching her from the verandah. She could see the glow of his cigarette.

'What you doin' out there? Time you was indoors.'

Matilda heard the slurring of his words and knew he'd been drinking. 'I hope you've had enough to make you pass out soon,' she muttered with feeling. Her footsteps faltered as her words struck a chill in her. They were an echo of her mother's.

Mervyn was sprawled in the rocking chair, legs stretched along the verandah, whisky bottle cradled to his chest. It was almost empty. As Matilda approached the front door, he slammed his booted foot against the frame, barring her way. 'Have a drink with me.'

Her pulse raced and her throat closed. 'No thanks, Dad,' she managed at last.

'It wasn't an invitation,' he growled. 'You'll bloody do as I say for once.' The boot thudded on the floor and his arm encircled her waist.

Matilda lost her balance and fell into his lap. She squirmed and wriggled, kicking her heels against the great trunks of his legs in an effort to escape. But his grip never lessened.

'Sit still,' he yelled. 'You'll spill the bloody grog.'

Matilda stopped fighting and went slack. She would wait for the right moment, then hopefully dodge the fist that would surely follow when she did get free.

'That's more like it. Now, have a drink.'

Matilda gagged on the stream of reeking, bitter alcohol he forced between her lips. She couldn't breathe, didn't dare spit it out. Finally she managed to push the bottle away. 'Please, Dad don't make me. I don't like it.'

His eyes were wide in mock surprise. 'But it's yer birthday, Matilda. You gotta have a present on yer birthday.' He sniggered, and his bristles rubbed her cheek as he nuzzled her ear.

His breath was rancid, and the stench of his dirty clothes made her heave. The air caught in her lungs and his arm was a vice around her waist as her stomach rebelled. She swallowed, then again. But her head was filling with thunderclouds and her stomach churned. She clawed his arm, desperate to be free. 'Let me go. I'm gonna . . .'

With one heave the regurgitated whisky splattered over them both. Mervyn gave a yelp of disgust and threw her from his knee, the bottle shattering on the wooden floor. Matilda fell hard on the broken glass but barely noticed the pain. The world was spinning out of control, and there seemed no end to the hot, gushing flow from her mouth.

'Now look what you done! Stupid bitch. You're all the bloody same.'

His boot connected with her hip and she crawled away, blindly searching for the door and the sanctuary of the house.

'Yer just like yer ma,' he yelled as he swayed over her. 'But then you bloody O'Connors always thought you were too good for the likes of me.' He kicked out again, sending her crashing into the wall. 'Time you learned some respect.'

Matilda scrabbled for the door, her eyes never leaving him as he returned to his chair, a fresh bottle in his hand.

'Bugger off,' he growled. 'You ain't no use to me. Just as yer ma wasn't.'

She didn't need telling twice. Stumbling to her feet, she edged towards the door.

Mervyn took a long pull from the bottle. He wiped his mouth on his sleeve and eyed her belligerently. Then he sniggered. 'Not so lah-de-dah now, are ya?'

Matilda slipped into the house. With the door closed behind her, she leaned against it for a moment and took deep, shuddering breaths. The pain in her hip was nothing compared to the pain in her leg, and on closer inspection she understood why. A jagged piece of glass was deeply embedded in her thigh.

Hobbling to the pantry, she pulled down the medicine box and swiftly dealt with the wound. The sting of antiseptic made her bite her lip, but once the glass was out and a clean bandage drew the lips of the ragged cut together, it didn't seem so bad.

Alert for the sound of Mervyn leaving his chair, she hastily stripped off the filthy dress and left it to soak in a bucket while she washed. There was nothing but the creak of the rockers on the bare boards and his unintelligible ramblings.

Matilda limped across the kitchen to the tiny room where she slept. With the door firmly jammed by a chair, she fell exhausted on to the bed where she lay wide-eyed and vigilant. Night sounds came to her through the shuttered window, and the outback smell of eucalyptus and wattle, dry grass and cooling earth, drifted between the gaps of the clapboard walls.

She fought to stay awake, but it had been a long, traumatic day and her eyelids drooped. Her last thought before sleep was of her mother.

The sound was alien and woke her instantly.

The door handle was turning. Rattling against the wood. Matilda edged up the bed, the thin sheet drawn to her chin as she watched the chair being rocked.

She cried out as a great weight was thrown against the door, splintering the panels, rasping the chair across the floor. The screech of rusty hinges was loud as the broken door slammed back against the wall.

Mervyn's towering bulk filled the frame, the light of a candle casting deep shadows around his staring eyes.

Matilda shuffled to the furthest corner of the bed. Her back was pressed to the wall, knees drawn to her chest. Perhaps if she was small enough, she could become invisible.

Mervyn stepped into the room, the candle held high as he looked down at her.

'Don't.' She put out a hand as if to ward him off. 'Please, Dad. Don't hit me.'

'But I've come to give you your present, Matilda.' He walked unsteadily towards her, fumbling with his belt.

She thought of the last time he'd beaten her, and how the buckle had bit so deep she'd been in agony for days. 'I don't want it,' she sobbed. 'Not the belt. Please, not the belt.'

The candle was carefully placed on the beside table. Mervyn belched as he pulled the belt free. It was as if she hadn't spoken. 'It ain't the belt you'll be getting,' he hiccuped. 'Not this time.'

Matilda's sobs came to an abrupt halt and her eyes widened in horror as he fumbled to undo the trouser buttons. 'No,' she breathed. 'Not that.'

The moleskins dropped to the floor and he kicked them aside. His breath was ragged, eyes bright with more than whisky. 'You always were an ungrateful bitch,' he grunted. 'Well, I'm gonna teach you a lesson in manners, and when I'm through you'll think twice about giving me lip.'

Matilda dived off the bed as he climbed towards her. But he was between her and the door, and the window was tightly fastened against the mosquitoes. There was nowhere to go, and no one to turn to – and as he grabbed her she began to scream.

But the screams bounced off the corrugated iron roof and were lost in the great silence of the Never Never.

Dark clouds swirled in her head. Matilda thought she was floating in a cocoon. There was no pain, no terror, just endless darkness which welcomed her, drawing her into its depths, offering peace.

Yet somewhere in that darkness was the sound of another world. Of cocks crowing and early-morning birdsong. The darkness faded to grey, the first rays of light banishing it to the furthest reaches of her mind. Matilda willed the clouds to return. She didn't want to be torn from this protective womb and thrust into cold reality.

The sunlight broke through the cloud, warming her face, forcing her to return to awareness. She lay for a moment, her eyes closed, wondering why there was so much pain. Then memory hit and her eyes snapped open.

He was gone – but there on the mattress was the evidence of what he'd done. Like a demonic rose, blood blossomed across the kapok, its petals scattered on the sheet and the remains of her petticoat.

Matilda remained huddled on the floor. She had no memory of how she'd got there, but guessed she must have crawled into the corner some time after he'd gone. Pushing away the images of that awful night, she gingerly dragged herself up the wall.

Her legs trembled and every part of her ached. There was blood on her too. Dried and dark, its coppery smell was laced with something else, and as Matilda looked down at her nakedness, she realised what it was. It was the smell of him – of his unwashed body and rough, demanding hands. Of his whisky breath and great forceful weight.

The sharp cry of a cockatoo made her flinch, but it also sharpened her resolve. He would never do this again.

With the trembling under control, Matilda pulled on a clean

24

petticoat and moved painfully round the bed to gather her meagre possessions. The locket was drawn from the hiding place under the floorboards, her mother's shawl taken from the bed post. She added her two dresses, one skirt and blouse, and her much-darned underwear. Last of all, she picked up the prayer book her grandparents had brought with them all the way from Ireland. She wrapped everything in the shawl, leaving only her moleskins, boots and shirt to change into once she'd washed.

Creeping past the discarded, broken chair, she hesitated just long enough to satisfy herself Mervyn was still asleep then began the endless journey across the kitchen floor.

Every creak and groan of the house seemed magnified. Surely the noise would bring an end to the snoring from the other room?

She paused again, blood singing in her ears, the pulse of it drumming in her head. The snoring was rhythmic and uninterrupted as she reached the door. She held her breath. Her hands were wet with perspiration as she took the water bag down from its hook. It was heavy, and thankfully full. Now for the front door.

The hinges shrieked – the snores stopped – bed springs groaned – Mervyn muttered.

Matilda froze. Seconds stretched into infinity.

With a grunt, the snoring began again and Matilda breathed once more. Slipping around the door, she eased past the screen and ran down the steps. One glance told her Gabriel and his tribe had not returned, neither had the drovers. She was on her own, and she had no idea how long it would be before Mervyn awoke.

Her bare feet stirred the dust of the yard as she hurried down to the creek. The banks were steeply cut and sheltered by willows, and as she slithered and slid towards the shallow, listless water, she knew she couldn't be seen from the house.

The water was icy, the sun not yet high enough to warm it, but it washed away the evidence of his filth, made her skin clean despite the lingering stink of him which she knew would always be with her. She shivered as she scrubbed. She might appear clean on the outside, but no amount of water could wash away the stains on her soul.

After drying herself roughly on her shirt, she dressed quickly. She dared not cross the yard to the tack room, the dogs would kick up a fuss and alert Mervyn. There was nothing for it, she would have to ignore the pain and ride bare-back. The decision made, she snatched up the shawl and, holding her boots, paddled along the creek bed until she reached the home paddock at the back of the house.

She looked over her shoulder. Nothing stirred behind those shuttered windows and the sound of his snoring drifted into the sleepy dawn.

With sharp, trembling breaths, she climbed the fence and dropped down into the paddock. Most of the horses were partially broken brumbies and would have meant a swifter escape, but the old mare was her only option. She'd been around for as long as Matilda could remember, and unlike the others could be relied on to return to the home paddock when set free.

The brumbies whickered and tossed their heads, milling back and forth as she approached Mervyn's bay mare. 'Shhh, Lady. It's all right, girl. We're just going for a ride,' she whispered, stroking the soft nose.

Lady rolled her eyes and stamped her feet as Matilda grasped her mane and hauled herself painfully on to her back. 'Whoa there, girl. Calm down,' she soothed. Matilda's cheek rested on the twitching neck as she whispered into the pricked ears, but her fingers were tightly woven into the coarse mane. Lady was used to Mervyn's rough handling and heavy weight – there was no knowing how she would react to this strange behaviour, and Matilda didn't want to risk being thrown.

With the canvas water bag slung over her back, and the shawl bundle hooked over her arm, she urged the mare forward and opened the gate at the far end of the paddock. Rounding up the others as she would a mob of sheep, she spent precious minutes encouraging the brumbies to leave their grazing and lead her out into the wider pastures of Churinga station.

Once they got a taste for the unexpected freedom they were off, and Matilda grinned as she kicked her heels into Lady's ribs and galloped after them. They would take a long time to round up, but it should give her a head start. For without a horse, Mervyn had little chance of catching her.

Thunder rumbled in the distance of his dream and Mervyn tensed, waiting for the flash of lightning and the drum of rain on the corrugated roof. When it didn't come, he turned over and burrowed more comfortably into the pillows.

Yet sleep, now broken, was elusive, and he found he couldn't settle. There was something wrong with the image of thunder. Something that didn't sit easily in his mind.

He opened a bleary eye and tried to focus on the empty bed beside him. There was something wrong about that too – but his head hurt and coherent thought was fogged by the need for a drink. His mouth tasted sour, and as he ran his tongue over his dry lips, he winced from the sting of a deep cut he had no recollection of receiving.

'Must have fell over,' he muttered, testing it with his tongue. 'Mary! Where the hell are you?' he yelled.

The drummer behind his eyes beat a painful tattoo and he fell back into the pillows with a groan. Bloody woman was never around when she was needed.

He lay there, his mind drifting aimlessly through the fog of pain. 'Mary,' he groaned. 'Get in here, woman.'

There was no answering rat-a-tat-tat of hurrying footsteps, no rattle of pots from the kitchen or bustle of activity in the yard. It was too quiet.

Mervyn rolled off the bed and gingerly stood up. His leg throbbed with the same rhythm as his head, and the wasted thigh muscle trembled as he put his weight on it. Where the hell was everybody? How dare they leave him here like this?

He lurched for the door and threw it open. It crashed against the wall, triggering off a memory that was fleeting and seemed to make no sense. He dismissed it and staggered into the deserted kitchen. He needed a drink.

As the last of the whisky slid down his throat and muffled the drummers in his head, Mervyn took stock of his surroundings. There was no porridge bubbling on the range, no billy steaming, no Mary. He opened his mouth to yell for her – then remembered. Mary was in the ground. Had been for more than two weeks.

27

His legs suddenly refused to support him, and he slumped into a chair. A coldness swept over him that no amount of whisky could warm as memory returned full force.

'What have I done?' he whispered into that terrible silence.

The chair toppled over as he thrust away from the table. He had to find Matilda. Had to explain – to make her understand it was the whisky that had made him do such a thing.

Her room was deserted. The splintered door hanging on one hinge, the bed a bloody reminder of what he'd done. Tears streamed down his face. 'I didn't mean it, girl. I thought you was Mary,' he sobbed.

He listened to the silence, then sniffed back the tears and stepped into the room. She was probably hiding but he needed to see her, to convince her it had all been a terrible mistake. 'Where are you, Molly?' he called softly. 'Come to Daddy.' The childhood endearment Mary had used was deliberate – he hoped she might respond to it more easily.

There was still no reply, no rustle to betray her hiding place. He flicked back the soiled sheet and looked under the bed. Opened the heavy wardrobe door and fumbled in its dark, empty recesses. He wiped his nose on his sleeve and tried to think. She must have gone to the barn or one of the other outbuildings.

He limped back into the kitchen, saw the bottle on the table and swiped it to the floor where it crashed with a satisfying explosion of glass. 'Never again,' he muttered. 'Never, ever again.'

His crippled leg dragged his foot on the floor as he hurried for the screen door, and as he was about to step on to the verandah, something caught his eye. It wasn't something that was there – but something which should have been.

Mervyn stopped and looked at the naked hook, and as he pondered the disappearance of the water bag, other things began to fit into place. The wardrobe had been empty. Matilda's boots weren't under the bed, and Mary's shawl was gone from the bedpost.

The tears dried as remorse and self-pity were replaced by fear. Where the hell was she? And how long had she been gone?

The sun was still rising, its glare hitting his eyes and making his head throb. He rammed his hat low and headed for the barns and outhouses. She had to be here – somewhere. Even Matilda wasn't stupid enough to run off, not with the nearest neighbours almost a hundred miles away.

He gave a brief thought to the drovers who'd ridden out with the mob a couple of days ago. She might come across them, but they would know to keep their mouths shut if they valued their jobs. Yet it was the idea of her making it to Wilga, and that nosy-parker Finlay and his wife, that truly bothered him. That would be bad enough – but what if she'd headed for Kurrajong and Ethan?

Icy terror made his pulse drum and quickened his shambling walk. He had to find her – and quickly.

Moments later he was approaching the home paddock, saddle and bridle in hand, a fresh water bag sloshing at his back. He was angry and afraid. If Matilda made it to Wilga or Kurrajong then his life at Churinga would be over. Fast talking and lies wouldn't save him this time.

He crossed the yard and came to an abrupt halt. The home paddock was deserted, the far gate open. The pastures beyond stretched emptily towards the horizon. Rage tore through him as he threw his saddle to the ground. Unlike Ethan Squires, his money didn't stretch to a ute and without a horse he would never catch the devious little bitch.

He lit a cigarette, then picking up his saddle, fretted and fumed his way through the long grass. She shouldn't have drunk that whisky and sat on his knee if she hadn't been willing. If she was old enough for that, then she was old enough for other things. Neither should she have looked so like her ma and treated him like dirt if she didn't expect to be punished.

And anyway, he thought as he finally reached the open gate at the far end of the paddock, she's probably not even my daughter. It was obvious something had been going on between Mary and Ethan – and if the rumours were true, it had begun long before Mary had become Mervyn's wife. That would explain Patrick's extraordinary offer of Churinga in exchange for his daughter's marriage to Mervyn, and why Mary and Ethan had plotted to cheat him.

Having convinced himself he'd done nothing wrong, he pushed back his hat and stared moodily into the distance.

Matilda had to be found. She must not be allowed to tell anyone what had happened. They wouldn't understand. And, besides, it was none of their damn business.

His heated thoughts stilled and he grew tense. Something was moving out there but too far away for him to tell what it could be. He shielded his eyes and watched the dark speck emerge from the shimmering heat haze. The brumby pricked its ears as Mervyn whistled, and after a few nervous twitches of its mane, curiosity drew it into a canter.

Mervyn stood rock steady, waiting for the animal to reach him. The horse was young and had obviously become separated from the herd. He'd found isolation bewildering and had returned to the only place he knew.

Mervyn's impatience was hard to contain as the horse dithered and twitched just out of reach. He knew from experience that rough handling or sudden noise would make the brumby bolt again so he took time to talk to it, to calm it before saddling up. Once astride, he studied the tracks of the other brumbies and followed them. The churned earth marked their passage well, but after an hour there were separate tracks of a single horse being ridden in a straight line.

That line headed south – towards Wilga.

Matilda had given Lady her head and the first few miles were covered swiftly. Now the mare was tiring and they'd slowed to an easy trot. No horse, let alone one as old as Lady, could be expected to gallop far in this heat. It was better to take it easy than to risk her getting injured or blown.

The morning was advanced, the sun high and fierce. Watery mirages shimmered on the parched earth and the silver grass rustled beneath Lady's hooves. The vast emptiness engulfed them, the sound of its silence coming back as a sibilant echo. If Matilda hadn't been so intent on escape, she would not have been afraid. For this harsh, beautiful land was as much a part of her as breathing.

Its grandeur piqued her senses, the raw colours jolting some deep part of her that yearned to embrace it – and be embraced by it. Yet within that ancient landscape was the soft beauty of delicate leaves, of pale flowers and ashen bark, the sweet aroma of wattle and pine, and the joyous trill of the skylark.

30

Matilda shifted on the mare's back. Her discomfort had grown more intense as the miles lengthened between her and Churinga, but there was no time to rest. She mopped the sweat from her face and adjusted the brim of her old felt hat. The water in the bag was warm and tasted brackish, but despite her thirst, she knew it must be rationed. The nearest water hole was still miles away.

After another long, sweeping search of the horizon behind her still revealed no sign of Mervyn, she settled as best she could on the mare's broad back and concentrated on the view between Lady's ears. The steady rhythm of plodding hooves became a lullaby, the heat embracing her in the languid cocoon of carelessness.

The snake had been coiled in a narrow cleft of corrugated earth, hidden from the sun by an overhang of scrub grass. The vibration of the approaching horse had woken it, bringing it sharply alert. Red-brown coils slithered in the dirt as forked tongue flickered and unblinking eyes watched the girl and the horse.

Matilda's chin rested low and her eyes were heavy-lidded with the enticement of sleep. Her fingers loosened their clutch on the mane as she drooped towards Lady's neck.

Sharp hoof rang on stony ground. Scrub grass tore. The snake whipped powerful coils, fangs unsheathed, yellow eyes fixed on their target. It struck hard and fast.

The mare reared as venom spewed. Her hooves flashed as she pawed the air and screamed in terror. Wild-eyed, she tossed her head, nostrils flared, back legs dancing over the shale.

Matilda grabbed for the wildly flying mane, her knees and feet instinctively clinging to the animal's sides.

The mare's flaying hooves crashed back to earth. Matilda's grip was torn from the mane and she clung to the sweating, straining neck. Lady reared again to resume the twisting, dancing fight for escape, and Matilda's desperate efforts to stay on board were over. The red earth rushed to meet her.

Lady pranced on her back legs, eyes rolling, lips peeled back as she trampled the ground. Matilda fought for breath as she rolled away from those crashing, deadly hooves – and all the while wondered where the King Brown had gone.

With a snort and a toss of her head, Lady wheeled around and tore back the way she'd come. Dust rose around her, the earth vibrated with the thud of her hooves, and Matilda was left far behind in a bruised heap. 'Come back,' she shrieked. 'Lady, come back.'

But there was only a cloud of dust tracing the mare's departure – and eventually even that had disappeared.

Matilda gingerly felt her arms and legs. There seemed to be no bones broken but through the tattered remains of her shirt she could see she was badly grazed. She closed her eyes in an attempt to still the spinning shock of the speed and ferocity of her fall, but the knowledge the snake could be close by meant she had little time to recover.

Hauling herself to her feet, she picked up the water bag and bundle and stood for a moment in the silence. The snake was nowhere to be seen, but that didn't mean it wasn't lurking.

'Pull yourself together,' she muttered. 'It's probably more scared than Lady after all that noise, and long gone by now.'

She settled her hat firmly over her forehead and hitched her belongings over her shoulder as she took stock of her situation. The elliptical rise of blue-grey the Aborigines called Tjuringa mountain was closer now. Wilga lay on the other side of the eucalyptus and pine-covered mountain but she knew it would take many hours' walking before she would catch first sight of it.

With a trembling sigh she scanned the horizon. Lady was gone but there was still no sign of Mervyn. Matilda lifted her chin and set out. There was water at the foot of Tjuringa, and shelter. If she could make it by nightfall, then she could rest.

Mervyn was driven by fear and uncertainty as to how much of a start she'd had on him. He dug in his spurs and the horse lengthened its stride, nimble feet racing over the hard, unforgiving ground. The sun was high, and after they'd been travelling for several hours, he knew the brumby was close to exhaustion. He'd ridden hard yet there was still no sign of her, still no dust plume following her trail. He reined in and slid from the saddle.

He could have done with a proper drink but water from the skin bag would have to do. Swilling the leather-tainted water around his mouth, he let it soak into his dry tongue before swallowing it. Then he filled his hat and offered it to the horse. The animal drank deeply, its sides still heaving from the ride, its neck flecked with sweat. When they had both had enough to keep them going, Mervyn rammed the wet, cool hat back on his head and led the horse forward. He would walk for a while in the animal's shade, and once they'd reached the water hole at the base of Tjuringa, they could cool off and drink all they wanted.

Flies swarmed as heat rebounded off the rough shale and jagged boulders. A hawk floated above the shimmering grass-land, an effortless predator in search of prey. Mervyn's thoughts were grim. Not for him the easy hunt or far-seeing eye of a hawk, but the endless trudge beneath a burning sun for a quarry that had so far out-witted him. The thought of how he would punish her when he did find her was what kept him going. That – and the fear of discovery.

His mind wandered back to Gallipoli. Back to the night he'd crept from the stinking hole in the ground that had become a graveyard for so many of his mates. The night discovery had been averted by his quick thinking and cunning.

He'd been in the thick of things for months, and the blast and crump of Turkish shells jangled in his mind long after the barrage was over. He'd twitched from it, relived every sight and sound of the carnage they had just come through. The stink of cordite and blood was always with him – as was the terror. It made him sweat and shake and cringe in the mud. Maddened him with a claustrophobic panic he could no longer control.

Mervyn remembered how he'd slipped away under cover of darkness, the survivors around him muttering in their sleep, rifles hugged to their chests for comfort. He'd scurried through the trenches, working his way further and further from the front line and certain death. Like a hunted animal, he'd searched for a bolt-hole, the merest shelter where the shells couldn't find him and death no longer rode his back.

Skirting the command post which nestled in a sheltered basin several hundred yards from the beach head, he'd finally found what he'd been looking for. He crawled past a dead body that must have been overlooked by the medics and into a narrow, dank cave where he slumped to the ground, hands over his head, knees drawn to his chin.

Sporadic fire echoed in the walls around him, making him whimper and cringe. He wanted it to go away – to leave him be. He couldn't bear it any longer.

He didn't hear the scrape of boots on the cavern floor or see the soldier's approach.

'Get up, you lousy coward.'

Mervyn looked up. A bayonet was inches from his face. 'Leave me,' he pleaded. 'I can't go back up there.'

'Dirty yellow dingo! I oughta shoot you right here and let you rot.' The bayonet stabbed the air between them. 'On yer feet.'

Mervyn's head was filled with a red haze. Terror of the trenches became secondary to the threat he now faced. The court martial would be swift, the firing squad a certainty. He was cornered. All he could do was attack – and before he realised what he was doing, the rifle he'd carried against the enemy was firing at a fellow Aussie.

The retort bounced off the walls and filled his head. A dull thud in his knee brought him to the floor and he lay stunned for a long moment, wondering what had happened. When the red mist cleared and his senses stopped jangling, he looked across the enclosed space.

The other man was down, rifle discarded beside him. There was no movement, no sound of breathing, and as Mervyn crawled towards him, he realised why. The man had no face. Mervyn's bullet had blown it away.

He inspected his own wound, the horror of what he'd done wiping away the fear and pain, bringing instead a cold calculation of what to do next. The other man's bullet had shattered his knee and driven up into his thigh before punching a hole in his hip. The pain would soon be all-consuming and the blood loss much too rapid for him to stay here any longer.

He eyed the dead soldier. He was small and lightly built. Shouldn't pose too much of a problem. Coming to a swift decision, Mervyn grabbed him and slung him over his shoulder. Using his rifle as a walking stick, he hobbled to the mouth of the cave. Guns were still going off on the Turkish side, lights still flickered in the hospital tent, and the command centre was alive with scurrying runners and shouted orders.

Mervyn hitched the man from his shoulder to his back, looping the dead arms around his neck, grasping the lifeless hands to his throat. He would make a perfect shield if a stray bullet came over the hill.

The steep climb down to the hospital tent had been agonising, but his arrival amongst the chaos had a gratifying effect – just as he'd known it would. He was the returning hero. Wounded, he'd risked his life for a cobber. He'd almost laughed when they solemnly told him his mate was dead, and looked at him with pity.

Mervyn came back to the present and stared into the sun. They'd given him a medal, and after many months in hospital, his ticket home. Luck and cunning had saved him that night, just as they would now – for there on the horizon was Lady.

He smiled as the grey mare galloped up to him. Catching the dangling reins, he remounted the brumby and spurred him into a gallop. If Matilda had been thrown, it wouldn't take long to find her.

With the sinking of the sun came the long, cool shadows, and with stumbling relief Matilda thrust her way through the clinging undergrowth and sought shelter beneath the canopy of trees. It hurt to breathe, to move, even to think. She was exhausted.

The bush sounds were all around her as she leaned against a tree trunk for a moment's respite, but it was the splash and trickle of water that drew her on again. There was no time to rest but she could wash and refill the water bag before moving on and the thought of that cold clean mountain fall revived her flagging spirits.

The waterfall began high up in the mountain, gushing down, gathering other springs along the way, until it fell hundreds of feet into the rocky valley below. Yet, as Matilda finally emerged from the dense, green light of the hinterland, she realised it was sadly depleted by the lack of rain. The water that trickled down the worn, glistening rocks was barely enough to fill the pools below. Great tree roots lay in naked arthritic tangles where once they'd been submerged. Forest ferns drooped scorched fronds, and thick ropes of withered ivy hung listlessly from creaking, parched wattle and King Billy pines.

Matilda climbed down to a broad, flat stone that jutted above one of the rock pools, and pulled off her boots. She didn't bother to undress, she was filthy and so were the remains of her clothes. As she lowered herself into the icy water, she shivered with pleasure. The blisters on her feet would soon heal, the scorch of the sun on her exposed arms would soon turn brown.

She closed her eyes and held her nose, then sank below the surface of the water. The dirt and sweat lifted away. The pain between her legs dulled in the icy caress. Her hair floated and her parched skin was replenished.

Emerging with a gasp, she cupped her hands and drank deeply before refilling the water bag. The birds which had fallen silent on her arrival were now in full song, and she gazed up into the surrounding trees. This had always been a special place. A place where Mary had told her about unicorns and fairies and the little people she'd called leprechauns. As Matilda looked around her, she could almost believe they existed – but harsh reality had a way of making such stories a nonsense.

She dragged herself reluctantly from the water and pulled on her boots. Wincing as the leather caught the angry blisters, the pain was not enough to daunt her – not after what she'd suffered in the past few hours – and she snatched up the bag and shawl bundle and headed deeper into the bush. It was a faster route through it than around it, and if she kept heading south she would come out on the crest above Wilga.

By the time she emerged from the humid green shadows and into the dying sunlight, she was sweating profusely. Yet she felt a jolt of achievement as she looked down on the great sweep of Wilga's pastures, and the thin spiral of smoke from the homestead on the horizon. She'd almost made it.

As the stands of trees grew sparse and the sun dipped even lower in the sky, Matilda picked her way over the tumble of boulders at the foot of Tjuringa. The water bag was heavy on her shoulder, the bundle cumbersome as she slid and stumbled over the loose, treacherous ground, but she had no thought of discarding either – they were precious. Creatures scuttled and slithered from beneath the rocks as she disturbed their late-afternoon slumber and the laughing jackass mocked her progress, but finally she reached flatter ground and stopped for a moment to catch her breath and take a drink.

It was almost twilight, and Wilga homestead was at least another three hours' walk away but she had to dredge deep to find the strength to carry on. Mervyn might have come across Lady and could be just a few miles behind her.

Thudding the stopper back into the neck of the water bag, she stepped out on to the plains and headed for the wisp of smoke on the horizon.

Time lost all meaning as she walked. She was aware only of the deepening shadows and the glimmer of Wilga homestead in the distance. Her boots scuffed the dry earth and silver grass as her thoughts centred on Tom and April Finlay.

Tom Finlay's family had owned Wilga for years. Old man Finlay had passed on a few months after his wife. Now Tom was married and ran the property with his wife. Matilda hadn't seen him in a long while – not since Mum got sick and Mervyn refused to let him visit. Yet she knew she would find shelter at Wilga. She and Tom had grown up together, and although he was several years older, Matilda knew he regarded her as the sister he'd never had.

She remembered him as a skinny boy who'd teased her mercilessly about her mother calling her Molly. What kind of name was that? he'd asked as he'd pulled her hair. But as they'd grown older, his tugs weren't quite so hard and he'd agreed that her pet name suited her. For Matildas were supposed to be rather stern people, not larrikins who climbed trees and played in the dust with their hair in their eyes.

Matilda smiled, despite her fear and weariness. How right he'd been, she thought. Great Aunt Matilda was very starched and proper if her portrait was anything to go by. No wonder her mother had changed her mind once her baby began to display less than immaculate behaviour.

A familiar sound disturbed her thoughts and in sharp antici-pation she looked around.

The drum of hoofbeats vibrated in the ground, and there, far behind her, was the unmistakable blur of a horse and rider.

At last. Someone had seen her and was coming to help.

She waved. 'I'm here. Over here,' she called.

Her cries went unacknowledged but the horse kept coming.

Matilda shivered as the first tingle of unease crept over her. There were two horses but only one rider. She took a step back. Then another. And as the outlines sharpened, the dread returned. There was no mistaking the solid figure on the back of the chestnut or the grey lumbering outline of Lady.

She began to run.

The sound of hooves grew closer. Wilga seemed an impossible distance away.

The adrenaline pumped as Matilda raced through the long grass. Her boots slipped and tripped over the uneven ground. Her hat flew off and dangled down her back. But her eyes were fixed on that distant glimmer that was her refuge. She had to make it. Her life depended on it.

The thundering hooves slowed to a steady walk.

She dared not look round, but guessed he was a couple of hundred yards away, playing with her as a cat toyed with a mouse, teasing, provoking, but all the while menacing. A sob of desperation mingled with the gasp as she stumbled again. He was waiting for her to fall. Waiting his moment. They both knew she couldn't outrun him.

The pastures stretched endlessly before her, the long grass hampering her escape, the earth seemingly set on making her stumble. Yet she found the strength to stay on her feet and keep going. The alternative was too awful to contemplate.

The steady plod of hooves followed her – never gaining but always there. She heard the soft, malicious chuckle and the jingle of harness. It spurred her on.

The homestead was nearer now, she could even catch a shimmer of light in one of the windows, and Mervyn wouldn't dare hurt her once she reached the fire-break that surrounded the property.

As her feet pounded over the earth, she searched desperately for a sign of life – of confirmation that someone was out there and would see her. Where was Tom? Why had no one come to help?

The pursuing drumbeat gathered pace. Nearer and nearer,

its approach filled the world with its sound until there was nothing else.

Her breath was ragged. Her heartbeat a hammer against her ribs as the chestnut gelding came up beside her. Sweat foamed its flanks, the great bellows of its lungs rasped as it came to a skittering halt in front of her.

Matilda twisted away.

The horse followed.

She ducked away from the trampling, stamping legs and weaved through the grass.

The horse closed in, the booted foot left the stirrup and kicked up.

The blow to the side of her head sent her stumbling, arms flailing, trying to catch hold of the harness to keep her balance. Then she was falling. Down, down, down she went – the earth rushing to meet her, embracing her in a cloud of dust and cruel stones, punching air from her lungs.

Mervyn's bulk blotted out the remains of the sun as he loomed over her. 'Just how far did you think you were gonna get?'

Matilda glanced through the grass at the silent, deserted homestead. If she hadn't taken time to rest she'd have made it.

His grasp on her arm was brutal as he yanked her to her feet. A gleam of sadistic relish was in his eyes as he tugged her hair and forced her to look up at him. Matilda knew he wanted her to cry out, to plead with him not to hurt her, but she wouldn't give him the satisfaction – no matter how much he was hurting her.

His breath was foul, his mouth inches from her face. His voice a low, menacing rasp. 'What happens on Churinga's no one else's business. Understood? You shoot through again, and I'll kill you.'

Matilda knew this was no idle threat. She lowered her gaze and tried not to flinch as his fingers increased their hold in her hair.

'Look at me,' he growled.

She dredged the last of her courage and stared back at him.

'There ain't no one going to believe you. I'm a hero, see, and I've got a medal to prove it.'

Matilda looked into his eyes and thought she saw something

else behind the threat – could it be fear? Impossible. For his words held the ring of truth and in those few seconds she knew she was truly alone.

# Chapter One

Sydney sweltered, and the graceful white sails of the new
Opera House gleamed against the dark iron struts of the
harbour bridge. Circular Quay was a kaleidoscope of colour
with its crush of people, and the water busy with craft of
every size and shape. Australia was celebrating as only she
knew how, the narrow streets of the burgeoning capital full of
noise and bustle. Jenny had gone to see the Queen open the
Opera House out of curiosity, and to help fill the hours of
another long day. Yet the great swarm of people who joined
her on the sun-drenched quayside did nothing to alleviate the
feeling of isolation, and she'd returned home to her house in
the northern suburb of Palm Beach as soon as the ceremony
was over.

Now she stood on the balcony and gripped the railing with
the same desperation as she'd clung to the debris of her life
during the past six months of mourning. The death of her
husband and baby hadn't come softly, with time to prepare, to
say the words of parting that should have been spoken – but
with an obscene swiftness that had swept everything else aside
and left her stranded. The house seemed too big, too empty,
too silent. And every room held a reminder of how it had once
been. Yet there could be no turning back, no remission. They
were gone.

The Pacific Ocean glittered in the sun, its reflection
mirrored in the windows of the elegant villas on the hillside
overlooking the shore, and the bright, purple heads of the
bougainvillaea nodded against the white stucco walls of the
house. Peter had planted them because they were the same

41

colour as her eyes. Now she could hardly bear to look at them. Yet it was the sight of the children splashing at the water's edge that most reinforced her loss. Two-year-old Ben had loved the water.

'Thought I'd find you here. Why did you run off like that? You scared me, Jen.'

She turned at the sound of Diane's soft voice to find her friend standing in the doorway. She was dressed as usual in a caftan, her dark curls anchored by a silk bandanna. 'Sorry. I didn't mean to frighten you, but after six months of shutting myself away, the noise and the crowds in the city were too much. I had to get away.'

'You should have said you wanted to leave. I'd have come with you.'

Jenny shook her head. 'I needed to be on my own for a while, Diane. Needed to make sure . . .'

She couldn't finish the sentence, couldn't put into words the awful hope she carried each time she left the house. For she knew the truth, had seen the coffins lowered into the ground. 'It was a mistake. I know that now.'

'Not a mistake, Jen. Just confirmation of your worst fears. But it will get better, I promise.'

Jenny eyed her friend with affection. The exotic clothes, garish jewellery and heavy makeup hid a softness she would have denied vehemently. But Jenny had known Diane for too long to be fooled. 'How come you know so much?'

There was a flicker of sadness in Diane's brown eyes. 'Twenty-four years of experience,' she said dryly. 'Life's a bitch, but you and I've survived this long, so don't you dare give up on me now.'

The kaleidoscope of their lives flashed through Jenny's mind as they embraced. They had met in the orphanage at Dajarra, two small girls clinging to the hope of finding their parents – and when that dream was shattered they'd built another. Then another.

'Remember when we first came down to Sydney? We had so many plans. How come it all went wrong?'

Diane gently pulled away from the embrace, her silver bracelets jangling as she smoothed Jenny's long brown hair away from her face. 'Nothing was ever guaranteed, Jen.

There's no point in lingering over what fate dished out for us.'

'But it's not fair,' she exploded, anger finally rising above the misery.

Diane's expression was enigmatic. 'I agree, but unfortunately there's nothing we can do about it.' She gripped Jenny's arms in strong fingers. 'Let it go, Jen. Get angry – cry – yell at the world and everything in it if it makes you feel better. Because you aren't doing yourself any favours by letting it eat away at you.'

Jenny waged an inner war as she turned away from that all-penetrating honesty and stared out over the bay. It would have been easy to rage, to give into tears and recriminations, but there had to be some part of her life still within her control and this enforced calm was all she had left.

Diane swept back her long sleeves, lit a cigarette and watched the inner battle reflected on Jenny's face. I wish I could do or say something to break down that great wall of resistance she always puts up when she's hurt, she thought. But, knowing Jenny, she'll come round to it when she's good and ready. It had been the same all their lives, and Diane could see no reason why she should change now.

Her thoughts drifted back to the orphanage and the silent, solitary little girl who'd rarely cried no matter how much she was hurting. Of the two of them, Jenny had always appeared to be the stronger. Not for her the tantrums and tears, the raging at what life had thrown at them – but Diane knew that beneath the façade of strength lay a soft, frightened core which was no stranger to pain. For how else could Jenny have sustained Diane through the hell of being told she couldn't have children? How else could Jenny have understood the agony when David had stood her friend up at the altar for a fertile tart he'd met at the office?

Diane stubbed out her cigarette as the old anger resurfaced. Two years and a lot of hard work in the studio had taken the sting off that rage, but a great many tears had been shed. They had been an intrinsic part of Diane's healing process, something Jenny too must accept if she was to have any kind of future.

Frustration at not being able to reach her friend made her

restless. She ought to be at the gallery they both owned, helping Andy display her sculptures for the forthcoming exhibition, but she didn't like to leave without making sure Jenny was all right.

Jenny turned from the balcony railing, her violet eyes fathomless in her pale face. 'I expect you want those paintings?' Her voice was toneless, her emotions tightly reined.

'The exhibition's not for a month yet, and I know how I want to display them. They'll keep for a while.' How the hell can she be so calm? thought Diane. If my husband had just dropped dead and taken my baby with him, I'd be climbing the bloody walls, not thinking about art exhibitions.

'I've already packed the canvases. They're in the studio.' Jenny flicked a glance at her watch. 'I have to go.'

Diane was startled. 'Go? Go where? Everything's closed for the day.'

'Solicitor's office. John Wainwright wants to discuss certain aspects of Pete's will more fully.'

'But probate was granted almost six months ago. What the hell's left to discuss?'

Jenny shrugged. 'He wouldn't tell me over the phone but it's got something to do with me being twenty-five yesterday.'

'I'll come with you.' Diane's alarm at her friend's unnatural calm made her voice rather sharp.

'There's no need, love. But do me a favour, take the paintings with you. I can't face Andy or the gallery at the moment.'

Diane had a sharp, mental image of their gallery manager. The limp-wristed Andy was inclined to go off the deep end if the slightest thing went wrong, but tantrums aside he was indispensable. For he saw to the day-to-day running of the gallery, leaving Jenny and Diane free to be creative. 'He's a big boy now, Jen. He'll just have to cope,' she said firmly.

Jenny shook her head, her glossy hair swinging over her shoulders. 'I'd prefer to do this alone, Diane. Please try and understand.'

She picked up her tote bag. It was pointless to argue when Jenny was like this. 'I wish you'd let me help more,' she muttered.

Jenny's hand was cold against her arm, nails bitten, fingers stained with oil paint. 'I know, darling, and you have. But like

Andy, I'm all grown up, and it's time I stood on my own two feet.'

Jenny drove the battered Holden down the steep hill and out on to the main road. Palm Beach lay on the central coast of the northern fringes of the great urban sprawl of Sydney, but despite being only an hour away from the harbour bridge it was another world to the hustle and bright lights of the city. Quiet inlets were home to sailing boats; tree-lined streets housed expensive boutiques and quaint little restaurants. Gardens were a riot of colour and leafy shade, and the houses that overlooked the bays had that understated elegance only money could bring. Despite her mood, she couldn't help but feel a certain peace here. She usually loved the buzz of the city, but the relaxed, seaside aura of the northern suburb had become her saviour.

Windsor lay somnolent in the heat of the Hawkesbury Valley, thirty-five miles north of Sydney. The houses were mainly clapboard and tiled with terracotta slates, shaded by great red gum trees. It was a pioneer town, settled in the days of Governor Macquarie, and its heritage was evident in the convict architecture of the Courthouse and St Matthew's Church.

Jenny parked up on the edge of the town and sat for a long moment, staring out of the window. Yet she saw nothing for she needed time to gather her thoughts before facing John Wainwright again.

The original reading of the will had passed without her registering how much it would affect her. Her loss had been too fresh, too sudden, and she'd lived from day to day in a protective vacuum where nothing could touch her. She had learned things about her dead husband she didn't want to acknowledge and had pushed them aside, hoping that somehow they could be faced if left long enough.

Now presumably she would have to face them. Have to question the things he'd done, and set them clear in her mind so she could deal with them.

Her emergence from that trance-like state made it hard to accept life had gone on despite the tragedy. Peter had been the rock on which she'd built the foundation of her adult life.

He'd been clever and resourceful, believing in her talent and encouraging her to exhibit her paintings. Yet his own dreams of returning to the land had never been fulfilled. He'd been too busy working in the bank and providing a home for his family to have time for dreams.

And yet his will had revealed another side to him. A side that was alien to the man she'd known and loved.

Jenny sighed. She wished they'd not been so certain time was on their side. Wished Peter had been honest with her and told her about the vast amount of money he'd tucked away – and had used to fulfil those dreams they'd shared. For what was the use of a fortune if they couldn't spend it together?

She stared off into the distance. Diane knew nothing of the will. Perhaps it would have been better to discuss it with her, to find out if her friend had seen Peter in a different light and had some inkling of what he was up to? But then, how could she? Jenny admitted silently. All marriages were conducted behind closed doors, and if living with Peter hadn't revealed the true man to her then how could she expect Diane to know any different?

Jenny checked her watch and climbed out of the car. It was time to go.

The offices of Wainwright, Dobbs and Steel were located in a solid Victorian building that had the dirt of years ingrained in its stone. She paused for a moment and took a deep breath. Control was everything. Without it, her world would crumble and she'd be lost.

Taking the short flight of steps at a steady pace, she pushed through the heavy doors. The building was gloomy, despite the heavy chandeliers, the light of the Australian summer deflected by the surrounding buildings. Yet the marble floor and stone pillars gave it a delicious coolness that was welcome after the heat of the park.

'Jennifer?'

John Wainwright was a short, round, prematurely balding Englishman, with rimless spectacles perched halfway down his long nose. The hand he offered was soft, like a woman's, fingers ringless and tapered, nails perfectly manicured. He'd been Peter's family solicitor for years but Jenny had never really taken to him.

She followed him into his gloomy office and sat down in a highly polished leather chair. Her pulse was racing and she had the strongest urge to get up again and walk out. She didn't want to hear, didn't want to believe Peter's secrecy, but knew that if she was to understand it, she must stay.

'I regret being so insistent, my dear. All this must be most distressing for you.' He polished his glasses on a very white handkerchief, myopic grey eyes soulful.

Jenny eyed the grey pinstripe suit, the stiff collar and discreet tie. Only a pom would wear such clothes in the height of an Australian summer. She forced a polite smile and clasped her hands in her lap. Her cotton dress was already clinging to her back. There was no air conditioning, no open windows, and a fly was buzzing overhead. She felt trapped. Suffocated.

'This shouldn't take very long, Jennifer,' he said as he selected a legal file and undid the red ribbon. 'But I have to be sure you understand the full implications of Peter's will.'

He eyed her over his glasses. 'I don't expect you took it all in before, and there are other matters which have to be discussed now you've reached twenty-five.'

Jenny shifted in the uncomfortable leather chair and eyed the jug of water on his desk. 'Could I have a drink, please? It's very hot in here.'

He laughed, a tight, brittle sound that held nervous humour. 'I thought you Australians were immune to the heat?'

Pompous ass, she thought as she drank. 'Thank you.' She put the glass on the desk. Her hand was shaking so much, she almost dropped it. 'Can we get on?'

'Certainly, my dear,' he murmured. The spectacles were pushed up on the bridge of his nose and he steepled his fingers under his chin as he scanned the document. 'As I told you before, your husband drew up his will two years ago when your son was born. There are several later codicils which are affected by your recent tragedy, but the gist of the will remains the same.'

He looked up at her then, took off his glasses and gave them another polish. 'How are you coping, my dear? Such a tragic business, losing both of them like that.'

Jenny thought of the policeman at the door on that terrible morning. Thought of the embolism that had struck Peter so swiftly, and with such deadly accuracy. It had wiped out her family in one cruel blow, leaving only the mangled remains of the car they'd pulled from the gully at the base of the coast road leading towards home.

They'd been twenty minutes away – and she hadn't known, hadn't felt anything until the police arrived. How could that be? she wondered for the hundredth time. How could a mother not feel the death of a child – a wife not experience some inner knowledge that all was not well?

She twisted the engagement ring on her finger and watched the diamond spark in the sunlight. 'I'll be right,' she said softly.

He eyed her solemnly then nodded and returned to his papers. 'As you already know, Peter was an astute investor. He took great care to protect his estate for his next-of-kin, and set up a series of trusts and insurances.'

'That's what I find hard to understand,' she interrupted. 'Peter worked in a bank and had a few shares, but apart from the house which is mortgaged, and the partnership in the gallery, we had very few assets – let alone spare cash to gamble on the stock market. Where did all this money come from?'

'The insurance has wiped out the mortgage, the partnership reverts to you and Diane, and as for where he found the capital to play the markets, that can be explained by the properties he bought and sold so astutely.'

Jenny thought of the long list of properties she'd been given. Apparently Peter had bought property all along the northern coast during the plunge in market values. Done them up and sold them on as the price index rose – and she'd had no idea. 'But he had to have had money to do that in the first place,' she protested.

Wainwright nodded and returned to the folder. 'He took out a substantial loan on your house at Palm Beach to buy the first few properties, then when he sold them, he used the profit to buy the rest.'

She thought of the large sum in her bank account, the years of scraping and penny pinching to pay the bills. 'He never told me any of this,' she murmured.

'I expect he didn't want to worry you with the financial side of things,' said the lawyer with a patronising smile.

She eyed him coldly and changed the subject. 'What's all

this about my birthday?'

John Wainwright shuffled through the papers on his desk and picked up another folder. 'This was Peter's special bequest – just for you. He wanted to present it on your birthday but . . .'

She leaned forward. Impatience and dread were a strange cocktail. 'What is it?'

'It's the deeds to a sheep station,' he said, opening the folder.

His words stunned her and she sank back into the chair. 'I think you'd better explain,' she said finally.

'The station was abandoned by the owners several years ago. Your husband saw his chance to fulfil a dream I believe you both shared, and took it.' He smiled. 'Peter was very excited about it. It was to be a surprise for your twenty-fifth birthday. I helped with the paperwork and so on, and worked out an agreement for the manager to remain on the property and look after it until you and Peter took possession.'

Jenny was lost in speculation as her mind struggled to take it all in. The ticking of the clock filled the silence as she marshalled her thoughts into some kind of order. Things were beginning to fall into place. Peter had told her her next birthday would be one she'd never forget. He had presented her with the locket she always wore on their last Christmas together and hinted it was connected to the forthcoming surprise but he had refused to divulge the secret of the locket, or the plans he'd obviously been making. But this? This was beyond her wildest dreams. Almost impossible to digest.

'Why didn't you tell me about it when you first read the will?'

'Because your husband's express instructions were not to reveal anything until your twenty-fifth birthday,' he said soberly. 'And Wainwright, Dobbs and Steel take a pride in maintaining our clients' wishes.'

Jenny lapsed into silence. It had all come too late. There was no way she could live out their dream – not on her own. But her curiosity was piqued.

'Tell me about this place, John. Where is it?'

'It's in the north-west corner of New South Wales. Or "back of Bourke", as you Australians put it. About as far into the outback as one can get. The name of the property is Churinga, which I'm reliably informed is Aboriginal for "sacred charm or amulet".'

'So how did he find this place? What was it that made him buy it? How come this Churinga was so special?'

He eyed her for a long moment, and when he finally spoke, Jenny had the impression he wasn't telling her everything. 'Churinga happened to be in our firm's portfolio of properties. The original owners left it to us to keep it going until we deemed it proper to pass it on. Peter happened to be in the right place at the right time.' He smiled. 'He knew a bargain when he saw one. Churinga's a good property.'

The silence weighed heavy, the ticking of a clock marking the passing of time as she waited for him to tell her more.

'I realise this has come as something of a shock, Jennifer, and I apologise for not having told you before. But I had a duty to Peter to carry out his wishes.'

Jenny recognised the apology was genuine and nodded. He was obviously not able to tell her anything more, but it left her feeling unsatisfied and curious.

'I suggest you think about it for a while, then come and see me in a few weeks' time to discuss what you wish to do with your inheritance.' He smiled his cold little smile. 'We can of course help dispose of the property should you decide not to take it over. I know several investors who would snap it up if it came on to the market. Wool prices are high at the moment, and Churinga is a profitable station.'

Jenny was still having trouble taking it all in – but the thought of getting rid of the sheep station before she'd even seen it didn't sit well. But she wasn't yet ready to voice her concern. John was right, she needed time to think.

He drew out the pocket watch from his waistcoat. 'I would advise you to sell Churinga, Jennifer. The outback is no place for a young woman, and I'm told the station is very isolated. Women don't easily survive out there, especially those who are used to the city.'

He eyed her delicate stiletto-heeled sandals and expensive cotton dress. 'It's still a man's world when it comes to sheep farming in Australia – but then I suppose you already know that?'

50

She almost smiled. The years of living in Dajarra and Waluna had obviously not left their mark. 'I'll think about it,' she muttered.

'If you could just sign these papers to confirm you have been given notice of this latest inheritance? We will need them for our files.'

She skimmed the legal jargon but couldn't make much sense of it. The signature was still wet on the paper when another folder was placed before her.

'This is a copy of your late husband's share portfolio, and I've made arrangements with the bank for you to draw the income. If you could just sign this, here, here, and here I'll set up the accounts.'

Jenny did as she was told. She was on automatic, out of control of the situation and almost at breaking point. She needed to get out of this claustrophobic office and into the sunshine. Needed time to think and digest the outcome of this extraordinary afternoon.

'I'll make another appointment for you in three weeks' time. By then you should have some idea of what you wish to do with Churinga.'

Her emotions were mixed as she stepped out into the street. Bewilderment, sadness and curiosity were a heady cocktail. As she walked back through the park, she tried to imagine the outback station. It was probably just like a hundred others – but special because Peter had bought it for them.

'Churinga,' she whispered, testing the feel of it on her tongue and in her mind. It was a lovely name. As old as time, mysterious and magical. She shivered with anticipation as she clasped the locket. Magic didn't exist, not in the real world, but maybe she could find solace in the outback.

Diane knew the minute Jenny walked into the gallery that something was wrong. A casual observer would have noticed only the long brown legs and slender hips, the easy, casual grace of the way she carried herself, and the startling violet eyes. But Diane knew her too well.

She turned to Andy who was nonchalantly flicking a duster over a sculpture. 'You might as well go. We've done all we can for today.'

His arch gaze drifted over Jenny before returning to Diane. 'Girl talk, I suppose? Well, I know when I'm not wanted, so I'll say ta-ta.'

Diane watched him flounce into the back room then turned to Jenny and gave her a kiss on the cheek. She was cold to the touch and trembling, but her eyes were fever bright.

'You'll never guess what's happened,' she stammered breathlessly.

Diane put a warning finger to her lips. 'Walls have ears, darling.'

They both turned as Andy emerged from the back room, his jacket slung over his shoulders. The pink shirt and flared trousers were as immaculate as ever, the gold medallion glinting against his perfectly tanned chest, but his eyes were narrow with curiosity.

'Goodbye, Andy,' the two women chorused.

With a disdainful lift of his chin, he slammed the gallery doors and ran down the steps into the street. Diane looked at Jenny and giggled. 'God, he's irritating! Worse than having a maiden aunt around the place.'

'As neither of us has a maiden aunt, I wouldn't know,' said Jenny impatiently. 'Diane, we have to talk. I've got some very big decisions to make.'

Diane frowned as Jenny pulled what looked like a legal document from her shoulder bag. 'Pete's will? I thought that had all been dealt with?'

'So did I, but things have changed.'

Diane led her into the back room and poured them both a glass of wine. She lit a cigarette and plumped down on one of the vast floor cushions she'd brought back from Morocco. 'What's upset you, Jen? He hasn't left you in debt, has he?'

Diane's thoughts raced. Knowing Peter, that was the last thing he would have done. She'd never known a man so organised, but there was no telling what could happen when the solicitors and tax men got hold of things, and she knew things had been very tight financially.

Jenny shook her head and smiled. She took the portfolio, the deeds and the will from her shoulder bag. 'Read those, Diane. Then we can talk.'

Diane shoved back her long sleeves and skimmed over the

first few paragraphs of the will. They were legal mumbo-jumbo and not designed to be understood by anyone. When the full impact of what she was reading began to sink in, she remained open-mouthed until the end.

Jenny silently passed over the portfolio, and Diane, who'd learned a thing or two from an old boyfriend about the stock market, was impressed by the investments. 'I wish I'd known Pete was into all this – I could have done with a few tips. There's some good stuff here.'

'I didn't know you played the market. Since when?'

Diane looked up, the cigarette burning away between her fingers. 'Since I sold my first sculpture. My boyfriend at the time was working in the city. I thought you knew?'

Jenny shook her head. 'Strange, isn't it? You think you know everything about a person, then something happens and all sorts of things emerge.'

'I don't tell you the dirty details of my sex life either, but that doesn't mean I don't have one or that I've anything to hide.' Diane was cross with herself, and with Jenny. There was absolutely no reason why she should feel guilty but she did – and it bothered her.

Jenny reached over and took the cigarette from her fingers and stubbed it out. 'I'm not accusing you of anything, Di. Just stating a fact. I had no idea you and Pete played the markets. No idea we were worth so much. And that's what worries me. How could he have been so secretive when I told him everything? Whey did we live on the breadline when there was money in the bank?'

Diane had no answers. She'd liked Pete Saunders because he obviously adored Jenny and little Ben. He'd also been faithful, unlike that bastard David who'd had the morals of a rat. But there had always been a sense of detachment about Peter, she acknowledged silently. A barrier she couldn't breach, and this had tempered her feelings toward him.

She was about to speak, to offer some cliché, when Jenny handed over the last of the legal documents. 'What's this?'

'Pete's surprise birthday present,' she said quietly. 'And I don't know what to do about it.'

Diane read the deeds, and when she'd finished the two women sat for a long moment in silence. It was all too fantastic and Diane could understand Jenny's bewilderment. Finally she cleared her throat and lit another cigarette. 'I don't know why you're panicking. You've got money in the back, a house without a mortgage, and a sheep station in the back of beyond. What's the problem, Jen? I thought that was what you'd always wanted?'

Jenny snatched back the documents and lunged out of the deep cushion. 'I do wish you'd get proper chairs,' she muttered, pulling her short dress back over her thighs. 'It's unladylike scrabbling about on the bloody floor.'

Diane grinned. At least she was showing spirit, and it was good to see it again after so long. 'You're avoiding the issue, Jen. I want to know . . .'

'I heard,' she interrupted. 'I've just had a shock and still can't take it all in. I'm rich. We were rich. So why do I drive a beaten up old Holden? Why did Pete work nights and weekends? Why did we never go on holiday or buy new furniture?'

She turned on her heel, her face white with strain. 'I was married to a stranger, Diane. He took out loans on our house, gambled on the markets, bought and sold properties I knew nothing about. What other secrets did he have?'

Diane watched as Jenny scrabbled in her bag and pulled out a sheaf of papers and waved them under her nose. This was good. This meant Jenny was finally emerging from the dark, secret place she'd been hiding in for the past six months.

'Look at this catalogue of past investments, Diane,' she hissed. 'A row of terraced houses in Surry Hills . . . a two-storey unit in Koogee, and another in Bondi . . . The list is endless. Bought, done up and sold on for vast profits which he used to buy shares.' She was trembling with fury. 'And while he was busy making a fortune, I was struggling to pay the sodding electricity bill!'

Diane rescued the crumpled papers and smoothed them out. 'So Pete was a closet capitalist. He only did what he thought best, even if it was behind your back – and the sheep station was something you both wanted.'

Jenny's anger seemed to ebb as swiftly as it had risen. She sank back into the floor cushions and chewed on a fingernail.

'Have a cigarette,' Diane said firmly, offering her the slim, flat box of Craven 'A'. 'You used to have lovely nails before you gave up.'

Jenny shook her head. 'If I start again, I'll never stop. Anyway, nails are cheaper than ciggies.' She gave a watery smile and sipped her wine. 'I lost it there for a minute, didn't I? But everything seems to have got out of control, and I sometimes wonder if I'm not going mad with it all.'

Diane smiled. The silver bracelets jangled. 'Artists are never sane, least of all you and me, girl. But I'll tell you when you finally flip, and we'll tumble into the depths of insanity together.'

Jenny laughed then, and although it held a note of hysteria, it was good to hear. 'So what are you going to do about his sheep station?'

There was a frown and she bit her lip. 'I don't know. There's a manager running the place at the moment, but John Wainwright suggests I sell it.' She looked down at her fingers, her rich brown hair falling in a veil over her face so Diane couldn't see her expression. 'It wouldn't be the same without Pete, and I know very little about sheep and even less about running a station.'

Diane sat forward eagerly. Perhaps Churinga was just the thing to take Jenny out of her misery and give her something else to focus on. 'But we were fostered out at Waluna, and you took to it like a dingo to a chook. You could keep the manager on and live like lady of the manor.'

Jenny shrugged. 'I don't know, Diane. I'm tempted to go and have a look at the place, but . . .'

'But nothing.' Diane's patience snapped. She didn't know this dour, helpless Jenny who dithered and prevaricated. 'Aren't you the least bit curious? Don't you want to see the surprise Pete bought you?'

She made an effort to remain calm. 'I know it won't be the same now he and Ben are gone, but this could be the chance to make the break for a while. To get away from the house at Palm Beach and all the memories there. Treat it as an adventure, a holiday with a difference.'

'What about the exhibition, and the Parramatta commission I haven't finished?'

Diane drew deeply on the cigarette. 'The exhibition will

have to go ahead because of the work we've already put into it. Andy and I can cope. Your landscape's almost finished.' She eyed Jenny solemnly. 'So, you see, there's no excuse really. You have to go. Pete would have wanted it.'

Jenny let Diane persuade her to eat a late supper in Kings Cross. It was a short walk from the gallery, in the heart of the bohemian sector of Sydney, and a favourite place for both of them. The neon lights blinked and flashed, music poured out of the bars and strip clubs, and the pavement traffic was as bizarre and flamboyant as ever, but Jenny was just not in the mood to sit back and take it all in as she usually did. The lights were too bright, the music too jarring, the street walkers and strutting exhibitionists seemed tawdry. Deciding not to go back with Diane, she made the hour-long drive to her own house.

It was a wonderful house, three storeys high, perched on the side of a hill overlooking the bay. They'd been lucky to find it so cheaply. In the first few years, before Ben came along, they'd sunk all their money into refurbishing. Now, with a new roof, air-conditioning, panoramic windows and fresh paint, it was worth much more than they'd spent. Palm Beach was suddenly fashionable, and although that meant an endless procession of weekend surfers and sun worshippers, neither of them had wanted to move. Ben had loved the beach, was just beginning to learn to swim and had thrown tantrums when it was time to wander back up the hill and home.

'I'd give anything for him to throw a tantrum now,' whispered Jenny as she put the key in the door to her attic studio. 'I wish. I wish.'

She unlocked the door and slammed it firmly behind her. All the wishing in the world wouldn't bring them back, but being here in the house only made the memories sharper, more painful. Perhaps Diane was right about leaving for a while.

The studio lights were necessarily harsh, for she often painted at night when the sun no longer shone through the cupola. Yet now she felt the need for softness and switched them off. After lighting candles and a stick of incense, she kicked off her shoes and wriggled her feet. The extra stub that grew over her little toe was red and sore, but it was her own fault. She'd refused to let this sixth toe make any difference to her life, and as the doctors had refused to do anything about it, she'd decided to ignore it as much as possible. But now and again it was rubbed raw by the fashionable shoes she was determined to wear.

She stripped to her underwear, took off all her jewellery but for the locket and curled up on the chaise-longue. It was very old, and the stuffing was peeking through the worn velvet, but it was comfortable, and she couldn't yet face that big double bed downstairs. It would feel too empty.

The sound of the sea came through the open windows, and the distant cry of a kookaburra defending his territory echoed in the stillness. As the candles flickered and the warm sensuous aroma of incense drifted above the familiar tang of paint and turps, Jenny finally began to relax.

She let her mind meander over the four short years she'd spent with Peter, pausing here and there on postcard pictures of the happy times, the moments caught forever in her memory. Ben on the sand, giggling with delight as the sea crept over his toes. Peter up a ladder repairing the guttering after a storm, his tanned body so lithe and sexy in those tight shorts.

They had met at a dance, shortly after she and Diane had come to Sydney. He was already working for the bank but his roots were firmly implanted in a cattle station in the Northern Territory which his two older brothers had inherited. He was bright and funny and she'd fallen in love with him almost instantly. They'd shared the same humour and the same interests, and when he'd talked about the land and his burning desire one day to have his own place, she'd recognised the same need within herself. Those years at Waluna had left an indelible impression, and Peter's enthusiasm had sparked her own.

Jenny curled further into the depths of the old day bed. God, I miss him, she thought. I miss his smell, his warmth, his smile, and the way he could make me laugh. I miss the way he used to kiss my neck when I was cooking, and the wonderful feel of him in the bed next to me. But most of all I miss not being able to talk to him. To discuss the day, no matter how trivial it had been, to marvel at how quickly Ben was growing and to share our pride in our marvellous little boy.

The tears finally came and ran slowly down her face as her resistance crumbled. Deep, choking sobs broke the dam and she gave into it for the first time since that awful day. Diane was right, she acknowledged. Fate was cruel, and there was absolutely nothing she could do about it. The dream of having a family of her own was shattered, just like the other dreams she and Diane had shared all those years ago in Dajarra. But beneath that tide of grief came the knowledge that Peter had given her one dream she could fulfil. He wouldn't be there to share it but perhaps his gift was a way of making a new life for herself.

The sun had already risen when Jenny opened her eyes again. Now it streamed into the studio, dust motes dancing on the rays, reflecting prisms of light from the crystals she'd hung from the ceiling. Her head hurt and her eyelids were swollen, but she felt a deep sense of calm and purpose. It was as if the tears of the previous night had washed away the false barriers she'd erected in the mistaken belief they would protect her, and brought her to a deeper understanding of what she must do next.

She lay there, savouring the moment. Then her gaze drifted to the easel by the window and the landscape she'd almost finished. The man from Paramatta had given her a photograph of a cattle station homestead. His wife had once lived there, and the painting was to be a gift for her on her birthday.

Jenny eyed the painting critically, looking for flaws, seeing a hint of carelessness in a brush stroke that would have to be remedied. She hadn't worked on it for some time, but now, in the light of a new morning, she felt the old, familiar surge of enthusiasm return. Climbing off the bed, she padded across the floor and picked up the palette. She would finish the painting then make plans.

As she mixed the paint, she felt a tremor of anticipation. Churinga. It seemed to be calling her. Enticing her from the cool blue of the Pacific towards the hot red earth of the centre.

Three weeks later Diane leaned back on the old chaise-longue. The many rings on her fingers sparkled in the sunlight that streamed through the cupola and windows. The tiny bells on her earrings tinkled as she adjusted the cushions and watched Jenny work.

The painting was almost finished. She wished she could have had it for the exhibition. Nothing the Australian public liked more than the glimpse of their own inheritance, a reminder of the true heart of their vast and wonderful country. Most of them had never been further than the Blue Mountains, and here, emerging from beneath Jenny's brush, was the real Australia.

Diane cocked her head and studied the painting more closely. There was a passion for her subject in Jenny's work, a feel for the great sweep of land and the isolation of the homestead that she'd never noticed before. 'I think that's the best thing you've done in a long while,' she murmured. 'It really speaks to you.'

Jenny stepped back from the easel, head tilted as she eyed her work. She was dressed in tattered shorts and a bikini top, her long hair twisted into a rough knot on the top of her head, anchored by a paint brush. She was barefoot – something she only did when she was alone or with Diane – and the only jewellery she wore was the antique locket Pete had given her for Christmas.

'I agree,' she muttered. 'Although I don't usually like working from photos.'

Diane watched Jenny's careful attention to the final details. She knew from experience these could either make or destroy all the hard work that had gone before. There came a time when enough was enough – and instinct was the only guideline.

Jenny moved away from the painting, stood looking at it for a long while, then began to clean up. The brushes were soaked in turps, the palette and knife scraped and stacked on the table next to the easel. She released her hair and shook it out, easing the stiffness in her neck and shoulders by stretching her arms to the ceiling. 'Finished,' she sighed. 'Now I can start planning.'

It's good to see her animated again, thought Diane. Great to have her back from the terrible anguish that almost destroyed her. She climbed off the couch, her gold sandals slapping against the wooden floor as she crossed the room.

Jenny turned and smiled. 'Are you sure you don't mind looking after the house while I go bush?'

Diane shook her head, earrings tinkling. 'Of course not. It'll be a bolt hole where no one can reach me, and I can get a bit of peace. What with the exhibition coming up, and Rufus plighting his troth all over the place, it's just what I need.'

Jenny grinned. 'He's not still after you, is he? I thought he went home to England.'

Diane thought of the robust, middle-aged art critic who wore loud shirts and even louder ties to compete with his voice and ebullient manner. 'I wish he would,' she said dryly. 'He's wearing me out with his pontificating about the rawness of Aussie art compared to the refinement of the English school.'

'He's only trying to impress you with his vast knowledge. He can't help being a pom.'

'Maybe not, but I do wish he wouldn't ram England down my throat all the time.' She stared out of the window. The beach was already crowded, and the latest Beatles song drifted up from a distant transistor. 'Having said that, I like him mostly. He makes me laugh and I think that's important, don't you?'

Jenny looked wistful as she came to join her at the window. 'Oh, yes,' she murmured. Then she turned her startling eyes to Diane. 'But promise me you won't go off and marry him while I'm gone? I know Rufus well enough to realise he can be very persuasive, and he's obviously besotted with you.'

Diane felt a surge of pleasure that surprised her. 'Do you really think so?'

Jenny nodded before turning away. 'Enough of him. Come downstairs and I'll make brunch, then you can help me sort out a plan and travel route to Churinga before I go and see John Wainwright.'

Diane looked into those lively violet eyes and knew for certain her friend was beginning to heal. Perhaps this new adventure would be the start of a new life – and even if it wasn't, she was grateful to Peter for having had the foresight to know Jenny needed to go back where she felt she belonged.

John Wainwright still wore his three-piece suit, the windows remained closed, and the only concession to the heat was a fan on the desk which did nothing more than stir the turgid air around the room.

Jenny watched as he neatly stacked the papers on his desk. He looked comfortable, at one with the panelled walls and leather-bound books. It was as if he'd been caught in a time warp, a small piece of England, transported like a convict, out of place and incongruous. She smiled at him and received a warm response. He seemed friendlier today, his eyes not quite so cold.

'Have you decided what you're going to do with your inheritance?'

She nodded. Yet the finality of accepting Peter's gift, and acknowledging that from now on she was on her own, was daunting. 'Yes,' she said firmly before she could change her mind. 'I've decided to keep Churinga. In fact, I'm planning to visit there for a while.'

Wainwright's fingers steepled beneath his double chin, his expression troubled. 'Have you really thought this through, Jennifer? It's a long journey for a young woman, and there are some rough types out on those lonely roads.'

This was exactly the reaction she'd expected, but as she was about to defend her decision, he thumbed through his diary and forestalled her.

'I could rearrange my schedule and come with you? But it couldn't be for another week or so.' He looked at her over his spectacles. 'I don't think it wise for you to be alone in such an out of the way place.'

Jenny's spirits tumbled. The last things she needed was this precise little man with his neat suit and his immaculate nails as a travelling companion. She had a mental image of him with his black umbrella, bowler and briefcase, walking down the dirt road of a distant outback town, and bit her lip against the smile it conjured up. She didn't want to hurt his feelings. After all, he was only being kind. Yet he would be of no use to her – one hint of trouble and he'd wilt.

She smiled to soften her words. 'You are kind, John, but I've gone bush before and know what to expect. It won't be as bad as you think. They really are quite civilised out there, you know.'

His relief was obvious, even if it was tinged with doubt,

and Jenny hurried on before he could protest. 'I've already made some travelling arrangements, and as you can see, I shan't really be alone at all.' She put the train and bus tickets on the desk. 'I'm going on the Indian Pacific as far as Broken Hill, then catching a bus to Wallaby Flats. I thought, as I have time on my hands, I might as well see as much of the country as I can. If you could contact the manager at Churinga and ask him to meet me at Wallaby Flats, I would be grateful.'

John eyed the tickets. 'You seem to be very organised, Jennifer.'

She sat forward and leaned her arms on the desk. Excitement was bubbling in her but she felt a little bit sorry for this man who would probably never venture further than his office now he'd made the transition from England.

'I'm leaving tomorrow afternoon, four o'clock. It will take at least two days to get to Wallaby Flats, but I can afford to take my time. From there, I hope to catch a ride or hire a car if the manager can't send someone to meet me.'

John Wainwright's blank stare was magnified by the thick glasses. 'Wallaby Flats is not a city, Jennifer. It's a forgotten mining town which boasts a few hovels, tin shacks and a pub frequented by swagmen, drovers and fossickers. It's in the middle of nowhere. You could be stuck for days before you found someone to take you out to Churinga.'

Jenny noticed his shudder of distaste. She'd been right in her opinion that he would only have been a burden if just the thought of the place could make him so uncomfortable.

'Then you'll just have to make sure the manager sees to it someone's there to meet me,' she said firmly. He might consider her stupid and wilful, but this was her adventure and she meant to see it through.

'As you wish.' His tone revealed his misgivings.

'I'm not afraid of the outback or of travelling alone, John. I was brought up in an orphanage at Dajarra, and have had to fend for myself all my life. I've met some of the roughest working men in the harshest of places during my years on a Queensland sheep station. They're only people like you and me. Honest, hard-working, hard-drinking people who wouldn't harm me. Believe me, John, I'm far more at risk here in the city.'

She fell silent for a moment to let him digest her words. 'Peter left me Churinga so I could return to the land. The outback is a part of me, John – I have nothing to fear there.'

Her impassioned speech seemed to decide him. 'Then I'll contact Churinga and let Brett Wilson know you're on your way. If you'd wait a moment, I'll try and get through now. I don't want you leaving here before I'm quite certain you'll be met.'

He raised an eyebrow and Jenny nodded her acquiescence. At least he seemed to care what happened to her, she thought. And she was grateful for that.

Three-quarters of an hour and two cups of weak tea later, he came back into the room. He was looking pleased with himself and rubbing his hands. 'I have spoken to Mr Wilson, and he's arranging for someone to meet the coach in three days' time. You'll probably arrive in the early evening so he suggests you stay in the hotel in case there's a last-minute hitch. He assures me it's quite proper for a young woman to spend the night alone in such a place.'

Jenny smiled and stood up. His handshake was warm but limp. 'Thank you for being so kind, John, and for your concern over my travelling arrangements.'

'I wish you well, Jennifer. And, may I say, I admire your courage. Let me know how you fare, and if there's anything you need . . . well, you know where I am.'

Jenny's footsteps were sure and light as she left the shadowed building and walked down Macquarie Street. She was at last looking forward to her future.

# Chapter Two

Jenny's emotions were mixed as she said goodbye to Diane, who as usual was decked in an exotic caftan, heavy eye makeup and too much clanking, jangling jewellery. 'I'm excited, nervous, and not at all sure I'm doing the right thing,' said Jenny, her voice not quite steady.

Diane laughed and gave her a hug. 'Of course you are. You don't have to stay there if you hate it, and I promise not to throw wild bohemian parties in your house.' She gave Jenny a little shove as the slam of train doors echoed around Sydney's central station. 'Now go, will you? Before I cry and make my mascara run.'

Jenny kissed her, adjusted the rucksack more comfortably on her shoulders and turned towards the train. Central Station was busy with people rushing out of the city for the weekend, many of them dressed as she was, in shorts, shirt and thick boots and socks. Her felt hat was crammed into the back-pack, along with insect repellent, plasters, drawing materials, and three changes of clothes. She wouldn't need much where she was going, and she certainly didn't envisage staying very long. This was just a reconnaissance to satisfy her curiosity, her need to return to the outback just once more to see if she could pick up the pieces of her old life again.

With a last wave to Diane, she stepped up into the old diesel train and found her seat in economy. Thrift was a habit, and her cheap seat meant she would have to sit all the way through the journey and not take advantage of the luxury sleeping compartments. Yet she felt at ease with that decision. It would give her a chance to meet and talk to the other passengers then perhaps she wouldn't feel quite so alone.

As the train pulled slowly out of the station, she experienced a twist of excitement. What would Churinga be like – and would she still feel the same way about the outback as she had as a child? She was more sophisticated now, older and hopefully wiser, soft from the years in the city with its air conditioning, shops, abundant water and cool, leafy parks.

Sydney slid by the window and she stared out at the suburbs. The old Holden would never have stood the journey, she was glad she'd chosen the train. Yet, as everything familiar began to fade into the distance, she wished Diane was beside her.

The train made regal progress out of the city and into the Blue Mountains. To Jenny it was like a majestic and magical picture book, spread before her in breathtaking panorama. Great, steep-sided gorges spilled waterfalls into wooded blue-green valleys. Jagged rocks, softened by the blue haze of eucalyptus oil, formed pinnacles which stretched endlessly into the distance and shimmered on the horizon. A scattering of holiday cabins peeked from between the trees and small settlements of older houses huddled on steep-sided plateaux, but nothing could mar the beauty of this awesome sight.

The tourist cameras were out, clicking and whirring beneath the excited chatter of the other passengers. Jenny furiously regretted not having brought her own, but as the miles of mountain track meandered on and on, she knew this scenery would be forever implanted in her memory.

Several hours later they had left one range of mountains for another. Passing through Lithgow, Bathurst and Orange, the train swept through the Herveys Range and on to Gondobolin, stopping only for a few moments to pick up passengers from dusty, remote platforms.

Jenny never tired of watching the sheep grazing this rough land which yielded only tough, yellow grass. Although the mountains had been awe-inspiring, the sight of scrubby trees and red earth touched something primal within her. A mob of kangaroos bouncing across the grasslands brought cries of delight from the others and she quietly enjoyed their pleasure in her beautiful country.

Night fell swiftly and Jenny was rocked to sleep by the

whisper of the wheels on the tracks. 'Going home. Going home. Going home.'

Day came with a sky of red and orange overhanging the land, reflecting its colours in the very earth it warmed. Jenny looked out of the window as she drank her coffee. The land seemed to be ripening in the heat. How beautiful it was, how desolate and achingly lonely. Yet what powerful emotions it evoked. How bravely the trees stood under the sun, their leaves wilting, bark bleached to ghostly grey. She was falling in love with her country all over again.

Another day, another night. Through the National Reserve, past Mount Manara and Gun Lake, the miles of sparsely populated land sprawled into infinity on either side. Small hamlets and deserted pastures, tranquil lakes and silent mountains, slipped by in majestic cavalcade.

Morning again, and Jenny's neck and back were stiff from sitting so long. Sleep had come fleetingly as her destination drew nearer, and she'd spent most of the night playing cards and drinking beer with a group of young English back-packers. The train slowed as it reached the desert oasis that was Broken Hill. The gauge on the line changed here, the next leg of the journey for the others would be in another train.

Jenny packed up her guide book and prepared to get off. Silver City, as it had once been called, lay on the banks of the River Darling, lush undergrowth and bright flowers jarring against the backdrop of dust and turn-of-the-century buildings.

The incongruous sight of the simple nineteenth-century iron mosque caused an excited babble amongst the others, who also talked of visiting the ghost town of Silverton which lay west of Broken Hill and was now used mainly for film locations. She would have liked to join them, and as she said goodbye to the back-packers, felt a twinge of regret that she couldn't complete the journey and go cross-country to Perth. There was so much to see and experience, so many places that had only been names on the map until now. Yet the bus would be waiting, and her journey would take her in a different direction. Perhaps another time, she promised herself silently.

Easing the straps of the pack, Jenny set off down the road. Broken Hill was a quaint mixture of outback village and city pretensions. Grand buildings from the age when silver mining

66

boomed, jostled alongside wooden shacks and colonnaded shops. The Catholic cathedral vied with the Trades Hall and post office clock tower for attention amongst the newer, rather brash hotels and motels.

The coach was waiting outside the Prince Albert Hotel that stood proudly in a lush garden. Jenny was disappointed. She had hoped to explore and take time out to shower and change her clothes, maybe get something to eat. But if she missed the bus, she would have to wait a week before the next one, and with Brett Wilson due to meet her at Wallaby Flats, this was not possible.

'Name's Les. I'll take this, luv. You hop on board and make yourself comfy. There's cold beers and cordial in the cool box, leave the money in the tin.'

The driver grabbed her rucksack and stowed it away. He was dressed in shorts, white shirt, boots and long white socks carefully turned over just below the knee. He seemed friendly, with a face leathered by the sun and a bright smile beneath his dark moustache.

She gave him an answering smile and clambered aboard. With a bottle of beer in her hand, she nodded and returned the other passengers' greetings as she passed down the bus to her seat. The space between them was narrow, the bus airless and flies buzzed around her face. She brushed them away, an automatic gesture as natural to an Australian as blinking, and took a long, refreshing pull of cold beer. Her excitement was building. In eight hours' time she would be in Wallaby Flats.

As the bus pulled away in a plume of red dust, the flies disappeared and a warm breeze came in through the windows. Hats and newspapers were used to stir the air, but despite the discomfort Jenny loved it. This was the real Australia. Not the cities and beaches, the parks and shopping malls, but the real essence of the country with all its faults.

The heat increased, the beer stock was depleted, and Les kept everyone amused with his constant chatter and terrible jokes. More beer was purchased in Nuntherungie, and this was repeated at every stop in the eight-hour journey. Jenny was weary from lack of sleep, the heat and too much beer and excitement. Lunch had been doorstep sandwiches at a small hotel in the middle of nowhere, but there had been no time for a wash and change of clothes.

It was almost dark, but thankfully cooler when the bus finally reached Wallaby Flats. Jenny stepped down with the others and stretched. Her shirt and shorts were dark with sweat, and judging by the look of the others, she knew she must look a fright. Yet her spirits were high for she'd come through the journey and was almost at her destination.

She stood in the twilight and sniffed the air. 'What's that awful smell?' she gasped.

Les grinned. 'That'll be the sulphur springs, luv. But you'll soon get used to the pong. No worries.'

'I hope so,' she muttered, retrieving her bag.

The Queen Victoria Hotel had a faded glory about it, despite the dilapidated sign that stood crookedly above the entrance. Years ago it must have been quite something, she thought. Now it just looks sad and worn out. The two-storey sandstone building was girded by a balcony and verandah. Paint peeled and the filigree ironwork was rusted and missing in places. Heavy shutters lay along the sides of the narrow windows, and wire screens kept out the flies and mosquitoes. Dusty horses were tied to a hitching post, their tails flicking, necks drooping towards the concrete water trough. The long verandah looked cool beneath the balcony and was obviously a popular meeting place for the local men. They sat in rocking chairs or on the steps, watching the tourists from beneath broad-brimmed hats which, by the look of them, had seen many years' service.

Jenny took it all in with an artist's eye. The oldest had stubbled chins, their weather-beaten faces and sun-dazzled eyes telling stories of hardship. I wish I could get to my drawing things, she thought as she climbed the steps. Some of these old blokes would make wonderful studies. She paused to take off the heavy pack. 'G'day. Been a hot one again.' Her gaze swept from one stoic face to the next.

Finally a grizzled old codger replied, 'G'day,' his eyes curious for a fleeting moment before he returned to staring at the darkening landscape.

Jenny realised they felt awkward, and wondered if the influx of so many people at once was an intrusion on their quiet, settled lives. Perhaps the isolation of their outback town had instilled a deep suspicion of outsiders.

She lugged the pack through the door and followed the others into the bar. A drink, a wash and something to eat would set her right for a good night's sleep.

Several men lounged against the bar, beer in hand, eyes following the new arrivals from beneath their hats. One flat-heeled boot was propped against the tarnished brass pole that was firmly bolted to the floor; shirts and moleskins bore traces of their day's labour. Conversation, if there had been any, was stopped, but there was no animosity in their silence, merely an amused curiosity.

A ceiling fan turned sluggishly through the humid air and fly papers hung black from every beam and picture rail. The bar itself was a long plank of wood which stretched the length of the room, presided over by a hawk-nosed, thin man who wore braces over his singlet and a belt around his baggy trousers. An array of dusty bottles lined the walls, the radio crackled with static, and ancient Christmas decorations did their best to brighten up the gloom.

'Ladies' lounge is out back,' said the landlord in a thick Baltic accent. He jerked his head in the vague direction of a door at the far end of the bar.

Jenny followed the other women. It was irritating to be treated as a second-class citizen. This was the Seventies, for goodness' sake. Yet as she sank into a cane chair and dropped the pack beside her, she knew better than to make a fuss. Even Sydney was not yet totally enlightened. Australian men didn't like to see their women in pubs – to them it was the break-down of a system that had suited them well for years and they didn't see why it should change. But change was coming, and the sooner the better, she thought, wondering if they would ever be served. She was parched.

A blonde came clattering into the room, her stiletto heels rapping a tattoo on the rough floorboards. She had obviously just applied fresh lipstick, but it clashed with the pink plastic earrings and tight orange skirt. Her over-developed cleavage bounced beneath a frilly blouse and numerous cheap bangles clattered on her wrists. She was in her late twenties. Jenny guessed, and probably too young to be the landlord's wife, but she seemed friendly enough and certainly brought colour and life to this dismal room.

'I've had enough beer, thanks,' Jenny replied to the offer of a drink. 'A cordial or a cup of tea would be right.'

'Righto. Nothing like a cuppa to settle the dust, is there?' The young woman's smile was bright as her eyelashes fluttered. 'Name's Lorraine, by the way. How'ya goin'?'

'She'll be right once I've had a drink, a wash and something to eat.' Jenny smiled. The aroma of roast lamb was sharpening her appetite. Reminding her that lunch was a distant memory.

Within minutes she was sipping her tea. It was strong and hot, and just the thing to revive her flagging energy. Lorraine had disappeared back into the bar, and Jenny could hear the to and fro of those high heels below the banter and raucous laughter. She looked around the quiet lounge room. Most of the women were half asleep; those that weren't merely stared into space, too tired even to make the most desultory conversation. Jenny wished she was with Lorraine. It sounded much more fun in the bar.

It was a good half hour before she returned, and after they'd followed her into the kitchen and she'd served the heaped plates of meat and vegetables, Jenny caught her attention. 'Are there any messages for me? I was expecting someone to meet me.'

Lorraine's over-plucked eyebrows shot up. 'What did you say your name was, luv? I'll check.'

'Jenny Sanders.' She was unprepared for the reaction.

Lorraine's face froze in mid-smile and her eyes grew sharp and predatory as they swept over her. 'Brett's not here yet.'

'But you do have a reservation for me?'

'Jeez, I don't know, Mrs Sanders. See, Dad's got the place full what with the bus and everything.'

Jenny looked into that artless face and wide, deceptively innocent eyes. She was lying – but why? 'Mr Wilson said he'd booked a room,' she said firmly. 'I have the confirmation here.' She handed over the telegram he'd sent to John Wainwright.

Lorraine remained unimpressed. She gave the telegram a

fleeting glance and shrugged. 'I'll see if Dad can squeeze you in, but you'll have to share.' She turned swiftly, a tray of empty glasses expertly balanced in one hand.

There was a murmur of disapproval from the other women, and Jenny shrugged and laughed it off. 'No worries. I could sleep anywhere, I'm so tired.'

'Well, I think it's disgraceful,' hissed a middle-aged woman whose broad girth was harnessed in sensible navy blue cotton. During the long bus ride, Jenny had learned that her name was Mrs Keen, and she was on the way to the Northern Territory to visit her grandchildren.

'If you've paid for a room, then you should have one.'

A murmur of agreement went round the table and Jenny began to feel uneasy. She didn't want to cause a fuss, and certainly didn't relish getting on the wrong side of Lorraine whom she'd clearly already upset. Though God knows how, she thought.

'I'm sure it'll sort itself out,' she murmured. 'It's too hot for a fuss, let's see what Lorraine has to say when she gets back.'

Plump Mrs Keen put her soft hand on Jenny's arm, and with a conspiratorial wink, leaned forward to whisper, 'It's all right, luv. You can bunk in with me. Lorraine obviously thinks you're after her man – that Brett you were supposed to meet?'

Jenny stared at her. Perhaps that was the answer. Lorraine had been fine until Mr Wilson's name had come into the conversation. God, she must be tired not to have realised sooner. But the whole thing was absurd, and the sooner she cleared it up the better.

'Brett Wilson's the manager of my sheep station. I can't see that I pose any threat to Lorraine.'

The older woman's laughter made her bulk quiver. 'I've never seen a woman so eaten up with jealousy in my life as when she clapped eyes on you, luv. And as for you posing no threat – well,' she dried her eyes, 'I reckon you ain't looked in a mirror lately.'

Jenny was lost for words but the older woman continued. 'I wouldn't mind betting Lorraine's got her hooks into your manager and is making plans. Mark my words,' she said solemnly. 'You want to watch that one.' This piece of advice was accompanied by a forceful spearing of lamb and potato.

Lorraine came back into the room as the conversation threatened to grow heated amongst the women. 'We're full so you'll have to share,' she said coldly. 'Or have a mattress on the back verandah. There's screens, so it'll be private.'

Mrs Keen mopped up the last of the gravy with a hunk of bread. 'I got a room with two beds. Jenny can come in with me.'

Lorraine's eyes were hostile as they switched between Jenny and Mrs Keen but she didn't reply.

Jenny finished her dinner and helped Mrs Keen with her things. They went through the back door and out on to the verandah. A flight of rough stairs took them to the room above the bar. The ceiling fan groaned as it moved turgid air in the small, gloomy room. Two cot beds, a chair and dressing table were the only furniture. The shutters were firmly closed against the night and the mosquitoes. The dunny was downstairs, outside, and the washing facilities were a bowl and pitcher of tepid water that was the colour of tea dregs.

'Not exactly the Ritz, is it?' said Mrs Keen, slumping on to one of the cotbeds. 'Never mind. After that bus ride, any bed will be heaven.'

Jenny turned to her back-pack as the other woman stripped off her dress and washed before climbing into bed. At least the linen was clean, she thought, and there are fresh towels and a bar of soap.

Mrs Keen was soon snoring softly into the pillows, and after a quick wash Jenny pulled on a thin cotton T-shirt and sat in the deepening gloom, relishing the peace and quiet after the long journey. After a while restlessness drew her out of the stuffy little room and on to the balcony.

She leaned against the railings and looked up into the sky. The night was velvet soft, the Milky Way splashing stars in a broad sweep against the inky black. Orion and the Southern Cross were bright and clear above the slumbering earth, and for a moment she wished she could sleep out here on a mattress. But the mosquitoes made it impossible.

How beautiful it all is, she thought. Then smiled. The soft, haunting chuckle of a kookaburra echoed in the stillness. She would have to reacquaint herself with this land called the outback, but knew she was already a part of it.

# Chapter Three

The first fingers of light came through the slats of the shutters and warmed her face. Jenny slowly emerged from a deep sleep and lay for a moment, eyes shut against the glare. The night had been dreamless for the first time in months, and although she felt refreshed there was a sense that Pete and Ben were drifting away from her. Faded silhouettes, growing dim on the horizon, the pain of their loss diminished by time and space – how soon the human psyche began the process of healing.

She slipped the photographs from under her pillow and looked at their faces. Then, with a kiss, she put them away. They would remain alive in her memory, no matter the distance between them.

Mrs Keen, who'd been snoring, woke suddenly, eyes bleary, hair tousled. 'Morning already?'

Jenny nodded and began to brush her hair. 'Comes early out here.'

'Too right, it's only five o'clock.' Mrs Keen stretched and had a luxurious scratch. 'I wonder when they serve breakfast?'

Jenny twisted her hair up on to the top of her head and anchored it with tortoiseshell clips. By the time Mrs Keen had returned from the dunny, she'd washed and dressed and was ready to explore. 'Catch you later,' she said quickly, squeezing past the older woman. It was too nice a day to be cooped up inside.

The dunny was a shed in the far corner of the back yard, well away from the kitchen. It was dark, smelled evil, and wasn't a place to linger. Jenny shuddered as she thought of lurking spiders and snakes, and was soon back in the early sunshine.

It was already warm, with a promise of more heat to come. The sky was streaked pink and orange, the earth reflecting the heat in an endless, shimmering horizon. As Jenny walked around the side of the hotel, she heard the rattle of saucepans and Lorraine's shrill voice. Digging her hands into the pockets of her shorts, she felt a return of the deep calm that had been missing in her for so long. It was a beautiful day and not even Lorraine could spoil it.

The dirt road meandered past the hotel and was lost in the desert. The houses on either side of this track were blasted by heat and dust. Paint was cracked and peeling, wooden shutters shrunken on rusting hinges. The river, now down to a trickle, ran parallel to the road, and was obviously in the habit of flooding during the wet, for every building was perched on stone pilings.

Jenny headed for the sulphur pools. Les had been right, she hardly noticed the smell any more, but at the sight of the bilious yellow water she decided against testing their therapeutic powers and went off to explore the mine shafts instead.

They were nothing more than deep holes punched into the ground, shored up by railway sleepers. According to her guide book, opals had once been big business around here, but these didn't look as if they'd been worked for years. She leaned over the side of one and almost lost her balance as a voice boomed in her ear.

'Wanna watch yerself there, lady.'

She spun round and came face to face with a gnome. Short and spare, with a gnarled nose and bright blue eyes, the little man glared up at her ferociously from beneath bushy white brows.

'G'day. This yours then?' She was finding it hard to keep a straight face now she'd got over the initial shock.

'Too right it is. Been digging here for two years. Reckon I'll hit the big one soon.' He smiled. There were only a few teeth on display – and they were rotten.

'So there are still opals here?'

'Yeah. Got me a beaut the other day.' He looked over his shoulder then leaned towards her. 'No point shouting me mouth off or some bludger'll come and nick me mine. I could tell you stories that'd make your hair curl, lady, and that's a fact.'

She had no doubt he could. Like most Australians, he'd obviously kissed the blarney stone, and there was nothing like a tall story to pass the time.

'Wanna have a look around?'

'Down there?' Jenny wasn't too sure. It looked awfully deep and horribly dark. Besides, there was probably nothing to see down there anyway.

'Yeah, she'll be right. There ain't snakes down there any more like the old days when the miners kept 'em for guards. C'mon, I'll show yer.'

His hand was rough to the touch, and she felt the strength in his fingers as he grasped her arm and showed her the best way to go down the ladder. He might have been small and goodness knows how old, but he was amazingly powerful. As Jenny balanced on the rickety rungs, she wasn't at all sure she was doing the right thing by going down a hole with him.

'Wait on,' he said as they reached the bottom. 'Let's get some light.' He struck a match and the warm glow of a kerosene lamp chased away the darkness.

It was cool down here in the ground, and as she looked around her she forgot her misgivings. It wasn't just a hole but an enormous web of tunnels, the earth chiselled away to reveal centuries of colour and texture.

'Beauty, ain't it?' He grinned with pride, then winked. 'But it's what's hidden in the earth that's really something.' He turned away and reached into a narrow shelf dug into the wall of the tunnel. Moments later he opened up a leather drawstring bag and spilled the contents into his hand.

Jenny gasped. The lamplight caught the opals, sending glints of red and blue and green through the milky white. And here and there were the rarest of them all. The black opals. Gleaming and secretive, they were flecked with spell-binding gold.

He took a particularly fine specimen and placed it in the palm of her hand. 'I polished it as best I could, but I reckon it'll get me a good price in the city.'

Jenny held it up to the light, turning it this way and that until the deep red fires flashed and danced. 'It's magnificent,' she breathed.

'Too right,' he smirked. 'Give you a fair price if you wanted to buy it.'

Jenny looked at the opal. She'd seen them in the jewellers in Sydney and knew how much they cost. 'I doubt I could afford it,' she said regretfully. 'Besides, aren't opals meant to be unlucky?'

The old man threw back his head, his laughter ringing in the labyrinth of caverns. 'Fair go, lady. You've been listening to blokes that don't know what they're talking about. They're only unlucky for the poor bastards that don't find them.'

She grinned back at him as he tipped the stones into the drawstring bag and returned it to its hiding place. 'Aren't you frightened someone might come down here and pinch them?'

He shook his head and reached for a tiny wire cage. 'Put me scorpions in there when I leave the mine. No bastard'll tangle with them.' He released the scorpions and shut them in with the pouch behind a thick slab of stone. 'Must be time for tucker. Lorraine cooks a fair brekkie, even if she does look like an accident in a paint factory.' He laughed again at his own joke, and set off up the ladder.

They walked in amiable silence back to the hotel. Jenny would have liked to ask about Lorraine and Brett Wilson, but knew that in such a small place her curiosity would cause comment. Besides, she acknowledged, it was really none of her business, so long as it didn't affect his work.

The kitchen was enormous and filled with noise. Long trestle tables were covered in plastic cloths and dishes, the benches crowded with the tourists from the bus, and the passing drovers and fossikers who'd stayed overnight.

'Cooee!' Mrs Keen's voice sailed above the general clamour. 'Over here, luv. I saved a place for you.'

Jenny had barely squeezed in beside her room mate before Lorraine dumped a plate of steak, egg and fried potato in front of her. She looked at it in horror. 'I don't usually eat breakfast. Just coffee, please.'

'We only got tea. This ain't some fancy hotel in Sydney, you know.' The plate was snatched away, the tea pot slammed down in its place.

'Too right it isn't,' Jenny snapped. Then instantly regretted it as the room fell silent and all eyes swivelled from her to Lorraine. She heard Mrs Keen draw in her breath.

'So why don't you push off back there?' Lorraine tossed her head, and with bracelets jangling, left the room.

Jenny laughed to hide her shame at having lost her temper so easily. 'And go through that bloody bus ride again? No, thanks,' she said to the room in general.

There was a relieved sigh and the others laughed with her. Soon the room was once again filled with chatter and the clink of cutlery. Yet Jenny knew she'd made a bad start to her stay here. There were few enough women out in the bush, she'd been stupid to alienate the first one she'd come across.

Mrs Keen left on the bus an hour later, and after waving goodbye Jenny sat on the porch with her sketch book. She was eager to begin for there were so many things she wanted to commit to paper. The colours were primary but each of them a shade deeper or lighter than the next, melding into one glorious tapestry of red and tan, orange and ochre. Impossible to capture in the softness of pastel or pencil. She wished now she'd brought her oils and canvases.

She was lost in her work, page after page filling with colour and movement as the desert vista was transformed by the rising sun.

'Mrs Sanders?'

She hadn't heard his approach but his mellow drawl didn't startle her. She looked up into grey eyes flecked with green and gold, and fringed by long black lashes. The sun had creased them at the corners, and the face that looked down at her was square and rugged beneath the shadow of his drover's hat. His chin was cleft, nose long and straight, mouth sensuous and curved by humour. He looked about thirty, but it was hard to tell a man's age out here once the sun had got to him.

'Brett Wilson. Sorry I'm late. Got held up back at the property.'

'G'day,' she managed once she'd got her breath back. So this tall, handsome man was the manager of Churinga? No wonder Lorraine guarded him against all-comers. 'Jenny's the name,' she said quickly. 'Pleased to meet you at last.'

He withdrew his hand, but his gaze lingered a fraction longer than was comfortable. 'Reckon it's better I call you

Mrs Sanders,' he said finally. 'People out here like to talk, and you are the boss.'

Jenny was surprised. It was most unusual for an Australian not to be on first name terms, even if they were a hired hand. Yet something in his eyes stopped her from saying anything. Quickly she gathered up her things. 'I expect you'll want to be getting back?'

He shook his head. 'No worries. Could do with a couple of schooners first. Want me to send Lorraine out with one for you while you wait?'

She didn't really, but if she was being forced to wait then the least he could do' was shout her a beer. 'Righto, Mr Wilson. But don't let's hang around for too long. I want to see Churinga.'

He tipped back his hat and Jenny had a glimpse of black, curly hair before the brim was firmly tugged back over his forehead again. 'No worries,' he drawled. 'Churinga ain't goin' nowheres.' He drifted into the hotel.

Jenny slumped back into the chair and picked up her sketch book. She would have to get used to this slower pace of life, even if it was frustrating.

Lorraine's excited chatter was followed minutes later by the sound of her high heels clattering over the wooden verandah. 'There you go. One schooner. Brett said he shouldn't be too long,' she said victoriously. The screen door slammed behind her.

'Silly cow,' Jenny muttered into her beer. It was as cold as Lorraine's eyes. Brett Wilson had better get his act together. She wasn't going to sit here all bloody day waiting while he messed about with a barmaid. A couple of schooners should see him right, then she wanted to get moving.

Finishing the beer, she left the verandah and went upstairs to fetch her back-pack. After washing her face and hands, she set to and brushed her hair. It always soothed her, and by the time it was gleaming, her humour had been restored. She would go back downstairs and enjoy the scenery. Brett was right. Churinga wasn't going anywhere, and neither was she until he was ready to take her.

The beer glass was still on the arm of the chair where she'd left it. Lorraine was obviously busy elsewhere. With a grin,

Jenny placed it on the floor and picked up her drawing things. She could still remember the way it had been with Pete in those early days. Snatching moments whenever they could. Tumbling into bed, unable to keep their hands off one another.

She sighed. Sex had been good with Pete, and she missed that intimacy, the feel of another skin against her own, the thud of a second heartbeat. With an impatient toss of her head, she snapped her thoughts back to the present. No point in dwelling on such things. They only brought back the pain.

Her attention was caught by the old opal miner sitting in a rocking chair at the far end of the verandah. As her pencil flashed over the paper, she forgot about Brett and Lorraine. The old man was a wonderful subject, hardly moving, staring into space, his broad-brimmed hat pulled back just enough from his face to expose the weather-beaten profile.

'That's real good. I didn't know you could draw, Mrs Sanders.'

Jenny smiled up at Lorraine. Perhaps this was a peace offering now Brett was firmly in her clutches. 'Thanks.'

'You should try and sell your stuff to the gallery at Broken Hill if you're planning on staying around for a while. The tourists love this sort of thing.'

Jenny was about to say her work was already quite well known in Australia, but held back. She didn't want to spoil this attempt at peace-making by sounding smug. 'It's just something to do to pass the time.'

Lorraine perched on the arm of the chair and watched as she finished the drawing. 'You got old Joe just right,' she said in admiration. 'Even down to the way his bottom lip sort of sticks out when he's thinking.'

Jenny tore the drawing from the pad. 'Then you have it, Lorraine. As a gift.'

Her eyes widened with surprise. 'You sure? Gee, thanks.' There was a hint of colour in her cheeks that had nothing to do with rouge. 'I'm sorry about ... you know. I don't usually blast off like that, and out here there's so few of us women it'd be a shame to fall out.' She put out her hand. 'Mates?'

Despite her misgivings, Jenny took the hand and nodded. 'Mates.'

Lorraine seemed satisfied and returned to the drawing. 'Do

you mind if I show this to Joe? He'll be tickled pink.'

'Of course not,' said Jenny with a smile.

'I'll shout you a beer for this. Brett shouldn't be too long now.' Lorraine hopped off the arm of the chair and trotted over to Joe to show him his picture.

The old man laughed and looked down the verandah. 'Good on yer, missus. Better than any mirror.' He lifted an empty glass in salute.

Jenny took the hint. 'My shout, Lorraine. Joe deserves something for being such a good model.'

Brett left the gloom of the bar and stepped through the screen door and out on to the verandah. Mrs Sanders was sitting next to Joe, listening to his tall tales of opal mining, and hadn't noticed him standing there, so he took those few moments to study her.

She was much younger than he'd expected, and quite a looker too with that shiny hair and those long brown legs. He regretted having been so short with her. But old Wainwright had just said she was widowed – hadn't prepared him for such a surprise. Yet it was her eyes that had unsettled Brett most. From the moment she'd looked up, he'd been fascinated by the way they changed from deepest purple to palest amethyst. She would never have made a good poker player – not with those eyes.

Brett nudged his hat back from his forehead and wiped away the sweat. She looked too delicate for Churinga. Probably wouldn't last more than a couple of weeks before scuttling back to Sydney. Lorraine was right. They were all the same, these townies. Big ideas about going bush, but when faced with the reality of no running water, fire, floods and drought, they soon left. Good riddance, he thought. I didn't reckon on taking orders from some skinny woman who wouldn't know a sheep's arse from its elbow.

He watched the sun catch the amber lights in her hair, saw how her hands fluttered as she described something to Joe, and revised his opinion. There was no sign of the trauma of her recent loss. She must have buried it deep – that took strength and courage, and on top of all that she'd made the journey out here alone, and seemed none the worse for it. Her

81

appearance was as exotic as some of the fantastic birds that inhabited the bush, and they flourished out here. Perhaps she was made of sterner stuff than he'd first thought.

She turned to look at him then, and he felt a jolt as her beautiful eyes met his. He jammed his hat further down and strode over. She's my boss – and everything depends on her. If she hates Churinga, then she'll probably sell up. But if she stays . . . Things could get complicated.

'I won't be a minute, Mr Wilson. Joe's telling me a story.'

Brett noticed how her eyes darkened to violet in the shade of the verandah, and knew she was playing him at his own game – the irony wasn't lost on him. He'd have liked to tell her he'd wait in the ute out back but Joe's stories were legendary and he liked the way Mrs Sanders tilted her head to listen. So he leaned against the verandah railings with an air of studied boredom, and lit a cigarette.

As the story finally came to an end she stood up. He was aware of long, slender legs, but kept his gaze firmly in the middle distance. She was tall, perhaps almost five feet six, but somehow it suited her. Brett Wilson, he silently berated himself, pull yourself together and stop mooning about like a galah.

'Bye, Joe. Catch yer later, mate.' He picked up her backpack. 'Let's get going,' he said abruptly. 'It's a long drive.'

He could hear the tramp of her feet on the floorboards as she followed him across the verandah and down the steps, but made no attempt to speak or look back. He wasn't much for small talk, and he doubted she would have much to say that would interest him anyway.

The battered utility smouldered in the sun at the back of the hotel. Brett slung Jenny's pack behind the seat, then grabbed the box of groceries from Lorraine and put them in the flatbed under the tarp. He wanted to get away quickly before she said or did something stupid. She'd been far too demanding lately, and he'd been avoiding coming to town. That was the trouble with women, he thought darkly. Give them a smile and a bit of pleasant company and they think they own you. He clambered aboard and slammed the door.

Lorraine leaned in at the window, her perfume filling the cab. 'Bye, Jen. I expect we'll meet up again soon.'

Brett turned the ignition key, his foot hard down on the accelerator to drown out her voice. He started as Lorraine's firm grip encircled his arm. The determination in her eyes made him go cold.

'See you soon then, Brett. And don't forget you promised to take me to the picnic races on ANZAC day.'

'Righto. See you later,' he said hurriedly. He pulled his arm free and slammed the ute into reverse. For a minute there he'd thought the blasted woman was going to kiss him right in front of Mrs Sanders. Lorraine was getting too damn possessive, and he didn't like it one bit. He slammed the ute into first. The sooner he got back to Churinga the better. At least he knew how to deal with the problems there. Animals were so much easier to understand than women.

Jenny witnessed the scene as an amused outsider. Poor Lorraine would have to work awfully hard to snare this particular moody individual. Did all bushmen have the same attitude when it came to women? she wondered. Or was Brett merely embarrassed in front of her? Probably, she decided. Lorraine was coming on strong, and it must be daunting to have your boss lady sitting right beside you when that happened.

She looked out of the window as the scenery opened up before her, and soon forgot the pair of them in her wonderment. Rusty brown termite hills stood sentinel by the side of the desert track. River beds, dry and yawning, jolted the wheels and threatened at every turn to have them over. Ghost gums, all silver bark and drooping leaves, wilted seventy feet above the grassland of pale green and yellow. The earth was ochre, streaked with black, the sky wide and incredibly blue.

Some day, she promised herself, she would borrow the ute and come out into the wilderness to paint. But before that she must contact Diane and get her to send oils and canvas.

They drove in a silence broken only by the whine of the engine and the scratch of a match on the dashboard as Brett lit an occasional cigarette. Yet Jenny preferred it that way. It gave her time to absorb the essence of the outback. Mindless, polite chatter would have marred its perfection.

Flocks of exotic birds wheeled above the trees, their colours acid bright and startling against the sky. White sulphur crested cockatoos squabbled, kookaburras laughed, and the hum of the heat on the earth was mingled with the rasp of crickets as Brett swung the utility from one almost invisible road to another.

They had been travelling almost ten hours before she saw a line of tea trees out on the horizon, and a long, flat-topped dome of rock.

'Tjuringa mountain. The Abos gave it its name because of the shape – like a churinga or a stone amulet. The mountain's one of their dreaming places, and sacred.'

Jenny grasped the dash as the front wheels jarred in a particularly deep fissure. 'When will I see the house?'

Brett gave a wry smile. 'In about an hour and a half. We've got fifty miles to go once we pass those trees.'

She stared at him. 'How big is Churinga station, then? Fifty miles from the trees to the house? It must be enormous.'

'Only a hundred and sixty thousand acres. That's quite small out here,' he replied nonchalantly, eyes screwed up against the sun, attention fixed on avoiding potholes.

Jenny wished she'd listened more carefully to John Wainwright. He must have told her all this but it had still come as a shock, even though she was well aware of the vast tracts of land that made up the heart of Australia's farming industry. 'Mr Wainwright said he'd signed you up to manage Churinga two years ago. Where were you before that?'

'Churinga. Me and the wife moved in ten years ago this Christmas. We took over from the old boy who was retiring. The bank employed me then.'

Jenny looked at him in amazement. There had been no mention of a wife and she'd assumed he was single. So what the hell was he doing messing about with Lorraine? No wonder he was embarrassed at her behaviour. She leaned back and stared thoughtfully out of the window. These particular still waters obviously ran deeper than she'd thought. It would be interesting to meet the woman behind the man.

'Churinga homestead up ahead,' Brett finally said quietly as the sun dipped behind the mountain.

Jenny heard the affection in his voice as he tipped his head towards the low building set against a backdrop of tall eucalyptus trees. And as the full glory of the place unfolded, she understood.

The house was an old Queenslander. Built of white clapboard, roofed with corrugated iron and perched on brick pilings, it was sheltered on the southernmost side in the shadows of the vast pepper trees which drooped, exhausted by the day's heat, pale green fronds humming with bees. A verandah ran the full width of the house, the railings covered in ivy and creeping bougainvillea. Screens were painted red, and the home paddock was acid green against the ochre of the clearing that made up the yard.

Brett pointed towards the paddock as he brought the ute to a halt. 'That's watered from the bore. We have to rely on underground springs to keep the stock alive, but we're lucky at Churinga, there's never really been a dangerous shortage because of the mountain streams. They say that during the war years, Churinga lasted out the ten-year drought.'

Jenny stepped down from the utility and stretched. They'd been travelling all day and she was stiff and aching. She looked at the horses in the paddock and envied them the shade of the trees. For despite the lowering of the sun, the heat was still intense.

'What are those buildings over there?' This was far bigger than Waluna – more like a small town than a single farm.

Brett pointed out each building in turn. 'That's for the stockmen, and that's the cookhouse beside it. The large shack over there is for the shearers, the smaller one's for the roustabouts and jackaroos. The slaughter yard and wood piles are in the yard behind them.'

He turned to point to the east of the house. 'That's the woolshed, sorting loft and dipping tanks. We can take up to twenty shearers at a time. The stock pens, dog kennels and runs are next door. Then there are the chicken runs, the piggery and dairy. Each main building has its own generator.'

'I never realised how self-sufficient you must be,' she murmured. 'It's just amazing.'

Brett scruffed his boot in the dirt and tilted back his hat. The pride in his eyes was unmistakable. 'We can do most things for ourselves, but we still rely on the Royal Mail for our groceries, petrol and kerosene. We buy in hay if the drought gets too bad, and corn, sugar and flour. Farm machinery has to be ordered by catalogue, but luckily we've got a good mechanic and he keeps our machines going 'til they fall apart. That barn over there is the store house for machinery and feed, and the forge is to the side of it, the carpentry shop at the end.'

Jenny was still taking it all in when Brett's tone became serious. 'Those tanks behind the house are fresh water tanks, Mrs Sanders. They're for drinking water only.' He turned and pointed towards a narrow runnel of water which crept sluggishly under weeping willows at the far western edge of the home paddock. 'Water for washing and household chores comes from that creek.'

Jenny decided it was time to enlighten him. 'I have lived beyond the black stump before, Mr Wilson. I know how precious water is.'

He eyed her with fleeting interest before returning to his monologue. It seemed he'd rehearsed what he wanted to say and nothing would side-track him. 'When the creeks run a banker, the yard's several feet under water. That's why all the buildings are on stilts. They're brick because of termites.'

'No wonder you love this place,' Jenny breathed. 'It's stunning.'

'It can also be cruel,' he remarked sharply. 'Don't go getting any romantic notions about it.'

Jenny realised nothing she could do or say would shake his belief that she was a townie and therefore ignorant, so she watched him turn away to unload the utility and said nothing. There wasn't a spare ounce of flesh on that long lean body, and he was as finely muscled as a young colt. He would make a wonderful subject for Diane to sculpt, but she doubted he'd think much of the idea. She snapped her thoughts into order.

'Is your wife in the house, Mr Wilson? I'm looking forward to meeting her.'

He stood beside her, his arms laden with groceries, his frown deep. 'She's in Perth,' he growled.

Jenny shielded her eyes from the low sun as she looked up at him. She recognised hurt in his eyes and in the tightening of his mouth. All was not well – perhaps the absent wife had found out about Lorraine?

Brett shifted from one foot to the other. 'She's not on holiday, if that's what you were wondering,' he said defensively. 'She's there permanently.' He strode up to the porch, hooked a toe under the screen door and slammed into the house.

Jenny hurried after him and finally caught up with him in the kitchen. 'I'm sorry, I didn't mean to pry.'

Brett kept his attention on the groceries he was unpacking. 'No worries. You're a stranger here, so why should you know about me and Marlene?' He turned suddenly, his face grim. 'She didn't like it here. Said she felt lost in all this space. Went back to Perth and the bar I found her in.'

There was a long silence. A moment when Jenny would have reached out to comfort him if only she'd known how.

'I didn't mean to snap,' he said by way of apology. 'But I hate gossip, and thought it best to tell you before someone else does. Now, is there anything else before I go? The men should be back soon, and I have work to do before it gets too dark.'

She accepted his apology with a smile. 'Who does the cooking around here for all the men? Have you got a house-keeper?'

The tension broke and Brett jammed his hands into the back of his belt, his face suddenly lit by a broad smile which deepened the creases around his eyes and made him even more handsome. 'Strewth! You townies have funny ideas. We mostly fend for ourselves, but in the shearing season – like now – we have one of the Sundowners' wives to see to the tucker.'

He tipped his hat and walked to the door. 'I'll tell you more about the place later. Tucker's in half an hour, and as it's your first night it'd probably be best to eat in the cookhouse. Ma Baker's in charge. She and her old man come every year, and she probably knows as much about this place as I do.'

Jenny didn't have time to thank him. He was gone.

Standing in the deepening shadows of the kitchen, she listened to the sounds of Churinga. The deep, ringing tone of hammer on anvil, the bleating of sheep and the shout of men were mixed with the chatter of galahs and the barking of dogs. She had expected silence but as she stood there she remembered how it had been as a child. As the memories returned she began to relax. She had come home to the land after too many years away – but the echo of it was hauntingly familiar.

Waluna sheep station was nestled in the heart of Queensland's Mulga country. The house was smaller than Churinga's but built on the same lines with a tin roof and shadowed verandah. The pastures stretched for miles around the homestead, and she could still remember the smell of the sun on the grass and the soft rustle of the breeze in the tea trees.

John and Ellen Carey had come to the orphanage at Dajarra a few months after Jenny had turned seven. She remembered that morning as if it was yesterday. The nuns chivvied her and the other children from their daily chores to line up in the drawing room under the austere gaze of the Reverend Mother. There was excitement in the air for the arrival of people at Dajarra meant one of them would be fostered, or even adopted if they were very lucky, and would be free of Sister Michael forever.

Jenny had held tightly to Diane's hand. They had made a pact not to be separated – and despite their longing to escape the nun's clutches, they knew that if they were to leave Dajarra, their real parents wouldn't be able to find them.

Jenny smiled as she remembered Ellen and John walking down the long line of children. Ellen had stopped in front of her for a moment, but Reverend Mother had shaken her head and pressed her forward. Jenny hadn't caught the muttered comment as they proceeded down the line, but knew that once again she and Diane were not to be picked.

The children were finally told to leave the room and scampered back to the library to finish the dusting. Jenny remembered feeling disappointed and glad all at the same time, but as this was nothing new she dealt with it as she had done before, and simply tucked it away out of sight.

The surprise had come when Sister Michael fetched them both and told them they would be going with the Careys. She'd looked up into that cold, emotionless face and wondered if this was just another way of punishing her. Yet within days she and Diane were on their way to a new life, a new home, with a promise from Reverend Mother that they would return immediately if their real parents turned up.

Jenny stared into the distance as the old doubts closed in. Other children from Dajarra were adopted, but for her and

Diane it had been different. And she'd always wondered why. She sighed. Ellen and John had been old enough to be their grandparents, but they had given them a good life and it was because of them she and Diane were able to face the world with a sense of worth. The years on Waluna had seen them flourish, and although those two wonderful foster parents were gone now, she still remembered the place and its people with deep affection.

She came out of her daydream and looked around. It was time to explore Churinga.

The kitchen was basic and utilitarian. A line of cupboards ran along one wall, filled with unmatched crockery and one good dinner service. A stained porcelain sink with wooden drainers was set beside rickety cupboards under the window and the centre of the room was dominated by a large, scrubbed wooden table. The two-way radio squatted in the corner, silent and brooding – the only life-line to the outside world.

She stood by the table and looked around. The kitchen had been extended so there was an area of over-stuffed chairs which looked out through long windows to the back of the house. Book shelves and several quite good watercolours lined the walls.

On closer inspection she could see that the paintings were all of the outback, but it was one particular painting of Churinga that caught her eye. It must have been done years ago, for the house was smaller and more dilapidated, the stand of trees less shady than now. There were only a few ramshackle sheds beyond the front yard, and the weeping willows by the creek were saplings, their fronds barely touching the water.

Jenny eyed the painting critically. There was no signature, and it was obviously amateur, but there was a certain quaint charm about it. The artist, and she was convinced it had been a woman, clearly loved her subject. But who was she, this woman with such a delicate touch? A squatter's wife, a Sundowner adding a few bob to her husband's wages, or a wandering artist earning bed and keep?

Jenny shrugged. It didn't really matter because whoever painted it had left a potent history of the property that was unassailable.

Returning to her exploration, she discovered a small bathroom complete with lavatory and shower. It was all a bit Heath Robinson, but no matter – a shower was a shower, and she couldn't resist. Peeling off her sweat-stained clothes, she stood beneath the sluggish drip of murky water and scrubbed away the dust of her travels. Then, with a clean towel wrapped around her, she padded down the narrow corridor to find the bedroom.

As she opened the first door, she realised she'd trespassed on Brett's territory. There was a clutter of boots and discarded working clothes on the floor. The bed was unmade and there was a strong smell of lanolin, shaving cream and the stable-yard. She eyed the mess, and wondered if she really wanted this moody, unpredictable man in quite such close proximity.

She closed the door and went on to the next room. It looked out over the paddocks at the back of the house, was freshly swept and polished, and someone had put a jam jar of wild flowers on the window sill. A thoughtful touch, but more likely to be Ma Baker's than Brett's she decided.

The head and foot of the bed was ornate brass, the covers a patchwork quilt of soft colours. A rag rug covered the wooden floor, and there was a chair and a white-painted wardrobe and dressing table. She stood for a moment in the twilight, trying to imagine the people who'd once lived here, but all she could see was the empty bed. All she could hear was the life going on outside in the yard. Her own bereavement swept over her unexpectedly, and she sank on to the bed. 'Oh, Pete,' she sighed. 'I wish you were here.'

Tears pricked and she brushed them away as she unpacked her things and pulled on fresh shorts and shirt. 'You're tired, hungry and feel out of place,' she muttered. 'But there's no point letting it get to you.'

With rather more determination than she felt, she grabbed the rest of her things and set about making herself feel more at home. As she opened the wardrobe door, she was assailed by the heady scent of moth balls and lavender. There was no sign of any clothes and she assumed Ma Baker must have cleared them away. Shame, she thought. Might have been interesting.

Restlessness filled her. Having seen everything in the house, she was drawn to the home paddock and the small cemetery she'd noticed earlier.

The evening shadows had lengthened as she stepped down from the porch and picked her way through the long grass. The back of the house overlooked the pasture where the horses drowsed beneath the trees and a smaller, overgrown plot that had been fenced in by white pickets. Wooden crosses marked burial mounds that were smothered in kangaroo paw and wild lilies. It was a peaceful resting place for the family who'd once lived here. So much more personal then a public grave-yard on a hill outside Sydney, she thought sadly.

She opened the gate, noticing that the hinges had been oiled and the grass recently cut. 'At least someone still cares,' she muttered, picking her way through the tangle.

There were eight grave markers still standing. The others were almost engulfed by the encroaching wilderness. Jenny read each of the epitaphs on the weathered crosses. The O'Connors had died in the late eighteen hundreds, and must have been pioneers from the old country. Mary and Mervyn Thomas had died within a few years of each other shortly after the Great War.

The smaller memorials were more difficult to decipher. The lettering was worn, the wood paper thin. The tiny crosses stood close to one another as if embracing, and Jenny had to clear away the creepers before she could read them. Each bore the same sad legend: 'Boy child. Taken at birth.'

She swallowed. Brett was right – Churinga country could be cruel.

She moved on to the two most recent headstones. Roughly hewn in the same dark rock, the lettering still glimmered white within the lichen – but the epitaph on the woman's gravestone made no sense at all, and she sat back on her heels and pondered why such a thing should have been put there.

'Tucker's ready.'

Jenny looked up, startled from her thoughts. 'Does that mean what I think it does?' she asked, pointing to the stone.

Brett tipped back his hat before jamming his hands into his pockets. 'I don't know. Mrs Sanders. Before my time. Rumour has it there was a tragedy here years ago. But it's only gossip, so I shouldn't let it worry you.'

'Rumours? What rumours?' Jenny stood up and brushed the dirt from her hands. She loved a good mystery.

'Nothing to get steamed up about,' he said nonchalantly. 'Come on. Tucker'll all be gone.'

Jenny stared at him but his gaze slid away. He knew something and had obviously decided to keep it to himself. She followed him out of the cemetery and across the yard, her appetite sharpened by the thought there might be a mystery attached to the history of Churinga.

# Chapter Four

Brett hadn't been surprised to find her in the cemetery; it was, after all, an intrinsic part of Churinga, and after being widowed so recently herself, it was logical she should go there. Yet he regretted having mentioned the rumours. Mrs Sanders was obviously inquisitive and resourceful, and like most women he'd come into contact with, would probably go on endlessly until he told her what he knew.

His thoughts were troubled as they crossed the yard to the cookhouse. He'd learned enough to know Churinga's past was better left buried.

He tugged his hat over his brow as she walked beside him. He was more accustomed to the smell of the wool shed than exotic perfume from Sydney. Mrs Sanders disturbed him. The sooner he was back in the bunkhouse the better. Should have moved his things from the house last night, and would have done too if his mare hadn't thrown a shoe and made him walk the five miles back.

Brett opened the screen door to let her pass, then slung his hat on to the peg beside the door. Ma had a strict rule about hats indoors. The noise in the cookhouse was loud and cheerful, but at the sight of Mrs Sanders it fell like a stone.

'This is your new boss, mates, Mrs Sanders.' Brett grinned as their astonished eyes took in her long legs and shiny hair. That fair shook 'em up and no mistake, he thought. 'Move up, Stan mate. And let me sit down.'

Ma came bustling out of the kitchen, wiping her hands on her apron. Brett liked Ma. She was easy to talk to, and her cooking stuck to your ribs. He winced as she cuffed him none too gently around the ear. 'What you do that for, Ma?'

'You've got no manners, Brett Wilson,' she retorted as laughter rang round the table. She turned to Jenny, a broad smile on her perspiring face. 'No one's got any manners around here, luv. Mrs Baker's the name, pleased to make your acquaintance.'

Brett surreptitiously watched Jenny's face as she greeted Ma and took her place at the table. Those eyes were fairly dancing, and he knew why – she was laughing at him. Bloody women. Always ganged up on a bloke just when he wasn't expecting it.

Ma had her fists on her broad hips as she surveyed the gaping mouths and curious eyes. 'What's the matter with yous lot? Never seen a lady before?'

Like the other men, Brett ducked his head and began to attack the heaped plate in front of him. It didn't do to cross Ma. The long drive had put an edge to his appetite and eating gave him the excuse to avoid the knowing looks and sly nudges from the others. They could think what they liked. She was just the new boss. Nothing special.

Jenny recognised friendship in Ma's broad smile. She was reminded of Ma Kettle from the old movies on a Saturday morning. A woman of indeterminate age, broad of beam and generous of spirit, who nonetheless stood no nonsense from the men for whom she cooked and washed.

Ma placed a heaped plate in front of her. 'There you go, luv. Nice bit of roast mutton. You look as if you could do with some feeding up. Too thin by half,' she said with dismay.

Jenny blushed, all too aware that despite their apparent interest in their food, the men were listening. It had been a mistake to come over and eat with them. She'd have been better off back at the house. Brett had brought enough groceries for a month.

As she tried to make a respectable dent in the food on her plate the men seemed to lose interest and, after a false start or two, returned to their own conversation. Sheep seemed to be the main topic, but as the nearest she'd come to one in the past ten years was in a butcher's shop, Jenny stayed silent and took in her surroundings instead.

The cookhouse seemed to be made up of a kitchen and this

vast room. The scrubbed table ran the full length of it, benches to either side. The vaulted ceiling was corrugated iron, slung over heavy wooden beams. The aromas of cooking, lanolin, horses and stables, and the honest sweat of a day's work, mingled headily.

As the meal progressed Jenny found it awkward to be surrounded by thirty or more men who, under the watchful eye of Mrs Baker, were obviously toning down their language and trying to display some sort of decorum. The tension in the room was almost tangible. She was ill at ease, and suspected they felt the same.

After what seemed an eternity each man left the table, the relief of escape clear in their rush for the door. She guessed they usually sat for hours over a beer and a cigarette, discussing the day's work, and felt more of an intruder than ever.

As the last man left the table, plate in hand for the kitchen, Ma came back with two cups of tea and a tobacco tin. 'You don't want to mind them too much,' she said, nodding her head in the direction of the noise and scuffling coming from the front porch. 'They're good blokes, but they only know how to talk to a barmaid. Not an ounce of heducation between 'em.'

Jenny bit back a grin and declined the offer of a roll-up, although she was tempted. It had been a fraught day. 'I spoiled their tucker, though. Perhaps I'll eat in the house from now on.'

Ma looked across the broad expanse of oilcloth, her expression thoughtful. 'It might be best, Mrs Sanders. After all, you are the owner now.'

'Call me Jenny. I'm not used to all this formality. Is it usual out here?'

Ma laughed and shut the tobacco tin with a snap. 'Lord, no, luv. Just our way of showing respect. You can call me Simone. I get pretty fed up with Ma all the time, makes me feel about a hundred.'

Jenny looked at her and smiled.

'Ridiculous name, isn't it? But my old mum read a book once, and the heroine's name was Simone – so I got lumbered. Well, I mean, look at me.' She laughed and the whole of her large body joined in.

Jenny grinned, enjoying the knowledge that here in this man's world there was at least one person she could talk to. 'Have you always followed the shearers, Simone?'

She nodded. 'Stan and me got together more years ago than I care to remember. I was looking after a squatter's kids out in Queensland then, and he'd come with the others to shear the mob.' She drank her tea, eyes misty with memory. 'He was a good-looking bloke in them days. Tall and straight, with arms like rope – all muscle.' She shivered at the recollection. 'Wouldn't think so now, would you? Shearing bends a man's back and makes him old. But my Stan can still get through more sheep in a day than most of those buckaroos.'

Simone snorted, her elbows on the table. 'Took me a while to catch the old bugger, though. Slippery as a dipped sheep. But I'm glad I did. We bought a horse and wagon, and from that day to this we've been on the road. Bit grim at times, but I wouldn't swop with the squatters and their fancy houses. Reckon I've seen more of Australia than anyone.'

Jenny felt a tingle of anticipation. Perhaps she knew about the previous occupants, and could explain that mysterious epitaph? 'You must have seen a great deal of change over the years, Simone. Did you come this way in the early days?'

She shook her head. 'Mostly Queensland. We only come this way about five years ago.'

It was strange how disappointed Jenny felt, but there was no point in dwelling on it, she decided. 'I didn't thank you for the flowers or for cleaning my room so nicely. It was lovely to be welcomed like that after such a long journey.'

'Think nothing of it, luv. Glad to do it.' Ma smoked her cigarette in silence.

'What happened to the clothes in the wardrobe? I assume there must have been some because of the mothballs.'

Simone looked away and became engrossed in the pattern on the cigarette tin. 'I didn't think you'd want those old things cluttering up the place. So I cleared 'em out.'

Jenny's curiosity was piqued. There it was again. The sideways glance, the studied air of ignorance. 'I'd love to see them. I'm an artist, you see, and one of the things I liked best at college was history of dress. If they belonged to the people who once lived here then . . .'

'You don't want to be messing about with the past, Jenny. It won't do you no good, never does. Besides, they was mostly old rags.' Simone's expression had grown wary, and she couldn't quite meet Jenny's eye.

Jenny kept her voice low and coaxing. 'Then there's no harm in letting me see them, is there? Go on, Simone. The more you try to hide them, the more I'm going to want to see them. Let's get this over with here and now, eh?'

Simone sighed. 'Brett won't like it, Jenny. He told me to burn the lot.'

'Why ever would he want you to do that?' she asked in horror. 'Besides,' she added roundly, 'they aren't his to burn.' She took a deep breath. 'For goodness' sake, Simone. If it's only a collection of old clothes, why the mystery?'

Simone eyed her for a moment, then seemed to make up her mind. 'Beats me, luv. I just do as I'm told. Come on, they're out the back.'

Jenny followed her into the kitchen where a mound of washing up was stacked by the sink. It was bright in here with checkered curtains and a scrubbed pine table. Stacks of fresh vegetables were piled in sacks on the floor, and pots and pans hung on hooks from the ceiling.

'I put everything in this old trunk. Seemed a shame just to burn it all.' Simone's expression was mulish, but there was a hint of colour in her face that had nothing to do with the heat in the kitchen.

Jenny knelt before the battered trunk and unfastened the leather straps. Her pulse was racing though she couldn't understand why. After all, she told herself silently, it was only a bunch of old clothes.

The lid slammed back against the wall and Jenny gasped. These were no old rags but a collection of shoes and dresses that dated way back into the last century.

Simone knelt beside her, her confidence suddenly deserting here. 'Course, if I'd 'a known you'd be interested, I'd 'a never . . .'

'It doesn't matter, Simone,' Jenny said softly, as she looked at the treasure trove. 'But I'm glad you didn't burn them.' One by one she lifted out the neatly folded clothes and inspected them. Finest lawn nightdresses that were handstitched and still perfect nestled in tissue paper. Victorian lace on the collars and cuffs of a nineteenth-century day dress was still as white as the day it had been made. She unwrapped the beautiful watered silk of a wedding gown that must have come all the way from Ireland and pressed its creamy softness to her face. She could still smell the lavender. There were cotton dresses a child might have worn in the first half of this century, and tiny, intricately stitched baby clothes that didn't look as if they'd ever been worn. There were dropped-waisted dresses of the early nineteen twenties, and post-war dresses of inferior cotton that still had matching belts and interchangeable collars.

'Simone,' she gasped, 'these aren't rags. They're probably collectors' items.'

Her round face reddened. 'If I'd known you'd want them, I'd have never taken them out of the house. But Brett said you wouldn't want them cluttering up the place.' She fell silent.

Jenny eyed her, her understanding of what Simone had really planned for these lovely things remaining tacit. She patted the workworn hand. 'They're still here. That's all that matters.'

She pulled out riding breeches and boots, scuffed and worn with work, and a beautiful silk shawl that had a tear in the fringing. Holding it to her face, she breathed in the scent of lavender. Had these things been worn by the woman whose picture was still in her locket! Then her eye caught a glimpse of a sea green peeking from beween the folds of a white linen sheet. It was a ball-gown, incongruous amongst the plainer working clothes. Soft, dainty and shimmering, its full skirt rustled with chiffon over satin, roses of the same material clinging to the tiny waistband and ruched shoulders.

'That colour would suit you,' said Simone. 'Why don't you try it on?'

Jenny was tempted, but something about the dress made her reluctant to share the moment and she put it aside. 'Look!' she cried. 'It's even got shoes to match. It must have been made for a very special occasion.'

Simone seemed unimpressed, her tone suddenly brusque. 'That's about it, luv. Only a load of old books and things in the bottom.'

Jenny stayed her hand as she began to pull the lid down. 'Books? What kind of books?'

'Look like diaries, but most of 'em are falling to bits.'

Jenny looked hard at the other woman. 'What is it about this place that makes everyone so secretive – and why the fuss over these clothes? Has all this got anything to do with that strange headstone in the cemetery?'

Simone sighed. 'I only know there was something bad happened here a long time ago, luv. Brett thought it best you shouldn't be worried by it, seeing as how you'd just had a tragedy of your own.' She paused. 'I was sorry to hear about your husband and little boy.'

Brett Wilson should mind his own bloody business! 'Thanks, Simone. But I'm not as delicate as everyone thinks.' Jenny dived back into the trunk and plucked out the books. How intriguing – they were diaries, but Simone was right, some of them were falling apart. The newer ones were covered in find, hand-tooled leather; the others and less recent were yellow and watermarked. There were twelve in all: some thick and heavy, spanning one or two years; others simply exercise books covering a few months.

While Simone watched disapprovingly, she carefully placed each of them on the floor in chronological order. They spanned the years 1924 to 1948. She riffled the pages, noticing how the childish, ill-formed writing had become a firm flourish as the years passed.

Yet the last diary was puzzling. The writing was jagged and almost illegible – as if it had been written by another hand.

'That's it then. Want me to help you put it all back?'

Jenny held the last diary close. It was as if she could feel the presence of the woman who'd written this – and it was such a strong feeling, she wasn't aware Simone had spoken.

'Jenny? You all right, luv?'

She drew away reluctantly from her thoughts. 'Yes, I'm fine. Let's pack the clothes up again and get the trunk over to the house. I'll carry the books.'

Minutes later the straps were tied and they were crossing the deserted yard. The murmur of voices was muted in the bunkhouse, and most of the lights had been dowsed. Once the trunk was deposited on the floor in the kitchen, Simone said goodnight.

'Ready for me bed. We start early out here before it gets too hot.'

Jenny looked at her watch. It was only ten o'clock, but she too was tired and ready for bed.

'You look wore out, if you don't mind me saying so,' said Simone. 'I put clean sheets on the bed. If you get cold in the night there are blankets on top of the cupboard. Keep the shutters closed or you'll be eaten alive by mozzies.'

'Thanks, Simone. I'll square this with Brett in the morning. Don't you want a hand with the washing up?'

'Nah. She'll be right. Besides, you're the boss. You shouldn't be helping me with my work.'

Jenny smiled. 'Good night then, and thanks.'

'Night, luv. It's been bonzer talking to another woman at last. Blokes are all right, but I get a bit tired of hearing about blasted sheep all the time.'

Jenny followed her out on to the porch and watched her disappear into the gloom towards the cookhouse. The air was warm, caressing her face, bringing with it the scent of the night flowers. The reality of what she'd inherited suddenly hit her, and she sank into a chair and stared out over the yard. She could hear the quiet rumble of men's voices over in the bunkhouse, and see the flicker of light from the jackaroos' bungalow and in the windows of the cookhouse. All of this belonged to her. The land, the stock, the house – everything. She had inherited a town. A community which would look to her for its livelihood and well-being.

The enormity of this realisation weighed heavy. She knew so little about this life – the few years as a child on Waluna had taught her only the bare essentials – and the responsibility was awesome.

With a long, deep yawn, she accepted what fate had thrown at her, and decided nothing could be accomplished by worrying about it tonight. She left the verandah and turned back into the house.

It was very quiet and she assumed Brett must already be asleep. Then she noticed the sheet of paper on the table. He'd moved out to the bunkhouse.

'That's a relief,' she sighed. 'One less thing to worry about.'

The trunk was a dark shadow in the gloom. It seemed to beckon her, to draw her towards the straps as if willing her to open them.

Jenny knelt before it, fingers hovering over the buckles. Then, before she could change her mind, the straps were drawn, the lid tilted back. The green dress lay shimmering in the pale moonlight, tempting her to pick it up, try it on.

The folds of chiffon and satin rustled as they slid over her nakedness. Cool and sensuous, the material caressed her, full skirt dancing against her legs as she moved. She closed her eyes, her fingers deep within the folds as a waltz from a distant life played in her mind. Then she was swaying to it. Moving around the room, her bare feet silent on the boards. It was as if the dress had transported her from this isolated farm to a place where someone special was waiting.

She felt hands on her waist, breath on her cheek, and knew he'd come. But there was no light, no joyous welcome, for the waltz had grown sombre and a shiver tingled down her spine as his fleeting kiss frosted her cheek.

Jenny's eyes flew open. Her dancing feet stilled. Her pulse hammered. The music was gone, the house was empty – and yet she could have sworn she hadn't been alone. With trembling fingers she undid the tiny buttons and the dress whispered to the floor. It lay in a pool of moonlight, skirts fanned across the boards as if caught in mid-swirl of the ghostly dance.

'Pull yourself together, for heaven's sake,' she muttered crossly. 'You're letting your imagination run away with you.'

Yet the sound of her own voice did nothing to dispel the feeling she wasn't alone, and Jenny shivered as she gathered up the dress and returned it to the trunk. Slapping the buckles taut, she picked up her discarded clothes and the diaries, and went to her room. After a hasty wash, she climbed between the crisp cool sheets and tried to relax.

Her back ached and her shoulders were stiff, but no matter how many times she plumped the pillows and turned from one side to the other, sleep refused to come. The memory of that music, of her ghostly partner in the dance would not be dismissed.

Lying there in the half light, her eyes were drawn to the diaries she'd left on the chair. It was as if they too were calling her. Demanding to be read. She resisted, unwilling to be drawn. But the haunting melody drifted around her . . . the feel of his hands, his passionless kiss making her tremble. Not from fear but from something else she couldn't explain . . . He was willing her to open those diaries, and before long she was unable to resist.

The earliest book was tattered and bound by cardboard. The pages were brittle and well thumbed, the fly-leaf inscribed in a childish hand.

*This is the diary of Matilda Thomas. Age fourteen.*

The ghostly music stilled as Jenny began to read.

# Chapter Five

Jenny slowly emerged from Matilda's world, tears wet on her face, to find the other girl had taken her through the night, tarnishing the magic of Churinga, showing her how it had become a prison. It was as if Jenny could hear the steady, ever-advancing thud of the horses' hooves as that bastard Mervyn caught her and brought her back. As if she could share the same fear the child must have experienced, knowing there was no one to hear her screams or offer help.

'Too late,' she whispered. 'I'm too late to do anything about it.'

Yet, as the tears dried and the images lost their sharp edges, she came to understand that Matilda must have learned to fight back – to survive the horror of life with Mervyn – or there wouldn't have been any diaries. Her gaze fell on the remaining books. There was the proof, and in those silent pages lay the answers to all the questions her night's reading had brought.

'Cooee! Breakfast.' Simone bustled into the room, her bright smile freezing as she looked at Jenny. 'Whatever's the matter, luv? Bad night?'

Jenny shook her head, her emotions too jumbled to convey. She was still with Matilda, out on the plains, running for her life.

Simone dumped the heaped breakfast tray on the floor and stood, arms akimbo, surveying the scattered books on the bed. 'I knew something like this would 'appen. You've been reading all night, haven't you? And now you've gone and got yourself all upset.'

Jenny was naked beneath the sheet, and felt strangely vulnerable beneath the older woman's concerned gaze. 'I'm fine. Really,' she stammered.

Simone clucked like an agitated chook and scooped up the offending diaries, dumping them on the dressing table. 'Never could make 'ead nor tail of all them words,' she said as she began to tidy up. 'Brett'll have something to say if he finds out. Told me to make sure you got plenty of rest.'

Interesting, thought Jenny dryly. I didn't realise he was that sensitive to my needs. 'Leave Mr Wilson to me, Simone,' she said firmly. 'I'm a big girl now and can look after myself.'

She snorted, picked up the tray and planted it on the bed. 'You'll feel better after a good breakfast.'

'Thanks,' murmured Jenny, eyeing the fried eggs and thick, fatty bacon with a shudder. How could she eat when Matilda was being held prisoner? How could she concentrate on Simone's chatter when all she wanted to do was return to 1924?

Simone left the room, and minutes later Jenny thought she could hear the clatter of pots in the kitchen. Her eyelids fluttered as a distant orchestra played a waltz, and the smell of lavender drifted into the room. The mists of the past enfolded her, drawing her through tunnels of time and into deep, unforgiving sleep where her dreams were haunted by dark shadows and advancing hooves – and strong, violent hands.

Sweat sheened Jenny's skin as her eyes opened several hours later. She lay there, confused and disorientated, until she found the strength to snatch at reality and hold on firmly to it. Sunlight chased away the threads of the nightmares, the sounds of Churinga silencing the screams.

'This is ridiculous,' she muttered, pulling the sheet around her as she swung out of bed. 'I'm acting like a fool.'

Yet, as her gaze fell on the pile of books Simone had tidied away, she knew she would return to them. 'But not yet,' she said firmly.

Wrapping the sheet more securely around her, she padded down the hall to the bathroom. The clatter of pots in the kitchen came to an abrupt halt and Simone appeared around the corner.

'You didn't eat your breakfast,' she said sternly.

'I wasn't hungry,' Jenny replied defensively. Why did Simone make her feel like a recalcitrant child?

The older woman gave her a thorough scrutiny, then sighed. 'Thought you was crook so I made some nice soup.' She led Jenny firmly into the kitchen and pointed to the bowl of vegetables and meat and the hot damper bread she'd laid out on the table.

Jenny clutched the sheet, all too aware of her own nakedness. 'I'm all right, Simone. Just tired after that long journey.' She forced a smile. 'But the soup looks bonzer.'

Simone sat the other side of the table, thick white cup between her hands, tea the colour of mud steaming into her face. She watched closely as Jenny took three hearty spoonfuls of soup.

'Delicious,' she murmured. And it was. Rich and filling, and just what she needed to chase away the remnants of the nightmares. The bowl was soon empty. 'Now I must have a shower and get dressed.' She looked at her watch. 'Is it really that late?'

'If you're sure you're okay?' Simone didn't seem convinced, but she too glanced at her watch, and it was obvious she had other things to do. 'I'll be in the yard feeding the chooks. If you need me, just holler.'

Jenny watched her clamber down the steps to the yard then disappear around the corner. Once she could no longer hear her footsteps, she headed for the shower.

Dressed and out on the porch several minutes later, her hair still wet but deliciously cool against her neck in the ferocious noon heat, she breathed in the aroma of sun on baked earth and watched the bustle of men at work. The shearing season was in full swing, and she was eager to see how much had changed since her childhood at Waluna.

The shearing shed was the largest building on Churinga. It stood high on firm brick pilings, surrounded by ramps. The air around it was laden with dust and the sound of men and sheep. Behind it was a labyrinth of pens.

As the shearers finished one sheep, another was sent up the ramp to replace it. The jackaroos, mostly young and black, herded the animals, voices high with excitement as they shouted commands to the dogs that raced over the woolly backs, nipping and snarling their bleating mob into some kind of order.

Jenny watched for a moment, the scene reminiscent of those days long ago when she'd stood just like this, by the sheep pens of Waluna. Nothing much changed out here, she thought. The old ways are still the best. She wandered off to the other side of the shed where naked sheep trampled down the ramps to the dipping tanks. Strong, sure arms lifted them out, dye stamped them, drenched and injected them before setting them free to complain in nearby pens. The work was hard beneath the merciless sun, but the men seemed cheerful, despite the sweat and strain it took to control the stupid beasts, and one or two of them took the time to shout a 'G'ay, missus', before returning to the struggle.

Jenny nodded and smiled. At least they aren't ignoring me, she thought, turning away finally. But they must be wondering what the hell I'm doing here. Pete would have handled this so differently. He would have known what to do and say. Sensed how they felt about things and been able to put them right. She sighed. Being a woman counted for very little out here. Sydney and her burgeoning career as an artist seemed light years away.

Her aimless footsteps led her to the front of the shearing shed. In her years at Waluna, she remembered, as a child and then a teenager she'd fetched and carried and helped load the bundles on to the trucks. Shearing brought great excitement to the place, with extra men drafted in, the sheep herded in great numbers in the home paddocks, and an air of expectancy lifting the spirits. The woolshed had always been a place of wonder to her then. A place where men sweated and swore but were always cheerful. Now, after a hesitant pause, she climbed the steps.

And caught her breath. The cathedral arch of the roof brought light and space into a shed twice the size of the one at Waluna. This shearing hall was long and wide and echoed with the hum of electric shears and cheerful oaths. The smell of lanolin and wool, sweat and tar, was intoxicating, taking her back to her childhood, reminding her of all the years she'd missed since leaving for Sydney. Digging her hands into her pockets, Jenny stood quietly in the doorway and watched the bustle.

There were twenty shearers, each stripped to the waist, back bent over the complaining sheep clasped between their knees. The tar boy was about ten and skinny, with big brown eyes, very white teeth and skin the colour of molten chocolate. The tar bucket seemed too heavy for such frail arms, but as he raced to cauterise a nasty gash on a ewe's side, Jenny realised this was not so. That whippet frame was made of sturdy stuff.

Three men collected the newly shorn fleeces, threw them on the long table at the far end of the shed, skirted, classed and pressed them into bales, then added them to those already stacked and waiting to be transferred by truck to the nearest railhead. Jenny knew this was the most important job in the shed. It took real expertise to judge the quality of the fleece, and she wasn't surprised to note that Brett was one of the sorters.

She leaned against the door jamb and watched him work. Like the others, he'd stripped off his shirt. His broad shoulders and muscled chest gleamed with sweat beneath the harsh lights. White moleskins hugged slim hips, and the ever present hat was for once discarded. Thick, unruly black hair curled over his forehead and down his nape, the light catching its blue depths as he moved.

He was definitely the tall, dark type beloved of romantic novelists, and very handsome, but frankly strong, silent men could be a pain in the neck. You never knew what they were thinking, and it was impossible to have a decent conversation with them.

Good thing Diane's not here, she thought. She'd love all this masculine flesh, and would have Brett posing on one of her Moroccan cushions in five minutes flat. The image this conjured up made her giggle, and she looked away.

It took a few seconds for her to realise that the mood in the shed had changed, but as the giggle subsided she became aware of silent shears and eyes turned towards her. She searched one hostile face after another, her confidence wavering. Why were they looking at her like that? What had she done?

Brett's heavy tread shook the boards as he strode the length of the shed. His face was thunderous, hands clenched at his sides. The silence was deafening as dozens of eyes followed his progress.

She had not time to speak. No time to think. His hand was a vice around her arm as she was forced from the doorway and hustled down the steps to the yard.

Tearing away from him, Jenny rubbed the bruises he'd surely left on her arm. 'How dare you?' she hissed. 'What the hell do you think you're playing at?'

His grey eyes were as sharp as flints. 'Women aren't allowed in the shed. It's bad luck.'

'What!' She was so astounded words almost failed her.

'You heard,' he said grimly. 'Stay out of there.'

'Of all the arrogant . . . How dare you talk to me like that?' Her fury was stoked by the knowledge that the men in the shed as well as the yard had stopped work and were taking a sharp interest.

'I'm the manager and what I say goes around here, whether you're the boss or not. Shearing shed's no place for women. They cause accidents,' he said firmly.

She was about to give him a piece of her mind when he turned away and disappeared back into the shed. Aware of curious eyes and listening ears, she bit down on the angry retort and fumed silently. Bastard! Who the hell did he think he was?

She thought about going back into the shed and having it out with him then and there, but knew it would only cause her more humiliation. So she scuffed her boot heels in the dust, rammed her fists into her pockets and headed for the paddock. Of all the insufferable, pig-headed, rude men she'd ever had the misfortune to meet, that one took some beating. And, boy, did he know how to wind her up.

The stock horses looked at her with mild curiosity before returning to crop the grass. She leaned on the top bar of the fence and watched them, her temper cooling, the heat of her embarrassment waning as the minutes ticked by. What's the matter with me? she wondered. I'm usually so calm, so in charge of my emotions. Why did I let him get under my skin like that?

A warm breeze rippled through the grass as if invisible feet had danced through the paddock. She shivered. The magic of Churinga was touched by something dark and powerful. She could feel its presence, hear the music it brought with it.

108

Her thoughts turned to the diaries and the still silence of the cemetery. Like Matilda, she'd been enchanted. Now she was wary – perhaps afraid. Her reason for coming had been curiosity, a need to find the roots she'd left far behind in her search for fulfilment – yet she couldn't help feeling the agenda had been changed. She was really here because of Matilda. Here because a fourteen-year-old girl needed to tell her story to someone who would understand.

Jenny sighed. She should never have come. She had hoped for too much, had looked to Churinga·to show her the way now Peter and Ben were gone – and Churinga had merely brought confusion.

She left the horses to their grazing and wandered listlessly around the other buildings. There were barns full of hay, sheds full of machinery and oil drums, men bent to their chores, sheep bleating and fussing in the pens. Her footsteps led her finally to the dog breeding kennels.

The puppies were enchanting: bright eyes, wobbly legs and fluffy wisps of tails. She scooped one up and nuzzled him. His tongue rasped her face and she laughed. There was nothing like a small animal to chase away the blues.

'Put that bloody pup down!'

Jenny froze, the puppy squirming in her arms. She'd had enough of Brett Wilson for one day. 'This isn't the wool shed, Mr Wilson. I'll put it down when I'm ready,' she retorted.

The silence stretched as grey eyes held violet.

'Those dogs aren't pets. Everything around here has to earn its keep – and that includes the pups. If they don't make good sheep herders, they're put down.'

'I bet they are,' she snapped. 'Pity they don't do the same for rude managers.'

Gold flecks glinted in his eyes and the corners of his mouth twitched. 'Shooting the manager seems a bit drastic, Mrs Sanders.'

Jenny buried her face in the puppy's silky fur. The man was laughing at her, and she didn't want him to see the answering mirth in her own eyes.

He jammed his hands into his pockets. 'Reckon we got off to a bad start, Mrs Sanders. How about calling a truce?'

'It wasn't me who declared war,' she said firmly as she

looked up at him.

'Neither did I,' he said with a sigh. 'But in a place like this there have to be rules. Accidents happen in a shearing shed when the men are distracted. And, believe me, you would distract them.'

His eyes settled on her for a long moment, the glint of humour still in evidence. 'As for the pups ...' He sighed. 'It's more difficult to kill them once you've made a pet of them.'

There was silence as he took the puppy from her and returned it to its mother. Then he tipped his hat and strolled away.

Jenny watched him cross the yard, acknowledging silently that she'd enjoyed their sparring. At least he has a sense of humour, she thought. Pity he doesn't show it more often.

With a last, lingering look at the puppies, she turned back to the house. She had no skills to contribute to the running of the property but was filled with a restless need to do something. Envy of Simone swept over her. Now there was a woman who knew the rules and could effortlessly cook a hundred meals in the heat of an outback summer. She knew her place, knew she could contribute and earn her keep. 'God,' sighed Jenny. 'I feel so damn' useless. There must be something I can do.'

Taking the steps two at a time, she went into the kitchen and made herself tea. Adding biscuits to the saucer, she went back out to the verandah and the long swing seat suspended by hooks from the rafters. The gentle creak of heavy rope through metal rings was the sound of summers long passed, and as she swung back and forth, she felt distanced from the bustle of the yard and pens. It was hot, even in the shade of the verandah. Not a breath of air stirred the leaves of the pepper trees or the petals of the bougainvillaea. Birds called and fussed in the eucalyptus, and a couple of possums scampered back and forth on the verandah roof.

As her tea cooled and the sun slowly moved overhead, her thoughts turned to Matilda. Churinga had been smaller then, less successful, but if she were to return now, she would still see much that was familiar.

Jenny looked into the heat haze and thought she could see

that slight figure, wrapped in a colourful shawl, running bare-foot over the yard down to the stream. She shivered as the figure turned to look at her, beckoning her to follow. She was trying to communicate – to pull Jenny back to those long, dark days and make her witness the evil that had gone on here. But why? Why had she chosen to reveal her story to Jenny?

Her tea forgotten, she stared into the horizon. She felt strangely drawn to the child of the outback. Felt they were kindred spirits, their lives somehow entwined – and knew that no matter how terrible the road, she could not abandon Matilda's journey along it.

Returning to the shadows of the house, Jenny carried the second diary over to the bed. With a long, trembling sigh, she opened it and began to read.

Life at Churinga had changed. Matilda moved within the shadows, becoming at one with them. Yet her spirit remained unbroken, her mind working feverishly as she plotted revenge for the things Mervyn did to her on those long nights after her return.

As days turned into months, she grew resourceful and quick-witted. His drinking became her salvation, and although it depleted their meagre wool cheque, she encouraged it. Once in a stupor, he posed no threat. But that didn't make her sleep easily. Night after night, weary from the day's grind, she would lie awake, face turned to the door, senses honed for the sound of his footsteps.

A sharpened stick became a deadly weapon in her small, darting hands as she tried to protect herself, but was often turned against her. Foraging for poison berries and leaves to put in his food proved useless. It was as if nothing could touch him. Her spirit dwindled as the months of abuse took their toll. There seemed to be no end to this torment, no lessening of his greed. She would have to kill him.

The axe was sharp, glinting in the lunar light that spilled through the shutters. The blood was pounding in her ears as Matilda stood in the silent house. She had dreamed of this moment, plotted and planned and waited for her courage to mount enough to see it through. Now she stood in the kitchen, the axe in her hand, the latest bruises livid on her arms and face.

The floor creaked as she tip-toed across the kitchen and she held her breath. His snores remained undisturbed behind the closed door.

She reached for the latch. Lifting it inch by inch, pushing the door until it whined on its hinges. Her pulse drummed, roaring in her head, making her hand tremble. Surely he must be able to hear it?

She could see him now. He was on his back, mouth open, chest rising and falling as he snored.

Matilda crept to the side of the bed. Looked down at that hated face, those strong, violent hands and heavy body – and raised the axe.

Light glinted on keen steel. Breath was tight in her throat. Pulse hammered as she stood poised above him.

Mervyn grunted, one bleary eye rolling towards her.

Matilda wavered. Fear made her weak, dissolving her courage. She fled back to her room, the tears bitter, the failure devastating. Her spirit had finally died.

Summer burned its way through Christmas and into the New Year. Clouds gathered on the horizon, black and swirling, heavy with promised rain. Matilda rode out with Mervyn and Gabriel to bring the depleted mob closer to the house. The dirty, woolly backs jostled before them, Bluey racing from one side to the other to keep them together. Choking dust rose beneath the trampling hooves, blinding the riders' eyes, filling their throats.

She dug her heels into the gelding's side and urged him up the steep bank after a ewe that had leaped for freedom. She rounded it up, whistling for Blue to chase it back into the pack. The mob trundled through the vast, dry grasslands and Matilda looked at the numbers in despair. They had lost a great many lambs to the dingos and the drought this year. They could no longer afford to pay wages – and there was too much land for two men and a girl to cover.

Mervyn's visits to the pub had become more protracted, and although Matilda was grateful for this small respite, she knew they would soon be bankrupt. The house was ramshackle, the once fine barns crumbling because of the termites. Creeks needed clearing, fences re-posting, fields disentangled from the ever-invasive bush. Water was down to a trickle and the need for a new bore hole had become urgent.

She gave a defeated sigh and urged her horse on towards the home pasture. Ethan Squires had made no secret of his desire for Churinga, and Mervyn had tried to bully her into selling. But she'd clung to her inheritance. Ethan Squires was not going to take it away from her – and neither was his stepson.

Matilda's smile was grim beneath the handkerchief she'd bound tightly over her nose and mouth to keep out the dust. Ethan probably thought he was being clever, but she'd seen through his devious plan. Andrew Squires might be handsome and educated, but she felt nothing for him and never would. She was damned if she would barter herself in marriage just to escape her father. Churinga meant too much to her, and marrying Andrew would mean she would lose it.

Churinga pastures were yellow beneath the unforgiving skies, and once the mob was released and the gates barred she headed for the house. It couldn't be called home any more, she thought sadly. Merely the place where she survived another day.

Mervyn slid from the saddle and led the tired horse into the corral. Separating Lady from the others, he fumbled with bit and bridle. The mare rolled her eyes as he swung on to her back. 'That's it then. I'm off to Wallaby Flats.'

Matilda rubbed down her own horse and set him free in the paddock. The relief was sharp, but she daren't let him see it in her eyes so concentrated on gathering up the tack.

'Look at me, girl. I'm talking to you.'

She heard the dangerous stillness in his voice. Her expression was deliberately calm and unreadable as she turned towards him. But inside she was quaking.

'Ethan and that young pup of his are not to come on our land. I know what he's after – and he ain't having it.' He glowered down at her. 'Is that clear?'

She nodded. It was about the only thing they agreed on.

Mervyn's riding whip flicked lightly against her cheek, the stock coming to rest beneath her chin, tilting back her head, making her look up into his face as he leaned down from the saddle. 'No kiss goodbye, Molly?' He was mocking her.

113

The cold, hard nugget of hatred settled deep inside her as she stepped forward and brushed his stubbled cheek with numb lips.

His laugh was humourless, laced with sarcasm. 'Not much of a kiss. Perhaps you're saving yourself for Andrew Squires.' Eyes the colour of pewter glared down at her, held her frozen for an endless moment, then released her. 'Remember what I said, girl. You belong to me – and so does Churinga.' Digging in his spurs, he galloped out of the yard.

Matilda watched the plume of dust until it faded into the distance. The silence of Churinga enfolded her, bringing back peace of mind, a renewal of energy. She looked up at the sky. It was still threatening rain, but would it be yet another empty promise? For the clouds were breaking up, moving away towards Wilga.

With the pigs and chooks fed and shut in for the night, she crossed the yard to speak to Gabriel.

The old man was squatting over a smoking fire, the billy simmering a stew of kangaroo meat and vegetables. 'Rains coming, missy. Cloud spirits are talking to the wind.'

Matilda took a deep breath. He was right. The wind had changed, she could smell the rain. 'Better move your gunyahs. When the creak runs a banker you'll be flooded out.'

His yellow teeth glistened as he smiled and nodded. 'Tucker first. Plenty time.'

And he was right. There were two more days of searing heat and dry winds before the wet arrived. Thunderous rains hammered the corrugated iron roof and lashed the windows. Water filled ditches and creeks, running over parched earth in torrential rivers. Lightning turned night into day, cracking like pistol shots across the black sky. Thunder rolled and crashed, sending tremors to the very foundations of the little house.

Matilda sat huddled over the smoking fire of the old cooking range. There was nothing more she could do. The horses were warm in the barn, Gabriel and his family secure in the hay loft. The mob would have to take their chances, but the other animals were securely shut away in their kennels and pens. Of Mervyn, there had been no sign.

'It's you and me, Blue,' she murmured, stroking the silky head of the old Queensland Blue. He seemed to understand her

114

need for his company, and licked her hand.

Matilda pulled the shawl more tightly around her shoulders. The house had been built to catch every breath of air in the heat of the outback summers. Now it was icy. The smoking fire gave little warmth, and the light of the kerosene lamp barely dispelled shadows in the corners of the room. And yet she felt safe. The rain was her friend. It kept Mervyn away and brought new life to Churinga. Soon the desert would be covered in kangaroo paw and wild blue anemones, thick grass and stout saplings.

She leaned back as her eyelids grew heavy. She could sleep without fear tonight.

Heavy hammering shocked her awake, bringing her sharply to her feet and reaching for the rifle. Bluey growled deep in his throat, his front legs straddled, hackles high.

'Who is it?' she yelled above the thunder of rain on the roof.

'Terry Dix from Kurrajong. Let us in, luv.'

Matilda edged towards the window where runnels of water obscured everything beyond. Shadows were visible on the verandah. 'What do you want?' She rammed a bullet into the rifle chamber and drew back the hammer.

'We got yer dad. Let us in.'

Matilda frowned. If it was Mervyn, then why all the rumpus? Something was wrong. She edged closer to the window. The shadows moved, divided into two figures and became clearer as they approached the window. They seemed to be carrying something heavy. Mervyn must have passed out again and his mates had brought him home.

She sighed. At least he wouldn't cause any trouble, not in that state.

The rifle was steady in one hand as she unfastened the door with the other. It flew open, the wind tearing in behind it, bringing rain and leaves and bits of tree. The two men pushed passed her, Mervyn slung between them. His body hit the table with a dull thud and the three of them stood for a moment in silence.

Matilda looked from the bedraggled muddy heap on the table to the two drovers who were dripping water from their capes. There was something about Mervyn that was too still. Too silent.

Terry Dix took off his sodden hat and ran his hands through his hair. His eyes didn't quite meet Matilda's, and his usually light, cheerful voice was hesitant. 'We found him tangled up in a tree root on the boundary of Kurrajong. No sign of his horse.'

Matilda thought of Lady and hoped fervently the mare was all right. She looked at Mervyn. 'He's dead then,' she said flatly.

Terry's eyes were round with surprise, his reaction to her lack of emotion clear on his young face. He looked away quickly to the other man, then down to the floor. 'About as dead as a man can get when he's caught in a flash flood.'

Matilda nodded and walked back to the kitchen table. Mervyn's clothes were torn and stained with mud. His skin bore the evidence of gouging tree roots and gashing stones, and was grey with death. He didn't appear as large or threatening as he once had. But when she looked at those closed eyes she felt a tremor of fear. She could imagine them suddenly opening, staring at her.

'We'll help you bury him, luv. If that's what you want?'

Matilda took one last look at the man she hated, and nodded. 'Yeah. He's too big to manage on my own.' She crossed the room to the range and put the big smoke-blackened kettle over the heat. 'Have a cuppa first and get warm. You must be frozen.'

She stoked the fire and cut hunks of bread and cold mutton, but her eyes never settled on the body in the centre of the room as she worked around him.

The two drovers ate their food and drank their tea in silence. Their clothes steamed as the fire brightened, glances drifting between them, their curiosity unspoken except in their expressions.

Matilda sat by the fire staring into the flames. She was unconcerned for their thoughts or feelings. They didn't know Mervyn the way she'd known him – or they would have understood.

'We'd better get going, luv. The boss'll be sending out a search party for us soon, and the horses need feeding.'

116

Matilda calmly wrapped her shawl around her shoulders and stood up. 'Come on then. There's spades in the shed. I'll get Gabriel to help you.' She picked up the discarded flour sacks. They would do for her father's shroud.

The two drovers fetched the spades whilst Matilda woke a reluctant Gabriel. The three men hauled the body off the table and struggled through the narrow door of the kitchen and out into the rain. They could hardly hear one another above the thunder, but Matilda pointed to the burial plot and led the way. She didn't really want him buried alongside her mother or her grandparents, but it would raise too many questions if she just put him in the ground outside the home paddock.

She stood bare-headed in the rain, her cotton dress clinging like a second skin, feet cold and wet as the water seeped into the thin soles of her shoes. She saw how the soft earth lifted easily under the spades. Watched as they lowered Mervyn Thomas into the deep hole and covered him with the flour sacks. Counted the spadefuls of earth it took to bury him. Then, without a word, she walked back to the house.

The drovers followed shortly after, and she wondered if they'd thought it strange she hadn't prayed over Mervyn – given him a Christian burial. She lifted her chin and watched the rain teem from the verandah roof. She'd leave it to Father Ryan's god to decide what to do with him.

Gabriel hurried by on his way back to the barn and his warm, fat woman. The two drovers said goodbye and left for Kurrajong. Matilda stood on the verandah for a while, then turned back and closed the door behind her. She could have gone with them, but had no further need to escape. It was over. She was free.

The rains lasted two months, and Matilda had plenty of time to take stock of Mervyn's legacy. He'd left her with a rundown sheep station. A will to succeed where he'd failed. And a child in her belly which would always be a reminder of the dark years.

# Chapter Six

'Stan's organising two-up behind the bunkhouse. You in, Brett?' The shearer's voice was a gravelly whisper.

Brett glanced towards the kitchen. If Ma knew Stan was involved, then the lot of them would be in trouble. He nodded. 'But I've got a couple of things to do first.'

'Wouldn't have anything to do with our new lady boss, by any chance?' George winked, his elbow digging into Brett's ribs. 'Quite a looker, eh? Reckon you'd do all right there, mate.'

He laughed. 'You need to get out more, mate. One whiff of perfume and you lose all sense.'

George shrugged, his humour still intact. 'Better than smelling bloody woollies all day.' He sighed. 'If I was twenty years younger and not so crook, I might have 'ad a go meself.'

Brett eyed the crooked nose, the grizzled chin and thinning hair. George's courting days were far behind him. 'At your peril, mate. She's got a fair temper, that one. Sharp as knives too.'

George's eyebrows shot up, but he said nothing.

Brett returned to the last of his dinner as the other man took his plate out to the kitchen, then left. I'll have to watch what I say, he thought. Shearers love nothing better than a bit of gossip to spread on their travels.

'Where's Stan?' Ma came bustling out of the kitchen, wiping her hands on her apron.

Brett shrugged and concentrated on his dinner. He wasn't going to dob in a mate to his missus, even if he did think the man was a fool.

Ma sighed and sat opposite him. She snapped open the tin of tobacco and began to roll a cigarette. 'Why do blokes always disappear just when you want them? Promised he'd help fix that table in the kitchen.'

Brett finished the last of the suet pudding and licked his lips. 'I'll do it, Ma. No worries.'

She lit her cigarette and stared at him through the smoke. 'He'd better not be playing two-up,' she said quietly. 'Doesn't know when to quit.'

Brett pushed the bowl away and reached for his cigarettes. 'Reckon he'll be right,' he muttered.

Ma's look was penetrating, but she said nothing more and they smoked in companionable silence. Yet Brett could tell by her frown that something other than Stan was worrying her.

'Mrs Sanders had a word with you, Brett?' she said finally.

He dragged himself back from thoughts of flashing amethyst eyes and a laughing mouth. He'd been hard on her today, but she'd given as good as she'd got. 'What about?'

Ma looked uneasy, her gaze drifting away, fingers restless on the tobacco tin.

'Is something wrong, Ma?' She had his full attention now. He didn't like to see her out of sorts.

She shook her head. 'I just wondered if she'd said anything about those old clothes . . . and things?'

He frowned. 'Why should she? You cleared them out and burned them.' He saw the flush of guilt slowly rise up her neck. 'Didn't you?'

Her plump fingers twisted the tin in circles, gaze firmly fixed on the table. 'Sort of,' she muttered.

He took a deep breath and chewed his lip. The damn' woman had let Jenny see those diaries! 'What do you mean, Ma?' His voice was soft, more reproachful than accusing, but he was furious, and it took a lot of will-power to remain calm.

She finally stopped playing with the tin and stared across at him. 'I don't know what you're getting all steamed up about,' she said defensively. 'It was only a lot of old clothes, and she took such pleasure in them. I didn't think it would do any harm to let her have them.'

Brett stubbed out his cigarette. 'You've heard the rumours. And after what she'd just been through, I didn't want . . .'

'Didn't want her to hate this place and sell it on?' she interrupted with spirit. 'You and your precious Churinga,' she said scornfully. 'This bloody place is cursed and you know it.'

He shook his head. 'No, it isn't, Ma. You don't understand.'

She eyed him belligerently. 'Yes, I do,' she retorted. 'You got a nice set-up here. If she sells, you'll probably be out of a job. Good riddance, I say. Better off away from this place.'

He was silenced by her scorn, and by how close she'd come to the truth. Churinga was everything to him. He'd been left to run the place as if it was his own, had taken pride in making it one of the best stations in New South Wales. But if Jenny did decide to sell, then he might have to leave – and he couldn't bear the thought of walking away from all he'd achieved.

Ma's pudgy hand rested lightly on his arm. 'Sorry, luv. But you got to face it sooner or later. What does a young girl like that want with a place like this anyway? She's got no man, no roots in the outback – and certainly no experience of running a sheep station.'

'So you reckon she'll decide to sell then?' His spirits plummeted.

'Well, you haven't exactly made her feel welcome, have you?' she said acidly. 'I heard about the rumpus in the woolshed, and about the pup.' She heaved a great sigh. 'Men,' she said with feeling.

'She gave as good as she got,' he said defensively.

'That's as maybe. But you got to remember, she's all alone out here. Things are bound to feel strange. Give all that macho nonsense a rest, Brett. Don't be so hard on her.'

He eyed her in silence. Ma was right. He shouldn't have bullied Jenny like that.

Her voice was conciliatory. 'I know it's hard for you, luv. But this isn't your place. Never was. You shouldn't have got to care for it so much.'

He ran his fingers through his hair in frustration. 'But I do, Ma. This is the place I always dreamed of having. I could never afford anywhere half as good – not after paying off Marlene with so much of my savings.'

'Then don't you think a little friendliness, a little kindness, might make her feel more at home here? This is a trial visit, Brett, and first impressions are important.'

He nodded. 'I did apologise, Ma. And I tried to explain about the woolshed and the pup. I think she understood, 'cos the last time I saw her we called a truce.'

'So why haven't we seen her about the place this evening?' she said flatly. 'Why's she over at the house on her own?'

He dug his hands in his pockets and eyed Ma coldly. 'She's probably reading those damn' diaries,' he hissed.

She shrugged. 'What does it matter? The past can't hurt her, and she's a right to know what went on around here.'

'You haven't read them,' he said bluntly. He thought of Matilda, and the early years of Churinga, and shuddered. 'If anything makes her want to leave, it'll be those blasted diaries.'

Ma's gaze was steady as she regarded him. 'I think you might be surprised. Jenny doesn't strike me as the sort to run away from anything. Look how she left Sydney and came out here on her own – and so soon after her loss.' She shook her head. 'Reckon she's tough and bright, and will make up her own mind.'

Brett sat in thoughtful silence as Ma took his bowl and waddled back to the kitchen. Jenny Sanders was an enigma. Yet he admired her spirit and her sense of humour. Perhaps he should stop worrying about what the men thought, and get to know her a little better. For if she was reading the diaries, she would need to be shown that things had changed since Matilda's time – that the old ghosts had long since gone and there was nothing to fear.

But not tonight, he thought, looking at his watch. By the time I've fixed Ma's table it'll be too late to call.

Jenny momentarily drew back from the faded writing. Matilda's courage shone through the pencilled scrawl, making her feel ashamed. How modern life had softened her.

She closed her eyes and tried to picture the girl whose powerful story was unfolding. The girl who'd had enough spirit to buy a sea green dress and waltz to beautiful music. Her presence was almost real – as if Matilda had come back to Churinga and was watching as she turned the pages.

121

Forgetting the time and her surroundings, Jenny returned to the diary. Stepping once more into the past where life was hard. Where only a woman of steel, such as Matilda, could survive.

Mervyn's mare returned two weeks later, on a day when the rains let up for a few hours and a watery sun turned the sky gun-metal grey. The sound of her hooves brought Matilda into the yard, and with a gasp of surprise and pleasure she caught the dangling reins and led her to the barn.

Lady was thin, her coat matted and dirty, and she'd cast a shoe – but she seemed happy to be home. Matilda gave her a good feed and a bucket of fresh water, then, when she'd had her fill, set to with a curry comb to restore her gloss. She stroked the matted mane and ran her fingers down the long neck, relishing the feel of her strong heartbeat. With her face pressed hard to the bony ribs, Matilda breathed in the musty, dusty smell of her. 'Clever Lady. Good girl,' she crooned. 'Welcome home.'

The wet petered out, and finally the sky was blue again. The pastures had come alive with strong green grass and colourful wild flowers, and a mob of 'roos had taken up residence amongst the ghost gums. Birds with bright plumage darted back and forth, and the air was clean and fresh after the rains. It was time to round up the surviving mob, take stock and see how much she could salvage from the devastation.

She was dressing to ride out when the drum of hoof beats came from the yard. Reaching for the rifle, Matilda checked it was loaded and went out on to the verandah.

Ethan Squires sat astride his black gelding, a vicious brute that stamped and snorted, kicking up the mud in the yard, its eyes rolling as he reined it in. Squires' waterproof coat reached his booted ankles and a brown slouch hat shadowed his face. But she could see his determined chin and the steel of his eyes. This wasn't a social call.

Matilda cocked the rifle and held it steady, barrel pointing straight at him. 'What do you want?'

He swept off his hat. 'I'm here to offer my condolences, Matilda. Would have come sooner but the weather was inclement.'

She eyed the fine clothes and expensive horse. Was he mocking her? She couldn't be sure. But Ethan wouldn't have come all this way just to pay his respects for a man he'd detested. 'Perhaps you'd better say what's on your mind, Squires. I've got things to do.'

His lips curved into a smile but Matilda noticed how it failed to reach his eyes. 'You remind me of your mother. All fire and bristle. There's no need for the rifle.'

She held it more firmly. 'That's for me to decide.'

He gave an elegant shrug. 'Very well, Matilda. If that's how you want it.' He paused for a moment, eyes moving from the rifle to her face. 'I've come to ask you to reconsider selling Churinga.' He held up his gloved hand as she was about to interrupt. 'I'll give you a fair price, you have my word on that.'

'Churinga's not for sale.' The rifle was steady, directed at his chest.

Squires' laughter roared into the quiet morning, making his horse skitter and toss its head. 'My dear girl, just what do you hope to achieve here?' He waved towards the surrounding waterlogged paddocks and crumbling barns. 'The place is falling down around you, and now the wet's over, Mervyn's creditors will be demanding to be paid. The pigs, the machinery, the horses, and probably the rest of the sheep will all have to be sold.'

Matilda heard him out in cold silence. He was a powerful man – and she was only fifteen. If she let him get away with thinking she was easy meat, then she could lose everything. Yet she knew he spoke the truth, and spent sleepless nights worrying about the debts and how she could pay them. 'Why should any of that concern you?' she retorted. Her pulse raced as she had a sudden, nasty thought. 'He didn't owe you anything, did he?'

His expression softened as he shook his head. 'I promised your mother I'd look out for you and lend Mervyn nothing.' He leaned forward in the saddle. 'Despite your misgivings, Molly, I'm an honourable man. I admired your mother, and it's because of her I'm here today. If Churinga is to be mine, then I'll have it through fair means.'

She eyed him steadily as her heart hammered. 'Even if it

involves marrying me off to your son?'

His silence was eloquent.

'I'm not stupid, Squires. I know Andrew's only doing what you tell him – that's why I'll have nothing to do with him. You can tell him to stop sending me invitations to his parties, I'm not interested, and Churinga's not for sale or barter.'

His expression hardened, his eyes bright with lost patience. 'You silly little girl,' he hissed. 'Where else will you get a better offer? My step-son's willing to give you a lifestyle you could only dream of, and you'll still have Churinga.'

'But it would be swallowed up by Kurrajong,' she said flatly. 'No deal, Squires.'

'How the hell do you think you can run this place on your own, and without stock?'

'I'll manage.' Her thoughts were racing. There had to be a way to avoid Mervyn's creditors. Churinga's survival depended upon it.

Ethan shook his head. 'Be reasonable, Matilda. I'm offering you a chance to begin again, without debts. Let me come in to discuss my terms. You'll be surprised at how much this place is worth, despite the state it's in.' He stood in the stirrups to swing his leg over the saddle.

Matilda lifted the rifle. 'Miss Thomas, to you, Squires. And I'm not a silly little girl,' she said fiercely. 'Now get back on your horse and clear off.'

Ethan's mouth was a thin line, his eyes hard as he settled back into the saddle. He jerked the reins, startling the gelding, making it dance in the mud. 'Just how long do you reckon you'll survive out here on your own? You might think you're as tough as your mother but you're just a kid.'

Matilda looked along the barrel of the rifle, her finger hovering over the trigger. 'I'm older than you think. And I'll thank you not to patronise me. Now clear off before I put a bullet through that fancy hat.'

He steadied the prancing gelding, his eyes never leaving her face. 'You'll be sorry, Miss Thomas.' His sarcasm was as heavy as the hand on the reins. 'I'll wager you won't last more than a month. Then you'll be begging me to take it off your hands. But the price will be much lower.'

Matilda watched him wheel the horse away from the

verandah and gallop towards Kurrajong. There were over a hundred miles between the two stations, but Matilda had no doubt she would see him again. Squires was a wily opponent. He wouldn't give up easily.

She lowered the rifle and wiped the sweat from her palms as she watched the diminishing figure. She was trembling but elated despite the threats. Squires would have to be watched – but the opening salvo in the first battle for Churinga had been hers and she'd come out the victor.

Bluey came running at her whistle, ragged ears pricked, eyes bright at the promise of work. Trotting at her heels, he followed her to the barn where he sat impatiently waiting while she saddled Lady.

As she rode out to the pastures with Gabriel to begin the spring round-up, Matilda knew the mob would be sadly depleted. But they were hers – and she meant to succeed where her father had failed.

Jenny closed the diary. Her back ached and her eyelids felt heavy. As she glanced at the clock she realised she had been living in Matilda's world for more than twelve hours. Night had fallen and Churinga slept, but despite her weariness Jenny felt the first tingle of excited hope. Matilda was about to embark on an adventure into the unknown. Where there had once been despair, there was spirit and determination.

She climbed out of bed and padded into the kitchen to the trunk. Opening it, she drew out the sea green dress and held it to her face before slipping into the silken folds.

As she closed her eyes and danced to the distant music, she wondered if her ghostly partner would join her. Yet it didn't really matter if she danced alone tonight, for she knew Matilda was teaching her a lesson in survival she would never have learned anywhere else.

# Chapter Seven

Jenny woke to the sound of galahs gossiping in the pepper trees outside her window, and the soft chortle of a kookaburra defending his territory in the ghost gums. She felt rested and relaxed, despite the lack of sleep over the past couple of days, and stretched luxuriously before clambering out of bed.

Today, she decided, she would learn more about Churinga, and take time to watch and listen to the men as they went about their work. It was Saturday, half day according to Ma, so there would be plenty of opportunities to talk to the shearers and drovers, perhaps even the Aborigines. She was determined to learn about the way of things out here, the problems and pitfalls of the everyday struggles Matilda must have come across.

Having dressed and made a cup of tea, she decided that one of the first things she must do was get back on a horse. It had been years since she'd ridden, and she'd loved it, but a nasty fall as a fifteen year old at Waluna had shaken her confidence, and now she was wary of rolling eyes and prancing hooves. Yet the only way of understanding Matilda's world was to get right into the heart of it – not hide in the house while everything went on around her.

With her hair twisted up into a knot, Jenny pulled down an old felt hat from a hook in the kitchen. She eyed it for a moment, wondering if perhaps Matilda had left it behind, but decided it was probably just an old hat of Brett's and rammed it low over her brow. He would have taken it with him if he'd needed it.

It was pleasant outside, the sun not fully risen, the sky a

cool blue. The yard was already busy, despite the early hour. Dogs barked and men and horses prepared for the day's work. Like Waluna, the place was alive with excitement for a new day of shearing. A day that would bring them closer to the wool-cheque and pay day.

She took a deep breath, appreciating the fresh air that was scented with wattle, and laughing at the galahs that were hanging upside down so the dew could wash their feathers. Daft beggars, she thought. But the impromptu shower was a good idea. With her shirt tucked firmly into her jeans, she rolled up the sleeves before crossing the yard to the cookhouse. Several men tipped their hats and hurried past, and Jenny acknowledged their greeting with what she hoped was a confident smile.

As she neared the shearers' quarters, she realised it was Brett who'd stripped to the waist by the water pump and was shaving. Her footsteps slowed. Perhaps it would be better to avoid him until they'd both had their breakfast. For although they'd come to a sort of stand-off, the episode in the yard yesterday was still fresh in her mind and she had no way of knowing if his mood was still conciliatory.

She was about to take another route to the cookhouse when their eyes met in the mirror he'd balanced on the pump handle. Caught, Jenny had no alternative but to speak to him. But she was damned if he was going to upset her again. 'G'day, Mr Wilson. Nice morning,' she said brightly.

'Morning,' he said gruffly as he hurried into his shirt and fumbled with the buttons.

'Don't bother to dress on my account,' she said pleasantly. She was rather pleased to have caught him at a disadvantage, and the view wasn't bad either.

His hands stilled. His eyes were steady on her face as he slowly stripped off his shirt again and resumed his shave. Each stroke of the cutthroat was sure and efficient as he looked at his reflection in the mirror.

'I want to go riding,' said Jenny, dragging her thoughts back to her intentions rather than the tanned perfection of his back. 'Is there a horse I could borrow after breakfast?'

Brett arced the blade carefully around the dip in his chin before replying. 'They're not hacks, Mrs Sanders. Some of them are barely broken.' He fell silent again, his attention on his shaving.

Jenny recognised that gleam in his eyes as he glanced at her through the mirror. Saw the uptilt at the corners of his mouth as he washed the blade in the water. He was making fun of her. She took a deep breath and remained calm. She would not rise to the bait.

The blade was clean, gleaming in the sun as he looked at her thoughtfully. 'I'm sure we can find you something suitable. There's a couple of steady mares around the place that would probably do. I'll get one of the boys to escort you.'

She smiled at him. 'There's no need, Mr Wilson. I'm sure I can find my way round.'

He was mopping up the last of the shaving cream with a scrap of towel, eyes bright in the morning sun as he turned to face her. 'You're not to go on your own, Mrs Sanders. It can be dangerous out there.'

She tilted her head and eyed him thoughtfully. 'Then you'd better be the one to come with me, Mr Wilson,' she said firmly. 'No doubt I'll benefit from your wisdom, and you look strong enough to protect me from any dangers I might come across.'

'In case you hadn't noticed, Mrs Sanders, we're in the middle of shearing. I can't be spared.' His hands were on his hips. There was a dab of shaving cream still beneath one ear.

'How wonderful to be indispensable,' she murmured, eyeing the sparkle in his eye and knowing it was reflected in her own. 'However, as it's Saturday and half day, I'm sure you'll find a way of delegating responsibility for just a while.'

Laughter tugged at his mouth and danced in his eyes. 'Then it'll be my pleasure, Mrs Sanders.' He sketched a bow before returning to the water pump and dowsing his head.

'Thanks,' she muttered, watching the water glisten down his back. Then she turned away, knowing he was watching her – knowing he understood the effect he'd had on her.

Damn man, she thought crossly. He really was infuriating. Yet, as she approached the cookhouse, her sense of humour got the better of her and she grinned. It might be interesting to spend the day with him.

*

Brett stood in the morning sun, his hair dripping into his eyes, the nick on his chin stinging like the blazes. It had been years since he'd cut himself shaving, but it was almost impossible to keep a steady hand when you were trying not to laugh.

Riding, he thought scornfully. What the hell does she think this is – a dude ranch? If madam wants to go riding then I'll find her a horse, but I bet a dollar to a cent she won't be prancing about giving orders tomorrow. Nothing like a long stint in the saddle to bring her down to earth.

He watched her disappear into the cookhouse, admiring the neat curve of her bottom in those tight jeans. Then he snatched up the towel and roughly dried himself. That one was trouble, and the sooner he knew what she was up to the better.

As he put on his shirt, he ran through the things he wanted to say to her. The questions he needed answering. But none of them sounded right. She didn't appear to be the sort of woman who would understand a man's love for the land. She was a spoilt city woman who thought of Churinga as an adventure, and would soon tire of the place once the excitement had worn off.

He looked across at the cookhouse. Mrs Sanders held his future in her hot little hands. New owners probably wouldn't want the expense of a manager, and even if she did decide to stay, there was no guarantee she would keep him on. The thought of leaving Churinga left a physical ache deep inside him, and he realised Ma was right. The only way to give himself half a chance was to be nice to her – which under different circumstances wouldn't have been difficult – but she seemed intent on winding him up, and as he had little experience of city women, he didn't quite know how to handle it. He jammed his hat on to his head.

'Bugger it,' he muttered, and went in to breakfast.

Jenny was the first person he saw. Hard to miss her, with her hair up like that, showing off her slender neck and the shadows of her breasts where the shirt dipped low. He looked quickly away as her violet eyes sought him out, and found a space at the furthest end of the table. He poured a cup of tea from the enormous metal pot and stirred in four spoons of sugar. He would need all the energy he could get if he had to spend the day with her.

'Morning, Brett.' Ma placed a plate of steak, eggs and fried potato in front of him. 'That should set you up for your ride with Mrs Sanders. And I've done you a packed lunch.'

Conversation came to an abrupt halt as a dozen pair of interested eyes turned towards him.

'Probably be back for lunch,' he mumbled, attacking his steak.

Ma chose to ignore his embarrassment as if intent on making things worse. She winked at her audience, hands on hips. 'If you say so. But it seems a shame to hurry back when there's no need.'

Cheerful ribbing buzzed around him, and Stan Baker nudged his elbow. 'Looks like trouble, mate. Take it from me, son. When women start making plans without asking a bloke, it's time to shoot through.'

A rumble of agreement greeted this piece of wisdom.

'Put a sock in it, Stan,' mumbled Brett through the steak. 'Let a bloke eat his tucker in peace.'

'The trick is not to let 'em catch yer,' Stan cackled as he lit his smelly old pipe and turned to the others to share his joke.

Brett glanced down the table to Jenny. He could see no compassion in her eyes for the way his morning was turning out, and as she picked up her plate and left the room, she even had the audacity to wink at him.

His appetite vanished and he pushed the half-eaten breakfast away and lit a smoke. She and Ma had made him look daft, and although he was used to being teased, having been brought up as the youngest of four brothers, he knew it could only get worse, no matter how well-meant. Ma had a lot to answer for, and when he had a moment, he would take her to one side and tell her to stop match-making. She did it every year. That was how he'd been cornered by Lorraine.

He smoked his cigarette and poured another cup of tea. At least Lorraine was at a safe distance, and as long as he kept it that way, she couldn't get her claws in. And he wouldn't throw fuel on the fire of the other men's amusement by hurrying after his lady boss, but would take his time and finish his tea first.

Stan puffed away at his pipe, his scrawny chest still rumbling with the cough his laughter had brought on. Brett eyed him thoughtfully and wondered how many more seasons he had in him. He had to be at least sixty, yet he was still one of the fastest shearers in New South Wales. Strange how that skinny frame and hunched back never seemed to tire.

'Time to go to work,' said Stan, ramming his smouldering pipe into his jacket pocket as he stood up. 'Ma chased me all over Queensland before she caught me, but it was only 'cos I let her.' He smiled. 'Just remember, son, never let a woman know you want to be caught – it gives 'em ideas.'

Brett eyed the smoking pocket. 'One of these days you'll go up in flames with that bloody pipe.'

The old shearer pulled out the offending object and tapped the dottle into a saucer. 'No worries, mate. I intend to die in me bed with me missus next to me.' He looked thoughtful for a moment, sucking at his gums. 'About time you let one of the ladies catch yer, though. A man gets crook out here without a bit of female company.'

'Don't do me any favours, Stan. I like things the way they are,' Brett retorted. He stood up, towering over Stan, and pulled on his hat. The conversation was taking him places he had no wish to visit.

Stan laughed as they pushed through the screen door, then set about relighting his pipe. Once alight and pulling satisfactorily, he stamped out the match and headed for the shearing shed.

Brett watched him go. No one stamped out a match or cigarette more thoroughly than a bushman. They had all witnessed the power of fire and the devastation it brought. He moved away from the cookhouse, his thoughts on what the old man had said – and although he was reluctant to admit it, Stan was right. He was lonely. The nights weren't the same since Marlene had left, and the house felt too empty with no one to talk to about things unrelated to sheep. And since moving back into the bunkhouse, he missed the privacy of listening to music or reading in the silence of the long evenings. Men were great company, but now and again he yearned for the smell of perfume and the touches that only a woman could bring to a home.

He glowered into the fast-rising sun. His thoughts were getting him nowhere fast, and impatient with himself and everything around him, he stomped off to saddle up the roan mare for Mrs Sanders.

Jenny sat on the five-bar gate and watched Brett catch and saddle the roan. Like the other men on Churinga, he was so much a part of this place, she couldn't imagine him anywhere else. He was tough and brown like the earth, wiry like the grass, and as enigmatic as the existence of such exotic birds and delicate wild flowers in the harsh landscape.

She'd regretted his embarrassment at breakfast, and would have put a stop to it if she'd thought it would have done any good. But she'd had no way of knowing Simone would blurt out their plans like that in front of the others and knew her interference would only have caused more comment. She had a sneaking suspicion Simone was trying her hand at match-making, and decided that, after the ride, she would have a quiet word. Brett was, after all, totally different from any man she'd met as an adult. Their life-styles collided at every turn, and they had nothing in common. Except for Churinga. And even that wasn't enough on which to build more than friend-ship. It was too soon – much too soon.

Jenny climbed down from the gate, picked up the saddle bag with the picnic and crossed the paddock. The man and the two horses were waiting for her, and although they made a pleasant picture against the backdrop of Tjuringa mountain and the tea trees, she wished it was Peter who stood there with the reins in his hands. For this was his dream – his plan for their future – and she wasn't sure it was right to live it without him.

The wistfulness must have shown on her face. Brett's grin faltered as he looked down at her. 'Not having second thoughts, Mrs Sanders? We could always postpone this.'

Jenny put thoughts of Peter and Ben to one side and pulled on her riding gloves. 'Not at all, Mr Wilson. If you could please give me a leg up?'

He cupped his hands beneath her boot and hoisted her into the saddle. His grin was firmly re-established as he swung up from the stirrup and settled into his own. 'We'll head south to begin with. Then we can rest up for tucker in the shade of the moun-tain.' He eyed her quizzically. 'That sound all right to you?'

132

Jenny nodded as she took hold of the reins. The mare was quietly tearing the grass and chewing contentedly. She was old and gentle, and Jenny was relieved and not a little ashamed of her uncharitable thoughts towards Brett. She'd had a nasty suspicion he might have given her a half-broken brumby to ride, just to teach her a lesson, but he'd proved less spiteful then she'd thought. Yet even this old mare was a challenge after so long, and it would take all her concentration not to make a fool of herself by falling off.

They moved away from the homestead, the long grass swishing around the horses' legs. As they left the paddock and headed out across the grazing pastures, the horses broke into a canter.

'You seem at home in the saddle, Mrs Sanders,' shouted Brett. 'A little tense, but that's to be expected on a strange horse.'

Jenny gritted her teeth and attempted a confident smile. His surprise at her capabilities was nothing compared to the struggle she was having to stay on board. The effort of hanging on with knees and hands was making her tremble. She was out of condition and out of practice, and wished she could have had time on her own before coming out with him.

And yet, as she looked out over the silver grass to the distant Tjuringa mountain, she realised how vast and empty the land was, and was relieved he'd come with her. To ride out here alone would be foolish, for if she fell or hurt herself, it could take hours for anyone to find her.

She thought of Matilda and her desperate run for freedom. Thought she could hear the pounding of her boots on the solid, dry earth, and the echoes of her cries for help. The child must have come this way all those years ago.

'We'll head towards the mountain,' Brett called over his shoulder. 'You wanted to see more of Churinga, now's your chance.' He spurred his horse and set off at a gallop.

Jenny's thoughts snapped back to the present, and she tentatively urged the mare on. Sweat was running down her ribs as her hands gripped the reins and the mare set off after the gelding. Jenny rose in the saddle and leaned close to her neck, knees glued to her sides. This was going to be a real test of nerves, and she almost wished she hadn't suggested it. But there was no way she'd let Brett know how scared she was.

Then, as if by magic, she lost her fear and the tension left her. Her grip on the reins relaxed, and she gave the mare her head. The old felt hat flew off and bounced against her back, restrained only by its thin leather strap. Her hair streamed and the sheer joy of freedom surged through her. It was exhilarating to feel the warm wind on her face, and the steady sure-footedness of the animal beneath her.

Brett was some distance ahead, his torso barely moving as his horse stretched its legs and flew over the ground, man and beast in perfect harmony against the rugged backdrop of Tjuringa mountain. How wonderful, she thought. I could go on like this forever.

As the mountain came more clearly into view, Jenny realised it was partially covered in thick bush. Ancient trees formed a cool oasis at its base, and as they drew nearer, there was the distinct sound of falling water and bird-song. Perhaps this was where Matilda had come – but Jenny wouldn't let gloomy thoughts spoil this wonderful day.

She followed Brett through the tangle and into the coolness of the green canopy until they reached the rock pool and splash of the falls. She reined in and grinned across at him. She was out of breath, and knew she'd be stiff tomorrow, but for the moment there was only the joy of the ride.

'That was bonzer,' she gasped. 'Thanks for coming with me.'

'No worries,' he muttered, swinging out of the saddle and coming to stand beside her.

'You don't understand,' she said, catching her breath. 'I didn't think I'd ever ride again after the accident. But I did it. I really did.' She leaned over the roan's neck and gave her a pat. 'Good girl,' she murmured.

Brett's expression was inscrutable. 'You should have said. I'd have given you more time to get used to old Mabel here. I didn't realise.'

She shrugged. 'Why should you? I was fifteen and the horse wasn't properly broken. It took fright, I fell off and didn't get out of its way in time.' She spoke the words lightly but still remembered the pain as the heavy hoof caught her shoulder and ribs. The broken bones had taken months to heal.

'Better rest a while then, Mrs Sanders. You've had a long ride and the water's good to drink.'

Jenny let go of the reins and swung a leg over the saddle. Then, before she realised what was happening, she was being lifted down by strong arms. She could feel the thud of his heart, and the warmth of his hands at her waist as he held her close before planting her firmly on the ground. She swayed against him, light-headed not only from the exhilaration of the ride.

'You all right, Mrs Sanders?' His look of concern was momentary, and she wasn't sure if the colour in his face had more to do with embarrassment at their closeness than with the exercise.

She drew away from him. 'I'm fine. Thanks. Just not used to riding any more. Reckon I'm out of condition.'

His eyes flickered over her before returning to her face. His expression was eloquent, but he remained silent as he turned away and led her through the undergrowth to the rock pools.

'What about the horses? Shouldn't we hobble them?'

'No need. Stock horses are trained to stay where they are once the reins are dropped.'

They used their hats to collect the water. It was icy cold, burning its way down her dusty throat, refreshing the heat in her face and aching body. After drinking their fill, they sat in silence as the horses took their turn.

Brett lit a cigarette and stared off into space and Jenny wondered what on earth she could say to him. Polite conversation would bore him, and she knew so little about his work her ignorance would merely make her look stupid.

She sighed and took a long appreciative look at her surroundings. Tjuringa mountain was made up of dark rock that was slashed with bright orange and piled like giant building bricks into haphazard order. The waterfall came from a deep fissure that was almost hidden by overgrown scrub, and the rock pools lay in flat basins that mirrored the centuries-old Aboriginal stone paintings on the mountain walls.

'What happened to the tribe who used to live here?' she asked finally.

'The Bitjarra?' Brett studied the end of his cigarette. 'They still turn up now and again for a corroberee, because this

135

place is sacred to them, but most of them have gone to the cities.'

Jenny thought of the itinerant Aborigines who got fat and drunk on the streets of Sydney. Lost in so-called civilisation, with their ancient culture forgotten, their tribal lands taken by squatters, they lived from day to day on hand-outs. 'That's sad, isn't it?'

Brett shrugged. 'Some of them stay true to the Dreaming, but they have a choice like everyone else. Life was pretty hard for them out here, so why stay?'

He eyed her from beneath the brim of his hat. 'You're thinking of Gabriel and his tribe, I suppose.'

She nodded. It was no surprise he'd read the diaries – for how else could she explain his reluctance to let her see them.

'They left a long time ago. But there's a couple of Bitjarra jackaroos working for us at the moment, who're probably distantly related. Great horsemen, the Bitjarra.'

'It was a good thing for Matilda Thomas they were around back then. Must have been hard for her once Mervyn was gone.'

Brett crushed out his cigarette. 'Life's hard out here anyways. You either take to it, or it kills you.' His gaze was penetrating before it drifted away. 'Reckon you'll be wanting to sell up and move back to Sydney before too long. It's difficult out here for a woman – especially when she's on her own.'

'Maybe,' she murmured. 'But Sydney's no picnic, either. This might be the Seventies, but there's a long way to go before women are accepted as equals.'

Brett snorted, and Jenny wondered what cutting remark he was about to make before he changed his mind.

'I haven't always lived in the city, you know,' she said firmly. 'I lived in Dajarra until I was seven, then went to live on a station at Waluna with John and Ellen Carey until I turned fifteen and left for art college in Sydney. I met my husband in the city so I stayed, but we always meant to return to the land one day.'

He eyed her thoughtfully. 'There's nothing much but a big Catholic orphanage at Dajarra.'

She nodded. 'That's right. I called it home for a while, but it's not somewhere I plan on visiting again.'

He sat up and chewed on a piece of grass. 'Look, Mrs Sanders, I'm sorry if I was rude the other day. I thought . . .'

'You thought I was some rich city woman come to give you a hard time,' she finished for him. 'But I didn't tell you about my past so you could feel sorry for me, Brett. I just wanted to put you straight, so there could be no misunderstandings.'

He grinned. 'Point taken.'

'Good.' She turned away and watched a flight of budgies cast a rainbow through the trees. When she looked back, Brett was sprawled on his back, his hat over his face. Conversation was obviously at an end.

After several minutes she became restless and decided to take a closer look at the Aboriginal paintings. They were as clear as if they'd been painted yesterday, depicting birds and beasts running from men with spears and boomerangs. There were strange circles and squiggles marking what she guessed were tribal totems, and handprints smaller than her own, tracing a passage into the scrub.

She picked her way through the bush, delighting in each new find on the ancient rock. Here was a cave, delving deep into the mountain, with fantastic creatures adorning the walls. There was a finely etched Wanjinna, a water spirit, drifting from a fissure in the rock up towards the waterfall. She moved deeper into the bush and began to climb. Clay mourning caps circled a long dead fire on a shallow plateau, and the bones and feathers of the feast that had once been eaten here littered the ash. She squatted down and looked out through the tree tops on to the grassland. It was almost as if she could hear the throb of the didgeridoo, and the hollow tap of the music sticks. This was the ancient heart of Australia. Her heritage.

'What the hell do you think you're doing, wandering off like that?' Brett came crashing through the bush and up the rock to stand breathlessly beside her.

She looked up into his thunderous face and took her time to get to her feet. 'I'm not a child, Mr Wilson,' she said calmly. 'I know how to take care of myself.'

'Really? Then how come you haven't noticed that scorpion on your boot?'

Jenny looked down in horror at the tiny creature, poised

and ready to strike where her boot ended and her socks were her only protection. She stood rock still then with lightning speed flicked it away with her gloved hand. 'Thanks.' She said grudgingly.

'You might have been brought up in Waluna, but you still have a lot to learn.' He growled. 'Thought you'd have had more bloody sense than to climb about up here on your own.'

'Perhaps I didn't like the company down by the pool,' she retorted.

'It was you insisted I come with you.'

Jenny rammed her hat more firmly over her head and pushed past him. 'My mistake. I won't bother again.'

'Good. 'Cos I've got better things to do than baby-sit a silly woman who thinks it might be fun to go walkabout right next to a scorpion's nest.'

She turned on him, furious to have been caught unawares by the scorpion, hurt pride making her sharp. 'Just remember who you're talking to, Mr Wilson,' she hissed.

'It would be difficult not to – believe me. But if you didn't behave like a brat, you wouldn't be treated like one,' he retorted.

'How dare you?' said Jenny with dangerous calm.

Her hand was caught in mid-flight as she aimed to slap his face. He pulled her close. 'I dare because if anything happened to you, I'd be blamed.' He released her as swiftly as he'd caught her. 'Time to go. I've work to do.'

Jenny clambered after him, out of breath and still raging. 'What is it with you? Are you always this rude?'

They reached the pool and Brett gathered up the horses' reins. He turned to her, his expression enigmatic in the cool gloom of the green canopy. 'Fair go, Mrs Sanders. If you play with fire, you should be prepared to get burned.'

The rage left her and confusion came in its stead. She looked into his eyes, saw no humour there, nor in the set of his determined chin. She snatched the reins from him, and without waiting for his help, clambered into the saddle.

They rode in silence back to the property, his strange words ringing in her head. What had he meant and why was he so touchy? She'd done nothing more than explore an ancient Aboriginal Dreaming Place. Why should that and the episode

138

with the scorpion make him so rude – so belligerent?

Jenny shifted in the saddle. She didn't like the way he made her feel so . . . So what? Uneasy? Guilty? Awkward? She sighed. There was no describing the effect he had on her, and she was frustrated at not being able to understand why that should be.

As they reached the paddock, Jenny slid from the saddle. Her back and arms ached, and her extra toe was chafing against her boot. Next time she would wear her worn-in boots instead of these new ones, she decided ruefully. And she would go with someone else. One morning of Brett Wilson's company was more than enough.

'Thank you,' she said coldly. 'I hope I haven't taken up too much of your precious time. You can go back to work now.' It was a spiteful thing to say, and she regretted it instantly – but she was damned if she was going to apologise after his earlier rudeness.

Brett took the reins, unsaddled the horses and walked away. His only acknowledgement of her thanks was a curt nod.

Simone was in the kitchen with a cup of tea and a plate of cheese salad in front of her. Her face was bright with curiosity. 'You're back early. How'd it go?'

Jenny threw her hat on to the table and sat down. Muscles she didn't know existed were tight and sore, and her foot was throbbing. 'The ride was ripper, but I can't say the same for the company.'

Simone's hand stilled as she lifted the teapot. 'You and Brett had a falling out?'

Jenny nodded. 'He was rude – and I won't bloody stand for it.'

'I'm sorry, luv, but I find that hard to believe. What happened?'

'Nothing,' she replied tartly. It all seemed so childish now. No point in expanding on it.

'Perhaps that was the problem.' Simone smiled as she poured the tea.

Jenny eyed the smugness in the older woman's smile. 'What do you mean by that?'

Simone laughed and patted her hand. 'Nothing, luv. Nothing at all. Strange you find him rude, though. Brett's

139

usually such a nice bloke. There's lots of girls would've given their eye teeth for a morning's ride with him.'

'Then Lorraine and the others are welcome to him. I can think of several things I'd rather do than spend the morning with Brett Wilson.'

'Wait on, Jenny. There's nothing more than Lorraine's imagination between her and Brett. He ain't looked at a woman seriously since that wife of his shot through.'

Jenny saw the hostility in Simone's face, and wondered what the departed Marlene could have done to upset her.

'And she was no better than she deserved to be,' Simone finished. 'Led poor Brett a fine old dance.'

'What do you mean?' Simone obviously had a soft spot for Brett, and doubtless thought he could do no wrong, that no woman was good enough for him.

'She sang in a bar over in Perth, by all accounts,' she said, arms tightly folded beneath her bosom. 'But I reckon it wasn't only her voice the men came for, if you know what I mean.'

She paused and pursed her lips. 'Poor Brett. Thought he'd got himself a pretty little wife who'd stay faithful and fill his house with kids. Caused a lot of trouble round here, that one. Couldn't keep her hands to herself.' Simone's bosom heaved with disapproval.

'No wonder he's so touchy around women. Must think we're all tarred with the same brush. How come he's got involved with Lorraine? By the sound of it, she and Marlene are sisters under the skin.'

Simone shrugged. 'She's young, attractive and willing. A man has needs, Jenny – and Brett is the same as any man – but I don't think he's been that daft yet. But she's mistaken if she thinks she can hook him that way. He's after something far more permanent after Marlene.'

Jenny thought of Lorraine's expectant face, and the way her colour and spirits rose once Brett had arrived at Wallaby Flats. 'Poor Lorraine,' she sighed.

Ma snorted. 'That's as maybe. Don't want to waste energy on feeling sorry for that one. Had more blokes than you and me 'ave 'ad 'ot dinners,' she said scornfully.

Jenny stirred her tea. 'He and I just don't seem to get along. After Peter, my late husband, he seems so taciturn, so unapproachable. Have I upset him in some way – is that it?'

Simone laughed. 'Not the way you think, no.'

Jenny frowned. 'What's that supposed to mean?'

The round, jolly face sobered. 'Nothing, luv. Brett's just worried you'll sell the place and leave him out of a job and a home. He's worked real hard for ten years to get it up this good, and it would break his heart to leave it.'

'He has a funny way of trying to impress me then,' said Jenny flatly.

Simone waved away this defence. 'It's only his way of hiding his feelings. Blokes are silly like that out here. They have to be seen to be tough and strong. My Stan comes back from the shed laughing and joking as if he hasn't a care in the world. But sometimes, when he thinks I'm not looking, he cries with the pain in his back.'

Jenny was silent as she finished her cup of tea. Brett's behaviour suddenly made more sense. His rudeness was covering up his fear. He was trying to prove Churinga was a place worth keeping. A place he could run efficiently and wisely. Her arrival had unsettled him – she was young, and a woman, and held his future in the balance.

She thought of his warm hands on her back and the beating of his heart against her own as he'd pulled her to him after she'd tried to slap him. There had been something in that moment which had almost broken through his defences – something she'd thought she recognised. And yet that was impossible.

'I'm real tired after that ride, Simone. Thanks for the tea and the gossip. See you later.'

'Right-oh. Time I got on with preparing dinner anyways.'

Jenny crossed the yard to the house, her mind playing over the morning's ride. Churinga was casting its spell over her, and soon she would have to decide what to do. But not yet, she thought. It's only been a matter of days, I'll not let Brett Wilson cloud my judgement.

The kitchen was cool and gloomy behind the closed shutters. She looked at the open trunk, the dress glimmering softly in the subdued light, and although she was exhausted, she knew it was time to read the next diary.

Kicking off her boots, she massaged her toes before

141

climbing on to the bed, and within minutes was back in Matilda's world.

The mob had been rounded up into the home pastures. They were a bedraggled lot, thin and depleted in number, the spring lambs not as plentiful as Matilda had hoped. The wool cheque would never cover her father's debts. She would have to find another way to pay them off.

As Matilda watched the mob crop the strong, fresh grass, she felt the baby kick inside her and knew she'd made the right decision to bring the sheep in early. Churinga was deserted but for Gabriel and his family, and soon she would find it difficult to patrol the far-flung pastures on her own. Crutch cutting could be done here just as well, and she could keep an eye on foot rot and the hundred and one other things that went wrong with sheep.

She felt the gentle swell of her belly and couldn't hate the child that grew there. Conceived in sin, it was blameless – she was determined to give it the best life she could.

The days grew longer and warmer, the grass lost its verdant freshness. Matilda rode out each day with Gabriel and Bluey to mend the fences and clear the streams of the storm debris that had been washed down by the wet. The nights were spent poring over the accounts and inventories. When the debtors came, she had to be ready.

The vegetable garden provided for the table, as did the dairy cows and the pigs. Yet her kerosene supply was way down, as was her store of flour, sugar, salt and candles. The shearing season was drawing ever nearer, and somehow, if she managed to keep hold of her stock, she would have to find the money to pay the shearers.

She fingered the locket her mother had given her. Matilda wore it most days now – there was no need to hide it from Mervyn any more. It was worth a lot of money but she would never sell it. Better to exchange some of Mervyn's rifle collection for seed and flour. Ethan's gloomy prophecy echoed in the silence of the deserted house, and despite her determination to prove him wrong, she could feel Churinga slipping away from her.

They came to find her a month after the short, violent wet

came to an abrupt halt. Matilda's condition was hidden by a loose shirt and a pair of Mervyn's old dungarees, and as they rode into the yard, she was perched on the top rung of the ladder, helping Gabriel fix the roof of the house.

She knew who they were, and why they'd come – and as she looked down at them, she wondered if they would give her the chance to outline her proposals. They had obviously worked out something between them – their turning up together was proof of that. And as she began the climb down the ladder, she steeled herself for the battle ahead.

They released their horses into the home paddock and were waiting on the verandah by the time she reached them. Matilda noticed they couldn't quite meet her eye, and how they twisted their hats in their hands. She decided not to waste time with small talk.

'I got no money,' she said firmly. 'But I aim to pay off Dad's debts one way or another.'

'We know that, Miss Thomas.' Hal Ridgley owned the feed store at Lightning Ridge, and despite his size, seemed to shrink before her direct gaze.

Matilda looked from one man to the other. Apart from Ridgley, there was Joe Tucker from the pub, Simmons from the bank, and Sean Murphy from Woomera. She took a deep breath and turned to Sean. He was well liked in the area, and his opinion was respected. If she could get him on her side, then she stood a chance of persuading the others to take her offer seriously.

'Dad still owes you for that ram and two ewes. I need the ram to increase the stock, but both ewes have had strong, healthy lambs, two a-piece. Will you take them in payment?'

His hair glinted grey in the sun as he thought over what she'd said. 'That ram's a good breeder. Cost me a fair packet, Miss Thomas,' he said finally. 'I don't know.'

Matilda's calculations had accounted for this reluctance. 'I'm offering the ewes as well, Sean,' she said quietly. 'But the ram has to stay here for another season if I'm to survive.'

He glanced at the other men who were watching for his answer, then nodded. 'Reckon that's fair, Miss Thomas.'

Matilda felt her spirits rise. She turned to Hal Ridgley and smiled. 'The wet came before I could use all the feed Dad laid in. You can take what's left, and I'll throw in his Spanish saddle to square things up.' She noticed a flicker of greed light his eyes and pressed her point. 'You've always liked it, and it's probably worth more than we owe.'

Hal's colour rose. 'That feed's probably full of weevils by now, and I reckon the rats have chewed it and all.'

'Not in my barn, they haven't,' Matilda said roundly. 'I put feed in metal containers with airtight lids.' She drew herself up to her full height and glared at his shirt buttons. 'Do we have a deal?'

An almost imperceptible nod came from the big man as Sean's elbow dug into his ribs, and Matilda smiled inwardly. Hal had always coveted Mervyn's ornate saddle – and although she'd probably have got more by taking it into town to sell it, she'd known he would find it hard to refuse.

Joe Tucker stepped forward and handed her a clutch of paper. 'These are Merv's IOUs. Some of 'em go way back.'

Matilda's pulse quickened. Unlike the other debts, she'd had no way of knowing how much Mervyn owed the landlord. As she read the scraps of paper with her father's scrawled signature, her spirits plunged. So much money. So many bets placed and lost. So much whisky. The sum was beyond her.

'Sorry, Matilda. But I got bills to pay too, and I can't afford to let these just go. Things ain't so good right now.'

She gave him a tremulous smile. Poor Joe. He was a kind man trying to do his best. It was obvious this was as painful to him as it was to her. She stared out across the yard to the home paddock and the horses grazing there. She had her own horse, the chestnut that was part broken, two brumbies that were still wild, and Dad's grey.

The silence was tense, broken only by the creak of the verandah chair as the banker, Simmons, rocked back and forth. Matilda shivered. It was as if her father had returned and was waiting to catch her out.

She pulled out of her thoughts and concentrated on Joe. 'Tell you what. You take the two brumbies and sell them on. Should get a good price if you can break them first, and they're both stallions, so why not try Chalky Longhorn over at Nulla Nulla? He's looking for new bloodstock.'

His expression was mournful. 'I don't know nothing about

breaking horse, Matilda. Now, if it was the chestnut as well as the brumbies, I could be sure of getting me money back.'

Matilda eyed the chestnut. She was a bonzer horse, fast and sure-footed, with just enough wildness still in her to put up a good show at the local races. Mervyn had put one of the jackaroos up last time and won a fair amount in side bets. But she couldn't afford to lose her as well as the others. It would leave her exposed if her own horse was injured. Lady was getting on, and soon she wouldn't be able to keep up with the work.

'The chestnut or the brumbies,' she said firmly. 'I can't let you have all of them.'

Joe's confidence seemed to have grown for his stance became more belligerent, his expression determined.

'Yer dad's owed me a long time, and it's only out of respect for you I haven't sold these IOUs to Squires. He was willing to settle them, you know. Can't wait to get his hands on Churinga.'

Matilda noticed how his eyes shone as he played his ace. She knew she was beaten. 'Thanks for coming to me first,' she said quietly. 'You can take all these horses if it means Squires keeps his hands off my land.'

Simmons rose from the rocking chair, his bulk making the loose verandah boards groan. 'None of this will make the slightest difference, Miss Thomas,' he said in his pompous voice. 'The bank won't be bought off with horses and feed and saddles. And if you can't repay the loan your father took out, then regretfully we'll have to call in the receivers. There should be no problem selling. We've already had enquiries.'

Matilda could see no regret in his expression as she took the IOUs from Joe and stuffed them in her pocket. No doubt Squires was the one who'd made the offer. She was aware of the other men leaving the verandah to collect their bartered goods but her whole concentration was on the man in front of her. She knew why he'd come, she'd found the papers after Mervyn was buried.

'You'd better come inside. We need to discuss this properly,' she said firmly. 'I don't want the others hearing what I got to say.'

He looked at her askance but followed her indoors without speaking. Once a cup of tea was placed in front of him, Matilda sat down, her arms on the table between them.

'Show me the terms of the loan, Mr Simmons,' she said quietly.

He opened his leather brief-case and pulled out a sheaf of papers, then settled back to drink his tea. His eyes remained firmly on her face, reminding her of a stalking dingo waiting his moment to grab a lamb.

Matilda read the papers, and when she'd finished pushed them back over the table. 'They aren't legal. I owe you nothing but the small loan Mum took out five years ago.'

He sat very straight in the hard wooden chair. 'I think you'll find they are, Miss Thomas,' he boomed. 'I had them drawn up by my own solicitor.'

'Then you should get rid of him, Mr Simmons,' she said acidly. 'Because he doesn't do his work properly.'

Simmons lost his composure. 'I hardly think you're in a position to question one of the finest legal minds in Australia, Miss Thomas.'

'I am when a loan is taken out on my property without my consent, Mr Simmons,' she fired back.

His pomposity and bluster were replaced by confusion. 'But I saw the deeds . . . Your father owned the land at the time of the loan.'

Matilda shook her head. 'He had the right to live here and farm the land until his death. Nothing more. Here's the rest of the paperwork. Read it for yourself. And if you don't like it, I suggest you question Mr Squires' lawyer. He set up the deed of covenant for my mother.'

Simmons took out a very white handkerchief and mopped his bald head as he read through the documents. His hands were shaking, and sweat darkened his shirt front.

Matilda waited until he'd finished reading. Her pulse was racing as she memorised the words of that important deed. Her mother had made her understand fully what she'd planned, and she knew the deed almost by rote.

'I'll have to take advice on this, Miss Thomas. It seems your father was not wholly honest with us.'

'He wasn't straight with a lot of people, Mr Simmons,'

Matilda said dryly.

'The debt will still have to be paid. It was quite a substantial sum and can't be just written off.'

Matilda stood up. 'Then take me to court. You don't get Churinga without a fight, Mr Simmons.'

He eyed her thoughtfully. 'How old are you?'

'Fifteen. But don't let that fool you.' Matilda folded her arms over her chest and stared him down.

'There's still the last of your mother's loan to clear. How do you propose to do that?'

Matilda heard the note of sarcasm and reached for the tin box she'd been so careful to hide from Mervyn. It represented almost a year of searching his pockets, of scrimping and saving and lying for just this one moment. It was all she had until the wool-cheque.

She tipped the coins on to the table where they glittered in the sunlight. 'This covers half of what we owe. The other half, as arranged by my mother, will come when this year's wool cheque is paid.'

He frowned as he eyed the pile of coins. 'By the look of your stock, Miss Thomas, I doubt you'll make much money this season – and how will you manage until then? This is all you have, isn't it?'

She didn't want his sympathy, Didn't want him in her kitchen. 'That's my business, Mr Simmons. Now, if that's all, I have work to do.'

She followed him out on to the verandah and watched as the four men filled their water bags and remounted their horses. Joe led the way to the first of the dilapidated gates, the brumbies and the chestnut on leading reins behind him. The lambs and ewes ran in a woolly bunch ahead of the horses. She waited until their dust was a speck in the distance before returning to her roof repairs.

Gabriel was straddled over the roof, his back resting against the chimney. He'd done nothing since the men had arrived, she noticed.

She caught her breath and eased the pain in her back as she reached the top rung. It was getting more difficult to move around quickly, and the baby was lying low and heavy beneath the concealing clothes.

'Let's get this over with, Gabe. Then we can have tucker.'

He grinned down at her. 'No nails, missy.'

'Then go down and bloody well find some,' she snapped.

# Chapter Eight

Matilda knew time was running out. Soon it would be impossible to disguise her condition, so a week after she'd dealt with the banker, she harnessed Lady between the wagon traces and with Bluey loping beside her, headed for Wallaby Flats. Supplies were dangerously low, and there was only one way of getting the money to restock.

As they trotted towards the distant town, she remembered her last journey away from Churinga. It had been a desperate run for escape then, but she'd been a child. Now she was a woman with her destiny firmly grasped. The debts were paid, Churinga was still hers, and the spring grass was fattening her sheep. Life was good.

She camped out that night, wrapped in a blanket under the wagon, Bluey growling and snuffling at the slightest sound, Lady's harness jingling as she cropped the grass. Then, as dawn filtered across the horizon, she rose to make tea in the billy, and eat the damper bread she'd brought with her.

Rooks cawed in the trees as she passed, and a mob of 'roos bounded out of her way as Bluey went off to chase them. She was hot in her father's long droving coat, but it covered her like a tent. Although it was nobody's business, she was not prepared to face the gossips and try to explain either herself or her father. If all went well this trip, she wouldn't need to return to Wallaby Flats until after the baby was born – but she would deal with that when the time came.

Wallaby Flats hadn't changed since Matilda had first been brought here by her mother as a child. It was still dusty and stuck in the middle of nowhere, reeking of sulphur and pitted with opal mines long since played out. The houses were weather-beaten, the pub still had gaps in the fretwork of the verandahs, and the men sitting in its shade still stared off into space.

She tethered Lady to the hitching post by the water trough, pulled the collection of rifles from the wagon bed, and stepped up on to the wooden walkway. The bell jangled as it had always done when she pushed her way into the general store. She was greeted by the heady aroma of sugar and coffee, tea and leather and kerosene. After the jolting, rolling ride in the wagon, this was too much for her stomach, and she swallowed hard until she had the nausea under control. Smells seemed to upset her lately, probably something to do with the baby.

She pulled the coat over the swell of her stomach and walked up to the counter where the shop-keeper was waiting. 'How much for the rifles?' She didn't recognise him, their supplies had always been delivered with the mail.

The man was thin, with a bad skin and a drooping moustache. He eyed her thoughtfully, then took the rifles one by one and looked down the barrels before checking the breech, the cartridge chamber, firing pin and the sights and balance. He grimaced and placed them on the counter. 'Already got a fair stock of rifles. These ain't up to much.'

Matilda eyed him coldly. She knew their worth. Mervyn had never stopped reminding her when he'd made her clean and oil them. She selected three of the seven – the most valuable. 'These two are Winchesters, this one's an Enfield.' She picked them up, drew back the bolt and clicked the firing pin. 'Smooth as silk. As good as the day Dad bought 'em.'

She waited as he pored over them, touching here, stroking there, his tongue darting over his lips in anticipation of a hefty profit. Matilda knew he was trying to decide just how far he could push his luck, and before he could insult both of them with a ridiculous offer, she broke the silence. 'I've got a list of supplies,' she said firmly. 'Those rifles should cover it.'

He rubbed his chin and pulled his moustache, his mean little eyes darting between the valuable rifles and the very long shopping list. 'It's not my usual way of doing business,' he said finally. 'But I reckon these should cover the list.' He looked at her more closely. 'Aren't you Merv Thomas' kid?'

150

She nodded warily.

His expression was mournful as he picked up the rifle. 'Thought I recognised the Enfield. Sorry to hear about yer dad. Told him he shouldn't have gone back when he did. But you know Merv.' He smiled. 'Old bastard never would be told. Good bloke. We miss him around the place.'

Matilda's answering smile was tight. She really didn't want to spend time discussing 'good old Merv'. She pushed the list over the counter. 'Can I have my supplies? Got the wagon out front.'

'Name's Fred Partridge, by the way. How you making out on yer own at Churinga?'

'I got Gabe,' she said quickly. 'And with the shearing season coming up, there'll be more.'

'Want me to put a notice up? How many you hiring this season?'

Matilda was distracted by his question – she hadn't prepared for it. She eyed the collection of notices on the board behind him. Shearing time brought an influx of men from all over the state and beyond. This store was their first call when they came looking for work. 'I'll let you know,' she said quickly.

'Have to be pretty quick, luv.' He took a scrap of paper and wrote out a hasty notice. 'I'll put you down for ten shearers and a cook. Reckon that should see you right.'

He pinned the notice on the wall with the others and Matilda's mouth dried. The only way she could afford to pay so many men was to send Gabe to market with the pigs and two of the cows. That would leave her with very little stock.

'Make it nine shearers. Peg Riley does the cooking every year, and Bert's still shearing.'

He eyed her closely. 'Feeling crook, luv? Sit down and I'll get the missus to make you a cuppa.'

Matilda pulled herself together and shook off the nausea. 'I'm fine,' she lied brightly. 'Don't bother.'

Her protest wasn't quick enough. As if she'd been waiting behind the curtain that divided the shop from house, his wife appeared with a cup and saucer in her hand. 'Matilda Thomas? Pleased to meet you.' Her gimlet eyes danced swiftly over Matilda's long coat, and when they returned to her face they were bright and curious. 'How's it going up there on yer own, luv? Hear you put Simmons in his place. I don't know how you done it, but good on yer. About time that sour piece of work got a taste of his own medicine.'

Matilda wasn't surprised by the speed with which word had spread, and although she did wonder what else was being said, she knew better than to ask. Those sparrowhawk eyes were too sharp, and she didn't relish getting entangled in the lies she would have to tell to keep her secrets. 'She'll be right once the wool cheque comes in,' she murmured, gulping the scalding over-sweet tea. 'Thanks for the cuppa, but I've got other things to do in town. I'll be back for the supplies.'

Matilda pushed her way through the door, heard the screen slam behind her and knew the storekeeper's wife was watching. She hurried across the dirt street to the little church around the corner and sank gratefully into one of the highly polished pews. Her back was one dull ache and the baby was squirming. She'd stay here and rest a while in the cool where no one could see her.

'It's Matilda Thomas, is it not? Well, well. Aren't you a sight for sore eyes?'

Matilda took a deep breath. She'd hoped the priest was on his vast parish rounds. They usually took up to three months – it was just her luck he should be at home. She finally looked up into Father Ryan's' kindly face. He was young and friendly, and had been a regular visitor when her mother was alive. The last time she'd seen him was two months ago, when he'd come to say a prayer over Mervyn's grave.

'Hello, Father.'

'How are you managing, Matilda? It can't be easy, a slip of a thing like yourself all alone on a big place like Churinga. I suppose you'll be selling up?'

She shook her head. 'No, Father. I'm staying.'

'Surely to God that's not wise, Matilda? Doesn't seem right for one so young to have such responsibilities.' His face was concerned, his Irish brogue echoing up into the vaulted roof of the wooden church.

Matilda had heard this once too often. 'I was on my own most of the time Dad was alive, Father,' she said dryly. 'I do now what I did then. Gabe and his family are there. They help.'

The priest smiled. 'Ah, Gabriel. One of God's more idle children,' he said with a sigh. 'Not too reliable, I'm thinking. A bit inclined to go walkabout, as they say.'

'Fair go, Father. We all need time off now and again.' She stood up. 'Gotta go. I got supplies to pick up, then I'm back to Churinga.'

'Do you not want me to hear your confession, child? It's been a while.'

Matilda shook her head vehemently. God knew her sins – no point in telling Father Ryan as well. 'Haven't got time, Father. Maybe on your next visit.'

His smile was sad. 'That's what you always say.' He eyed the heavy coat she was clutching to her. 'Are you sure everything is well with you, Matilda?'

'Bit tired, that's all. Now, I gotta be getting back.' She left the church and hurried to the store. The sooner she was out of here the better. There were too many prying eyes, too much well-meaning sympathy.

Fred Partridge was loading the last of her supplies into the back of the wagon. His two little boys were peeking out from behind their mother's skirts as she leaned in the doorway and watched Matilda's approach.

Matilda checked the list against the things in the wagon. Everything seemed to be there.

'I've added a couple of things I thought you could probably do with,' said Fred. 'Nails, twine, and an extra bag of chicken feed. The wife thought you could find some use for the last of that bolt of cloth as well. Reckon Merv's rifles are worth it.' There was a flush of colour to those sallow cheeks, and his eyes were focused on a point over her shoulder.

Matilda eyed the bright blue gingham and thought of the things she could make with it. 'Thanks.' She climbed into the wagon and took up the reins, then smiled down at him and his family. There was no point in alienating them by saying she didn't want or need their charity. They were being kind, and she should be grateful. Yet she wondered how kindly they would be if there wasn't enough money from the wool and her supplies ran short again. Now the rifles were gone and the pigs and the cows earmarked to pay the shearers, she had nothing else to barter with.

153

She whistled and Bluey wriggled from beneath the store where he'd probably been chasing rats. She slapped the reins over Lady's sway back and they pulled away, heading down the dirt road and out of town. She didn't look behind her, but knew the men had come out of the pub to watch her pass, and curtains twitched at every window as she went down the street. She held her head high. They could make of her what they wanted. She would do things her way from now on – and no one would be owed a penny.

Jenny lay on the bed and stared at the ceiling. She tried to picture Matilda on that wagon behind the old horse, with Bluey loping alongside. Tried to imagine the back-breaking labour and sheer loneliness of those next few months as she repaired the roofs and walls, and virtually rebuilt the shearing shed. What had gone through her mind as she'd travelled over her land, and seen no other sign of life?

Jenny felt her isolation as if it was an echo within herself. She knew what it was like to be alone. Could understand the longing for someone who cared to talk to. The years at the orphanage had taught her the power of resilient silence, the need to keep the deepest emotions hidden behind a façade of cool control. For once exposed, the soft, inner core of fear and bewilderment would make her weak – a weakness Sister Michael saw as an invitation to exploit and punish.

Her thoughts turned to Dajarra and the orphanage of the Sisters of Mercy, the sound of children's voices breaking the silence, the memory of the nuns making her cold. They had ruled with sharp tongues and quick hands, but it was the voice of Sister Michael that brought back the terror of those early years.

'You're the Devil's child, Jennifer, and the Devil must be beaten out of you.'

She winced as if that cruel little whip Sister always carried had once more touched her back. Even now, after all the years in between, she couldn't enter a Catholic church without the dread returning, or hear the swish of a nun's habit, or the click of rosary beads without a shiver. They were sounds which filled her with an urge to run and hide.

Jenny swung off the bed and leaned out of the window. She

needed air and light to chase away those dark memories. The cruelty of those years would remain with her forever, but her salvation had come with Diane.

Left alone and sobbing, the four year old had been found on the orphanage steps one night after vespers. There was a scrawled note pinned to her thin dress.

*'Her name is Diane. I can't cope no more.'*

Jenny sighed as she remembered Diane's muffled sobs during the night, and how she'd crawled into bed with her and they'd clung together until morning. A strong bond had been forged – one that would never be broken – and it was at times like these, when she felt alone, that Jenny missed her the most.

'At least I have Diane,' she muttered. 'Poor Matilda had no one.

Her words drifted into the still of the late afternoon and she turned away from the window. Thoughts returned of a green dress and haunting music, of arms gently holding her as she danced. There had been someone for Matilda – someone who cared for her very much. Someone whose spirit still lingered at Churinga all the while her story needed to be told.

Matilda plunged the spade into the earth and pulled out the potatoes. She was in a hurry to be finished, for there was a lot to do before the shearers turned up tomorrow. Yet she was hampered by the deep pain that had been with her on and off all day. It was low in her back and she wondered if she'd pulled a muscle when she'd heaved the old generator into place behind the woodshed.

She stood for a moment, her fingers kneading the pain as she caught her breath. It seemed to be moving, spreading like a steel girdle in the pit of her belly. The child had stopped kicking several days ago and lay heavy and low, and as she ran her hand over the taut mound beneath her loose shirt, she wondered if it was time.

'Not yet,' she breathed. 'It can't be. There isn't time. The shearers will be here soon.'

She bent to pick up the potatoes and was struck by a searing pain that felled her. She dropped to her knees, the potatoes forgotten, all her concentration on the grinding pain that assaulted her. Eyes tightly shut, she curled into the agony, the warm earth pressing on her cheek. A keening grew in her throat as she rocked, and escaped in a long, low moan as the contraction finally subsided.

Staggering to her feet, she weaved a precarious path to the verandah. It was imperative she should get indoors before things went any further. But as she reached for the front screen, she felt the onslaught of another contraction. She sank into the rocking chair as it tore through her. 'Gabriel,' she screamed. 'Gabe! Help me.'

The gunyahs were deserted and nothing stirred but the sheep in their pens.

Pain was laced with fear. She was no stranger to birthing, she'd helped the ewes at lambing time – but things could go wrong. Many a ewe had been lost through a breech birth, many a lamb stillborn.

'Gabriel,' she yelled. 'Where the hell are you, you bludger?'

Sweat beaded her skin and stung her eyes as she waited for the answering shout. None came. 'Gabriel,' she moaned. 'Please come back. Don't leave me now. I need you.'

The contraction subsided, the yard remained empty, and Matilda knew she was alone. She pushed through the screen door and into the kitchen. Grasping an old blanket from a peg by the door, she laid it on the floor in front of the cooking range. The billy was boiling and the knife she used for gutting rabbits was on the table. She dropped it into the billy. She would need it later to cut the cord.

Her head swam as she stripped off the overalls and boots. Her shirt was soaked, but she kept it on. There was something too vulnerable about being naked and in pain. With a clean sheet set aside to swaddle the baby, she knelt on the blanket and whimpered for Gabriel. Where had he and his family gone? Why had he chosen this particular day to leave the homestead and take his women with him? It was not a good omen for Gabriel had an intrinsic feel for trouble, and was never around when it happened.

'Lazy, good-for-nothing bastard,' she spat. 'Trust him to shoot through when I really need him.'

The pains grew more ferocious, coming in quick succession

until she felt an urgent need to push the child out. The agony was everything. The urge to push too great. She felt herself descend into a swirling vortex where nothing else existed but the need to give birth to the life inside her.

Then, from somewhere far removed from the reality of what was happening to her, came the sound of a screen door slamming and feet treading on floorboards. Distant voices muffled by the roaring in her ears. Shadows flickered, moving around her like ghosts in the firelight.

'Oh, my lord! Bert, she's in labour. Quick – get my box from the wagon.'

Matilda opened her eyes and saw the familiar, friendly face of Peg Riley.

'It's all right, luv. You just relax. Peg'll see you right.'

'My baby,' she gasped, grabbing hold of Peg's arm. 'It's coming.'

'Too right it is, darlin', and in a hurry too. Grab hold and push.'

Strong arms held firm as Matilda gripped them. Teeth gritted and eyes tightly shut, she gave into the need to push – and with one final, mighty thrust, she felt the child slither out of her. Darkness came then. Welcoming and all-consuming. And she slipped into it with a grateful sigh.

Matilda opened her eyes, disorientated by the soft darkness and the sliver of moon touching the corner of her bedroom window. Something was different, something wrong. She struggled to escape the clutches of oblivion and remembered. How long had she been out, and where was her baby?

A dark shadow moved in the dim corner, and she yelped in fear. It was Mervyn. He'd come back from the grave to punish her and steal her baby.

'Shhh. It's all right, luv. Only me, Peg Riley.' A warm hand stroked back the hair from her forehead, and a cup of something that smelled strange but tasted very sweet was pushed against her lips.

Matilda looked into the familiar face of the Sundowner's wife as she drank from the cup and relaxed. She'd always like Peg Riley, and felt safe knowing she was here.

The cup empty it was taken away then the sheet was tucked

neatly beneath her chin. 'There you go, darlin'. It's all over. You can go back to sleep now. Peg's here to look after you.'

'Where's my baby?' she murmured. Her eyelids were heavy and sleep seemed impossible to resist.

'Don't you worry about anything, luv. What you need is a good night's sleep. Everything'll feel much better in the morning.'

'My baby,' she whispered. 'Is my baby all right?' The sound of her voice echoed in the room and in her head as sleep finally claimed her. Yet her dreams were uneasy, almost haunted, filled with the sound of disembodied voices and the tread of feet in a distant room.

She finally opened her eyes and found it was dawn. The cool, clear light was drifting between the new gingham curtains and settling on Peg who was sitting beside the bed with her knitting. Matilda smiled into the kindly eyes and took her reddened hands. 'Thanks, Peg. I was so scared. I don't know what I would have done if you hadn't turned up.'

'No worries, luv. We decided to come straight here instead of going into Wallaby Flats first. I like to get meself prepared before the shearers turn up.' She drew back her hands and gathered up her knitting. 'Can't say I was sorry to hear about yer dad, but I reckon you done all right for yourself. Mob looks healthy enough.'

Matilda lay back into the pillows. She felt exhausted despite the long sleep, and it was too much of an effort to talk. She watched Peggy move around the room, content to hear the swish of skirts again and the light footsteps of another woman.

'Drink this, darlin'. It'll help get your strength back.' She watched as Matilda screwed up her nose against the strange smell. 'I put a little something in it to help you sleep, luv. Won't do no harm.'

Peg waited until Matilda had drained the warm milk. Her expression was thoughtful as she took back the cup. 'Where's your man?' she asked finally.

Matilda could feel the heat of shame in her face. 'There isn't one,' she whispered.

Peg seemed unmoved by her reply. She merely nodded and tucked the sheets more firmly beneath the mattress before turning to leave the room.

'Where's my baby, Peg?'

The Sundowner's wife stopped in the doorway, her back straight, her hand resting lightly on the latch. The seconds ticked away and Matilda was speared with dread as the woman finally turned to face her. Peg's expression was solemn, her eyes downcast.

Matilda tried to raise herself on her elbow, but was too weak. 'What's wrong, Peg?' she muttered.

Peg's weight tilted the bed as she sat down. Her arms reached for Matilda, enfolding her in a warm, smothering embrace. 'Poor little thing was dead, darlin',' she crooned. 'There was nothing we could do.'

Matilda let herself be rocked in that soft embrace, moulded to Peg's generous chest, the words going round and round in her head and not making sense.

'My Bert's making a fine box. We'll see the poor little mite has a decent burial.'

The effects of the drink Peg had given her made it difficult to think and Matilda fought the black waves of sleep that threatened to drown her. 'Dead?' she whispered. 'My baby's dead?' Truth dawned through the encroaching darkness and bitter tears ran unheeded down her face. She'd known there was something wrong. The child had been too still inside her. She should have gone into Wallaby Flats to Doc Peterson and got help. It was her fault the baby was dead.

Peg held her until the darkness claimed her.

Sounds drifted in, at first distant, then more sharply focused. The complaint of sheep, the hum of a generator, the excited chatter of men, all came together to rouse her from the lethargy of sleep. Matilda listened to the familiar sounds, knowing the men had arrived for the shearing and feeling content that Peg and Albert would see to them.

Truth hit with searing ferocity. Her baby was dead. Peg and Albert were planning a funeral. She couldn't lie here and do nothing. 'Peg? Where are you?' She swung her legs out of bed, the sheets entangled in her nightshirt.

There was no reply.

'Must be over at the cookhouse,' she muttered. Her head felt as if it had been stuffed with wool, and her legs trembled

159

when she tried to stand. Leaning heavily on the bedside table, she waited for the swirling vertigo to dissipate. There was an emptiness inside her she'd never experienced before, and an aching reminder of her baby's entrance into the world. She took a series of deep, tremulous breaths, fortifying herself for the walk into the kitchen.

As her head cleared and she was able to focus on the bedside table, she realised something was missing. It was important, but as lucid thought had escaped her, she couldn't figure out what it was. 'I'll remember soon enough,' she muttered.

Pulling on a loose shirt to cover her nightclothes, she shuffled into the kitchen. It was deserted, but she wasn't really surprised. With the shearers arriving, Peg would have a lot to do in the cookhouse. But it looked as if she'd left a note.

With slow, unsteady steps, Matilda shuffled to the table, picked up the scrap of paper, and slumped into a chair to read it. The writing was almost illegible.

*Bert took ill. Had to leave. We done our best for the baby.*
                                                              Peg Riley

Tears blurred Matilda's vision as she screwed up the note and looked around the deserted kitchen. She was sorry to hear Albert was ill, but how on earth would she manage now? She'd been depending on Peg to help through the season.

Yet as she realised they'd taken flour and sugar from her precious store, and the side of mutton from the meatsafe, the tears dried. A cold anger at her own weakness blew through her. That was the last time she would trust anyone, she vowed. She had come this far on her own – she would find the strength from somewhere to carry on.

She got up and went out on to the verandah. The clatter and bustle of Churinga drifted around her as she leaned on the railings and watched Gabriel taking charge of the jackaroos. At least he's come back, she thought. But I wonder who's in charge of the woolshed?

She pushed thoughts of the shearing to one side. She had to see where they'd buried her child. Had to say goodbye. Her legs were still unsteady, her head light, as she stumbled around the house to the family cemetery. But she refused to give into what she saw as a weakness. There wasn't time for self-pity.

The newly dug earth was covered in stones to protect it from dingos, and marked with a crude wooden cross. Matilda knelt on the hard-baked earth amongst the wild flowers. She reached out and touched the pathetically small mound, the tears coursing down her face as she thought of the tiny child beneath the earth. Her child. The child she'd never seen or held.

She tried to pray, but couldn't find the words. Tried to transmit her feelings through her touch on the roughly hewn cross – but knew it was too late. She was being punished for her wickedness and that of her father. The child, innocent of all sin, had been taken to heaven. Perhaps it was for the best, she thought after the tears had dried. For what kind of life could I have given it? Gossip would have spread, poisoning our lives, and my knowledge would destroy us both in the end.

She picked some wild flowers and placed them against the cross. Stumbling to her feet, she stood for an endless moment looking at the brutal reminder of the past.

'I'll survive this, as I've survived everything else,' she whispered. 'But one day, I promise, you'll have a proper headstone.'

Jenny closed the book, tears running unheeded down her face. She understood the pain of losing a child. Knew how deeply Matilda must have mourned, remembering her own sweet Ben. His sunshine smile and bright yellow hair. Chubby legs and clutching fingers that had been a delight.

But at least she'd been allowed to get to know him. To love him before he was snatched away. Matilda had no photographs, no memories to cherish – merely a rough cross over a mound of earth.

Jenny covered her face in her hands and wept for them both.

# Chapter Nine

Brett hesitated before knocking. He'd acted on the spur of the moment, which for him was unusual, but after the ride this morning, he felt a certain respect for the surprising Mrs Sanders and wanted to apologise.

Ma was also instrumental in his coming here. She'd told him in no uncertain terms what she thought of him, and having regarded himself as an easygoing sort of bloke, he'd been shocked to realise just how rude he'd been. Jenny had obviously been afraid of that horse but she'd stuck to it, literally and metaphorically, until she'd gained her confidence. No mean feat after a bad fall in the past.

The black and white pup squirmed in his arms, paddling with his feet to get down, but Brett held on, unsure if coming here tonight had been such a good idea after all. He'd seen the lights from across the yard and assumed she was still awake, yet there appeared to be no one about and his knock remained unanswered.

He waited another moment, then pushed through the screen door. She must be here, he thought. Where else could she go? But the thought she might be asleep came as a relief. He could leave now, and apologise in the morning.

The silence in the house surrounded him, and he cleared his throat to announce his presence. He was reluctant to disturb her privacy, knowing how precious it was in a place like this but not wanting to startle her if she wasn't asleep.

Then he heard the muffled sobs coming from the bedroom and panicked. Perhaps he should leave now, before it was too late and she caught him listening. Women were one thing but tears were way out of his league. He stood there for a moment, unsure of his next move, the wriggling pup in his arms. Perhaps his churlish behaviour was the reason for her tears. He hoped not but one never knew with women.

The pup made the decision for him. With a last, desperate wriggle, it landed with a thud on the floor and scampered towards the bedroom door. With his front paws scrabbling at the wood it began to whine.

The crying stopped abruptly. 'Who's there?' Jenny's voice was muffled but edged with alarm.

'It's me, Mrs Sanders. Nothing important. I'll come back tomorrow,' Brett said hastily.

'No, don't go. I'll be out in a minute.'

He scooped up the pup, took off his hat and stood awkwardly some distance from the bedroom door. He could hear her moving about in there, the muffled sigh, the hasty snuffle of tears all telling him he was intruding. He wished he was back in the bunkhouse. Wished he'd never come.

The door opened to reveal her tear-streaked face. Brett took a step back. The sight of those wonderful eyes awash with tears was having a strange effect on him. 'I brought you a peace offering,' he stammered. 'But I can see it's the wrong time. I'll come back tomorrow.'

He was gabbling, and probably not making sense, but she seemed not to notice. 'For me? Oh, beauty,' she gasped, her eyes wide with pleasure. 'How kind. Thanks.'

He transferred the pup to her arms where the little animal set about licking away the remains of her tears. Brett looked into those violet eyes. He was suddenly finding it hard to breathe, and all the carefully rehearsed words he'd meant to say were wiped from memory. He wanted to reach out and touch her – to stroke the glossy hair from her damp cheek and kiss away the tears.

The realisation shocked him from his stupor and he backed away. What the hell was he thinking of? She was his boss. He must be going mad. He cleared his throat and drew himself up to his full six feet two inches.

'Just to say sorry for this morning – and yesterday,' he stammered. 'Thought you could do with a bit of company. He's a ripper little bloke, but he's not house-trained.'

He could feel the colour rise in his face as she looked back at him and twisted his hat in his hands as he slowly backed towards the front door and the safety of the verandah.

Jenny giggled as the puppy squirmed and licked and whined. 'He's a bonzer boy, aren't you?' she crooned, ruffling his silky head. 'Thanks, Brett. He's the best present you could have given me.'

'It's late,' he said gruffly. 'See you in the morning.' He reached behind him for the door handle, his eyes firmly fixed three feet beyond her shoulder.

'Do you have to go? Please stay and have a beer. You can help me find a name for this little bloke.'

Brett heard the loneliness in her voice and recognised the plea for company in her eyes. 'Well,' he began. He was torn between wanting to stay, and knowing he should leave.

'Please.' Violet eyes looked back at him in appeal.

He was lost. He remembered Marlene's loneliness, her accusation that he'd spent no time with her and didn't listen when she wanted to talk. Guilt had a way of eating at you, and the thought of Jenny needing him made him leave the doorway and follow her across the kitchen. One beer wouldn't hurt.

He stood awkwardly by the table, hat in hand as he watched her pour milk into a saucer. The pup promptly stood in it, then licked the milk from the floor and his paws, large brown eyes watching for their reaction.

Jenny laughed, stroked the pup's head, then turned to fetch the beers from the gas fridge. She opened them, passed one to Brett and tipped the other to her lips and took a long drink.

He watched the way her neck arched and her throat moved and looked quickly away, wondering what game she was playing. She had to realise what effect she was having on him. He'd finish this beer and go.

Jenny sat across the table from him and watched the pup chew a pair of her shoes. 'Thanks again. That was real nice of you, Brett.'

'No worries,' he mumbled. He saw fresh tears in her eyes and looked firmly at his beer. He would have liked to ask what was troubling her, but he didn't know how. He just hoped she didn't start crying again. Dammit, he thought. Wish Ma was here. She'd know what to do.

'I mean it, Brett. It was thoughtful and kind, and although I probably don't deserve it after being such a bitch this morning, I need a friend just now.'

Brett looked across the table as she flicked her hair over her shoulders and gave a tight, false laugh. This woman was hurting, but it wasn't his place to pry into the reason why. It had to have something to do with her bereavement, and no doubt the diaries weren't helping.

She must have sensed his awkwardness. She turned away and watched the pup for a moment before speaking again. He'd discovered a pair of socks and was happily snuffling and chewing his way through them.

'Reckon his name should be Ripper,' she said finally. 'What do you think?'

'Too right,' he said quickly, relieved the tense moment was over. 'Bit of a larrikin, that one. Runt of the litter, but full of energy.'

The silence grew and Brett took a swig of beer. He didn't know what else to say and as the moments passed began to feel more uncomfortable. He was on the point of getting up from the table when her hand crept across and rested on his fingers.

It was as if he'd been jolted by a cattle prod. He was transfixed, staring into violet eyes that now seemed too close to his.

'Talk to me about Matilda Thomas, Brett.'

Her eyes weren't just violet, he realised. Now he was closer, he could see gold and flecks of blue, surrounded by the deepest black. He reluctantly pulled away from her and clasped the neck of the beer bottle to steady himself. He should have known this would come. But did it have to be tonight when she was already upset and he was tongue-tied?

'What do you mean, Mrs Sanders?' It was the best he could do. He needed time to get his brain in gear.

'You know very well what I mean, Brett Wilson,' she said in exasperation, her eyes dark and angry. She pushed away from the table, her chair scraping on the floor. 'And if you don't stop calling me Mrs Sanders, I swear I'll smash this bloody bottle over your bloody head.'

They stared at one another, shocked at her words, then

165

broke into simultaneous laughter.

'This is ridiculous,' Jenny giggled. 'We're both adults, for goodness' sake, how the hell did we get to be so scratchy with each other?'

Brett shook his head, the grin still firmly set on his face. 'Beats me. My fault probably. But fair go, Mrs – I mean, Jenny – you were a bit of a shock. I expected someone older. Less . . .'

'Bossy?' she finished for him.

That wasn't what he was thinking at all, but he let it go. He noticed how the laughter shone in her eyes as she tilted her head and looked at him. 'How was I supposed to know you'd be so young . . . and everything.' He tailed off. He'd said too much.

She grinned. 'I'll take that as a compliment, Brett. Have another beer.' She passed the bottle and raised her own in a toast. 'Here's to a better understanding of each other.'

'Yeah, why not?' The beer was cold, just the way he liked it, and yet he couldn't remember her leaving the table to fetch it. He was aware only of her face and eyes. He would have to watch it, or he'd find himself in too deep with the lovely Jenny Sanders.

'Tell me about the history of this place, Brett,' she said, her expression serious. She held up her hand to silence his objection. 'You and Ma mentioned rumours. Come on, I need to know.'

His thoughts were jumbled. Since reading the diaries, he'd come to realise the rumours were nothing compared to the truth, and yet he had no idea how much she'd already learned. He decided to tell her the positive things he knew about Churinga's history. But where to begin? He took a sip of beer to prolong the moment and collect his thoughts.

'The O'Connors came here as pioneer squatters back in the early eighteen hundreds. They were poor Irish, like most of the settlers back then. Sick of British rule and desperate to own the land they worked. Churinga homestead started out as a shack in the middle of the bush. There was water and grass and protection from flooding on the higher land near the mountain. But the bush had to be cleared before they could increase the stock they'd brought with them.' He stared thoughtfully into the distance, imagining the years of back-breaking work this must have entailed.

'They didn't have tractors and sophisticated machinery, of course. Most of the work must have been done by axe and hoe. But as the land cleared and their sheep prospered, they began to increase their acreage. When Mary took over, Churinga was almost a hundred thousand acres, and the shack was now surrounded by barns and sheds.'

'Mary was Matilda's mother?'

Brett nodded. 'She ran the place during the first world war, when her husband Mervyn was away in Gallipoli. She brought in the Merinos and the dairy herd, and with the money she made from the wool, she improved the homestead. The rumours have it that Mervyn resented her success, and when she died, he tried to sell Churinga to Ethan Squires.'

'But he couldn't,' murmured Jenny. 'It belonged to Matilda.' She finished her beer. 'I've read some of the early diaries, and they aren't pretty. But I'd like to know what others thought of Matilda. What about these rumours you mentioned?'

'Matilda Thomas was a legend around here before she turned twenty. She was unusual because she was a woman alone in a man's world. She was thought odd, perhaps eccentric, living the way she did with her Aborigines, and people are always a little afraid of what they don't understand so she was left very much to herself. There were rumours about a baby, of course, prying eyes don't miss much. But when there was no sight of it, that was all forgotten.' He stopped, knowing there was more but reluctant to spread what he considered to be vicious speculation.

'But she made Churinga what it is today?'

He nodded. 'She was respected for what she achieved here, although the other squatters and their wives disapproved of her.' He grinned. 'She was a bit of a larrikin, by all accounts. Charging around in men's clothes and not giving two hoots what anyone thought of her.'

'What about her father? What did the rumours say about him?' Jenny's voice held a low urgency he understood.

'He came back from the Great War a hero. But it wasn't until after the flash flood when he drowned that the truth came

167

out. He wasn't shot while bringing a mate back through enemy lines but by one of his own who'd found him hiding from the fighting. Mervyn killed him, put him over his back and returned to base camp. He was awarded the Victoria Cross and after a year or more in hospital was sent home. He thought he'd got away with it, but a man down in Sydney recovered from his amnesia and made a statement to his commanding officer. He'd been overlooked when they'd searched for the wounded near Mervyn's hiding place, and had seen it all.'

'I'm not surprised he was a coward,' Jenny said grimly. 'A man like that could never be a hero.'

Brett drank his beer and wondered how much all this was affecting her. She was, after all, recently widowed, and the diaries were a graphic account of the Churinga years. Had her tears tonight been for her personal loss or the loss of Matilda's innocence?

'Tell me about Matilda.'

'You've read the diaries. You know as much as I do,' he countered.

She shook her head. 'Not all of them, Brett. I want to know what happened after the baby died. And what part the Squires family had to play.'

He was on dangerous ground. Although the diaries never revealed much about Ethan's involvement, truth and rumour had a nasty habit of melting into one another, and he didn't want to speculate. He looked across at her, knew he would have to say something, so decided to stick to what he knew as the truth.

'No one saw much of Matilda after the baby died. She went into town a couple of times a year on that old horse of her father's, and got reacquainted with her neighbours Tom and April Finlay over at Wilga. As Churinga prospered, she modernised and bought a utility but she never travelled far.'

He lit a cigarette and stared off into the distance. 'Talk has it she got to be a hermit. She was alone with her Bitjarras except at shearing time, never went to the picnic races or dances, didn't socialise. Andrew Squires made a play for her, but she knew he was only after the land and sent him packing. Squires' youngest son, Charlie, was said to be keen on her, but nothing came of it.'

'But she did have someone, didn't she?' Jenny leaned forward, her fingers inches from his on the table.

Brett shrugged. She'd find out soon enough if she finished the diaries, but he wasn't prepared to enlighten her so soon after her crying storm. 'Don't know, Jenny. Sorry.' He said finally.

She eyed him solemnly then leaned back in the chair, her expression thoughtful. 'According to the diaries, Ethan Squires was after her land. And according to my solicitor, the family is still interested.'

Her eyes were on him, direct and penetrating. 'What is it about Churinga that makes them so hell-bent on owning it?'

'Water,' he replied promptly. 'Kurrajong has bore holes and a good river, but Churinga has three rivers running through it as well as deep artesian springs. The O'Connors knew good land when they saw it, and Squires never got over being too late to stake a claim.'

'Tell me about the Squires family.'

Brett sighed. Why couldn't she just let things drop? If only Ma had done as he'd asked and burned those bloody diaries, none of this would concern her. 'Ethan's father was the youngest son of a rich farming family in England. He was sent out here in the early eighteen hundreds to make his fortune, with just enough money to see him right for his first few years. He started out in Queensland, learning the differences between English sheep and Australian, then came south. He saw the land, realised this was a good place to settle, and built Kurrajong. But with Churinga expanding to the south and east of him, he had no option but to spread north. It's drier there. Much less rain and fewer rivers.'

'So the feud began?'

Brett shrugged. 'I don't think it ever came to blows, but Ethan's father certainly made it known he resented the O'Connors and did everything he could to hinder them. He passed on his legacy to Ethan, who tried to marry off his step-son to Matilda, but she ruined his plans by refusing to co-operate. Ethan's still bitter about that.'

'I thought you said Charlie Squires was interested? Why didn't anything come of that if his father was so keen?'

Brett shrugged. 'I have no idea,' he said truthfully.

She looked at him thoughtfully. 'Is this place cursed, Brett? Is the Churinga an evil amulet?'

He snorted. 'That's ridiculous. This place is like a hundred others. Lonely, cut off and surrounded by the harshest elements in the world. What happened to Matilda could have happened to anyone out here. You have to remember what she achieved despite the setbacks, not dwell on your vivid imagination. There's nothing evil here – just life in the raw.'

'You really love this place, don't you?' she murmured. 'Despite losing your wife because of the isolation.'

Brett was relieved at the turn in the conversation. He began to relax. 'Marlene was a city girl. She liked the shops, the cinema, new clothes and lots of parties. I should have known she'd hate it here,' he said quietly. 'I tried my best to keep her happy, but it wasn't enough.'

It was suddenly important to her to see Churinga as he knew it – as it really was. 'Don't get the wrong idea about this place, Jenny. It might be cut off, but there is a certain primal spirit about it. Think about Matilda. She didn't have the luxuries we have today or the men to help in those early years. Yet she stayed. She worked and struggled for years to make this place what it is today because she loved it. She loved the land, the heat and the wide open spaces – and despite all the things she went through, she wouldn't be beaten by any of them.'

Not all of them anyway, he thought. But Jenny doesn't need to know that yet.

He fell silent. He'd said more than enough, and she seemed satisfied. The urgency had left her face, the intensity was gone from her eyes.

'Thanks, Brett. But the more I read of those diaries, the less I feel I should stay. Churinga seems to cast a spell over the people living here. It's as if Matilda still haunts the place. There are times when I know she's in the house. Drawing me further and further into her world. And I'm not sure I like it.' She shivered. 'It's as if she knows I'll understand her pain. But it's too soon after losing Ben and Peter. My own wounds are still too raw to take hers on board.'

He reached for her hand and held on. 'Then throw the diaries away. Burn them. Leave the past where it belongs before it destroys you.'

She shook her head. 'I can't do that, Brett. Matilda's taken hold of me and I have to know what happened to her. Have to try and understand what kept her here.'

'Then let me show you the Churinga I love. Let me help you understand why we stay on this land even though it makes us old before our time. This is my home, Jenny. There's nowhere else I'd rather be. And I want you to love it too.' He could feel the heat rise in his face as he realised how impassioned he'd become. She'd think he was a fool.

'You're afraid I'll take it away from you, aren't you?'

He nodded, unable to speak. He could feel the thread of her pulse running through her fingers, warming his own, echoing in the beat of his heart. 'Do you think you'll sell?' he asked finally, dreading her reply but knowing he would have to be strong and face up to it.

'I don't know, Brett,' she said thoughtfully. 'It's beautiful here, and I think I can understand your love for the place. But those grave markers haunt me.' She pulled away from him, folding her arms across her chest as she shivered. 'I'm sorry I can't give you a definite answer. I know how much your future depends on it.'

He breathed a sigh of relief. At least she hadn't decided yet – there was still hope.

'Your imagination's running away with you, that's all. And it's not surprising after what you've been through recently. But all stations have their graveyards – there's no time to take people into town for burial. You should concentrate on the life you're living and what you can make of it. Let the past alone and enjoy what you have.'

Jenny fixed him with a penetrating stare. 'You're very philosophical for a station manager,' she remarked dryly.

'Learned that from me mum,' he admitted with a grin. 'She was always going on about life and death. Reckon some of it must have stuck.'

He fell silent, the cigarette burning low between his fingers. 'Mum and Dad were good people. I still miss them. Reckon me and my brothers were lucky to have them.'

For a fleeting second he remembered his mother's face. Then it was gone. There were only childhood memories left of the woman who'd struggled to make sure her children had the things she'd never known as a child. A loving home, clean clothes and an education.

Jenny's voice broke into his thoughts. 'I envy you. Dajarra fed me and gave me an education but the Sisters of Mercy didn't have it in them to spare time for affection.' She sighed. 'That sort of start makes you wary and perhaps too self-sufficient – so you trust no one. Reckon that's what makes me cautious about this place.' She looked up at him and smiled. 'And you,' she added mischievously.

Brett's opinion of Jenny was changing fast. This was no spoilt Sydney brat but a scared little girl who hid her loneliness and pain behind a wall of false assurance. She reminded him of a colt he'd once had. It'd been beaten by its owner until it trusted no one. It had taken many months of patience and gentle handling before it was healed.

'I didn't realise it was that bad,' he murmured. It was all he could think of to say.

Jenny swept aside his sympathy. 'Tell me about when you were a kid, Brett.'

He stubbed out his cigarette and scooped up the puppy, which promptly fell asleep in his lap. Jenny grinned back at him. A grin that told him they were friends.

'We lived in Mossman up in Queensland. My dad was a cane cutter so we never saw much of him. There was always one more season to see through until he had enough money to buy a place. It did for him in the end. The cane's a bastard. Full of vermin and biting insects which infect the cuts and sores you get from the fields.'

Jenny had his full attention, but he lit another cigarette and shifted the pup to a more comfortable spot on his lap. He didn't want to depress her with tales of the grinding poverty of his childhood, but neither did he want to sweep it aside as if it meant nothing. Mum had struggled too long and hard in that rented shack for him to do that. The cane had killed her eventually but in a different way from his father.

'There were four of us kids. John the eldest stayed in the cane fields with my other brother, Davey. I reckon they couldn't get enough of the smell of molasses.' He grunted. 'I hated that smell. It was sweet and overpowering. Always in the house, your clothes, your hair.'

'What was it like? I lived in Dajarra until I was seven and although it was in the heart of cane country we were surrounded by grazing land and mountains. The sheep station in Queensland where I was fostered wasn't far enough north to grow cane.'

'It's another world. Hot, humid, fly-infested and snake-bit. The heat saps your energy, the sweat's constant, the cane demanding.' He paused, remembering how it could be. 'Beautiful, though. You should see a field of cane in the wind – like a great, green sea, shifting and floating. But there's few white Australians who'd work it. It takes a special breed of man to survive that life.'

He stroked the pup's ear and thought about how things were changing in the cane. Soon there would only be machines to do the work of hundreds, and men like his brothers would have to find something else to do for a living.

'After the war the immigrants took over and it was difficult to find anyone who spoke the same language. The orientals, the Italians and the Greeks are the best cutters, but times are changing and once the machines take over there will only be the legends of the cane fields left.'

Jenny pushed another beer across the table. 'Go on,' she said quietly.

He took a long drink before he spoke again. It was almost as if he needed to rid himself of the taste of molasses and the memory of the thick, choking smoke when they burned the fields prior to cutting.

'We moved from one rented shack to another. Always a few miles away from the fields so Dad could visit. But we never saw much of him even then. He was always off with the other cutters. They had a strange kind of fellowship, those blokes. Women didn't figure much in their lives and I wonder now why Dad ever got married. He must have seen us as a burden, and his promise of a proper home was something I think even he knew was a day-dream.'

'So you had it tough, too?' she said with quiet understanding.

He stubbed out his cigarette and began to stroke the sleeping puppy. He must have said more tonight than he usually did in a whole month. But she was easy to talk to and he didn't regret it.

'What you never had, you never miss,' he said lightly. 'We were happy enough, and Mum did her best to make us feel special.'

Brett fell silent, thinking about the bad times. There had been days when Mum was too tired to take in the washing, and he and his brothers would sweat over the old copper so the money wouldn't stop coming in. To this day he didn't know how his frail, slender mother had managed to lift out those heavy, boiling hot blankets and sheets in that steam furnace of Queensland's cane country. But she did. Day after day after day.

Jenny remained silent, as if she understood his need to keep some of his thoughts private.

Brett had slipped back into the past. He remembered the times when Dad had been too crook to cut cane. Jaundice attacks were frequent, each one making him weaker, until he no longer had the strength to return to the fields. The end was slow in coming, and Brett thought of his father, broken and yellow, waiting to die in that dingy shack. To this day he would never understand what drove a man to kill himself for the cane.

'Dad was a big bloke,' he said finally. 'He could pick us all up in those great arms of his, and carry us around the room at a run. But after the cane got to him, he died weighing not much more than six stone.'

'I never realised cane could do that to a man,' Jenny said quietly. 'We take sugar so lightly, without a thought for where it's come from or the price some man has paid to get it cut. I'm sorry your dad had to die like that.'

Brett shrugged. 'He chose to live that way, Jenny. And someone's got to do it. I decided early on it wasn't for me, though. John and Davey stayed on after Mum died, but Gil and I moved south to jackaroo on the sheep and cattle stations. Gil stayed in Queensland and eventually bought a property, but I moved further south. I've worked with sheep since I was sixteen and never regretted it.'

He saw her stifle a yawn and picked up the pup. 'Reckon this little bloke needs his kip. About time I was off as well. I

174

expect you're sick of me running off at the mouth.'

'No,' she said quickly, her expression serious. 'Thanks for telling me about your life, Brett. I hope it didn't bring back too many bad memories. They can be painful – I know.'

He smiled and shook his head. 'Why don't you come riding with me tomorrow morning, and I'll show you the rest of Churinga? Perhaps, if you see it the way I do, you'll understand why it's special.'

She cocked her head, eyes bright with mischief. 'Are you sure you can be spared?'

He laughed. 'I won't be missed. It's Sunday.'

'In that case, Brett, I'd love to.' She took the puppy from him and nuzzled the sleepy head with her lips.

'See you in the morning then? We'll leave early so it's still cool.'

She nodded, her smile lighting up her face.

Brett pushed through the screen door. He was very tired, but he doubted he'd sleep at all tonight.

Jenny stood in the doorway, the pup in her arms as she watched him cross the yard. He walked with a long, easy stride, his hands deep in his moleskins' pockets. She smiled and kissed the top of Ripper's head. Brett was good company once he'd lost that arrogant, bossy veneer, and his gift of the puppy had been just what she needed after those tears for Matilda.

The pup whimpered in its sleep, paws paddling as though he was running. He lay warm and heavy in her arms as she carried him back into the kitchen and made up a bed and dirt box for him. With a blanket stuffed into a vegetable crate, she settled him down for the night.

As she undressed for bed, she knew she couldn't just put the diaries to one side and forget about them. They were meant to be read – it was why Matilda had left them.

Yet Brett was right. She must look to the future and place less importance on the things which had happened here so long ago. It was up to her to find the same music he and Matilda had found here. Then perhaps she too could call it home.

# Chapter Ten

It was Sunday, and Ma's clanging of the tucker bell was an hour later than usual. Jenny lay for a moment, luxuriating in the cool comfort of early morning. Then, as she remembered her plans for the day, she climbed out of bed. She soon discovered she ached all over from the previous day's ride, and her extra little toe was almost rubbed raw from the pressure of the new boots she'd worn.

Ripper's eyes peeked between the folds of the sheets, one ear flattened to his head, and Jenny laughed as she untangled him. 'Bad dog,' she murmured. 'I made you a bed in the kitchen.'

He was unrepentant and licked her face as she carried him out to the back porch, then scampered off into the grass and cocked his leg.

Jenny limped back into the kitchen to find some ointment and a plaster for her toe. She glanced at the clock and groaned. It was still only five-thirty. Would she ever get used to these early starts and siestas in the afternoon?

With her toe firmly bandaged, she set about making breakfast. With a cup of tea, boiled egg and toast in front of her, Jenny realised something was missing. The clatter and slap of a newspaper being thrown from a passing bike on to the verandah was a Sunday morning sound so familiar, she'd hardly noticed it in Sydney and yet, this morning its very absence was acute.

She thought of lazy days on the balcony, overlooking the sea, of the arts and review pages, the supplements with their gossip and glossy pictures, the financial and sports sections

Peter always grabbed first when he was at home. Ben's favourite had been the cartoons. He would sit on her lap while she read them to him.

She sliced the top off the egg with one decisive swipe of the knife. 'I'm just going to have to get used to being alone again,' she muttered. 'No point in whingeing.'

Ripper's stubbly tail brushed the floor, his head cocked as if he understood.

They sat in the sun-drenched kitchen, the puppy taking small pieces of toast from her fingers with all the delicacy of a prissy spinster. Then, with breakfast over, she showered and dressed. Loose cotton strides, cotton shirt, old boots and the battered hat would keep her comfortable. She was putting away her jewellery and hunting for her riding gloves when a knock rattled the screen door.

'Wait on, Brett. Just coming,' she called. The gloves had somehow fallen beneath the bed and she was on her hands and knees trying to reach them. Ripper wasn't helping. He thought it was a game.

'Andrew Squires, Mrs Sanders. I hope it's not too early to call?'

Jenny froze. 'Andrew Squires? This should be interesting.

She finally managed to get the gloves away from Ripper, and despite her curiosity to meet the man who'd courted Matilda, took time to calm herself. Squires could wait. What ungodly hour was this to come visiting anyway? she thought acidly.

She checked her appearance in the mirror. The sun had tanned her skin and brought colour to her face, and as she scooped up her hair and twisted it into a knot, she decided to add a touch of lipstick to her mouth, and a dab of perfume to her neck. Knowing she looked good gave her confidence.

His back was to her as he leaned on the verandah railings and watched the early-morning bustle in the yard. A brand new Holden was parked by the hitching post, covered in a veil of red dust that somehow couldn't dim the sparkle of chrome bumpers.

Ripper growled deep in his throat, stubby legs planted stiffly on the verandah floor.

'Mr Squires?'

177

He turned to face her, and she was startled by his incongruous appearance. He was tall, square-built and still handsome although he had to be at least sixty-five, but despite having arrived by car, he was dressed in jodhpurs, tweed jacket and gleaming English riding boots, his crisp white shirt open at the neck to display a fancy cravat. His moustache and hair were still fiery red, and his eyes very blue as they returned her frank stare.

'Good day, Mrs Sanders.' His accent was more English than Australian. He reminded her of John Wainwright. 'I do hope this isn't inconvenient but I wanted to catch you before the day got too hot.' He sketched a bow. 'Welcome to Churinga. Andrew Squires, at your service.'

Jenny shook hands, noting the petulant twist to his lips and how the sun glinted on his copper hair. His handshake was limp and rather unpleasant. 'G'day,' she replied, quickly retrieving her hand. 'Won't you come in and have a drink?'

'After you, dear lady.' He opened the screen door and followed her inside.

Jenny quickly shut the snarling Ripper in the bedroom before making tea and finding a decent pair of cups and saucers. With a few biscuits to accompany the tea, she sat down at the kitchen table. At this hour of the day he wasn't going to be offered anything stronger, and she certainly wasn't going to cook him breakfast. Besides, she thought as she caught him arrogantly surveying the room, I never did trust red-headed men.

He took a cup of tea, eyed her with open curiosity and crossed one elegantly clad leg over the other. It was a strangely feminine gesture – one that did nothing to change her opinion of him.

'I understand you live at Kurrajong,' she said to fill in the silence. 'I suppose that's Aboriginal, like Churinga?' He was making her feel uncomfortable. There was calculation in his eyes, and an air of weakness about the mouth and chin she recognised as greed.

'Of course,' he replied. 'Kurrajong means evergreen, Mrs Sanders. And has been Churinga's neighbour for almost a century.' His smile was condescending.

Jenny sipped her tea, wishing Brett would hurry up. This

man wasn't here for small talk – he was after something. 'I know something of Churinga's history, Mr Squires. But most of it seems to be conjecture. Do you remember Matilda Thomas at all?' Her expression was deliberately artless.

Andrew Squires began a close inspection of his manicured nails. 'I was educated abroad, Mrs Sanders, and only returned once I'd been accepted at the Bar. My practice is in Melbourne. Kurrajong is merely a retreat from the hurly-burly of the city for me.' His eyes were very blue as they looked back at her. 'I never had the pleasure of meeting the Thomas woman. But I understand my father knew her well.'

Liar, she thought as she returned his gaze. 'Then perhaps I should return your visit, Mr Squires. It would be interesting to talk to your father about those early years.'

He looked down his long nose, his expression cold, his voice drawling, 'I doubt if he could tell you much. They didn't mix socially.'

He's a self-important clothes horse as well as a liar, Jenny decided. And he was sitting in her kitchen drinking her tea as if he owned the place. It was time he went.

'You really should have called first, Mr Squires,' she said coolly. 'I have plans for today, and I'm running late as it is.'

Andrew seemed smugly amused by her heavy-handed attempt to make him leave. He selected a gold-tipped cigarette from a silver case and fitted it into a short ivory holder. He lit it with a silver lighter, and blew smoke to the ceiling before answering her.

'You don't make a chap feel terribly welcome, dear lady. Especially when he's taken such a long drive to visit you.'

'Was there a particular purpose for this call?' She glanced towards the door. Where the hell was Brett?

'My, my,' he drawled. 'Such a businesslike approach. How refreshing. I think you and I will get along famously, Mrs Sanders.'

'That depends on what business you have to discuss,' she said coldly.

He eyed her through the cigarette smoke. 'You seem a sensible woman, and God knows they're rare enough. With your artistic talents and growing reputation, you must obviously feel more at home in the city than in this godforsaken place.'

'Get to the point, Mr Squires. I don't have all day.'

He smirked as he tapped ash into a saucer and Jenny wondered what it would be like to come up against him in court. He was a cold bastard, the sort you chose to be on your side not with the opposition.

'I understand Wainwright has already told you of our interest in Churinga, Mrs Sanders. I'm here this morning to make you an offer.'

Jenny was about to speak when he raised his hand to silence her. 'At least have the courtesy to let me finish, Mrs Sanders.'

'Only if you have the courtesy to remember this is my home and you have no right to come in here throwing your weight about,' she retorted. 'This isn't a court of law – I'm not in the witness box.'

'Touché.' His smile was cold as his gaze swept over her. 'I like a woman who speaks her mind, Mrs Sanders. One gets so tired of sycophants, don't you agree?'

Jenny eyed him disdainfully. 'I wouldn't know.'

He seemed unfazed by her rudeness. 'As I was saying, I'm willing to offer you more than a fair price for the property. If you agree to sell, then I'm sure we can come to an arrangement that will suit both parties.'

Jenny leaned back in her chair, keeping a tight rein on her rising anger. The Squires just wouldn't give up, and because of what Brett had told her last night she knew they never would. Now Ethan had sent this snake to do his dirty work – just as he had all those years ago with Matilda.

She forced a smile but her pulse raced and she itched to slap that reptilian smile off his face. She would play him at his own game. 'What figure did you have in mind?'

Animated at the thought of achieving his goal, Squires sat forward. 'Three-quarters of a million dollars. Plus stock at value.'

Jenny was astounded, but made sure it didn't show on her face. She'd seen the balance sheets and valuations, and knew the price he offered was way above what it was worth. This game was too dangerous to take any further. She could demand a million – and knowing how much he wanted Churinga he just might agree.

'It's certainly a good price, Mr Squires,' she said more calmly than she felt. 'But what makes you think I'm in the market to sell?'

He lit another cigarette, his movements liquid, all sign of nonchalance dissipated in his confidence she could be bought. 'I've done my homework, Mrs Sanders. You're a widow. An artist with a fast-growing reputation and a partnership in a city gallery. You've had to scrimp and scrape most of your life. Now you have the opportunity to be rich beyond your wildest dreams. What possible use is a sheep station in the middle of nowhere to a woman alone when you could be set up for life back in the city?'

The bastard had done his homework, and it took all her will-power not to let him see how that affected her. 'All true. But my late husband bought this place for me. It wouldn't seem right to sell.'

He sat forward eagerly. 'That's just where you're wrong, Mrs Sanders. He bought Churinga for you both, planning to move here with your son and start a new life. He didn't mean for you to struggle on your own, to live out here with no family or friends to keep you company.'

Jenny watched his face, and vowed that if she ever did sell Churinga, it would never be to this particular snake.

Andrew was warming to his subject. 'Just think, Mrs Sanders. You need never worry about money again. You'd be free to travel to Paris, Florence, Rome, London. You could visit the Louvre and the Tate, paint for pleasure not just a living.'

'I've already travelled extensively and I didn't care for London,' she said flatly. 'Churinga is not for sale.'

Surprise flashed momentarily in his eyes and was swiftly veiled. 'I realise this comes rather soon after your bereavement, Mrs Sanders. Perhaps you need more time to collect your thoughts before you rush into any hasty decisions.'

He's a cold fish, Jenny thought. That smile's still in place even though my refusal obviously came as a shock. 'I don't need time to consider your offer. Churinga is not, and will not be, for sale in the foreseeable future.' She stood up. 'I have a lot to do today. So if you don't mind . . .'

Squires reached into an inside pocket of his neat tweed

jacket. His face was tinged with colour, anger emanating in waves from beneath rigid politeness.

'My card. If you should change your mind, Mrs Sanders, please call me. The price is of course negotiable, but only for so long.'

Jenny took the heavily embossed card, looked from the gold lettering to the blazing blue of his eyes. 'Thank you. But you already have my answer.'

She walked to the door, the thud of his boots on the wooden floor like hammer blows as he followed her. They reached the verandah and she stepped outside with relief. The house had become claustrophobic.

Andrew Squires adjusted his soft, narrow-brimmed hat and pulled on his gloves. Jenny almost gasped at his audacity when he caught her hand, and after a courtly bow, kissed her fingers. 'Until we meet again, Mrs Sanders.'

She stood transfixed as he went down the steps to his car, gunned the engine and roared off towards Kurrajong in a cloud of dust. The feel of his lips remained with her, and she wiped the back of her hand down her trousers.

'What did he want?'

She turned to see Brett at the far end of the verandah. He was clutching the reins of two horses saddled and ready to ride, his eyes flint sharp in the morning sun.

She told him.

Brett dropped the reins and strode across the verandah. He grabbed her by the arms, pulling her close, forcing her to look up into his face. 'He's poison, Jenny. Just like his father. Have nothing to do with any of them, or everything Matilda built up here will be destroyed.'

'You're hurting me, Brett,' she protested.

He let her go and ran his fingers through his hair. 'Sorry, Jen. But I meant what I said.'

'I've met his kind before. Cold, calculating and greedy, used to buying their way through life – but I'm no fool, Brett. I can handle his sort.'

'How did you leave it with him?' His face was still grim.

'I told him I wouldn't take his three-quarters of a million bucks.'

'How much?'

Jenny laughed. 'You should see your face! Thought that would shock you.'

'Bloody hell. Even I would've been tempted by that much money,' he said in wonder. 'I had no idea Churinga was worth so much.'

'It isn't, believe me,' she said dryly. 'But he was willing to pay over the odds. I can't pretend I wasn't tempted, but it didn't seem right to sell to a Squires after all these years. Besides, he knew too much about me and my business. I reckon he's had someone spy on me.'

'I wouldn't put it past him.' Brett muttered.

Jenny took a deep appreciative breath of the cool, early air. 'Never mind about him. Sun's up, the horses are ready, and so am I. Let's go for that ride.'

'Andrew and his family can't just be swept aside like that, Jen. They're wealthy, powerful people – and not to be trusted.'

Jenny looked up into Brett's face and saw he was haunted by the thought of things changing and having to move on. 'I know,' she said solemnly. 'But I'm not poor like Matilda – I've got the means to fight them – and it's me who owns Churinga, not them.' She put a conciliatory hand on his arm. 'I'll never sell to them.'

She plastered on a smile. 'Forget the Squires family and show me your Churinga,' she said brightly. The conversation with Andrew had left a sour taste but she wasn't going to let it spoil her day with Brett.

They caught the reins and slowly walked across the hard-packed earth of the central clearing. They didn't speak and Jenny hoped Brett's mood wouldn't last for too long. She wanted Andrew and the Squires family out of her mind so she could see Churinga as Brett did.

She needn't have worried. He was soon pointing out the various buildings, taking her to see the stock pens and explaining the seasonal rituals.

'We move the sheep according to the weather, the water, the grass and the grade of sheep. To ensure good breeding and the finest wool, all the sheep on Churinga are Merinos.'

Jenny stood by the stock pens, looking over the woolly, shifting backs. 'Why pack them in so tightly? Surely there's no need?'

He grinned. 'Because they're the silliest buggers on earth. They take it into their heads to shoot through, and when one goes they all follow. If it wasn't for the dogs, we'd never get the damn things shorn.' He eyed her solemnly for a moment. 'They're only penned like this for a short time. The shearers work fast. They have to. Most of them are on a tight schedule to get to the next shed, and there's always a bonus for quick, efficient work.'

'It seems cruel to shear them just as winter's coming. Surely they need all that wool to keep them warm and dry?'

Brett shook his head, a knowing smile twitching at the corners of his mouth. 'Common fallacy of the city dweller,' he murmured. 'Wool is king out here. Sheep are a commodity. To ensure a thicker, better fleece, they have to be shorn now.'

Jenny eyed the penned animals, realising that bleeding heart sympathy was of no use out here where only the strong and useful survived. 'So, what does a year on this place entail? I suppose winter's about the only time you can relax.'

Brett lit a cigarette and meandered along the labyrinth of pens. 'Sheep have to be looked after all year round – there's never much time for anything else. We move them from pasture to pasture, grade them, separate them, breed them. After shearing, they're dipped and marked, then drenched to get rid of internal parasites. If the rains don't come and the grass is poor, then we scrub cut and try to feed the blasted things by hand.'

He tipped back his hat and smeared sweat from his forehead. 'Sheep are the most witless things on earth. They won't eat anything that isn't from their own pastures and refuse point blank to take the scrub we give them unless the Judas eats first.'

Jenny smiled. 'Sounds familiar. I remember John Carey going on about the Judas sheep. The leader of the pack. Devil and saviour – blasted nuisance.'

'Yeah. But if you don't get it through the open gate first, the rest of the idiots will stand about and get burned to a cinder in a bush fire because they haven't got the sense to see escape is only inches away.'

She looked up at him. 'But you love your work, don't you?'

184

He nodded. 'Most of the time. Not so much fun at lambing though. Each one has to be caught, its tail ringed, ear tagged, and if not wanted for breeding, castrated. Crutching's not my favourite job, and neither is shooting lambs who've had their eyes eaten by crows and are still running around the fields.'

Jenny shivered despite the heat of the rising sun.

'I never promised it would be pretty, Jenny. It's life, that's all. We breed the finest Merino sheep. Everything here is geared to perfect wool. None of the sheep are sold for meat. When they're past wool-producing years, they're shipped off for skins, tallow, lanolin and glue. Everything is used – there's no waste.'

Jenny eyed the pens and fields beyond. She was still finding it hard to believe she owned all this. 'How many sheep are there?'

'We have about two sheep for every acre of pasture. That's about three hundred thousand head in all, but the numbers fall rapidly in the droughts or if there's a fire or flood.'

They moved away from the sheep pens, past the carpenter's shed where the pungent aroma of fresh wood shavings brought back memories of Waluna. There had been a small timber yard nearby and she'd loved the smell of it as a child, often slipping beneath the wire to gather the shavings which she kept in a box by her bed.

The hen house was a rough lean-to, fenced in by wire, the cockerels strutting amongst the hens with pompous majesty. The dairy was spotlessly clean, the milking machines glistening against the white tiles.

'We only keep a few head of cattle. They're not as profitable now as sheep, but they provide us with milk, butter and cheese, and the occasional steak to vary the diet of mutton.'

Brett moved on to the stockyard which sprawled over several acres behind the jackaroos' bungalow and leaned on the fence. 'Most of these are hard-mouthed, bad-tempered bastards, but can turn on a pin and will give you a good day's work. We rotate them so they don't get blown. No stockman will ride the same horse two days running unless he's out in the pastures and can't get back.'

'Do you breed them here?'

He shook his head. 'They're all geldings or mares. Stallions are a pain in the neck, so we don't keep them. If we need new stock, we buy in.'

Jenny stroked the twitching neck of the bay mare. The flies were swarming around her eyes, and her tail never seemed to stop flicking at them. 'She seems quiet enough.'

'She's one of the few, but she's still a good stock horse.' He took the reins and climbed into the saddle. 'Come on. I'll take you to the dog pens, then we'll head out.'

The pens were fenced, the kennels merely rough, low shelters filled with straw. The blue-grey dogs snapped and snarled, leaping at the wire, teeth barred.

'We keep the bitches separate so we can breed them properly,' he said pointing to the far pen where puppies suckled their mothers. 'We have some Kelpies, like Ripper, but there's nothing like a good Queensland Blue for herding sheep. Reckon it's all that a dog should be – intelligent, aggressive, alert. Not like the pampered lap dogs in the cities.' His sideways glance was mocking.

'Everything out here seems to be half wild,' she said quietly as two cats came storming out of a nearby barn and rolled in a frenzy of fur, claw and tooth.

Brett drew his heavy stock whip from the saddle and flicked it with deadly accuracy at the snarling, hissing flurry, the crack thunderous, centimetres above their ears. They ran off as if scalded, and he and Jenny laughed.

Jenny climbed into the saddle, turned the mare's head and followed him out into the paddock. 'How many men are left here after the shearing?'

'Usually ten, sometimes twelve. Stockmen are notoriously hard to keep for more than a couple of seasons. They're always moving on to what they think are bigger and better stations, real swaggies if the truth be told. But we still have to look after the animals all year round.'

Jenny screwed up her eyes as she looked out over the dry, silver grass that shone glaringly bright in the morning sun. Blasted trees stood as lone sentinels in the sweeping acres. The bark peeled in stiff ribbons down the trunks, and tiny whirlwind spirals of dust moved dead leaves and grass from one listless heap to another. One careless match, a tin can in the grass or a piece of glass, and Churinga would perish.

As they rode through the stand of box, coolibah and stringybark, a swarm of budgies darted and weaved above them, joined by a pink cloud of galahs which finally settled in the two pepper trees on the far edge of the timberland. Bell birds called their fluting song, and a kookaburra chortled a warning before descending with a flap of brown speckled wings on to a low branch in front of them. Vast spider webs laced the leaves of the trees, crystal drops of dew sparkling in the sun, their hairy, long-legged inhabitants making Jenny shudder. She was used to the redback spider in Sydney, but these were monsters, and probably twice as deadly.

She began to relax as they left Churinga homestead behind. Despite the heat, the flies and spiders and snakes, it was majestic. But could she live here?

She was used to the city now, enjoyed the sea and the feel of salt spray on her face. She thought longingly of soaking in a tub of gin-clear water instead of the sludge green showers she'd endured recently. Thought of Diane and her other friends who understood her need to paint. Who shared her interest in the theatre and art galleries, and brought colour and life into her world. Once Simone moved on to the next shed, she would be the only woman on Churinga. Alone amongst men who said little, who lived for the land and the animals they cared for – and probably resented her being there.

'How you doing, Jenny? The heat and dust got to you yet?'

She grimaced. 'I seem to be permanently covered in dust. It's everywhere, and I've given up trying to clean the house. But the flies don't bother me, and I'm used to the heat.'

They rode in silence as the crows cawed and the cockatoos shrieked. And yet Churinga was growing on her, she realised. There was something here which seemed so familiar – so much a part of her that although this was her first visit, it felt like coming home.

'We're on Wilga land now,' said Brett an hour later. 'See the trees?'

Jenny shielded her eyes against the glare. Thick lime green fronds dipped in perfect symmetry towards the ground, offering sheltered arbours from the sun. 'Does the wind make them that shape? They look as if someone's come out here and done a bit of barbering.'

Brett laughed, and she noticed the attractive way it crinkled up the corners of his eyes. 'You're part right. The sheep do the cropping until they can't reach any higher. That's why all Wilga trees are round.'

The horses plodded through the tinder dry grass. 'Won't the owners mind us trespassing? Should we call in first?'

Brett pulled on the reins and his cranky gelding snorted and stamped as he looked across at her. 'I thought you knew. Didn't Wainwright explain?'

'Explain what?'

'This all belongs to you. It's part of Churinga.'

Jenny absorbed this information with astonishment. 'But I thought you said we didn't breed cattle? And what happened to the Finlays?'

Brett eyed the prime beef herd that grazed all around them. 'We don't at Churinga, but Wilga's run separately, with a manager to look after it. The Finlays left after the war.'

The mare dipped her head to crop the grass, her harness jingling pleasantly in the still, warm air. 'Why the different names? Why not all under the Churinga banner?'

'Used to be a separate station. The trees gave it its name, of course, and I suppose no one thought to change it when it became part of Churinga.'

'Everything out here sounds musical.' Jenny sighed. The smell of the baked earth was strong, the sound of the birds and crickets harmonious with their surroundings.

'The Abos have a musical language. You should hear them jabbering on when they get together for a corroboree. Most of the places out here are called by their Abo names, except for a few which reminded the original squatters of homes back in Europe.'

'That's true all over Australia,' Jenny said with a smile. 'Tassie's littered with them.'

They rode side by side through the pastures. 'Have you travelled a lot, Jenny?' he said finally.

'A fair bit. When I left the foster home at Waluna, I went to art college. Then after I'd finished, I travelled with Diane through Europe and Africa for a year to study the history of art.' She thought fondly of Diane's flowing caftans and outlandish jewellery. 'Diane fell in love with all things exotic after we went to Marrakesh but I loved Paris best. Montmatre, the Left Bank, the Seine, the Louvre.'

He must have heard the wistfulness in her voice. 'Do you wish you could go back?'

'Sometimes. Maybe I will some day, but it wouldn't be the same. Things never are. The people we knew back then would have moved on, things would have changed. Besides I'm older now, perhaps less careless of the dangers.'

'Nothing in Paris could be as dangerous as the Tiger snakes you get out here surely,' he said thoughtfully.

Jenny thought of the rat-infested lodgings she and Diane shared, and the lecherous, Frenchmen who thought all young girls were there to be seduced. 'There are snakes everywhere,' she said bluntly. 'Not all of them crawl on their bellies.'

'Cynic,' he teased.

She laughed. 'That's what travelling does for you. Perhaps I'll take my chances here. There are worse places to live, but at least you know what to watch out for.'

'I'll remember that.' He gathered up the reins. 'Come on. I'm going to show you my favourite place. It's similar to where we went the other day, but on the other side of the mountain. It's not far now, and I don't think you'll be disappointed.'

They galloped over the endless plains, through the timber, past the sentinels of blasted trees, and on towards the shimmering blue of the distant mountains. Spidery fingers of acid green traced a web through the grass – evidence of the bore head water that must drain into the pastures somewhere up ahead.

Her joints ached, and her limbs trembled, and as much as she was enjoying the ride, Jenny looked forward to getting off for a rest.

'Almost there,' Brett shouted about half an hour later.

Jenny saw that the leaves were fat and green on the trees and the grass verdant, startling against the surrounding mirror-bright silver. The thought of water made her urge the mare on until they reached the shade of the outlying trees. Sliding down from the saddle, she took off her hat and wiped away the sweat. Flies buzzed around her, settling, darting, drinking the moisture on her face and arms.

Brett took the reins of both horses and led the way through the thick scrub. The heat beneath the canopy of trees reminded her of Queensland, damp, humid, buzzing with insect life. Sweat drenched her clothes and ran down her face as she followed closely behind him. Would this walk never come to an end? she wondered.

Then suddenly they were in a clearing of pure, golden light, where the sound of a waterfall cooled the heat of the day. Brett stood aside and she gasped. It was an oasis, hidden in the folds of the mountain. Trees, verdant and lush, bent their fronds to the wide pool which lay still and clear at their feet. Tumbled, jumbled rocks sprouted flowers and vines which trailed, picture book bright, down crevices and along fissures. Birds, disturbed by their presence, flew in an agitated cloud above their heads. Bright scarlet and blue rosellas swooped with green and yellow parakeets. Tiny finches, sparrows and starlings fluttered and called as they flew from perch to perch. It was as if the world consisted only of birds. They swooped and dived in their hundreds before settling, bright-eyed and inquisitive, to watch the intruders.

Jenny laughed with the sheer joy of it, and the sound caused a flutter of wings as a flock of cockatoos flew out of the trees above them.

'I told you it was special,' he said, smiling with pleasure.

'I never thought such a place could exist out here. Not in this wilderness.'

'You don't have to whisper,' he said with a smile. 'The birds will soon get used to us.' He caught her arm. 'Look. There in the mud bank.'

Jenny followed his pointing finger. Crayfish claws were visible in the slimy grey mud, dozens of them. 'Yabbies,' she exclaimed. 'We'll have to take some back for supper.'

'Later,' he said firmly. 'What we could both do with now is a swim.'

Her spirits fell. The water looked so inviting in that clear pool, but to swim fully clothed would take away the pleasure. 'You should have warned me. I didn't bring anything to wear,' she protested.

Brett grinned, and like a conjurer, pulled something from

his saddle bag and threw it across. It was lurid orange with purple flowers dotted all over the nylon ruching. 'It's Ma's. I expect it's a bit big, but it's the best I could do.'

Jenny looked at it. It was enormous and hopelessly old-fashioned, but if she tied the straps together at the back, and used her trouser belt to cinch in the waist, it would do. But to be on the safe side, she'd keep her underwear on.

When she'd finally tied and belted and tucked the vast costume around herself, she hesitated before stepping out from the bushes. She was barefoot and although her little toe was covered with a plaster it was still obvious – she always dreaded it when people commented on it and asked questions. It was something the nuns had believed to be the sign of the Devil, and although she knew better now, she was still ashamed of it.

The heat and the sound of the water was too enticing. Jenny took off her locket and peeked from behind the bushes. Brett was already in the water. He was wearing black trunks that showed off his muscular legs, flat stomach and broad chest to perfection. As he floated on his back, the sunlight glinted on his dark hair, turning it almost blue.

Jenny hutched the straps over her shoulders. Ma was blessed with a comfortable bosom, and no amount of tying and hitching could disguise the fact that Jenny had rather less to cover. She dived into the water and surfaced quickly. It was freezing, taking her breath away. But as she broke through the clear green depths into the sunlight, she realised Simone's costume had filled with water, and was ballooning around her like an inflatable life-jacket.

What the hell? she thought as she floated luxuriously. I'm decent enough, and this water's wonderful after those showers.

She watched as Brett struck out with clean, sure strokes to the other side of the pool where a small waterfall plunged through creepers and down the rocks. He swam beneath it then stood in the shallows, the water tumbling over his head. He gave a whoop of delight, sending the birds into startled flight.

Jenny laughed with him, and as she felt the costume sink further and further, decided she'd rather swim in her underwear than drown. Unfastening the belt, she pulled it off. It landed with a soggy plop on to an overhanging rock, and she kicked out and swam free. Diving into the cool depths after having swum back and forth for several minutes, she resurfaced on the far side where the rocks lay in great slabs beside the trees, and hauled herself out.

She lay there, gasping with the cold and the effort, basking in the warm caress of the dappled sun and the stones. The sound of Brett's splashing and the birds' chattering began to fade as weariness from the long ride took over. Her eyelids grew heavy and with feline pleasure she fell asleep.

'Jenny . . . Jenny.'

His voice came from far away. It was almost a lullaby in tune with the orchestra of birds and water.

'Jenny, wake up. It's time to eat.'

She reluctantly opened her eyes and found herself mirrored in clear grey that was flecked with blue and gold. Like precious opals, they gleamed with fire. She sat up, confused by the things she read there, and shook out her wet hair to cover her embarrassment. 'Have I been asleep long?' she asked quickly.

'Drifted off a bit there. You looked so peaceful – seemed a shame to wake you.' His voice was different, as if he was having difficulty breathing, but before she could analyse it he became brisk. 'Come on. Ma's packed us another picnic and there'll be hell to pay if we don't eat this one.'

He held out his hand, and as she grasped it, pulled her to her feet. They were closer now, the warmth of their bodies mingling in the dappled sunlight. She noticed how his eyes had darkened, felt the tremor of his fingers, heard the catch of breath.

'Mind your step,' he said gruffly as he released her hand and turned away. 'It's slippery.'

Jenny dragged herself back from the spell he'd woven and followed him through the undergrowth. Common sense told her she'd misread his signals. He was merely being polite to his boss, showing off his Churinga, pleased with her reaction to it. But a small, insistent voice niggled deep in her subconscious. She'd thought he was going to kiss her – and she'd been disappointed when he hadn't.

192

As she stumbled into the grassy clearing on the other side of the pool, she realised with horror that her wet underwear was transparent. Grabbing her shirt, she dived into the bushes and covered herself quickly. Hot with embarrassment, she chided herself for being a fool. No wonder there'd been a change in him, seeing her like that, as good as naked, stretched out on that bloody rock. It wasn't surprising he hadn't bothered to wake her. Must have got a real eyeful.

She fastened the buttons, tucked the shirt into her trousers and pulled on socks to hide her toe. As reason returned, she acknowledged that at least he'd been a gentleman about it. Most red-blooded males would have jumped her – but, with her being his boss, he'd obviously decided discretion was better.

But how to face him again? How to brazen it out and act as if nothing had happened? She took a deep breath and stepped out of the bushes. Nothing *had* happened, and if he didn't say anything then neither would she.

Brett had his back to her as he laid out the picnic on the rocks. There was chicken and ham, damper bread, cheese, tomatoes and a large bottle of homemade lemonade as well as beer and a flask of tea.

Jenny avoided eye contact and tucked in. She hadn't realised how hungry she was and the chicken was delicious. Brett was either unaware of her earlier discomfort or had decided nothing had happened to merit comment. He spoke only of Churinga.

She listened as he told her about wool and sheep auctions, and about the problems of transport and finding reliable men to work the place. The minutes slipped past with no mention of the swim and she began to relax and enjoy his company.

When the sun dipped behind the trees they fished out a dozen yabbies to take back for supper and made their way back to the homestead. Jenny was bone weary, and yet it was a satisfying feeling – one that came after a pleasant day and exercise. As they approached the home paddock, she looked forward to a good night's sleep.

With the horses unsaddled, rubbed down and fed and watered, she and Brett leaned on the fence as the world softly descended into night. A canopy of stars covered the earth, so bright and clear she felt she could reach out and touch the Southern Cross. Take it in her palm and hold it close. 'It's been a wonderful day, Brett. Thanks. I've seen some beautiful sights today.'

He looked down at her, mouth twitching, eyes glittering with humour. 'So have I,' he said, and he loped away towards the bunkhouse before she could think of a cutting reply.

# Chapter Eleven

As the shearing season was in full swing and the mobs had arrived from the smaller stations to be shorn, Brett had little time to spare so Jenny would take off with her sketchbook and spend hours capturing the essence of this red earth country. Their evening rides out into the pastures were cool and leisurely after the heat of the day, and as the weeks went by she came to look forward to them and was disappointed when Brett's work made them impossible.

The days were full of noise and bustle. More than four hundred thousand sheep needed to be sent up the ramps to be shorn before the shearers could move on to the next shed. She watched the animals skitter down the ramps where they were grasped by strong brown hands and dipped. Those same hands plunged syringes down their throats, drenching them of intestinal parasites before releasing them into the pens where Brett and the stockmen divided the wethers from the breeding rams, the lambs from their ewes.

Castration of the male lambs was swift and bloody, the slaughter of the sheep past their wool prime inevitable, their carcasses fit only for the tannery or the knacker's yard. Life at Churinga was harsh, there was no room for sentiment. Even the cats which slunk between barns and pens were lean and predatory, each one a practised, cunning killer. Never hand-fed or petted, they were expected to keep the property clear of vermin. As Brett had said, everything on Churinga had to earn its keep.

When Jenny rode out with the stockmen and listened to their stories she began to understand the enormity of what

Matilda had taken on. The size of the property meant the men took it in turn to patrol the pastures, their rifles and stock whips always to hand. They would sleep in the fields guarding the sheep, shooting rabbits that ate the grass and dingoes and rooks hunting the lambs. Wild pigs, black and hairy and as big as a cow, could create havoc in a tightly packed feeding mob and the men were extra vigilant if they knew one was around. One thrust of those long curved tusks and a man could be ripped in half.

Jenny soon got used to being in the saddle for hours on end and even began to learn how to use the impossibly long and heavy stock whip the men seemed able to flick so effortlessly over the sheep. She became immune to the dust lifted by thousands of Merino feet and the swarms of flies that drifted in black clouds, waiting to settle on shitty back-sides, as she followed the mob to winter pasture. Her skin glowed from the sun and her hands grew calloused. She fell into bed at night and didn't stir until the cookhouse clanger rang in another day.

Ripper, whose creamy paws, chest and eyebrows had been reddened by the dust, followed her everywhere with adoring eyes and lolling tongue. He seemed to know he wasn't expected to work like the other Kelpies but watched over them all the same, his canine grin revealing a certain superiority.

A month passed, then half another. The shearers were packing up and moving on. The bustle of the yard and wool-shed died to a murmur and Brett travelled with the trucks to ensure the wool transportation went smoothly.

Jenny felt peace descend, stillness creep over the quiet stock pens and empty home pastures. Simone and Stan would be leaving tomorrow. Life was about to change once again – returning, perhaps, to the isolation Matilda must have experienced.

She thought wistfully of the unread diaries, and of the green dress in the trunk. The enticing music of the past was growing louder as the days passed, and she knew she would soon have to return to that world. Return to the haunting but familiar threads of a life she was only just beginning to understand.

The kitchen was sweltering, the temperature way up to a hundred and ten, and as Jenny sweated over dinner she admired Simone's tenacity. To cook in this heat deserved a medal, but to do it every day for such vast numbers of men was worthy of sainthood.

Dinner was to be eaten at ten when the day was done and with it the fierce heat. Jenny was dressed in a cotton shift and low-heeled shoes when her guests arrived promptly at nine-thirty.

Simone was tethered into bright yellow cotton, her face for once made up, her hair in tight curls. Stan, who could never look anything but a shearer with his elongated arms and hunched back, was unusually smart in an ill-fitting suit and water-slicked hair. He shuffled his feet, looking sheepish and uncomfortable out of his usual singlet and flannels.

Jenny led them through the kitchen, where the aroma of roast beef and Yorkshire pudding wafted from the oven, and out on to the back porch. The French windows of the extension had been flung open, the chairs pulled outside into the cool evening. She'd spent most of the day polishing and dusting, sweeping the verandah and arranging great bowls of wild flowers on the small tables she'd set beside the chairs. The kitchen table was outside as well. It was hardly recognisable beneath white linen and fine china. Silver glittered in the moonlight, and a vase of wild lilies stood between the candlesticks she'd unearthed from the back of the kitchen cupboard.

Simone stood and looked at everything, eyes wide with pleasure. Jenny watched as she wonderingly touched the napkins and the silver cutlery. Perhaps she'd gone too far. These were poor working people, as rough and resilient as the land they worked, not go-getters from Sydney.

'Jenny.' It was a sigh of pleasure. 'Thank you for making dinner so special. You don't know how much I've wanted to sit down at a real nice table with flowers and silver and candles. I'll always remember this.'

'I was worried you'd think I was showing off,' she admitted. 'I got a bit carried away when I found all this locked in the cupboards. If it makes you uncomfortable, I can always put some of it back.'

Simone turned horrified eyes on her. 'Don't you flamin' dare. I'm just Ma to most people. They forget me when they've got full bellies. This is the nicest thing anybody's done for me in years.' She poked Stan in the ribs. 'And that goes for you too, mate.'

Jenny poured sherry.

Simone eased her bulk into an overstuffed chair and sipped her Amontillado with relish. 'This is something I'll remember for a long time,' she said wistfully. 'Living on the road does have its drawbacks.'

Stan sat on the edge of the couch, his long arms dangling between his knees as he looked around. 'You made it nice, Mrs Sanders.'

'Thanks. Here, I know you'd prefer a beer. And, please, take off that tie and jacket. It's far too hot to be formal.'

'Oh, no you don't, Stan Baker,' roared Simone. 'Just for once in yer rotten life youse gonna do things proper. Keep that flamin' jacket and tie where they are.'

Jenny saw determination on Simone's face, resignation on Stan's. She topped up Simone's drink. Perhaps she'd relent once she'd eaten.

The roast beef and Yorkshire pudding was a success, and Jenny served peach pavlova and thick cream for pudding. She'd made the meringue earlier that day, and had had to keep it in the gas fridge to stop it from wilting. It was devoured with relish, and followed by coffee and brandy.

Leaving the table, they returned to the softer chairs and looked out over the sleeping land. 'I'll miss you, Simone. You're the only woman I've talked to since Wallaby Flats,' Jenny told her wistfully.

'None of your city friends got in touch then?'

'Diane's written several times, but the phone line is so bad it's impossible to have a decent conversation.'

'Have you decided what you're going to do yet? You seem to be settled here, now you and Brett have got over squabbling.' Simone slipped off her shoes. Stan's jacket and tie had been surreptitiously removed and slung over the back of a chair.

'I haven't made up my mind yet. This place has a strange hold over me, and yet there's so much I still haven't done in the outside world. I don't know if I'm just using Churinga as an excuse to run away from reality.'

'Humph,' grunted Simone comfortably. 'Nothing unreal

about this place, luv. You see all of life out here.'

Jenny looked out over the moonlit pastures. 'The harsh side of life, maybe. But there's so much more of this country to explore. Such a big world to travel.' She thought of Diane's last letter. Of Rufus' offer to buy Jenny out of the gallery and rent her house if she wanted to stay at Churinga. But she couldn't let go that easily. The house, the gallery, her friends were all a part of her. And she wanted to paint. Needed to paint. Her sketchbook was full of drawings that cried out to be put on to canvas. Painting was an itch demanding to be scratched, and if she stayed away from it too long, she got edgy.

'It's lonely, I grant you. I been traipsing round New South Wales and Queensland all my adult life, and I seen a lot of changes. Women have to be tougher than the men, stronger-willed and immune to the bloody flies and the dust. We stay because of our men and our children. Because of the thing that's born in us – the love of the land. I reckon you'd be happier in the city.'

Jenny eyed her as sadness welled. Simone was right. There was nothing to keep her here but lost dreams. She had no husband and no child to care for any more, no consuming passion for the land to tie her to Churinga. Yet she didn't want the mood of the evening to spoil, so she changed the subject. 'Where you headed next, Simone?'

'Billa Billa. Bloody good shed, and the cookhouse is fitted out real nice. Then we're off up to Newcastle to see our daughter and the grandkids. Ain't seen 'em for a while, have we, Stan?'

A man of few words, he merely shook his head.

'We got three kids. Two girls and a boy,' Simone said proudly. 'Nine grandchildren in all, but we don't get to see them much. They're spread all over the bloody country, and if the sheds we work are too far away, we don't see 'em from one season to the next.'

She stared out into the soft darkness. 'That's when we mooch around looking for casual work. The money soon runs out if there's no work between shearing seasons, and Stan's too old to go back to the cane.'

'What are your plans for when shearing gets too much,

Stan?' Jenny couldn't imagine him in a unit by the sea.

'Reckon I got a few seasons in me yet,' he mumbled around his cigarette. 'I always promised Ma we'd have our own place when the time comes. Not too fancy, mind. Just a small place, with about a thousand acres so I can keep me hand in.'

Simone snorted. 'Promises, promises! There's always one more shed, one more season. Reckon they'll carry you out of a bloody shed in yer box.'

Jenny heard the disappointment behind those sharp words and wondered if the idea she'd been harbouring was so silly after all. 'If I decide to stay,' she began, 'and I'm not promising I will, would you and Stan consider living here?'

Simone glanced quickly across at her husband, a flicker of hope instantly quashed as she looked back at Jenny. 'I dunno, luv. We been moving around for so long, won't seem right being in the same place all the time.'

'You could live in the bungalow by the creek, help me keep house and organise the food for the shearers. Stan could help in the yards and oversee the woolshed.'

His expression was as dour as always, the lack of response more telling than words.

Simone looked at him and sighed. 'Sounds like heaven to me, luv. But Stan ain't one for settlin' down. Got itchy feet.' She shrugged, her smile forced.

'No worries, Simone,' Jenny said hurriedly. 'I haven't decided what I'm going to do yet, but if I do stay then I'll write. Perhaps by then we can twist Stan's arm a bit.'

Simone bit her lip as she looked from Jenny to Stan, who was peering into the depths of his beer as if the answers were to be found at the bottom of the glass. 'Me and Stan are right with the way things are for now, Jen. But I'll give you the address in Newcastle anyways. Our daughter will see we get your letters.'

Stan drained his beer and stood up. 'Thanks for the tucker, Mrs Sanders. Ma and me really appreciate all you done, but we got an early start tomorrow.'

Jenny shook his hand. It was soft from years of handling wool, the lanolin a natural protection from calluses. Simone's embrace was warm and comforting, and Jenny realised she would miss her dreadfully. This cheerful, stoic woman was the nearest she'd come to a mother since Ellen Carey, and the thought they may never see one another again was hard to accept.

She went with them out on to the front verandah, and watched them cross the yard to the cookhouse. With a final wave, she turned back into the house. It already felt deserted, the sight of the dishes in the sink and the empty chairs merely highlighting that sense of emptiness. The dust had returned, silently and almost secretly as it always did. The polished tables were dulled by it, the bright flowers wilting beneath its gossamer weight.

Ripper was released from the bedroom to be fed the scraps, then turfed out for his nightly run while Jenny saw to the dishes. Then, with a final cup of coffee, she plumped down into an easy chair and breathed in the scent of the night.

The warmth caressed her. The rustle of leaves and dry grass lulled her. The music was playing again. Drawing her back – back to a gentle embrace and the whisper of satin. The time had come to open the diaries again.


Dry winter was followed by rainless summer. There was no time to mourn her baby, for the knee-high, tawny grass was crisp beneath a merciless sun, the trees stark, their leaves shrivelled and wilting. Rabbits in their thousands and vast mobs of 'roos came ever southward to the grassy plains as the great outback dried up and sweltered.

Matilda looked out over the pastures, her hat low on her brow, shielding her eyes from the glare. Thanks to Tom Finlay, and his help with overseeing the shearing shed last year, the wool cheque had covered the final payment on the bank loan. This left her with just enough to see her through another summer. She was under-stocked for a station as large as Churinga, and if it wasn't for the rabbits and 'roos, the grass just might last out. There were a thousand head of Merinos left of the once great mob, yet their depleted numbers would make them easier to keep an eye on. If the rains didn't come, then she would have to scrub cut and hand-feed them.

With their meagre supplies in saddle-bags, Matilda and Gabriel patrolled the pastures. She learned to sleep on hard-packed earth, boots on, rifle cocked, alert for the rustle of a wild pig or the stealthy creep of dingo or snake. Searing days followed freezing nights. With Bluey trotting at her side, she rode amongst the widespread mob. Each dead sheep made her want to cry, but she buried it in grim silence, knowing there was nothing she could do about it.

Lambing time came, bringing a race against the natural predators. Matilda checked the pens she and Gabriel had put up on the far western corner. With a depleted mob, it would be easier to have the ewes all in one place before they dropped their lambs.

Each lamb had to be caught and graded, its tail ringed and ear tagged. Castration was a bloody, filthy job, the testicles popped between the fingers, chewed off and spat out. It repelled her, but after her initial hesitancy she learned to do it swiftly. For if she was to maintain a superior quality wool, it was a necessary evil.

So was crutching – an arduous, repulsive task that had to be carried out in the fields. No self-respecting shearer would touch a dirty fleece unless he was paid double rate and she couldn't afford to run a learning shed like Kurrajong, where the young shearers learned their trade on wets, cobblers, dags and fly-blowns.

The rear end of a sheep is the dirtiest thing this side of the black stump. Covered in excrement and buzzing with egg-laying flies, the wool gathers in black lumps or dags. Matilda and Gabriel wrestled with the squirming, brainless beasts and cut the wool close to the papery skin. Gabe seemed unaffected by the flies, but Matilda had to stitch bobbing corks to the brim of her hat – it was her only protection from the black swarms that never seemed to leave them.

As the shearing season loomed closer, she and Gabriel began the muster. The mob was graded in each pasture, some penned, others brought down to the paddocks near the homestead. Matilda followed them over the dry, dusty land and began to fret. Her mob had increased, and although it was nowhere near the numbers it had once been, she couldn't afford to pay a quid a hundred to have them shorn.

She stood in the silent shearing shed and looked up at the cathedral roof where dust motes danced in beams of light. The smell of sweat and lanolin, of wool and tar, hung in the air.

202

She breathed it in with deep pleasure. This was what it meant to be a squatter, a keeper of sheep, a provider of the best wool in the world. Her glance fell to the floor and the bleached circles on the wood where generations of shearers had dropped their sweat. Then she eyed the tar buckets in the corner and the generator. It had been fixed by a passing swaggie in return for a couple of meals and a bed for the night. The ramps and sorting tables were sturdy with new wood, but what use were they when she had no shearers, no tar boys, no shed hands or sorters?

The sigh came from deep within her. Shearers wouldn't wait to be paid. But no men meant no wool. And without the wool cheque, she couldn't survive.

'G'day, Matilda. See you got the muster under way.'

She turned and smiled at Tom Finlay whose Irish ancestry was evident in his dark hair and green eyes. She shook his hand. 'Yeah. Almost done. How're things on Wilga?'

'Mob's almost in. Bonzer lot of lambs this year despite the lack of rain. Been a fair cow trying to hand-feed the buggers, though.'

Matilda nodded her understanding. 'Come into the house for a cuppa. I might even have a bottle of something stronger somewhere.'

'Tea'll be right.' He walked with her across the acre of cleared, flattened earth. 'Good to see you looking well, Molly.' His endearment made her smile. He'd always called her Molly, and she'd always liked it. 'Had me and April worried when you took crook last year. She wanted to come over and visit after I finished managing your shed, but you know how things are.'

She pushed through the screen door and headed for the range. 'Probably wouldn't have found me,' she said as she cut hunks of cold mutton and stuffed them between slices of bread. 'Spent most of the year patrolling the pastures. With only me and Gabe to keep an eye on the mob, there didn't seem much point in coming back here much.'

'What about the young Bitjarras? Surely you and Gabe could have used them?'

She brought the rough meal to the table and shook her head. 'Worse than useless. Most of them are too young, the others only get in the bloody way. Besides, I haven't enough horses for all of us, so I left the boys here to sort out the barns and sheds and to tidy up after winter.'

They ate in silence, and when they'd finished, leaned back in their chairs with mugs of good, strong tea.

Tom regarded her thoughtfully. 'You've changed, Molly. I remember a skinny little girl who wore ribbons in her hair and liked to dress up in her Sunday best for the picnic races and barn dances.'

Matilda took in his handsome Irish looks, the character etched in fine lines around his eyes, the sunbaked skin, the broad, capable hands. 'We all change,' she said quietly. 'You're a man now. Not the horrid little boy who used to pull my hair and rub my face in the dirt.' She sighed. 'The time for ribbons and party dresses is over, Tom. We've both had to grow up.'

He leaned forward. 'That doesn't mean you can't have fun, Molly. You're young and pretty under those old rags. You should be going to the parties and looking for a husband. Not sleeping rough and up to your armpits in sheep shit and daggy wool.'

Matilda laughed. She felt a hundred years old, and knew she must look a sight in her father's old flannel trousers and much darned shirt. 'If you think that, then you've been out in your own fields for too long, Tom.'

He shook his head. 'This is no life for a young girl on her own, Moll. And there're plenty who'd like the chance to get to know you.'

Her amusement died. 'Men, you mean?' she said sourly. 'Andrew Squires still sniffs around, and there've been one or two others, but I send 'em off with a flea in their ear.'

His green eyes were full of humour, and she glared back at him, daring him to laugh at her. 'I don't want or need a man about the place unless he's a shearer and leaves when he's done his job.'

Tom pushed the pouch of tobacco towards her then rolled himself a cigarette. 'Talking of shearers,' he drawled, the humour still making his eyes dance, 'how many head do you reckon you got?'

'Just under the fifteen hundred,' she said promptly as she

inexpertly tried to roll her own. 'But I'll manage this year. No worries.' She kept her eyes on her cigarette, afraid to let him see the hope in her eyes.

'I got the shearers coming next week. If you can get your mob marked, crotched and over to Wilga by then, they can be done with mine.'

'How much will it cost?' Tom's kindness was overwhelming, but she had to be practical.

He grinned. 'Well, now, Molly,' he drawled. 'That all depends.'

She raised an eyebrow and looked into his face.

'I got me a deal with Nulla Nulla and Machree. They're bringing their mobs to me this year, and they can both afford an extra penny here and there to cover your expenses.'

She grinned back. 'Crafty.'

He shook his head. 'Not at all. Old Fergus can well afford a few pennies, and so can Longhorn. Tight-fisted bastards, the pair of 'em. Now, what do you say?'

'Thanks,' she said simply, real appreciation in her eyes, offering the firm handshake of a deal agreed.

'Another cuppa wouldn't go amiss. Me mouth's like a drover's armpit.'

She poured him more tea, wishing there was some way in which she could repay him. But Tom Finlay had always been able to read her mind and age apparently hadn't dimmed that particular talent. 'You'll live in the house with me and April, of course, but you'll not be getting your sheep sheared for nothing, mind. There's plenty of work you can be doing, and you'll be too tired at the end of it for gratitude.'

Matilda smoked the last of her cigarette in silence. One day, she promised herself, she would repay Tom. He was the only one out of a dozen neighbours who'd offered help, and she would never forget it.

After he left, she crossed the yard to the Abo gunyahs. 'Gabe, I want you to ride out with me tomorrow and finish mustering. Your two eldest boys can stay here and make sure they're kept in the home pasture. We're taking the mob to Wilga.'

'Bloody good shed here, Missus. Why we going Wilga?'

She eyed the bony figure in the thin blanket. 'Because we

can get the job done cheaper there.'

He frowned, his mind working slowly. 'Big job, Missus. Taking mob to Wilga. Me and the boys is tired,' he said mournfully.

Matilda swallowed her impatience. She was tired as well, exhausted if the truth be known, and Gabriel was a lazy good-for-nothing bludger. 'You want sugar and baccy, Gabe?'

He nodded with a grin.

'Then you'll get it when the mob's back here from Wilga,' she said firmly.

His smile disappeared and he looked slyly at his wife. 'Can't leave the missus. Baby coming.'

Her exasperation reached boiling point. 'There are six other bloody women to look after her, Gabe. This is her fourth kid, and you never stuck around when the others were born.' She eyed the grubby children playing around the encampment in the dirt. They ranged from crawling babies to adolescents, from rook black to pale coffee. Most of them had the wild, black hair of their ancestors, but some were tow-headed, almost blond. A drover or two had obviously got lonely for female company on his way through. 'Where are the boys? I'm going to need them too.'

Gabriel looked into the distance. 'Kurrajong,' he muttered. 'Good money for jackaroo there.'

If it's so damn good, she thought furiously, then why the hell didn't the whole bloody lot of them move over there? She kept her thoughts to herself, though. Until things improved around Churinga, she would have to encourage them to stay. They cost little to keep, but God almighty they were irritating.

'One sack of sugar and flour now. Another when the mob's in from Wilga, plus some baccy.'

They stared at one another for a long moment of silence. Then Gabriel nodded.

The two young boys he brought with him were as nimble as Blue at herding, chasing and gathering in the strays. But the muster still took almost three days. Days where the sky grew dark with thick black clouds and distant thunder growled a promise of rain. Yet as one by one the pastures were emptied, each herd brought to the home paddock and fenced in before they went back for the next lot, the clouds held their precious

206

cargo, scudding away on the hot, dry winds that rustled the grass and made the sheep nervous.

It was not yet dawn on the fourth day. Matilda had packed her saddle-bags with the things she would need for the coming few weeks, and with Lady saddled and ready, she stood by the fence and looked over the shifting woolly backs. Despite the lack of rain, Churinga grass had held out, and the fat, fleecy animals looked healthy and strong. Some of that tallow would be worked off in the coming trek to Wilga, but the quality of the wool was the important thing.

'Storm coming, missus,' said Gabriel who was astride her gelding.

She looked up at the sky. The clouds were gathering again, the air electric as though sky and earth were giant fire sticks rubbing together. 'Then let's go.' She signalled to the boys to open the gate.

Blue sank to his belly at her sharp whistle, moving swift and sure-footed over and around the mob as they poured into the paddock. With a nip here, a nudge there, a race over woolly backs to collar a Judas, he kept the mob tightly packed.

Matilda rode at the back of the mob with Gabriel, cajoling them forward, flicking the stock whip with consummate ease above their stupid heads, eating the dust of fifteen hundred sets of feet. The electricity in the air was making her tingle, lifting the hairs on her arms and at the back of her neck. Storm clouds gathered in layer upon ominous layer, blotting out the early sun, bringing pewter dullness to the day.

'Dry storm, missus. Not good out here.'

Matilda nodded, the dread returning. She had to get to Wilga before it broke. There was nothing more terrifying than a dry storm and at the first crack of lightning she would lose control of the mob.

Bluey seemed to sense the urgency. He raced after a frightened ewe, chivvied a dawdler, and kept an eye on the Judas. He nipped and snarled, ran in circles and across their backs, hovered, belly in the dirt, until the right moment to head off a stray. It took all that day but finally, as the defeated sun disappeared behind the mountain, they reached the pastures of Wilga and the welcome sight of drovers coming to meet them.

The sheep were finally herded into the small paddock behind the shearing shed, separated from the other three great mobs by the vast labyrinth of pens.

'You can sort and grade them tomorrow,' said Tom. 'Looks like the storm's about to hit.'

Matilda finished her counting and breathed a sigh of relief. 'I haven't lost any on the way. Good thing we came when we did.'

They looked up at the rolling waves of thunderous clouds. 'Gonna be a fair cow,' Tom said grimly as he walked with her to the corral. Her two horses joined the others, their flanks twitching with apprehension at the approaching storm. 'April's indoors. Come on. Time for tucker.'

April was perhaps three, maybe five years older than Matilda, her hands reddened from work, slender figure looking too frail to survive this heat as well as her pregnancy. She was drawn and obviously tired, her feet restlessly taking her in a never-ceasing round of table to stove, sink to table. The sleeves of her dress were rolled to her elbows, hair trailing pale damp wisps across her face where it had escaped the knot on top of her head.

'Nice to see you again, Molly,' she said, her smile weary but welcoming. 'I could certainly do with another pair of hands around here just now.'

Matilda looked away from the swollen belly. Sadness welled and she pushed it aside with remorseless determination. April had chosen to marry and have babies. They didn't fit into her own plans, so why feel anything but unshackled?

Wilga homestead was bigger than Churinga, sprawling across the crest of a low hill, its verandahs looking out over the creeks and home pastures. Wilga trees gave shade to the men's barracks, and box and coolibah lined the creek banks. Like Churinga, there were no trees too near the house. Too much of a fire hazard.

April poured hot water from the kettle into a tin bowl, and handed Matilda a scrap of towel and a bar of homemade soap. 'Have a wash and a bit of a rest, Moll. Tucker won't be for a while.'

Matilda's room was at the far eastern end of the house. It looked out towards the stock pens, was small and cramped with heavy furniture and a vast brass bed. But it smelled wonderfully of beeswax polish and the floor had been recently swept with fresh wood shavings. She listened to the sound of the children playing in the yard. How many did Tom have now? she wondered. Four, or was it five?

She shrugged, caught sight of her reflection in the mirror and stared in horrified fascination. Was this brown-skinned, wild-haired woman really her? She hadn't realised how much she'd grown, how thin she was, or how old the lines around her eyes made her look. If the hair was a shade darker, the eyes a little bluer, she could have been looking at the ghost of Mary Thomas.

With a rueful grimace she eyed the flannel trousers she'd cut down to fit. They were stained and worn, tied at the knees and ankles with bowyangs, the strips of 'roo-hide a necessary addition to stop creepy crawlies from climbing up her legs. The grey shirt had once been blue but had been bleached by the sun and too many washes in lye soap.

She sighed. Mary Thomas had liked to wear the rough, easy clothes of the drover, but hers had always been immaculately clean and mended, not like these disreputable rags.

She thought of April and her neat cotton dress, and remembered how Tom had said she should put on a dress and go to the parties and dances. Grimacing, she stripped off the soiled clothes and began to wash. It had been a long time since she'd bothered to dress up, and now she probably never would. She had chosen her way of life, and if that made her more like a man, then so much the better. Women had it too tough anyway, and she meant to survive.

Matilda had fallen asleep on the feather mattress when the tucker bell was rung. She hurried to join the others in the kitchen. It was daunting to eat in company, to be the focus of six pairs of eyes that followed every move she made.

The four children, all boys, had not inherited the pale yellow hair and gentle face of April but the stormy black brows and Irish green eyes of their father.

'The men arrive day after tomorrow,' said Tom, shovelling in stew and following it up with a chunk of bread. 'Should get around to yours sometime around the middle of next month.'

Matilda nodded, her mouth too full to speak. After living

on cold mutton and damper bread for months, she didn't want to waste time talking.

'April's almost finished clearing out the barracks. You can help with the stock pens, or in the cookhouse. It's up to you.'

Matilda glanced at April's wan face and decided that although she'd have preferred working in the pens, she was needed more in the cookhouse and barracks. They would need scouring and the beds repairing. The shearers would bring their own cook, but Wilga had a lot of men working for them and there were always vegetables to prepare and bread to make. Then there were the children to watch over. April couldn't possibly be left to shoulder that on her own.

'How you off for water, Moll? Got enough in the tanks to see you right if we don't get rain?'

She pushed back her plate and began to roll a cigarette. She was sated. 'Yeah. Those tanks are about the only thing Dad kept in good order,' she said dryly. 'We've got the bore head, of course, but the river's down to a trickle.'

'Your grandad was wise to put up all those tanks. I put an extra couple on just before the rains two years back but we're lucky here with the creeks and the rivers. The artesian well waters the fields, but it's too full of minerals and doesn't help the house any.'

A deep, ominous rumble silenced them and all eyes turned to the windows.

The world and every living thing in it held its breath, suspended in terrible expectancy. Endless seconds followed, dragging out the suspense, filling each of them with dread. The younger children crept from the table to burrow into the folds of April's apron like small, timid creatures.

Her face was white, eyes round and unblinking. 'It's all right,' she said mechanically. 'We've got a conductor. It can't touch us.' She shivered. 'Please God, it can't touch us,' she added in a whisper.

The crash rocked the house, tore the sky apart and spilled its fury. Blue flares of forked light streaked through the lowering clouds, turning night into a day brighter than any of them had seen before. Electricity cracked like a stock whip, lashing from one cloud to another, ripping the heavens apart as if possessed. The earth trembled as thunder crashed and rebounded off the iron roof. Jagged blue and yellow seared the hills and paddocks, touched the sentinel finger of a lone tree in the middle of a distant pasture, and sizzled a demonic halo around the bark before dying. The storm echoed in their heads and rang in their ears. Blinded them with its light, deafened them with the sheer weight of its force.

'Got to check the stock,' yelled Tom.

'I'll come with you,' Matilda yelled back.

They stood on the porch and watched the awesome display of nature's pent-up fury, knowing there would be no rain, no remission for the parched earth and tinder-dry trees. The air was so thick Matilda could hardly breathe, the electricity making her hair dance and weave, spark if she tried to tame it. They hurried to the pens where the other men were already checking the fences and gates. The sheep rolled their eyes and bleated, but they were tightly packed with nowhere to go.

Matilda ran across the yard to the paddock. The horses shied, pawing the air, their manes flying, tails stiff with fear. No one could catch them and after a fruitless chase Tom and Matilda decided they would have to take their chances. The dogs howled and whined in their kennels, the cattle lowed and sought shelter by hugging the earth. It was as if the whole world was writhing in agony.

The storm went on all through the night and into the next day. Thunder crashed, clouds stripped the sun, and lightning slivers burned blue fire through the sky. They became immune to the noise, the children creeping to the window to watch in awed silence. But none of them could voice the fear they all felt. One blade of grass could be struck, one hollow tree, dead and forgotten in the midst of a pasture, could attract the lightning bolt that would begin as a tiny blue flame and spread in seconds.

The shearers arrived along with the extra jackaroos, drovers and tar boys. Work in the cookhouse became a ceaseless succession of meals, of bread and mutton, cakes and pies, anything to take their minds off the storm. The sweat ran down Matilda's ribs, plastering her clothes to her skin as the barometer crept up to a hundred and twenty degrees. The kitchen sweltered, and although she was used to the hard work of the fields, she was drained by the end of the day and filled with admiration for April. Eight months pregnant and with over eighty people to feed, she never stopped and never complained.

At the end of the second night the winds came. They coiled the earth into spirals, barrelling across the ground, knocking down anything in their path. There was no way of fighting the willy willies. You just had to pray they didn't grow into tornadoes and come your way.

Tom watched from the verandah as they swept over his fields, ripped trees and fence posts from the ground and tossed them like matchsticks to the four corners of Wilga. Great tunnels of wind kicked up the earth, raced in one direction then turned in another, each giving birth to smaller ones, which whipped up the shallow water in the creeks and spewed it out in the spinning, ceaseless vortex. Roofs clattered and flapped, the wall of the machine shop tilted and swayed then collapsed with a crash against one of the empty stock pens. Shutters slammed and the air was full of choking dust.

But the winds blew the storm away and by noon on the third day the land was quiet. The people of Wilga emerged like ship-wrecked survivors to assess the damage.

The willow trees by the river had survived, their long, pliant branches bending towards the stony bed where only pools of murky water remained. The ghost gum at the end of the nearest pasture had split. It lay on the ground, its silver trunk cloven in two branches clawing fruitlessly skyward. Two of the six precious water tanks had blown over and were the first thing to be repaired. Corrugated iron roofs needed replacing, the machine shed to be demolished and rebuilt. Luckily it hadn't crushed any of the animals in the pen, just given them a scare and made them more jumpy than usual.

One of the stockmen returned from mending fences, his face grim and dirty after his long ride. 'Found five cows, Tom. Sorry, mate. Must have got the full brunt of the wind. They was miles away from their grazing. Dead as doornails.'

Tom nodded was resignation. 'At least it wasn't more. And the mobs are right, despite the shed almost falling on 'em.'

Matilda fretted about Churinga as she and April returned to the broiling kitchen. The devastation wrought on Wilga could quickly be repaired with so many willing hands, but what if

Churinga had been wiped out? The tanks spilled, the house and sheds ripped from the earth? With stoic determination she put her worries aside. Her mob was safe – she could survive.

The shearing shed was fully operational within hours of the storm's departure, the shearers making up for lost time. A gun shearer can get through over two hundred sheep in a day. They wielded the narrow boggies with a co-ordination of grace, strength and endurance, sweeping the length of the sheep's body, keeping the razor close enough to the loose, fragile skin to free the wool in one piece and please the most demanding shed boss. It was exacting work, done in an atmosphere of sweat, noise, flies and the stink of a thousand woolly backsides.

When Matilda could escape the kitchen, she would hurry to the woolshed to watch these master craftsmen, for unlike some sheds, Tom had no qualms about women helping in his. She would grab a bucket of fresh water and a ladle, and pass each stooping shearer a drink. Each man would need about three gallons of water a day in this heat. She watched them work. Most of them were short, wiry little men who had the permanent stoop of a life-long shearer and the elongated arms necessary to sweep the boggies through the fleece that went right down to a Merino's hoofs and nose.

There were no dreadnoughts in Tom's shed this year, she realised. None of the rare breed of men who could shear over three hundred in a day, and who made a fortune on side bets. She watched the shed boss stride up and down the lines of sweating, cursing men. His word was absolute and the shearers were expected to reach his high standards. No second cuts and no ripping of that fine skin.

Fergus McBride and Joe Longhorn patrolled the lines as their sheep came to be shorn. They tipped their hats to Matilda but in their shyness found it awkward to strike up a conversation and concentrated on their woolly harvest instead.

It was almost six weeks before the shearing was over. The days had been filled with a keener heat, as if soaked by the storm. Matilda sweated in the kitchen and sought relief in the pens and sheds, where it was just as hot, but less humid. She felt stifled, being shut in the house all day, and liked to feel the sun on her face, and the weariness of hard labour in the stock pens.

As McBride and Longhorn followed their newly fleeced mobs to their own winter pastures, the shearers climbed into their wagons and left Wilga. The wool was already baled and on its way to the rail head at Broken Hill.

Matilda had wondered if she would see Peg and Albert this year, but no one could remember seeing them for a long time and she supposed they'd gone back up towards Queensland this season. Probably too ashamed at having filched her meat and flour, she thought. No, she wasn't surprised they'd decided not to show their faces around Churinga this season.

Her last supper with Tom and April was over, the dishes washed and put away, the children finally in bed and asleep. Matilda sat on the veranda with the others, in her mind turning over the words she wanted to say to these kind people. And yet she was finding it hard to express her thanks in a way that would truly show the depth of her feeling for she'd learned too well how to hide her emotions. 'Thanks, Tom,' she said finally – knowing it was inadequate.

He seemed to understand. He nodded, patted her shoulder awkwardly and returned to his perusal of the yard. 'Reckon me and some of the blokes better come with you tomorrow, Molly. The storm fair kicked up a lot of damage and I wouldn't like to think of you stranded for the winter.'

'No,' she said quickly. 'You and April have done enough already. I'll manage, Tom. Really.'

'You always were stubborn,' he said without rancour. 'April could never have fed all them men on her own, Moll. I reckon you earned the cost of your shearing.'

'But you've got to get the mob to winter pasture, Tom, and there's things to do here yet,' she protested.

'No worries,' he said calmly. 'Our repairs are almost finished, the drovers can muster the mobs. And besides,' he looked at her with laughing eyes, 'what the hell are neighbours for if they can't help one another now and again?'

April put down the sock she was darning. The mending basket was overflowing as usual, and despite the long hours she'd spent doing the household chores, she couldn't sit idle even though she seemed permanently tired. 'We'd be happier if we knew you was all right, Molly. I don't know how you can bear it out there all on your own.' She shuddered. 'It's bad enough here when Tom's away with the mob. I don't think I could survive at your place.'

Matilda smiled and picked up a sock. 'It's surprising what you can do when you have no choice, April.'

The other woman watched her thread the needle and inexpertly begin to darn one of Tom's socks. 'But I thought Ethan offered to buy you out?' she said softly.

Matilda stabbed herself with the needle, watched the drop of blood blossom, and stuck her finger into her mouth. 'He did,' she mumbled. 'And I told him where he could stick his offer.'

Tom roared with laughter. 'You sounded just like your mum then, Molly. Good on yer. You'll make a squatter yet.'

They were up before dawn, breakfast eaten as the light diffused a soft glow over the land. Matilda kissed the boys who rubbed their faces and raced off yelling, then turned to April. 'It's been good having another woman to talk to,' she said. 'Nothing like a gossip about the neighbours to get the day going.'

April wiped her hands on her apron and took Matilda into an embrace. 'It's been lovely,' she said wistfully. 'Please promise you'll come again.'

Matilda felt the unborn child squirm between them and pulled away. The pain was returning, making her weak, grinding her aspirations to dust. She forced a smile. 'I'll try and get over sometime, but you know how it is.'

They moved off the verandah and crossed the broad sweep of yard that until yesterday had been busy with men and horses and thousands of sheep. Blue heard her whistle and leaped out of the dog pens to follow closely to heel. Gabriel, who'd been sharing a gunyah with three other Aborigines, drifted towards the paddocks and collected the two horses. The sheep were released from the stock yards, the dogs began to work, and they all headed towards Churinga.

Matilda could follow the path of the wind through the grass, and saw changes on the horizon. Trees had been blown down, fence posts uprooted and left in a tangle of wire fencing. Familiar landmarks, like the old blasted tree, were gone forever. And yet the mountain never changed. It was as solid as ever, still covered in thick, green trees. Still the sentinel of Churinga station.

She was breathing a sigh of relief when they came to the home paddock for there seemed to be no real damage.

'Jeez. Will you look at that?' Tom's hoarse whisper made her follow the direction in which he was pointing.

One of the cast iron water tanks had been blown on to the roof, smashing its way into the house. It lay drunkenly amongst the remains of the south wall, the corrugated roofing rising above the devastation like great rusty wings.

Matilda turned to Tom, relief and anguish mixed curiously within her. 'You saved my life,' she whispered. 'If I hadn't come to Wilga . . .' She licked her lips. 'That fell right on top of my bedroom.'

He took immediate charge. 'You and Gabe see to the sheep. We'll see to the repairs. Looks like you escaped the worst of the storm, there's not much more damage.' He eyed her closely. 'Thank God you were with us, Molly.' Then wheeled his horse towards the house, shouting orders to the drovers who'd come with them before Matilda could think of a reply.

She and Gabriel mustered the sheep into the stock pens. It wouldn't hurt to have them there a few days while the repairs were done. Gabriel returned to his newly erected gunyah and his new baby – now he'd received his baccy and flour, he considered his work over.

Matilda couldn't get into the house, even though most of the damage was only on one side, so she dug a pit in the yard, circled it with stones and built a fire. With a billy and a rather battered old frying pan, she managed to cook for Tom and the two drovers over the next few days, and at night they slept wrapped in their horse blankets.

Tom and the others rigged up a pulley and sweated and strained to get the heavy tank back on its pilings before turning to the repairs of the fences then the house. The timber walls were splintered into a thousand pieces, the windows smashed, the verandah railings snapped like twigs, the roof just a jumble of corrugated iron. He took off his hat and scratched his head. 'Reckon we should start again, Moll. This old place is falling down round your ears.'

216

She looked at him in dismay. 'You haven't got time to do that, Tom. What about your sheep?'

'Bugger the sheep,' he drawled. 'The men are looking after them, and I want to make sure you're warm and dry for the winter.' He stomped off before she could say anything more.

The men worked flat out for more than a week. One drover returned from Wallaby Flats with a wagon load of timber he swore was being given away by an old squatter who'd decided to pull down one of his sheds. Matilda looked at him in disbelief, but as he seemed set on sticking to his story, she realised there was nothing she could do but believe him.

Tom had a way with the Bitjarra too. He set Gabe and the boys to hold the cornerposts while he and the drovers hammered the new wood of the walls. Gave them hammer and nails to replace the roof, and taught all of them the intricacies of putting new glass into a window frame.

With a new front door, mended screens and shutters, and a fresh coat of paint, Churinga gleamed in the late-summer sun. The verandah now swept all the way around the house, shaded by the new sloping roof and rough pillars.

'April's put flowers all over our roof, and up the tank stands. Reckons in a couple of years you won't see the ugly old things. You should try it, Moll.'

She eyed her new house, speechless with pleasure, almost blinded by the tears of gratitude. 'Reckon you could be right, Tom.' She turned to him. 'How can I ever thank you? You've given me so much.'

He put his arm around her and held her close. 'Let's just say this is to say sorry for all the times I pulled your hair and dunked you in the river. Sorry we haven't been as close since your mum died too. We're mates, Molly, and that's what mates are for.'

She watched the men ride away, then with Blue at her heels stepped into her new house and shut the door. There were no words to describe how she was feeling when she placed her mother's watercolour of Churinga on the wall, but she knew that at last she had found a man she could trust. An honourable man who could be called friend. Perhaps there were others. Good people in the community she'd shunned until now.

217

The courage to face them returned and she decided that after taking the sheep to winter pasture she might ride into town and buy a dress. And one day, she promised silently, she would find a way to return Tom's kindness.

Jenny marked the place in the diary. She could understand how Matilda must have felt. Such kindness after the brutality was bound to leave her speechless, perhaps confused – and yet it had given her courage. A different kind of courage from that needed in the pastures and paddocks, one that allowed her to open up – to meet people and learn to trust again.

She eyed the pup who was scratching enthusiastically at his fleas. 'Come on, Ripper. Time for bed. And in the morning, young man, you are going to have a bath,' she said sternly.

He looked up at her, his adoring eyes following her around the room before he scampered off. Jenny took a long, last look at the silent paddocks and the high black sky that was splashed with a million stars. It was beautiful and cruel – but always rewarding. She was beginning to understand why Matilda and Brett loved it.

# Chapter Twelve

The silence had become a living thing that pressed in on Jenny and as the days passed she became more aware of her isolation. And yet she found comfort in her own company, and in that of the men who still remained on Churinga, a kind of peace she had never before experienced.

During the long days she wandered the vast acres on horseback, her sketchpad in a saddle-bag, and in the frosty nights, when dew glittered on the pastures, she swept and dusted and kept house. She washed curtains and bedding, painted the cupboards in the kitchen and moved the trunk into the bedroom. The dresses belonged in the wardrobe, she decided. Not hidden away.

She took out the sea green dress and held it against her. The memory of lavender drifted into the room as the ghostly orchestra struck up the waltz. Matilda's spirit was with her as she danced but there was an echo of sadness in that music too. A tenuous thread of dreams unfulfilled running through the refrain that she couldn't capture or understand.

Jenny closed her eyes, willing the images she'd formed of the ghostly dancers to return. For it was they who were guiding her through the pages of Matilda's life. It was their story that demanded to be told.

'Jenny? You home?'

Her eyes flew open, the music fragmented and was gone, the images faded. It was as if she'd been snatched from one dimension into another, but despite being disorientated her first thought was that Brett must not find her like this. 'Wait on. I'll be out in a minute,' she called.

The slam of the screen door was followed by the tread of his boots on the kitchen floor as she hung the dress in the wardrobe. His voice was a baritone against Ripper's sharp yaps of excitement as she left one reality for another and quickly changed into shirt and strides. She took a deep breath and opened the bedroom door.

'G'day, Jen.' Brett looked up from the pup who was chewing enthusiastically on his fingers.

She smiled, curiously pleased to see him. 'I wasn't expecting you back so soon. How did the wool transport go?'

'OK. We got a good price at auction, and I banked the cheque as usual.' He fished in his pocket. 'I had to take out the wages and expenses, but here's the receipts.'

Jenny glanced at the figures. This was more money than she could imagine. 'Is the wool cheque always this big?'

Brett shrugged. 'Depends on the market. But that's about average.'

He seemed so nonchalant. As if such a vast sum meant nothing, she thought in wonder. She folded the receipt and tucked it into the pocket of her jeans. But of course it wasn't his money so why should he get excited over it?

'Got a beer, Jen? Been a long drive.'

She fetched two bottles and popped the tabs. 'Here's to the wool cheque.'

'Too right.' He took a long drink then wiped his mouth with the back of his hand. 'By the way, picked up something for you at Broken Hill. It's been there waiting for Chalky White to bring it out with the Royal Mail.' His slow smile reached his grey eyes, bringing warmth and humour to the flecks of green and gold as he lugged the enormous parcel in from the verandah.

Jenny gasped. 'Diane's sent my stuff.' She tore back the paper and struggled with the string until she came to the battered wooden box of oil paints, the rolls of pre-prepared canvas and clusters of brushes. 'She's even thought to add my lightweight easel,' said Jenny in surprise and delight.

'Reckon you're set for the winter.'

Jenny nodded. She was too engrossed in her tubes of paint, the gleaming palette knives, the little bottles of white spirit and linseed oil, to speak. Now she could bring Churinga alive on canvas. Bring colour and light to the drawings she'd made over the past month, and perhaps even attempt to capture the images sparked by the diaries. The restless energy returned. She was impatient to make a start.

'That's if you decide to stay, of course. Nothing much goes on around here for the next couple of months, what with the drovers out in the winter pastures.'

She looked up at him, her hands still amongst the tubes of paint. 'Now I've got these, I won't mind the isolation. There's so many things I want to paint, so many of my sketches I need to get on to canvas. There's the house, the paddocks, the stretch of land leading to that wonderful waterfall and pool. The mountain, the oasis where we swam, the wilga trees, the shearing shed and stock yards.' She paused to catch her breath. 'And I'll have you and Ripper for company in the evenings.'

Brett shuffled from one foot to another, hands in his pockets, eyes firmly on his boots. 'Well . . .' he began.

Jenny sat back on her heels, her spirits plummeting. 'What's the matter, Brett?' she asked quietly. He looked uncomfortable. There was something bothering him but he was obviously finding it hard to put into words. 'Is it the thought of being stuck out here with me? Because if it is then you don't need to worry. As long as I know there's someone around, we don't even need to see one another,' she said firmly.

Brave words, she thought. Why don't you just admit you were looking forward to spending time with him? Time when Churinga's demands were not so urgent. Time to get to know one another.

His eyes were the colour of woodsmoke as they rested on her face. 'That's unfair, Jen. I don't like the thought of leaving you here alone – wouldn't do it if it wasn't totally necessary,' he said softly.

'So what's made it necessary?' she asked a little too sharply as she thought of Lorraine.

'There was a letter waiting for me at Broken Hill. From Davey, my brother up in Queensland. John's real crook this time, Jen. And this is the only chance I've got of seeing him this year.'

Jenny could see the agony of indecision in his face. 'How long will you be gone?' Her voice was calm, despite the bitter disappointment.

'A month. But I'll cancel my flight if you don't want to be left that long. You must have felt pretty isolated these last couple of weeks.'

Jenny was furious at the surge of jealousy she'd experienced, furious with the relief of knowing he wasn't planning to spend his leave seeing Lorraine, and ashamed she'd jumped the gun and come to the wrong conclusion. And yet why should that affect her? It was none of her business. Brett was merely a friend and friends should trust one another, not be suspicious of the other's motives.

'Of course you must go,' she said firmly. 'I'll be fine. I've got all this to keep me occupied, and there's always the two-way radio to keep me up with the gossip and if I should need help.'

'I don't like the thought of you out here alone. This isn't like the cities, Jen.'

'Too right it isn't,' she said lightly as she brushed dust from her jeans and stood up. 'But I'll be okay. Go and see your brother, Brett. I'll be fine.'

He didn't seem convinced, and hovered uneasily in the doorway.

Jenny put her hands on her hips and looked him in the eye. 'I'm a big girl now, Brett, I can fend for myself – and if things get too much, I can always go back to Sydney. Now go and leave me to paint.'

He looked down at her for a long moment, his expression thoughtful, eyes sweeping across her face as if searching for something. Then he was gone. Through the screen door with a clatter and over the porch, his boots ringing a tattoo on the wooden boards.

Jenny gave a long, deep sigh as the silence closed in. She'd been looking forward to his return much more than she cared to admit – and the realisation came as a shock. The house seemed emptier with him gone, the silence deeper, the isolation of Churinga more profound. The long weeks stretched endlessly before her and she thought she heard soft laughter and the rustle of silk.

With a snort of impatience, she reached for the box of oils. She was letting her imagination run away with her. Churinga and the people who had once lived here were having a strange effect on her and the sooner she got on with her painting the better.

It hadn't taken long to throw a few things into a holdall. Now he was back on the verandah, looking through the screen door.

Jenny had been busy in the few minutes he'd been away, Brett realised. The furniture had been moved from the windows at the back of the house, the floor and table covered in sheets. Her easel had been set up on the table, the brushes stuffed into jars at her side, the oils laid out in regimental lines. She'd chosen her spot well. Light streamed in from the paddocks, the warm breeze ruffling the curtains.

He watched as she stretched canvas on to the frames Woody had made in the carpentry shed and felt the weight of his disappointment. She didn't need him. Probably wouldn't even notice he was gone. She had all she wanted.

With a sigh, he turned away and crossed the yard to the utility. The ten-gallon water and petrol cans were in the back, the spare wheels and tools firmly lashed to the flat bed. He threw his bag on the passenger seat and climbed in. There was a long journey ahead of him, but he couldn't help feeling he might have been easier about going if he could have had one last glimpse of those beautiful eyes.

He cursed softly as he turned the key in the ignition. He was being a fool and it was time he put some miles between himself and Churinga.

As the utility rattled over the stony ground, he forced himself to concentrate. One false move and he would be over-turned. The lonely road to Bourke was no place to break down. From Bourke he would travel north to Charleville in the heart of the dry Mulga country, catch a plane to Maryborough and fly north to Cairns where he'd arranged a lift on a Cessna out to the cane fields where Davey would meet him.

He hated flying, especially in little planes, and would have preferred to drive all the way, but with over one and a half thousand miles to travel, he needed to save time. It was unusual for Davey to write at all, and his letter about John was a shocking first. He had been ill before and it had gone unmentioned during their brief and infrequent phone calls. Brett had only found out on his occasional visits up north. But this time it sounded serious and the thought of being too late to do anything was urging him to take risks he would never have contemplated in normal circumstances. Yet he forced himself to calm down and take things easy. He'd be no good to either of his brothers if he ended up in a wreck.

Mile followed jolting mile. Day turned to night and he slept fitfully, anxious to resume his journey at first light. Churinga seemed a world away, but the lonely hours spent behind the wheel meant that although his brother John was always on his mind, he couldn't quite rid himself of thoughts of Jenny. Of how the light caught the copper in her hair. Of how she moved. Of the long limbs and slender body that had baked in the sun that day they'd gone swimming. He berated himself for the fool she was making of him. Tried to put her out of his mind and concentrate on the reason for his journey. But as the miles between them grew, she remained firmly in his head and he wondered how she was doing on her own and if she was thinking of him.

He finally stepped off the light aircraft that had brought him to this backwater in the cane fields. His senses were immediately assaulted by the all-too-familiar stink of molasses, taking him swiftly back to his childhood and provoking memories he'd thought long dead. It was cloying and all-pervasive, lingering on the humidity in a smothering blanket. Within seconds of stepping off the plane he was drenched, his shirt clinging to his back.

'How's it goin', mate? Good to see you.' John was wearing the cane country uniform of khaki shorts, boots and a singlet. His skin was the colour of old parchment, his wasted arms and legs covered in scars.

Brett stared at the man before him. They hadn't seen one another for three years and as they shook hands he tried to disguise his shock and assimilate this grey-haired, stooped old man with the muscular giant he remembered. Davey was right to be worried. The cane was killing his older brother just as it had killed their father.

'What the hell are you doing here, John? I thought Davey was going to meet me?'

'He's tying up a deal for next season,' John replied. 'And I've had enough of lying about like a bludger all bloody day. Fresh air'll do me good.'

Brett glowered. 'Nothing fresh about this, mate. Just liquid sugar.'

John grinned, the sharp contours of his skull clearly visible through the papery skin. 'Looks like New South Wales agrees with you. You got it soft down there, you bludger. Looking after a bunch of woollies ain't what I'd call man's work. You ain't even got grey hair,' he added ruefully as he slicked back the thin remains of his own.

Brett tried to make light of it, but inside he was aching for his brother. 'Fair go, John. You're an old bloke now – over forty.' He slapped his brother's back to take the sting out of his words and felt him wince before he pulled away.

Brett eyed him closely. 'Just how crook are you, John? Give it to me straight.'

'I'll be right,' he mumbled as he led the way to the truck. 'Just a touch of Weils. Once you got it, you always got it. You know that.'

Brett climbed into the truck and watched his brother turn the ignition and head through the cane fields. Weils disease explained the yellow of John's skin and the stewed fruit complexion. It also explained the wasted arms and legs, the premature aging and painful joints. 'Davey said you went down with this last attack a month ago. And by the looks of it you should be in bed.'

John lit a cigarette, and after a hacking coughing fit, left it to dangle from his bottom lip. 'Nah. She'll be right. Just need a couple of weeks off the cane.' He kept his eyes on the winding dirt track that led right into the heart of the cane. 'Was real crook when Davey wrote. But like I told him, I always get better.'

Brett felt impatience rise. Hadn't John learned anything from Dad?

His brother seemed unaware of his concern and swung the utility with cavalier recklessness around the potholes. 'Picked a good time to visit, Brett. Season's over and Davey reckons we can get work in the refinery to see us through. But that won't be for a coupl'a weeks.'

'I heard things are changing up here. What you going to do next season if the farmers are bringing in the machines?'

'Ah, she'll be right. Machines cost money and Davey's cutting a bonzer quota, almost as much as me when I were his age. He's up there with the Greek at the top of the cutter's league so I reckon we'll be working for a few more years yet. Soon have our own place. Seen a bonzer property out near Mossman. Owner's retiring, and he's willing to take a cut in the price.'

Brett eyed his brother and saw the false optimism shine in those fevered eyes. He was forty-five and looked sixty. Why did he and Davey live like this when life could be so much healthier for them in the dry heat of New South Wales? What was the attraction of rat-infested cane, the day to day slog in this draining humidity, and the dubious honour of being the fastest cutter in the league? And as for the idea of having their own place – it was just a pipe dream. They'd been talking about it for years and could probably afford the place at Mossman three times over by now. But they would never settle down. Cane and the cutter's way of life had got into their blood.

Brett sighed. He would have to try and persuade John to come back with him. There were plenty of jobs he could do around Churinga. Jobs that would give his body a chance to recover. For if John stayed here, there wouldn't be many more seasons left to him.

Brett turned and looked out at the cane fields of burnt stubble which spread as far as the eye could see to either side of the ribbon of road. He wished he hadn't come. John didn't need him, wouldn't listen to any of his advice. He no longer belonged here, hadn't in a long while. Brett stripped off his shirt and wiped away the sweat. The humidity was sapping his strength at every passing mile, and he thought longingly of Churinga's green pastures and shady wilga trees. And of Jenny.

He stared out at the burnt fields but didn't see them in the blinding flash of realisation. He loved Jenny. Missed her, needed to be with her. What the hell was he doing here when she was alone at Churinga and probably making up her mind to return to Sydney? The look on her face when he'd told her he was leaving for a month had been enough to make him realise she could never settle beyond the black stump. It was too lonely, too isolated for such an intelligent, attractive woman. She would sell up, move on, and he'd be left with nothing. No home, no work, no woman.

He almost turned to John and demanded they go back to the airfield – but reason took over, keeping him silent. Regardless of his fears over Jenny, John had to be his first priority. There had to be some way of persuading him to leave the cane, if only for a break. He would achieve nothing by returning home so soon.

'Deep in thought there, Brett. Problems?' John had one hand on the wheel, the other hanging out of the window.

'Nothing I can't handle,' he said shortly.

John chuckled as he swung the truck into the parking bay of a ramshackle building that called itself a hotel. 'Oh, you mean a woman?' He switched off the engine and turned to face his younger brother. 'Love 'em and leave 'em, bruv. They tie a man down, make demands on his time and his money. You take my advice, mate, travel alone. It's quicker.'

'Not as simple as that,' Brett mumbled, reaching for his bag. John had always had little regard for women, and his attitude was already beginning to grate.

'I'd have thought you learned your lesson with that wife of yours. What was her name? Merna? Martha?'

'Marlene,' Brett said flatly. 'This one's different.'

John hawled phlegm and spat. 'All cats are black in the dark, Brett. Take it from one who knows.'

'One night stands don't interest me. I want a wife, children, a place of my own.'

John eyed him scornfully. 'You tried that before. It didn't work. Reckon you'd be better off with that barmaid you mentioned last time we spoke. Seems a willing sort, and you wouldn't have to marry her.'

'Lorraine's good company, but that's as far as it goes.' He thought of her and of the way she'd been angling for more than friendship. He'd been stupid not to put a stop to it.

227

Arrogant in thinking he could have things as he wanted them without committing himself. Of course she'd wanted more from him. More than he'd been willing to give. 'You're wrong about the marriage part, John. I reckon she sees me as a meal ticket out of Wallaby Flats.'

His brother grimaced. 'Could be right, mate. Most women want something from a bloke. Now come on, I need a beer.' He winced as he shoved open the door and climbed out. His face was grey with pain and dewed with sweat.

Brett knew better than to offer to help, so he followed the shambling figure across the parking lot and up the steps to the front door. It was all very well for John to spout his dubious wisdom, he thought. His life was already tied to the cane, which was far more demanding than any woman. Only he would never see it like that so there was no point in arguing.

The hotel was perched on stilts halfway up a hill. Surrounded by tropical trees and bright creeping flowers and vines, its verandahs and open windows caught the slightest of breezes. The air was less humid, up here in the hills, but the smell of the molasses was still strong as it wafted up from the refinery chimneys in the valley.

Brett followed his brother along the cracked linoleum in the dim passageway to the uncarpeted stairs. John threw open the door of his room and collapsed on the old iron bed. 'Beers are in the fridge,' he said wearily.

Brett grimaced as he took in the room he'd be sharing with his brothers. Even the jackaroos on Churinga had better accommodation than this. There were three beds, a side table, no curtains, no carpet, bare light bulb. The paint was peeling, mould grew in the corners, dust lay inches thick on everything, and the bedding looked as if it hadn't been washed for months. A ceiling fan squeaked listlessly and the fly papers obviously hadn't been renewed for weeks. He dropped his bag on the nearest bed and opened the fridge. The sooner he could persuade John out of this hell hole, the sooner he could take the plane back to Maryborough.

The beer was ice cold, burning his mouth and throat, freezing his taste buds, sending a jolt of pain into his head as he swallowed. But nothing had ever quenched his thirst so well, or brought relief from this torpid heat so instantly. He drained the bottle, dumped it into the overflowing garbage can and uncapped another. Stripped to his shorts, boots and socks kicked to the floor, he collapsed on the bed. As fast as the beer cooled him, he sweated it out. He was exhausted.

'Why the hell do you live like this, John, when you know it's killing you?' Brett was deliberately blunt, because diplomacy was a foreign language to John.

His brother lay supine on the grubby mattress, his thin arms beneath his head. ''Cos it's the only life I know and I'm good at it.' He rolled painfully on to his side, his parchment pale face animated, high spots of colour on his sharp cheekbones. 'There's nothing can beat the feeling of knowing you're king of the cane. I can still cut with the fastest of them, and although I'm a bit skinny at the moment, I ain't beat. A couple more weeks and I'll be right. We all get crook, it's part of the life. But there ain't nothing like living with a bunch of cobbers, working your bollocks off and seeing the money build up in the bank.'

'What's the point of all that money if you aren't gonna use it? You been talking about owning your own place for years. Why don't you get out while you can, buy your own place, retire and let some other mug do the work?'

John sank back into the pillows. 'Nah. Place I want will take all Davey and I got, and more. Should be about there in a coupla years.'

'Bullshit! You sound just like Dad. There won't be a place for you and Davey, John, and you know it. Just another bunkhouse, another rundown hotel, until you get too old and sick to work. All that money you've been saving will be eaten up with hospital bills.'

John seemed untouched by his younger brother's outburst. 'Remember me telling you about that place at Mossman? Real nice it is, with a house and everything. I reckon me and Davey'd be just fine there if we could get the bucks together.'

'How much do you need? I'll stake you the shortfall if it means getting you out of the fields.'

'Thanks for the offer, but me and Davey can manage without your handouts.' John finished his beer and reached for another.

Brett noticed how his hand shook, and the painful way he

229

swallowed. This was a very sick man, and although he probably had more money tucked away than Brett could imagine, his stupid pride would never let him leave the fields until he dropped down dead. The offer of part of Brett's own savings would have meant his dream of a sheep station would never be fulfilled – but it would have been worth it to see John well and strong again.

He eyed his brother for a long moment. The years between them and the great distance of their separate lives had made them strangers. If someone had asked, Brett couldn't have told them what John felt about anything other than the cane. His life was a mystery, neither of them understanding the pull of the other's different ambitions, neither acknowledging their mutual estrangement. His reason for coming this year was obvious. But why had he come all those other years? The ties of blood were tenuous – almost at breaking point – and yet something drew him back to the roots he despised. Something intangible and ultimately frustrating.

His thoughts were shattered by the crash of the door and before he could escape he was almost flattened by Davey. Laughing and choking, Brett tried to fight him off but his brother had a stranglehold on him that was unbreakable.

'Okay, okay,' he yelled. 'I give in. For Christ's sake, let go of me, you wowser.'

Davey disentangled himself and pulled Brett to his feet and into a bear hug. 'How are ya, mate? Jeez, it's good to see you. This miserable old bludger won't wrestle, just lays around all day feeling sorry for hisself.'

Brett grinned. Nothing about Davey ever changed but his size. Taller by two inches, his shoulders and chest broader than ever, his arms were muscled, his skin tanned. At least the cane hadn't begun to wither him.

Brett's own wiry strength was no match and only the promise of beer brought an end to the friendly tussle. 'Look a bit crook there, Davey,' he teased.

'Bugger off.' his brother grinned. 'Bet I'm stonger than you.'

Brett had only just caught his breath from the last bout of wrestling. He held up his hands. 'Too hot for all that. I believe you. Have another beer.'

Davey drained the second bottle and reached for a third before collapsing on the end of Brett's bed. 'So. What's life like out in the Never Never where men are men and the sheep are nervous?'

Brett raised his eyes to the ceiling. It was an old joke. 'Might have to leave Churinga soon. New owner's turned up,' he said nonchalantly.

Davey eyed him over the lip of the beer bottle. 'Tough going, mate,' he said finally. 'This mean you'll be coming home?'

'Not bloody likely! Cane's not for me. Never has been. Reckon I'll have to find another station, that's all.' Now Brett's thoughts were out in the open they were more painful than ever but he knew better than to whinge to his brothers.

John plumped the damp pillows and dragged himself up the bed. Sweat beaded his skin and Brett could hear the rattle in his lungs as he fought for breath. 'What's yer new boss like? Mean bastard, is he?'

Brett shook his head, reluctant to discuss Jenny. 'It's a woman,' he said flatly. Then rapidly changed the subject. 'How about another beer? I've sweated the last few out,' he finished in a rush.

Davey's eyes were round with shock, but it was John who grimaced and voiced their opinion. 'Strewth! No wonder you want to leave, with a bloody woman in charge. Tough luck, cobber. Have another beer. We're wasting good drinking time talking.'

Brett took the beer, thankful that neither of his brothers wanted to know more and yet disappointed they weren't even interested in his problems.

John seemed to be pulling through. Hanging on to life with grim determination against all the odds. And yet Brett knew this could be the last time he would see him. His coming here had been a mistake – he'd achieved nothing – and John would just go on until he dropped. Yet the cutters knew how to have a good time, admitted Brett after ten days of solid drinking and carousing. The bagpipes had howled far into the night for the dancing, the beer had flowed in gallons, the fights had been legendary and his hangover seemed to have taken up

231

permanent residence behind his eyes.

He rolled out of bed on that last day, looked at himself in the fly-blown mirror and grimaced. The diagnosis was worse than he'd thought. It even hurt to shave and comb his hair.

After a breakfast of stewed tea, fatty bacon and over-fried eggs, he climbed into the truck with his brothers. 'Ready?' Davey's expression was serious for once, making him look older, more careworn.

Brett nodded. This pilgrimage was probably the real reason for his visit – the only tie that truly bound him to this place.

The little wooden church nestled in a deep, green valley where palm trees provided umbrella shade from the blistering sun and the lush rainforest crept right up to the clapboard walls. The garden of rest was a carefully tended oasis against the backdrop of riotous wilderness, the marble headstones and crude crosses glimmering in the sun, lined in regimental order over several acres. This was how the cane repaid those who worked it.

Brett knelt by the twin slabs of marble and placed the bunch of flowers they'd brought in the stone urn. Then he joined his brothers and stood in silence as each of them remembered their parents.

His own thoughts returned to his mother. She'd been small and slim, but with a steely inner strength that he now understood had been born of necessity. She'd been a kind and loving mum, despite the poverty and daily grind to make ends meet, and he still missed her, still wished he could talk to her. She was the rock on which their family had been built and now she was gone, that foundation had crumbled.

He looked at his father's headstone. The cane had taken him, just as it had so many of those buried here – just as it would John and Davey if they didn't leave. Dad had been a stranger during their childhood. A man who, most of the time, remembered to send a money order. He'd followed the cutters up north and lived in barracks and flop houses, preferring the company of his cobbers to that of his wife and children. To his older sons he'd been a hero. But to Brett and Gil, he'd remained an enigma.

Brett's memory of him as a young man was vague, but seeing Davey again was a reminder of the strong, boisterous presence that had punctuated their lives. Yet his only true memory was of a wizened old man gasping for breath between sweat-soaked sheets, and the deathly hush in the house as they waited for him to die.

It was only in maturity that Brett had come to understand the strong bond between his parents. The cane was all his father knew and his mother had accepted that because she loved him. Together they had forged a kind of living in the humid hell of the north to raise their kids as well as they could. After Dad had died, Mum just seemed to give up. It was as if she'd lost the will to fight on without him. Her boys no longer needed her, now she could finally rest.

Brett turned away and walked out of the churchyard. It was time to leave the north. The mountains were shutting out the sky, the rainforests closing in, the heat too stifling to endure. He yearned for wide open spaces and the dust of a mob of sheep, wilga trees and ghost gums against pale green grass. Churinga – and Jenny.

Back at the hotel, he threw his clothes into his bag and ordered a taxi. John had insisted upon going to the refinery with Davey today, despite his hacking cough and poor condition, and Brett knew there was nothing he could do to stop him.

'Time I was gone,' Brett said to John as he drew him into an awkward embrace. He saw the grimace of pain, heard the sharp intake of breath and the rattle in his lungs. 'Go see a quack. Spend some of that damn money on proper medicine. And take a break,' he said gruffly.

John pulled away. 'I ain't no bludger,' he growled. 'Won't catch me pullin' a sickie just 'cos I got a bit of a cough.'

Davey gave Brett a bear hug then began to throw his belongings into a bluey which he slung over his shoulder. 'I'll watch out for the old bastard, no worries, Brett. You can give us a lift down. The ute's about had it and we won't need it for a while.'

The three of them rode in the taxi in silence. They had nothing to say to one another beyond small talk, and it was too hot to bother. The only tie they still had was one of blood, and Brett realised with overwhelming sadness that it was no longer enough.

He watched his brothers walk away, heading for the tall chimney stacks and red brick of the refinery, and knew he would probably never see them again. There was nothing here for him any more. He was glad to be leaving.

Arriving back at Charleville, he climbed into the utility and headed south. The air was light, hot and dry, with just a hint of winter sharpness to give it a refreshing edge. It didn't swamp a man's lungs in water and drain his body of vitality, but let him breathe. He took great gulps of it as he surveyed the familiar soft colours and contours of the south's endless grazing. It stretched in every direction – silver grass, white bark, green eucalyptus – soft colours after the citrus glare of the northern tropics, colours a man could live with.

He hadn't planned on visiting Gil, but after the depressing visit with John and Davey, he needed to see him, to catch his breath and put things into perspective. For if Churinga was to be sold, then he would have to start thinking about finding a new job or even a place of his own. And Gil had always been easy to talk to. He understood the same things, had a similar outlook on life.

Gil's place was about a hundred miles south-west of Charleville, deep in the dry Mulga country where sheep and cattle outnumbered the human population by thousands. The homestead was a gracious old Queenslander, with deeply shaded verandahs and intricate iron lacework decorating the railings. Stands of pepper trees gave shelter to the home paddocks, and the garden was a riot of colour as he drove up the long driveway.

'Where'd you spring from, Brett? Jeez, it's good to see you.'

Brett climbed out of the truck and hugged his brother. There was barely a year between them, and most people took them for twins. 'Good to see you too, mate,' he said, then grinned. 'Been up north to see John and Davey, and thought I'd look you up. But if I'm in the way, I can always get back in the ute and go home.'

'Not on your flamin' life, mate. Gracie would never forgive me if I let you shoot through.'

They climbed the steps on to the porch just as the screen door was slammed back and Grace hurled herself into Brett's arms. She was tall and dark, as wiry and slim as a boy despite the three kids she'd had, and Brett loved her like a sister.

She released him eventually and stood back to look at him. 'Still as handsome as ever. I'm surprised some girl hasn't snapped you up.'

He and Gil exchanged knowing looks. 'I see things don't change around here,' Brett muttered wryly.

Grace gave him a playful slap. 'Time you settled down, Brett Wilson, and gave my kids some cousins to visit. Surely there must be someone you like the look of down there?'

He shrugged, furious with the colour that surely must show in his face. 'How's about a beer for a bloke, Gracie? Mouth's as dry as a claypan.'

She shot him a look that told him she wouldn't be deflected from her mission in life, and went to fetch them a drink.

'Where's the kids?'

'Out with Will Starkey. Mob's gone to winter pastures and the kids are old enough to sleep out. Should be back tomorrow.'

Brett smiled as he thought of the two boys and their sister. 'Can't imagine those larrikins keeping a mob under control.'

'You'd be surprised. They ride as well as me, and I reckon all three of them will stay on the land when schooling's over.' He shot Brett a look. 'They've got that special feel for it. Like you and me.'

Grace came back with the beers and a plate of sandwiches to see them through until tea time, and the three of them relaxed in the comfortable chairs on the verandah and gazed out over the pastures. They talked of John and Davey, of the cane, and Brett's visit to the cemetery. Gil discussed the price of wool, the lack of rain, and the breeding of stock horses which was his latest venture. Gracie tried to persuade Brett to meet a couple of her unattached girlfriends during his stay, but eventually gave up when he threatened to leave.

She eyed him thoughtfully. 'Something's on your mind, Brett – and I get the feeling it has nothing to do with John and Davey.' She rested her arms on her knees as she leaned towards him. 'What's the matter, sunshine? Trouble on Churinga?'

Damn Gracie, he thought furiously. Blasted woman didn't

miss a trick. He took a long pull of his beer to gain time, but her direct gaze never faltered. 'Churinga's been sold,' he said finally.

'Jeez, that's a bummer,' she gasped. 'But you'll still have your job, won't you?'

He looked deep into his glass before draining it. 'I don't know. New owner's from Sydney and it's touch and go whether she stays.'

'She?' Gracie's eyes lit up, and she leaned back in the chair and folded her arms. 'So now we get to the nitty-gritty,' she said triumphantly. 'I knew something was up the minute you arrived.'

'Leave it, Gracie,' muttered Gil. 'Let the bloke get a word in edgewise.'

Brett was filled with restless energy. He stood up and began to pace the verandah as he told them about Jenny. When he'd finished he came to a halt, hands jammed in his pockets. 'So, you see, my time at Churinga could be over, and I have to think about what to do next. It's part of the reason for my visit.'

Gracie laughed until the tears ran down her face and the two brothers looked at one another and shrugged. No point in even trying to understand how a woman's mind worked.

She finally spluttered to a halt and eyed them with pity. 'Men,' she said in exasperation. 'Honestly. You have no idea, have you?' She looked at Brett. 'Sounds to me like you're in love with this young widow, so why the drama? Tell her, you galah! See what she has to say before you go steaming off in a panic.' She cocked her head, eyes as bright as a sparrow's. 'I reckon you could be in for a surprise.'

Brett felt his spirits rise only to plummet again as cold reality struck home. 'She's very wealthy, Grace, what on earth could she see in me?'

Grace snatched up the empty plates and glasses. There were two high spots of colour on her cheeks. 'Don't do yourself down, Brett. If she can't see what a bonzer bloke you are, then she isn't worth having.' She stood up and glared at him. 'You've waited a long time for the right woman to come along. Don't blow it. This could be your last chance.'

'It's not that easy,' he grumbled. 'She's rich, she's beautiful, and she's still in mourning.'

Grace balanced the plates as she tucked her boot under the screen door to open it. 'I didn't tell you to go stomping in with both feet,' she said with a sigh. 'Take your time, let her get to know you. Become her friend first, and then see how things develop.' She eyed him softly. 'If you care enough, it's worth waiting, Brett.' The screen door slammed behind her, leaving an empty silence.

'Reckon Gracie's right, mate,' said Gil thoughtfully.

Brett stared out over the home paddock, his thoughts in turmoil. 'Maybe,' he muttered. 'But if things don't work out, I'll be looking for another place.'

Gil leaned back in his chair, boots resting on the verandah railings. 'There's a nice little property coming on to the market in a few months' time. Had it straight from Fred Dawlish. He and his wife are retiring and moving up to Darwin to be with their grandkids. The place is too much for them now, and none of their sons wants to take over so they're letting it go.' He eyed his brother. 'It's just under a hundred thousand acres. Good sheep country, and the stock's top rate. Would suit you down to the ground, Brett – if you've got the money?'

He thought of the money sitting in the bank. It was less than he'd hoped after the divorce settlement but enough to cover the price Gil mentioned. Yet the thought of leaving Jenny and Churinga held him back. 'Sounds good, I'll have to think about it,' he said finally.

'You do that, and I'll have a word with Gracie. Now she smells romance, she'll be impossible.'

The two brothers grinned at one another then went off to inspect the new string of horses that had come in that morning. The hours passed and the day dwindled. Finally Brett fell asleep in the spare room surrounded by the children's discarded toys.

He stayed for a week, and it was over too soon. As he packed his things and threw the bag into the utility, he felt a stab of envy. Gil had done all right for himself. He'd found his place in the world and the right woman to share it with. The kids made it a home, filling the house with noise and vitality, bringing a purpose to the hard work of the station that would one day be their inheritance.

As he drove through the first of the fifteen gates, he turned to wave. He would miss the cheerful rumpus of the kids. Miss Gracie's cooking and enthusiasm for everything. This was the nearest thing he had to a home outside Churinga, and the thought of the empty manager's bungalow that awaited him there filled him with dread. Would Jenny be gone? Had the isolation proved too much?

He slammed into third gear and pressed his foot to the floor. He'd already wasted too much time – could already be too late – for after talking to Gracie, and thinking about the alternatives, he'd finally realised where his future lay. And he was determined not to let this chance escape him.

Driving south over the hundreds of miles between Gil's property and Churinga, his thoughts churned. Jenny was still grieving. Gracie had been right, he had to be patient, and give her time. Become her friend before he could take things further. But he knew his impatience could so easily spill over and realised that courting Jenny would be one of the hardest things he'd ever attempted. He wanted her so much it hurt but the first move would have to come from her – and he wasn't at all sure she was ready to see him as anything more than the manager of Churinga.

Brett finally drove into Wallaby Flats and skidded to a dusty halt outside the hotel. It had been less than three weeks since he'd left but it felt longer. Although he would have preferred to go straight back to Churinga there was something he had to do here first – and he wasn't looking forward to it.

Lorraine was drying glasses behind the bar as he walked in. Her bottle blonde hair looked as if a force ten gale wouldn't shift it and the thick make-up was smudged around her eyes by the heat. She let out a whoop of excitement and raced towards him. 'You should have let me know you were coming back,' she gasped as she grabbed his arm. 'Gee, Brett. It's good to see you.'

He was aware of a dozen pairs of eyes watching this little scene and could feel the heat rise in his face as he disentangled himself from her clutches. 'Can't stop long. Give us a beer, Lorraine.'

She poured it expertly into the long, chilled glass then watched him drink it down, her elbows on the bar so her low-cut blouse revealed a good deal of cleavage. 'Want another?' she purred. 'Or is there something else I can get you?'

Brett saw the promise in her eyes and shook his head. 'Just beer, Lorraine.'

Her mood seemed to change and her smile became brittle. 'So. How's life at Churinga, then? New boss coming up to scratch, is she?'

He gulped his beer, feeling the chill run down his throat and spread into his chest. 'Dunno. Been up north.' He didn't want to discuss Jenny. It wasn't his reason for being here.

She leaned over the bar, breasts billowing against the polished teak. 'I've heard about the blokes up there. The ones that cut the cane.' She gave a shiver of pleasure as she ran one painted finger nail along his arm. 'Supposed to be really something. Perhaps I should leave Wallaby Flats and go travelling?'

He pulled away from her and took his time to roll a cigarette and light it. This situation was more difficult than he'd thought. 'You're better off here, Lorraine, unless you fancy being second best to a field of cane.'

She pouted. 'What's to keep me here? A bunch of woollies and a bloke I see less than four times a year.'

He took a long pull of his beer and drained the glass. 'You and I aren't joined at the hip, Lorraine. Go travelling if that's what you want. Australia's a big place, and there's thousands of other blokes about.'

She flinched as though stung, and began furiously to wipe the wet rings off the bar. 'Reckon that puts me in my place, doesn't it?' she snapped.

'You said you wanted to travel,' he said defensively as he deliberately sidestepped the hidden agenda behind this conversation. 'I was only agreeing with you.'

Lorraine's hands stilled. Her eyes glittered and her voice was tight with suppressed spite. 'I thought I meant something to you, Brett Wilson. But you're just like all the other bastards around here.'

'Fair go, Lorraine. That's a bit strong. We were never that close, and I never promised you anything.'

She leaned closer, her voice a hiss. 'Didn't you? Then why take me to the dances and parties? Why come in here and spend hours chatting me up if you weren't interested?'

He took a step back, stung by the venom she was spilling. 'We had a good time, that's all,' he stuttered. 'Kept each other company. But I said right from the start I wasn't interested in getting involved again after Marlene.'

She slammed a glass on the bar. 'You blokes are all the flamin' same,' she yelled into his face. 'You come in here and drink yourselves stupid, talk about nothing but flamin' sheep and flamin' grass and the flamin' weather. I might as well be a piece of the flamin' furniture for all you lot care.'

A stunned silence filled the dusty room as all eyes turned towards them.

'I'm sorry, but if you feel like that then perhaps you'd be better off moving away.'

Black mascara tears rolled down her face. 'I don't want to go bloody travelling,' she snivelled. 'What I want is here. Can't you see how I feel about you?'

He felt like a dirty yellow dingo, and hung his head. 'I never realised,' he muttered. 'I'm sorry, Lorraine, but you got me wrong. I thought you understood.' He couldn't look her in the face, he was too ashamed.

'You bastard,' she hissed. 'It's that hoity-toity Mrs Sanders you're after, isn't it? Get her into yer bed, and you got Churinga. Well, you'll get yours, mate. You'll see. She'll go back to the city where she belongs and you'll be out on yer flamin' ear. But don't expect me to be waiting for you – I'll be long gone.'

'What the flaming hell is going on in here?' Lorraine's father still retained thick traces of a Russian accent that mingled strangely with his Aussie twang.

Brett looked at Nicolai Kominski and shook his head, relieved at the interruption. 'No worries, Nick. Lorraine's just letting off a bit of steam. She'll be right.'

The full glass of beer hit him in the face and drenched his shirt. 'Don't patronise me, you bastard!' she yelled.

Nick grasped his daughter's hand. He was shorter by several inches, and whip thin, but he seemed to have the measure of her. 'I flaming told you, girl. This man not interested. I find good Russian boy. You settle down. Have kids.'

Lorraine shook him off. 'I don't want some flamin'

immigrant. This isn't flamin' Moscow.' She left the bar, heels licking like castanets on the floorboards.

Nickolia shrugged and poured himself a vodka which he sank in one. 'Women,' he sighed. 'That girl cause trouble ever since her mama die.'

Despite the soaking, Brett couldn't help but grin. 'She fair let rip, Nick, and no mistake. I'm real sorry she's upset but I never . . .'

Nickolia waved away his apology and poured him a shot of vodka. 'I know, I know. You fine man, Brett, but not for my Lorraine. I get Russian boy for her, shut her up good.'

He laughed and slapped the bar with a bony hand. 'Women don't know what is good for them until a man tells them. I see to Lorraine. No worrying.'

Brett took the shot in one, then finished his beer and reached for his hat. He had no wish to get into a long drinking session with Nick; he'd done it before and ended up with a sore head that lasted for days. And his system was already overloaded after the sessions with John and Davey.

'See you at the races, mate.' He left the hotel and climbed into the ute. The episode in the bar had disturbed him. He was sorry he'd hurt Lorraine but had had no idea she'd felt so strongly. Hindsight told him he'd been playing with fire and had just been too bloody dumb to notice.

# Chapter Thirteen

Jenny and Ripper had fallen into an easy routine once Brett and the others had gone and in the peace and solitude of an autumnal Churinga she felt the healing begin. She had needed this space and time to find the inner calm that had been missing for too long. To evaluate her life and the tragedy which would always be with her, and deal with the anger. She found she could examine that rage now, distance herself from it, understand it was a necessary part of her healing and then put it away. Memories of Peter and Ben would remain throughout her life. although this was still painful, she'd come to realise it was time to let them go.

The days followed a seamless rhythm, melting one into another with a soothing influence that brought her inner strength with which to face the future. The mornings were spent tramping the fields or riding out to the winter pastures to capture the sights and sounds of the men and the great white flock. The stock horses were mean-mouthed and half wild, the men who rode them just as tough and unforgiving. Here was rugged colour set against pale grass and blue mountain, and as her pencil flew over the paper, Jenny tried to capture the movement and strength in the scenes.

Ripper trotted along beside her. When he was tired, she would put him in the saddle-bag where he sat grinning with pleasure as the cooling breeze flapped his ears. In the heat of the afternoon, they would find a cool spot on the verandah and Jenny would put the morning's work on canvas. She worked with a speed and skill she'd never known before – as if there was a time limit on what she was doing, an inner force that urged her not to waste a second.

With autumn slowly creeping towards winter, the early-morning dew sparkled in the grass and the nights became cold enough to light the cooking range and snuggle in a chair in front of it. Ripper snuffling at her feet, Jenny once more immersed herself in Matilda's world.

This was the largest diary, covering the greatest number of years. The writing was more forceful than in the previous books, the sentences shorter, as if Matilda had had little time to record the events of that busy time.

1930 brought the Depression into the outback. It had swept through the cities, leaving women and children to fend for themselves and collect the dole as their men went tramping. These itinerant swaggies humped their blueys from one station to another in search of food and employment. They were a ragged army of nomads, searching for something that existed only in their minds. There was a restlessness about them which drove them into the unknown, and they never stayed in one place for very long. It was as if the purity and vast loneliness of the land beyond the Black Stump encouraged them to drift and it beat sleeping in the Sydney Domain.

Matilda buried her money beneath the floorboards and kept a loaded rifle by the door. Although the majority of the swaggies were harmless, it wasn't worth taking the risk. There were rich pickings around Wallaby Flats, especially after word got out of an opal find in a long disused mine, and as the recession deepened it brought the bad men from the cities. Men who looked at her with eyes like Mervyn's. Men who wanted more than a hot meal and a bed in a barn.

But the women who accompanied their men Matilda admired and could empathise with. As tough as the land they traversed, this new generation of Sundowner meandered across the outback in wagons that clanked with pots and pans and billy cans. Like Peg some of them were cheerful, others sour – and yet she could understand why they hid the sorrows their lonely lives brought them. She knew that somewhere in the vast Never Never was a special tree or stone that marked the burial place of a child, a husband or a friend. These places might seem unimportant to others but their significance would forever be carried in these stoic hearts.

The men helped with the chores in return for flour and

sugar and a few shillings. And as food was cheap, Matilda always made sure they left Churinga with full bellies. When they left, they were replaced by another man, another wagon, another family.

Matilda knew what it was to fight for survival. Thanks to Tom, who still let her share his shed, the wool cheques enabled her to restock with good breeding rams and ewes, and to hire a couple of drovers. These men were generally easy to come by but finding the ones who would work for a woman was more difficult. The bushmen had their own set way of thinking, which did not include woman bosses, and yet this taciturn attitude soon turned to respect when they stayed long enough to discover that Matilda asked no more of them than she was prepared and able to do herself. She took on Mike Preston and Wally Peebles who'd come down from Mulga country where their boss had gone bankrupt, and was glad of their company with so many drifters coming on to the property.

Ethan Squires was proving a wily adversary. Although he never came to Churinga again she could feel his malignant influence on her land. Fences were dismantled so her mob wandered into his pastures, their markings obliterated by the green dye of the Kurrajong pine tree. Lambs were snatched as the ewes dropped them and one of her rams found with its throat too neatly cut to have been the victim of a boar or dingo. Yet she and her drovers had no proof against Squires. Despite the endless patrolling of her fields and the long nights spent sleeping rough it was impossible to cover every acre, and he always seemed to know where Matilda was most vulnerable.

It was winter, the air frosty enough to cloud her breath as she lay silently beside Lady in the dry gully that traversed the far corner of the southern pasture. The others were patrolling nearby fields where the breeding programme was in full swing. She'd opted for the more isolated corner of Churinga. It was quiet in the darkness, the thin blanket poor insulation against the chill. Even the sheep huddled together in miserable silence.

The sound that jarred her from a light sleep was soft, stealthy and very close. Too sly to be a wild pig, but careful enough for a dingo. Matilda eased back the firing pin and crouched in the shadows. Her night vision was good and she soon spotted the moving figures near her fence. These hunters came on two legs, and their purpose was obvious.

She moved silently down the gully, keeping low and in the shadows until she was behind them. Bluey followed her, teeth bared, hackles rising. There was tension in his stance, a pent-up readiness to spring in his powerful shoulders, but he seemed to understand the need for silence and waited for her signal to attack.

The three men began to cut through the smooth wire and dismantle the fence posts. The sheep shifted uneasily. Dogs whined. Matilda waited.

'Keep those bloody dogs quiet,' hissed a familiar voice.

The coldness that ran through her had nothing to do with the chill of winter but was akin to hatred. Billy, the runt of the Squires litter, was doing his father's dirty work.

'I wish I could see her face when she finds half her mob gone!'

'You bloody will if we don't get a move on,' rasped Squires' stockman. 'Get those dogs working. Now!'

Matilda waited until her mob was almost gathered then stood up, rifle poised, fifteen-year-old Billy Squires in her sights. 'That's far enough. One more move and I shoot.'

Bluey's growl accompanied her threat, but still he waited for her signal.

The three men froze but their dogs kept working the sheep nearer and nearer to the gap in the fence.

Her shots thudded into the ground at Billy's feet, kicking up dust and making him jump. The sheep took fright as she knew they would and scattered to every corner of the field. She pumped two more cartridges into the barrel and held the stock firm. 'Call off the dogs and get off my land,' she yelled.

Blue's belly scraped the earth as he sidled towards another Queensland Blue – a brute of a dog, the leader of the pack, with long fangs and a nasty snarl. Still the three men hesitated.

'You ain't gonna shoot that thing, Matilda. You wouldn't bloody dare.' Billy didn't sound as confident as his words.

'Try me,' she replied grimly. Her finger squeezed the

trigger, the boy clear in her sights.

The men muttered uneasily but it was Billy who first broke away and headed for Kurrajong land on the other side of the fence.

The two dogs were at stand off. Drooling, wild-eyed and with hackles high, they circled each other on stiff legs. 'Call it off or I'll kill it,' she warned.

The sharp whistle was almost lost in the thunder of approaching hooves. Matilda didn't have to take her eye off Billy to know Wally and Mike had heard her shots. 'Round 'em up, boys. They've got a fence to mend and sheep to catch.'

The men from Kurrajong ran for their horses, but they were no match for a stock whip, a lasso and a very angry dog. Matilda climbed on to Lady's back and joined Mike and Wally whose rifles were covering the working men. Once satisfied her fences were back in place, she turned to Mike. 'Tie them up. It's time Billy boy went home to Daddy.'

Mike grinned as he helped to round up the horses and truss the squirming, furious men over their saddles. With Bluey snapping at their dangling feet and hands, they began the long trek to Kurrajong homestead.

The sun had almost set on another day as they passed through the final pasture and saw Kurrajong sprawled before them. There were lights glimmering from every window of that elegant stone house, spilling over the formal gardens that swept down to the river, highlighting the deep shadows in the trees and surrounding barns.

Matilda hauled in the reins and all three of them stopped to stare at the majestic sight. Known as one of the richest stations in New South Wales, it had nevertheless come as a shock to see it for the first time. She gaped at the two-storey house with its fine balconies and intricate iron lacework. Sighed when she saw the lush lawn and the sweep of rose bushes and weeping willows. How beautiful it all was.

Then her gaze fell on Billy and her admiration drained away. Squires already had more than enough. How dare he encourage his youngest son to steal? She took the reins more firmly and kicked Lady forward. It was time to give that bastard a piece of her mind.

With the others following closely behind they made a strange procession down the immaculate driveway, but Matilda's anger was far too great for such grandeur to distract her. With a signal to the others to stay put, she climbed off Lady and marched up the steps to hammer on the front door.

Squires emerged, filling the frame, almost blotting out the light which streamed from the hall behind him. He was obviously startled to see her.

Matilda caught a glimpse of rich carpets and crystal chandeliers – and she wasn't impressed. 'I caught Billy stealing my mob,' she said coldly.

His jaw dropped as he saw the three helpless bundles thrown across the saddles. Then hardened as he noticed Mike and Wally's rifles pointed at his youngest son. His glacial stare returned to Matilda. 'They must have wandered on to your land by mistake,' he said with icy contempt.

'Bullshit!' she spat. 'I saw them taking down my fences. They even had their dogs with them.' She swept her arm towards the pack that snapped and snarled at one another between the horses' legs.

Squires' expression was inscrutable, but his eyes were emotionless as they looked down at her. 'Do you have proof of your accusations, Matilda? Perhaps you'd show me the damaged fence, and I'd be delighted to help you find your strays.'

She thought of the repaired fence and the scattering of her mob into their own pasture. How easily Squires had broken through her defences. How quick-thinking and clever he was. No wonder he was so rich and powerful. 'I have two witnesses. That's proof enough for me,' she said stubbornly.

'Not for me, Matilda.' He stepped on to the verandah, pushing past her as if she was nothing. 'I suggest you and your men leave Kurrajong before I have you all arrested for trespass and common assault.'

His arrogance astounded her. 'If I catch you or anyone else from Kurrajong on my property again, I'll take them straight to Broken Hill. It's about time the law knew what you're up to, Squires.'

He appeared to relax and took his time over lighting a cheroot. When he'd taken a puff, he drew it from his mouth and gave it close inspection. 'I don't think you'll find the police much help, Matilda. What I do is none of their business – and they are well paid to leave me alone.' He looked down at her, his smile vulpine. 'It's what real business is all about, Matilda. You scratch my back, I scratch yours.'

'I'd like to scratch your bloody eyes out, you bastard,' she hissed. Spinning away from him, she clattered down the wooden steps and climbed on to Lady. Gathering up the reins, she wheeled the mare to face him. 'Next time I shoot on sight. Even the police will find it hard to ignore the death of one of your men on my land.'

'Go home, little girl, and take up needlepoint,' he said with deep sarcasm. 'Or better still, sell up. This is no place for women.'

He'd moved off the verandah into the shadows of the drive-way, and although the light was behind him and his features were almost invisible, she knew his eyes were granite cold.

'I'm glad I've got you rattled, Squires. It means you finally understand you'll never beat me.' She turned the mare towards the gate. It had been a bad twenty-four hours but this was probably only the beginning. War had been openly declared between them, and it was time to employ more men to guard Churinga.

April had had another boy. Joseph was three years old now, an intelligent, energetic child whom Matilda loved as if he was her own. And as she watched him and his brothers grow, she never lost the deep yearning for her own child.

'You'll wear that kid out with all those kisses,' remarked Tom one night as Matilda dressed him for bed.

'Can't give a kid too much love,' she murmured, breathing in the delicious smell of his freshly bathed and powdered skin.

Tom watched her silently for a moment then opened his newspaper. ''Bout time you had kids of your own, Molly. Plenty of blokes about if you'd only give 'em a chance.'

Matilda picked Joseph up and straddled him across her hip. 'I'm too busy keeping Churinga safe from Squires to think about anything else.'

'You're only twenty years old, Moll. I just think it's a pity no one but me and April get to see your new dresses,' he mumbled. 'That's all.'

She eyed the sprigged cotton she'd bought on her one and only visit to Broken Hill. It draped from shoulder to hip where it gathered in a broad band to fall in pleats to her knees. She had thought the new fashion very daring after the high-necked, long gowns her mother used to wear but having seen similar dresses on women at the country shows she delighted in the freedom of movement it brought. 'No point getting dressed up to herd the mob,' she retorted. 'And if I turned up at the wool auctions dressed like this, no one would take me seriously.' She left the room and helped April put the children to bed. It was almost time to switch on the radio.

This was the latest miracle to arrive in the district and nearly every homestead had one. Matilda had weighed up the cost and decided she needed new stock horses more, but whenever she visited Wilga she barely moved away from it.

It was an ugly great thing, taking up most of the corner by the fireplace. But it was a link with the outside world and Matilda never quite got over the magic of being able to know there was a flood in Queensland, a drought in Western Australia or a glut of cane in the north. For the first time in her life she was able to explore the world outside Churinga, but she had no yearning to leave. The cities were dangerous places, she'd seen what they'd done to the men and women who'd been forced to drift far from their homes.

April had picked up her darning from the inevitable pile at her side and Tom was contentedly smoking his pipe as they waited for the radio to warm up. 'You should have babies of your own, Molly. And a man to look after you. You're so good with my lot.'

She stared at April then across to Tom. 'I've already had this conversation. Your babies are enough for me – what do I need a man for?'

'To keep you company,' April replied softly. 'To watch out for you.' Her needle darted in and out of the woollen sock. 'You must get lonely, Molly, and Tom and I would feel much better knowing you had someone to protect you.'

For a moment Matilda was tempted to tell her about Mervyn and the dead baby, but it had remained a secret so long she was unable to voice it – to give colour and shape to something she preferred to keep in her heart. 'I'm happy as I am, April. I tried going to a party once but I didn't fit in. Better to keep my own company and get on with things at Churinga.'

April's gaze was very direct. 'You never said. When was this?'

Matilda shrugged. 'The end of season party at Nulla Nulla. You'd just had Joseph.'

The pale blue eyes widened in the wan face. 'You went on your own? Oh, Molly. Tom would have gone with you if you'd said.'

'He was busy,' she said flatly.

'So what happened?' The darning was put aside, and Tom lowered his newspaper.

Matilda thought of that night and shivered. 'I'd finally decided to buy myself some proper clothes, and when the invitation came thought it would be a good idea to accept for a change. I would know most people there – the men anyway, 'cos I deal with them each year at the markets and auctions. The Longhorns put me up in the manager's bungalow with some of the other single women.' She fell silent, heat rising in her face as she thought of the purgatory of sharing a small space with five other women she didn't know and with whom she'd had nothing in common.

'You hated it, didn't you, Moll?'

She nodded. 'They looked at me as if I was something a dingo had dragged in, then after a lot of questions that I thought were too personal, just ignored me.' She took a deep sigh and began to roll a cigarette. 'In a way it made it easier. I couldn't talk about the latest singing heartthrob or the newest film on at the travelling pictures. They didn't know one end of a sheep from another. So I just got on with changing into my new dress, listened to their chatter about boyfriends and make-up and tailed after them when we left for the party.'

She thought of the way she'd been left sitting on the narrow bed as they chattered and giggled and painted their faces. She'd so wanted to become part of such a lively, happy group but they didn't want her and she wasn't going to make a fool of herself by pushing in. So she'd let them leave without her, and had taken her time strolling the short distance to the barn where the dancing was to be held. It had been a beautiful night, soft and starry, the air caressing the bare skin on her arms and legs. The dress had made her feel pretty when she'd bought it, but compared to the city gowns the others were wearing, she knew it was hopelessly dated and gauche for a seventeen year old.

'Charlie Squires met me at the door and got me a drink. He was real nice and asked me to dance and everything.' Matilda smiled. She'd liked Charlie, and had been surprised at how easily they'd got on. He was only two years older than her, but so sophisticated after those years in a Melbourne boarding school that she'd wondered why he'd wanted to spend time with her when there were so many other, far more beautiful girls to dance with. Yet his heart too was in the land and as they chatted and danced she knew she'd found someone who understood her feelings for Churinga.

April's eyebrows arched. 'You and Charlie Squires? Jeez. I bet his old man had something to say about that.'

'The others weren't there so I suppose Charlie felt free to dance with me.' She looked down at the barely smoked cigarette burning away between her fingers. 'Anyway, it was only one night, and I didn't go to another party after that.'

'Why, Molly? If Charlie was interested, why didn't he ask you to the other parties?'

She looked at April and slowly shook her head. 'It wasn't Charlie put me off. In fact he was on the two-way every day for a month, and even came over to see me once or twice.' She stubbed out the cigarette. 'We were getting on real well when suddenly he just stopped calling.'

'Well, aren't you the dark horse, Moll? You never said.' Tom's eyes were steady on her face. 'What happened to make him cool off? And why didn't you go to any more parties? You'd done the hard bit – it had to be easier the next time.'

'I don't know what happened with Charlie,' she said thoughtfully. 'I'd have thought old Squires would have been jumping fair to tie a fit, knowing his son was courting me after what happened with Andrew. But nothing was said, and now when I meet him Charlie just grins, says "G'day", and turns away. It's as if he's embarrassed to see me.'

Tom frowned. 'Strange. Something must have happened to make him change his mind, Molly. After all, he was only

251

nineteen and boys of that age are too busy sowing wild oats to get tied down.'

'Possibly,' she said lightly, masking the hurt of his rejection. She'd liked Charlie, he'd made her laugh and she'd felt attractive and girlish in his company. 'But I stopped going to the parties because of the other women. I can face a wild pig or a dingo and shoot it between the eyes, but I can't do that with the gossiping, snide remarks and inverted snobbery of the wives and daughters of the other squatters.'

April's work-reddened hand covered hers. 'What happened, Moll? Were they terribly unkind?'

Matilda took a deep breath. 'I overheard them talking as I was fixing my hair in the bathroom the next morning. They laughed at my dress, at the way I walk and talk, the state of my hands and my underwear . . . But I didn't really care about that. It was what they said about me and Charlie that really did it.'

She paused as she thought about those humiliating sniggers behind the closed door of the bathroom. They'd known she was in there. Known she could hear them.

'They said Charlie was just being nice to me because old man Squires wanted my land. They said no man in his right mind would ever marry me, that I'd probably end up having a string of Abo kids because only a black man would find me attractive. They suggested things about me and Gabe, awful things, that made me burn with fury. I stormed out of there, gave them all a piece of my mind and left. But I could still hear them laughing as I collected Lady and rode back to Churinga. And the sound of it's still with me sometimes – reminding me I should keep my own company and know my place.'

'That's terrible,' Tom protested. 'Longhorn would be horrified if he knew anything about it, and so would his wife. Why didn't you say something?'

'And cause more fuss?' Matilda smiled. 'It wouldn't have made any difference, Tom. They would still keep their opinion of me, and I would still keep mine of them. I'm happy the way I am. And as for Charlie . . . It was nice to be courted for a while, but even I realised it could never come to anything because I would always wonder if Ethan had been behind it and Charlie had only done it because of Churinga.'

'It seems such a shame, Molly,' murmured April.

Matilda's laugh was light. 'I've enough problems trying to keep the bloody drovers in line without a husband hanging on to my boot straps. You have the babies and I'll love them. But I'll stick to the land and sheep instead of the social rounds. I know where I am with them.'

They fell into a comfortable silence listening to the evening news which was followed by a concert from Melbourne. Matilda's thoughts of that awful night and Charlie's subsequent snub faded into the past where they belonged. Her life was settled and she was happy enough on her own. Why wish for more?

She was humming the refrain of a particularly lovely waltz as she stepped out on to the verandah for a last cigarette before going to bed. Tom came to join her and they sat on the creaking porch chairs in companionable silence for a moment – Bluey stretched between them, his snores making a pleasant bass rhythm against the chaffing of the crickets.

'That dog of yours has been sniffing round one of my bitches and I think she's in pup. If they're good, we'll share them. What d'you say?'

'Good on yer, Bluey. Didn't know you still had it in you.' Matilda laughed. 'Flaming right you'll share, Tom Finlay! If they prove to be half the dogs old Blue is, then I can find them work.'

He became thoughtful as he rocked in his chair. 'You don't want to take too much notice of April. She just wants to see you settled, that's all. I hope we didn't upset you, making you talk about that do at Nulla Nulla? Couldn't have been easy for you, girl.'

Matilda sighed. Tom meant well but she wished he'd just leave things alone. 'I'm about as happy as I'll ever be, I reckon. I have my mates, my land and a few bob in the bank. What more could a girl ask for?'

'Rain,' was his terse reply.

She looked up at the clear star-speckled sky and nodded. It hadn't rained properly for four years, and although she hadn't overstocked, grass on Churinga was getting scarce.

*

253

As the fourth year of drought dragged into the fifth, Matilda began to see more black ink in her account books but knew that if it went on much longer that would soon change. Bluey's pups turned out beaut. Eight in all, two of them bitches. With one bitch each, she and Tom divided up the litter. They were intelligent and obedient, and soon she was able to take them with her to the paddocks and harness their inbred skills for mob herding.

She moved her sheep from pasture to pasture as the grass dwindled to dust, and finally corralled them in the home pastures where the grass remained lush from the bore. She had sold some of her stock and put the money in the bank. Sheep couldn't be forced to eat, and it was cheaper to keep her mob to a minimum than to try and feed them from expensive store-bought feed.

Everyone was hurting. Wilga, Billa Billa, even Kurrajong. The poor quality wool was being sold for the lowest price ever and Matilda wondered if this was the end of everything she'd worked for. The grass was thin, silver and whispering as she trudged the fields. The sheep were listless and drooping in the incredible heat.

Then the storms came. Dry and harsh and filled with electricity, they crackled overhead and left the squatters hot, on edge and desperate. They thickened the air with their heavy, rain-filled clouds, blackening the sky so she had to light the lamp during the day. Matilda and her drovers looked constantly to the heavens for the long hoped-for rain, but when it came it did little to soothe the parched earth. It was too lightly scattered and windblown to stay more than a few seconds.

She lay in bed, aching for sleep after another long day of moving the sheep to another pasture where the grass was only slightly better than the last. She was unbearably hot and rest-less, and Bluey lay beneath the bed quivering in terror. The sound of the electric storm filled the house, thundering over the roof and reverberating in the foundations. It was as if the world was on fire, waiting for that final whip crack of light-ning that would bring Armageddon.

She must have finally drifted into sleep for when she next opened her eyes she realised that although it was still dark outside, and the thunder was continuing to roll across the land, something was different. She leaned on one elbow and sniffed the air. The temperature had dropped several degrees and a cooler, fresh breeze drifted in from the window.

'Rain!' she yelled, leaping out of bed. 'It's going to rain.'

With Bluey tight on her heels, she raced through the house and out on to the verandah. The first heavy drops splashed on to the roof and darkened the dry earth of the firebreak. They grew in number, following swiftly one after another like a great drum roll until the deluge became a thunderous roar.

Matilda forgot she was in her nightshirt. Forgot she was barefoot. Tears mingling with the wonderful, sweet rain, she stepped off the verandah and stretched her arms to the sky. 'At last, at last,' she breathed.

Gabriel and his family crawled out of their gunyahs and stood laughing and dancing in the cold, wet downpour. Wally and Mike emerged bare-chested and sleep-tousled from their bungalow. Even from this distance, she could see their grins.

'It's raining,' she yelled unnecessarily.

'Too bloody right it is,' laughed Wally, the younger of the two, as they came to join her in the yard.

Matilda was filled with a restless energy, a longing to celebrate, and after watching Gabriel cavort with his wife in the mud, grabbed Wally by the hand and pulled him into a whirling, exhausting dance across the yard. Mike caught hold of Gabriel's young daughter and followed suit. Within seconds all of them were caked in mud and out of breath.

When they'd finally collapsed on the porch steps, they all just sat and watched the parched earth soak up the inches and inches of life-giving water. It was a miracle – and it hadn't come a day too soon.

Mike was the first to voice the concern they'd all begun to feel. 'Reckon we'd better move the mob to higher ground, Molly, before this lot takes hold. They're too near the river at the moment and if it runs a banker we'll lose the lot.'

As he gave her an appraising look, Matilda suddenly realised her cotton nightshirt was sodden and left little to the imagination. Blushing furiously, she gathered its folds. 'Let me get dressed,' she muttered. 'You see to the breakfast, Mike.'

She ran indoors and stripped off the filthy, sodden scrap of cotton. She washed quickly and scrubbed herself dry with one of the new towels she'd bought from Chalky on his last visit.

Chalky White, and his father before him, had been touring the outback for years. No one knew his real name, or age but his visits were eagerly looked forward to by the women for he always carried a collection of the latest dresses, as well as make-up and shoes, records, books, and all the things that made a house a home. He had once travelled by horse and wagon but now he drove in style in a converted fairground truck and came more than twice a year.

She eyed the new moleskins and boots, and decided against them. They would be ruined in the mud. But the long water-proof droving coat would be a godsend.

Breakfast was a hasty affair of mutton sandwiches and mugs of strong, sweet tea. Conversation was kept to a minimum as it was impossible to hear one another against the thunder of rain on the roof, but they left the house as one to saddle up the horses. Gabe was to stay behind to make sure the cows and pigs didn't drown, and to batten down the barns and hay lofts so the rain didn't spoil their precious stores.

The rain was heavy, almost bruising. Matilda tucked her chin into the collar of her waterproof and tipped her hat low over her eyes as she watched Blue and his three pups round up the sheep. The drovers' whistles were drowned by the sound of the rain punching the ground, but the animals were proving skilful and well-rehearsed.

Lady was skittish, dancing on her toes, tossing her mane, eyes rolling. Matilda took a firm grip of the reins and kicked her forward. It was going to be a long day, and tough going, but thank God for it.

Sheep hate getting wet. Newly shorn, they shivered in pathetic clumps, skittering this way and that to escape the bullying dogs and riders. But there was always something or someone there to stop them, to turn them back into the mob and press them forward. This made the exodus from the pastures slow, but it became steadier as the horizon was hidden behind a curtain of rain.

Matilda breathed in the wonderful fresh smell of soaked earth and wet scrub. An inch of rain meant nothing out here, but ten inches meant fresh grass – and grass to a squatter meant life.

They finally reached higher ground which lay to the east of Tjuringa mountain. The grass was spare but would soon flourish and there was plenty of water in the fast-flowing mountain streams. After checking the fences, they released the mob and began to make their way back.

It was three in the afternoon, but there had been no real sunrise that day. The clouds raced, black and heavy over a leaden sky, and a sharp wind blew darts of rain through the trees. The horses picked their way through the rivers and runnels of water which ran swiftly over the concrete-hard earth, their manes flicking rain, letting the water stream from necks and legs.

The long waterproof weighed on Matilda's shoulders and cold drips ran down her neck. But she didn't care. Couldn't possibly feel cold and miserable now the rain had come. Getting wet was a small price to pay for survival.

The steep-sided creek had run a banker. Where there had been only a trickle of water a few hours ago, now there was a raging torrent which swept everything before it. Matilda took a firm grip on the slick reins and urged Lady down the slope and into the water.

The old mare baulked as she slid and slewed in the mud, head tossing, eyes wild with terror as the water surged around her legs. Matilda tried to calm her and urge her forward, but the mare rolled her eyes and backed off.

Mike's black gelding was too close. As it reared up and whickered, she felt the answering shiver run through Lady. It was some minutes before both horses were under control. 'We got to cross, Molly,' shouted Mike above the deluge. 'There's no other way back – and if we don't do it now, we'll be stranded.'

'I know,' she yelled back. 'But Lady's spooked, and I don't think she'll make it.'

'It's that or wait for the rain to stop – and I don't reckon it will for days.' Wally's chestnut stood placidly on the edge of the raging water, seemingly unaffected by the skittishness of the other two. 'I'll go first and take a line with me.'

He uncoiled his rope and lashed it around the bole of a tree which in normal times stood several feet above the water on the bank but was now almost submerged. Tying the other end firmly around his waist, he took a couple of the pups and stuffed them inside his waterproof coat. The chestnut stepped into the fast-flowing water, and was soon swimming strongly against the tide.

Mike and Matilda held tightly to the rope, ready to pull Wally back out if his horse was swept from under him. They were lashed by the rain which stung their eyes and froze their hands, but their grip never faltered. The tide was strong, the undercurrent deadly as it rushed over the craggy bottom in whirlpools and eddies – and Wally's life depended on them.

He finally emerged, the gelding sliding in the mud as it tried to get a grip on the steep bank. Again and again the horse strained and struggled. Eventually Wally slid from his back and scrambled up the slope, dragging the gelding by the reins as he shouted encouragement.

The ascent was agonisingly slow for those who watched but eventually they reached dry ground and Wally tied the rope around a tree stump. Matilda and Mike breathed a sigh of relief as he took off his hat and waved it. He was all right. He'd made it.

'You go next, Molly,' shouted Mike. 'But if you feel the horse slip away, don't hold on to it. Just keep tight to the rope and pull yourself across.'

She nodded, but she had no intention of letting Lady slip from beneath her to certain death. They'd been together too long, shared too much for Matilda to abandon her. She tucked the remaining pup into her coat where he squirmed, his wet fur soaking her shirt. She waited for him to settle, then gently encouraged Lady back into the water. With one hand gripping the reins, and the other hooked around the rope, she used her knees and thighs to keep the old mare under control as the water swirled in vicious eddies around her feet.

Lady slipped and stumbled, her head rearing up as she whickered with terror. Matilda leaned over her neck, muttering soothing noises, coaxing her on until she found her footing and her courage to push against the tide.

The water surged over their legs and Matilda felt its tug as Lady began to swim. She clung like a limpet to her back, face almost touching her mane, hands grasping reins and rope, the puppy squirming between them.

'Good girl,' she crooned. 'Good girl. Steady now, Lady. Keep going, girl. Keep going.'

The rain fell in solid sheets, blinding them, adding to the flow of the river, making the banks slick and deadly. Wally stood on the other side shouting encouragement, but Matilda was deaf and blind to everything as she felt the old mare begin to tire. 'Come on, girl. One more push. One more and we're home,' she urged.

Lady heaved herself into the shallows and gamely ploughed up the slope. But there was no foothold, just sliding, slimy mud which slithered beneath her hooves and dragged her back into the water.

Matilda could hear the rasp of those great lungs, feel the bunching of those tired muscles, and leaped off her back. With her grip firm on the bridle, and feet squarely dug into the mud, she tried to pull her out of the water and up the slope.

Lady came snorting and struggling, fighting for a foothold, teeth bared in the effort as Matilda scrambled up the slope dragging her behind her. She shouted encouragement and once they were clear of the water, Wally slithered down to grasp the reins and add his strength.

Time ceased to exist in the mare's agonisingly slow progress, but then her hoof struck solid ground and she gave a final great lunge and stumbled to the top of the slope. She stood there for a long moment, sides heaving as she fought for air. Then her legs crumpled beneath her and she sank to the ground. Her long yellow teeth snapped, then her eyes rolled back in her head and she was still.

Matilda was on her knees in the mud, the pup slithering unnoticed from her coat and racing to its siblings. She stroked Lady's neck, following the familiar contours of her once powerful body as tears slid down her face and mingled with the rain. Lady had been a true friend – her only friend in that first year or so – she'd shown courage right up to the end.

'Mike's coming across,' Wally yelled close to her ear. 'Give us a hand.'

Matilda sniffed back the tears and grabbed the rope. Mike was already halfway across the river with Bluey riding pillion.

As the water swirled over the gelding's back, the dog almost lost his footing and Matilda held her breath.

Bluey had no intention of swimming. He crouched low against Mike and steadied himself, then gave a sharp bark and windmilled his tail.

'Little bastard's enjoying that,' yelled Wally as they pulled on the rope. 'I swear he's grinning.'

Matilda was speechless with fear and grief. She'd lost one mate today. She didn't think she could bear it if she lost another.

Mike's gelding struggled on the bank but was soon on firm ground. Bluey jumped off his back and shook himself all over them before lunging at Matilda in a whirlwind of muddy paws and darting tongue. She and the two men collapsed on the ground, winded and exhausted, no longer caring that they were growing colder and wetter by the minute. They'd made it.

After they'd caught their breath, Matilda climbed up behind Mike and they began the long trek home. The dogs ran beside them, eager for a warm kennel and dinner. Matilda could think only of Lady. They'd had to leave her behind – an ignoble end for such a brave horse. Matilda grasped her saddle close. She would miss her.

The rains had brought waist-high grass. The squatters of New South Wales breathed easily for the first time in five years. The stock that had survived the drought would grow strong, healthy wool. They would breed well and life would return to normal.

But life in the outback was cruel, the elements deceitful, and their relief was short-lived. The water which had fallen in such a deluge ran over the impacted earth and disappeared. The sun rose high in the sky, brighter and more searing than ever. The land steamed, and soon the lush grass was silver again, the pastures veiled in dust and heat haze.

Tom had lost a few sheep in one of the lower pastures but his mob was much bigger than Matilda's and he counted himself lucky it hadn't been more. Matilda bought one of his stock ponies to replace Lady, and life began the inevitable cycle of mustering, breeding, shearing and selling.

It had become a ritual for her to visit Tom and April at least a couple of times a month. The news from Europe wasn't good, and Prime Minister Menzies was warning it could be war if Hitler advanced his attacks in Europe.

'What will Hitler's invasion of Poland mean to us out here, Tom?' They were all sitting in the kitchen and the atmosphere was tense on that September night in 1938. 'Why should a war in Europe affect Australia?'

'It means we'll be dragged into it,' he replied thoughtfully. 'Only to be expected I suppose, seeing as we're part of the Commonwealth. Chamberlain needs to do something about it, and bloody quick.'

Silence fell and April's hands stilled over her knitting, her face pale in the lamp light. 'But you won't have to go, Tom? You'll be needed on the station. The country will be crying out for wool and tallow, mutton and glue. If there is a war,' she finished fearfully. She looked expectantly at her husband but he kept his gaze averted and switched off the radio.

'Depends on how things go, luv. A bloke can't sit out in comfort while his cobbers are being shot at. If they need me, then I'm going.'

Matilda and April looked at him in horror. 'What about Wilga? You can't just walk away from it,' Matilda said sharply. 'And what about April and the kids? How are they supposed to manage without you?'

Tom smiled at her. 'I never said it was definite. I just said I would go if I was needed. There might not even be a war.'

Matilda saw the excitement light his eyes and knew his words meant nothing. He was fired up by the thought. He could hardly wait for call up. She looked across at April and knew she'd seen that look in his eyes too, for her pallor was more pronounced than ever, her hands for once still in her lap.

Matilda bit her lip and came to a decision. She had vowed to return his kindness – perhaps now was the time to fulfil that promise.

'If you do go, Tom, then I'll look after Wilga. The sheep can be mustered together and I can use your sheds for the shearing. Hopefully some of the men will stay to work the land, but we'll manage somehow until you get back.'

April burst into tears and as Tom went to comfort her.

Matilda left the room and wandered out on to the verandah and into the pasture. They needed to be alone – and she needed space and time to think.

She stood by the home paddock and watched the horses for a moment, then looked up at the sky. It seemed endlessly wide, almost encompassing this small patch of earth in its star-studded embrace. Hard to believe the same sky looked down on war-torn Europe. Men would fight and die. Land would be left to women, and boys too young to know what they were doing. Or to old men who no longer had the strength to fight nature's onslaughts. For the first time in many years she was glad not to be a man. Glad she wouldn't be forced to leave Churinga for a foreign killing ground.

She shivered. She would do her best for April and the boys, but she still had memories of how it had been for her mother during the Great War. And God help them all if that should really happen all over again.

# Chapter Fourteen

The light was gone for the day. Jenny had stacked the finished canvases against the wall and was cleaning her brushes when she heard Ripper barking. She turned at the sound of footsteps on the verandah and felt a jolt of pleasurable surprise to see Brett standing in the doorway.

'Hello.' There was something wrong with her voice, it was too high, almost breathless. She cleared her throat and smiled. 'You're back early.'

He grinned as he took off his hat and mopped his brow. 'I see you've been busy,' he said, nodding towards the stacked canvases. He gave a long, low whistle. 'Strewth! You must work quick.'

Jenny turned her attention to the paintings. She was flustered by his unexpected appearance and needed a moment to escape those grey eyes and gather her wits. Whatever's the matter with me? she thought. I'm as twitchy as a schoolgirl.

'What do you think of my efforts?' she said finally as Brett stood beside her and examined the dozen landscapes.

He rammed his hands in his pockets and looked thoughtful. 'I don't know much about this sort of thing, but you've certainly got the feel of the place.' He pulled out one of the canvases and set it on the easel. 'I especially like this,' he murmured.

Jenny relaxed, her smile warm as she looked at the pastoral scene of sheep and drovers. 'I rode out with the drovers for that one. The light was extraordinary, and I wanted to capture the essence of what Churinga is all about.'

He looked at her and nodded. 'Reckon you did that all

right. I can almost smell the sheep.'

She glanced back at him, wondering if he was teasing her, but his expression was merely thoughtful, his attention still on the painting before him. She turned and kept her hands busy tidying brushes and scraping paint from the palette. She didn't know what to say to this tall, quiet man who stood so close to her she could almost feel his body heat. His absence over the past few weeks had made her realise he was a part of Churinga that really mattered to her – and her conflicting loyalties and emotions waged a silent, inner battle.

'Have a good holiday?' she finally asked when there was nothing left to tidy up and the silence had grown awkward.

'Brother John's crook and needs to go to hospital, or at least have a break from the cane. But he's a stubborn bastard, and there was nothing I could do to persuade him to give up and find something better to do with his life. The journey was wasted really, but it was nice to see Gil afterwards.'

'Fancy a beer and a sandwich?' She heard her own clipped tones and wondered again why she couldn't have a decent conversation with this man without her throat closing up. She took the makeshift supper out on to the verandah. She needed air.

Brett strolled out after her and leaned against the railings as he watched her set the table. 'It's ANZAC day tomorrow and the picnic races. Thought you might like to come along.'

This was safe ground, and his tone was almost impersonal, so perhaps she hadn't made too much of a fool of herself. 'Too right. It's over at Kurrajong, isn't it? I've been listening in on the two-way and it seems to be the only topic of conversation.'

He nodded. 'It's the biggest place around so it got to be the custom over the years. The shindig goes on for three days so be prepared to stay over.'

Jenny tried to hide the excitement in her eyes as she bit into a sandwich. The opportunity to meet and talk to the Squires family was too good to miss. 'Where will we stay? In one of the bungalows?'

'As the new owner of Churinga, I expect they'll put you up at the big house.' He glanced at her over the beer. 'It'll be quite something to have you as a guest, you know. The radio's been buzzing with speculation ever since you arrived.'

'I know,' she said with a giggle. 'I listened in.' She munched on her sandwich. 'Hope I come up to their expectations. I'm not used to such notoriety.'

He grinned. 'You have to do something bad to get notorious, Jenny. And I don't think there's much danger of that.'

She drank her beer in silence, thinking of Ethan Squires and his sons. Perhaps the old man could be persuaded to fill in some of the gaps Matilda had left in her diaries – and it would be interesting to find out why Charlie had dropped her so abruptly.

'So what happens exactly?'

'We have a memorial service in Wallaby Flats, then it's back to Kurrajong for the races. The elimination rounds are first – just about every man in New South Wales is hoping to make the final which is on the third day. There are several picnics, of course, and fireworks and fun fair. Then, on the last night, Kurrajong lays on a dance.'

'Sounds like fun.'

Brett's smile was slow, the warmth of it clear in his eyes. 'It is. The women love it just as much as the men because it gives them a change to dress up and gossip.'

'When do we leave?'

'Very early tomorrow morning. I've got a string of horses to take so you'd better drive the ute.' He eyed the pup that had fallen asleep under Jenny's chair. 'Ripper will have to stay here. The dogs at Kurrajong would have him for tucker.'

Ripper seemed to understand he was being discussed and came wriggling across the floor to have his tummy tickled. 'Whoa there, mate. I already washed.'

Brett's laughter was soft as he played with the eager little animal, and when he looked up at Jenny, she felt a tug of something akin to longing. She quickly looked away and took a long drink of tepid beer. Solitude was making her imagination work overtime. He was just being friendly – nothing more – and she was in danger of making a complete idiot of herself by thinking otherwise.

The sun was melting into the earth, casting an ephemeral veil of pink and orange over everything as they finished their supper. Jenny looked at her watch and yawned. 'Better call it a day if we have to be up so early,' she said casually. She didn't want to go to sleep – would have preferred to sit out here with Brett and watch the Southern Cross grow bright.

He looked at her as they both stood up. His eyes were fathomless, his expression enigmatic. There was a long silence in which she felt she was being drawn towards him, but the spell was broken when he jammed on his hat and turned away.

'Five o'clock tomorrow, then. G'night, Jen.'

She watched him amble across the clearing, his flat-heeled boots scuffing the dust, his easy, loping stride that of a man who'd spent many hours in the saddle. She smiled and wondered if he could dance, blushed at the thought of those strong hands holding her close, then snorted in disgust and went into the house. Who am I kidding? she thought. I'm his boss and he's Lorraine's boyfriend. And, she decided firmly, he probably can't dance anyway.

Yet excitement began to bubble within her. It had been a long time since she'd socialised – there'd seemed little point after Peter died, and friends weren't quite so keen on single women at dinner parties and dances. She thought of the boisterous dances she'd gone to when she was a teenager. It would be fun to dress up and be whirled across the floor until she was breathless.

Her daydream came to a grinding halt as she realised she had nothing to wear apart from jeans, shirts and shorts. 'I can't go,' she muttered to Ripper. 'Not when I know all the other women will be dressed up to within an inch of their lives.'

He yapped, then began an energetic search for a flea.

Jenny watched without seeing. An idea had formed but it seemed so outrageous she pushed it away. And yet. And yet . . . It might be possible. If she had the nerve.

She went into the bedroom and opened the wardrobe door. The soft perfume of lavender wafted into the room. It was a scent of bygone years, lingering like a memory. The ghostly refrain began to echo in the empty house and as she reached for the sea green dress it was as if Matilda had come into the room and was encouraging her to try it on again. As if she and her mysterious partner were willing Jenny to waltz with them.

The music was mesmerising as she shucked off her clothes

and stepped into the swirl of silk and chiffon, and as she looked at her reflection in the mirror, she thought she saw a glimpse of wild red hair and heard the soft laughter of another woman.

She closed her eyes and when she opened them again was almost disappointed to find she was alone.

Eyeing herself critically, she turned and twisted before the mirror, letting the lights from the lamps shimmer and dance in the silken folds. The ocean green was shot with violet – a perfect foil for her eyes and the chestnut lights in her hair. The bodice was boned and tight to the waist, with a sweetheart neckline and cap sleeves. It was a little short but that didn't matter. The mini skirt was all the rage in Sydney and Jenny knew she had good legs.

But as she stood there listening to the ghostly music, she realised the dress was hopelessly old-fashioned. She felt reluctant to tamper with something so beautiful – something that had obviously once meant so much to Matilda.

There was a soft sigh, and as if a warm breeze had come into the room, she felt the lightest caress on her arms. She was not afraid for Matilda was no stranger. This was merely a signal for her to do what she thought best. An acknowledgement that time had moved on and Matilda wanted her special dress to be worn again.

'Thanks,' Jenny whispered. 'I'll take good care of it, I promise.'

She slipped out of the dress and laid it on the bed. She would need shoes. Then she remembered the pair she'd found in the bottom of the trunk that were obviously meant to match. Digging them out of the wardrobe, she sighed with disappointment. They were just too small and with the extra toe on her right foot, no amount of pushing and shoving would get her into them. She would have to wear the low-heeled sandals she'd packed at the last minute. They were quite smart, and as they were the nearest thing to a dancing shoe they would have to do.

Taking the dress into the kitchen, she carefully unpicked the fabric roses at the waist and shoulder. Then, after a long moment's hesitation, she began to cut. When she put down her needle and thread two hours later, she had a strapless evening dress that could rival the most expensive in Sydney.

As she held it up against herself and eyed her reflection in the mirror, she realised there was just one more thing to do and the outfit would be perfect. Minutes later she tied the green ribbon of silk round her neck. The roses were now dusted with gold paint, stitched firmly to the choker and settled between the curve of her neck and shoulder.

Jenny stared at her reflection, amazed at the transformation. Then she giggled. 'Well, Cinderella. You really are going to the ball. And how!'

Jenny was awake and on the move before the sun came up. She had showered and washed her hair, and was dressed in cotton strides and a broderie anglaise shirt as she painted her nails. Her jewellery was necessarily sparse – just silver hoops in her ears and the locket Peter had given her and which she never travelled without. She eyed her reflection critically and with a faint nervousness. It had been years since she'd been to a country party and she wasn't at all sure she was fully prepared – but it was too late now. It would have to do.

Ripper had trailed her mournfully as she packed her rucksack and tidied the bedroom. Following her out to the utility, he sat hopefully at her feet as she draped the cloth-covered dress over the passenger seat. He knew something was happening and suspected he wasn't going to be a part of it.

She picked him up for a last cuddle. He would be going back to the kennels for the weekend and she would miss him. Yet she couldn't resist the sorrowful brown eyes that looked so appealingly up at her and after a moment's hesitation gave in.

'Come on then, you little bludger. Get in while no one's looking.' She tipped him into the utility and pointed at him sternly. 'But I'm warning you: one bark and I leave you behind.'

Ripper's tail wagged the rest of him but he seemed to understand the order of silence. Jenny climbed in after him and switched on the engine. She'd seen Brett on the other side of the yard, a string of horses milling around him from leading reins.

'Get on the floor, Ripper,' she murmured. 'We'll both be in

trouble if he catches you.'

The calvacade of horses and utilities was waved off by the two men who would stay on Churinga. As Jenny joined it through the first gate she realised it wouldn't be easy going. The route to Kurrajong was littered with potholes and the dust from the other vehicles was already billowing in a great cloud that stuck to her perspiring skin and made her feel uncomfortable. It had been a mistake to set out in clean clothes.

For five hours she ate their dust and watched the men in the flatbed of the utility in front. They were getting more boisterous by the mile. The beer was already flowing and judging by the erratic movement of all three vehicles the drivers were getting their fair share.

The main entrance leading to Kurrajong was a pair of freshly painted wrought-iron gates beneath an archway that had the evergreen emblem at its zenith. It was an imposing introduction that was nothing compared to her first sight of the house.

The colonial verandah and balcony against the warm honey of the bricks, the pillars intertwined with bougainvillaea and frangipani, gave it style and beauty. Its lush gardens and quiet grandeur whispered of wealth and power – and confidence in its own importance. It was as Matilda had described and for a moment Jenny experienced the same unease. Then she remembered Matilda's spirited defence of her own place in this vast land and knew she had nothing to feel uneasy about. What had happened was in the past. This was a new era – a time for things to settle down – a chance for the people of Churinga and Kurrajong to make peace.

'Impressed?' Brett leaned down from his horse.

'Probably not as much as I'm expected to be,' laughed Jenny. 'But it is spectacular.'

'You go on up to the house. I've got to see to the horses.'

'Aren't you coming too?' The thought of facing all those strangers on her own was quite daunting.

He shook his head and grinned. 'I'm just a hired hand. It's the bungalow for me. I'll catch up with you later.' He caught sight of Ripper who'd squirmed out of his hiding place at the sound of Brett's voice. 'I thought I told you to leave him behind?'

Jenny pulled the puppy on to her lap. 'He'll be right. He can sleep in the ute. I couldn't bear to leave him behind.'

Brett snorted. 'Women,' he muttered before leading the horses towards the paddock.

There was no time for any retort. Andrew Squires was coming down the wide steps of the verandah to greet her. He was handsome, Jenny acknowledged, and supremely confident. But he was a liar and a cheat, and she wasn't looking forward to his company.

His smile was bright, his handshake warm and firm. 'Good morning, Mrs Sanders. Such a pleasure to meet you again.'

Jenny smiled back. She was hot, dirty and in need of a drink – and his perfection annoyed her. How could anyone remain so clean in all this dust? 'You have a lovely place here,' she said politely.

'I'm glad you like it,' he said, collecting her bags and dress from the utility. 'You must let me show you around sometime.' His blue eyes held hers for a moment then shifted back to the utility as Ripper emerged from his hiding place. 'Hello. We seem to have a stowaway.'

The tension broke and Jenny laughed. 'He insisted upon coming. But he can sleep in here and I promise he won't get in the way.'

Ripper wagged his tail hopefully as Andrew patted his head. 'No worries. So long as he's house-trained, he's welcome.'

Jenny felt a shift in her opinion of Andrew. He couldn't be all bad if he liked Ripper. Perhaps this wasn't going to be as daunting as she'd first thought. She followed him up the steps and through the elegant front door into the hall.

It was as though she'd stepped into another world. The floors were covered in Persian rugs, the walls adorned with gilt-framed pictures and mirrors. There were flowers in crystal vases on the highly polished tables and antique porcelain jostled for position amongst silver trophies. She stood beneath the magnificent chandelier, her innate sense of beauty piqued by the way its crystal droplets splashed rainbows on the walls and ceiling.

'My grandfather brought that back from his grand tour of Venice many years ago. It's something of an heirloom,' said

Andrew proudly.

'I wouldn't like the job of cleaning it,' Jenny replied dismissively.

'We have servants to do that,' Andrew replied shortly. 'Come, I'll take you up to your room.'

'Don't you have servants to do that as well?' Her tone was mildly sarcastic, the bite of her words veiled in a smile.

He looked at her solemnly. 'Yes, we do. But as this is your first visit to Kurrajong, I thought you would appreciate a more personal introduction.'

Jenny looked away, ashamed of her own waspishness, and followed him up the sweeping staircase.

'A maid will unpack for you,' said Andrew as he put her bag and dress on the bed. The bathroom is in there. When you're ready, come down to the drawing room and meet the rest of the family and the other guests. I don't need to tell you they're curious about the new owner of Churinga.'

His smile was warm and enhanced his good looks – if she hadn't witnessed his other side, she might have been fooled into thinking he would make pleasant company. She thanked him and waited for him to leave the room before bending down and stroking Ripper. 'Bit different from what we're used to, eh, boy?'

Jenny eyed the cream brocade at the window and around the four-poster bed. A thick pale carpet was spread over the polished floor, a perfect foil for the rich lustre of the Victorian furniture. She crossed the room to the dressing table and examined the row of crystal perfume bottles and the tiny rosebud soaps that had been left in a Wedgwood bowl. Balmain, Chanel, Dior. Her hosts liked to display their generosity, but she couldn't help wondering if there was a hidden agenda behind this sumptuous welcome.

The thought of Churinga with its rough floors and simple furnishings made all this grandeur seem overblown and for the first time Jenny felt homesick for that lovely familiar place. For home was what it had become, she realised with a jolt. The house in Sydney seemed light years away. She yearned to be back amongst the rustic simplicity of her inheritance.

A discreet tap on the door interrupted her thoughts and Jenny turned to find herself being scrutinised by soulful black

271

eyes. The girl was dark-skinned and wore a blue and white cotton dress beneath the starched apron. Her feet were bare, her smile friendly.

'I alonga you, missus. Unpack bags, eh?'

Jenny smiled. 'I'll do it later.'

The girl's smile vanished and she shuffled her broad feet as she looked at Jenny through her lashes. 'Boss tell me, eh?'

Jenny saw her discomfort and gave in. There was no point in trying to buck the system but getting a maid to unpack a rucksack was taking things a bit far.

She bustled around putting underwear in drawers and hanging up the dress then pointed to Jenny's travel-stained clothes. 'Wash good, eh?'

Jenny grimaced. 'No time. I'm expected downstairs soon.'

The girl shook her head impatiently. 'Plenty time. Clean 'im good, eh?'

Jenny shrugged in capitulation and stripped to her underwear. 'What's your name?'

'Jasmine, missus.' The clothes were already bundled in her arms and she was halfway out of the door.

Jenny sighed and strolled into the bathroom. With nothing else to wear, she might just have time for a soak before she faced the Squires and their guests.

She stood in the doorway and gasped with horrified amusement. It was so opulent it wouldn't have gone amiss in a bawdy house. The taps were gold dolphins, the tiles hand-painted and Italian. An alabaster Venus de Milo stood in a corner niche surrounded by bottles of bath salts. Thick fluffy towels were draped over a warm rail, and crystal lamps made the silk dressing gown shimmer on the back of the reproduction Louis XVI boudoir chair. Obviously the people of Kurrajong weren't expected to bathe in sludge.

With water lapping around her ears, Jenny closed her eyes and rested back on the thoughtfully placed cushion. This was definitely more like it – and even if it was way over the top, she was determined to enjoy this chance to pamper herself.

She had no idea how long she'd been in the bath but when she next opened her eyes she found the water had grown tepid. With deep reluctance, Jenny climbed out and swathed herself in a warm towel before giving a hasty glance at the bottles of

272

cold cream and skin preparations that were lined up beneath the obsequious Venus. There wasn't time to experiment, she was already late.

Jasmine had worked a miracle. The strides had been brushed and pressed, the blouse laundered. How on earth she'd managed to get it all done so quickly was a mystery but one Jenny didn't have time to contemplate, she realised in horror as she looked at her watch. An hour had slipped by without her noticing.

As she hastily dressed and applied mascara and lipstick, she heard cars pull into the driveway and the murmur and bustle of people greeting one another. Her nerve faltered. She was a stranger – an object of curiosity and speculation. This called for a hefty dose of courage.

She eyed her reflection and remembered how it had been at her first exhibition. The butterflies had been fluttering that day too but she'd been able to hide behind the persona of an artist, acted out the part until she felt more at ease. Today would be the same – but instead of an artist, she was a squatter. The new, very wealthy widow from the city who was used to the social round. She took a deep breath.

'If I pull off this one,' she muttered, 'then I'll seriously think about taking to the bloody stage.'

Ripper whined and cocked his head as she headed for the door. 'Stay put,' she ordered. 'I'll take you out later.'

As Jenny reached the top of the stairs, she realised she only had to follow the voices to find the drawing room. Her heart was hammering and she wished Brett was beside her. With a deep intake of breath, she squared her shoulders and began the long descent. The curtain was up. Time for the first act to begin.

A handsome, smiling man of about sixty came through the open doors and waited at the bottom of the stairs. His admiring glance ran over her as he held out his hand, and she knew instantly that this was another of Squires' sons. 'Nice to meet you at last, Mrs Sanders. Charlie's the name. Can I call you Jenny?'

She warmed to him immediately. No wonder Matilda had liked him – she could see why. 'Jenny'll be right. Pleased to meet you, Charlie.'

He took her hand and tucked it under his arm. 'Now for the lions' den. Better get it over with quick then we can settle somewhere quiet with a bottle of bubbly. Are you ready to meet my father?'

She smiled. 'Only if you promise not to leave me in the arena.'

He eyed her thoughtfully. 'Far too tasty to leave anywhere,' he teased. 'I think you and me will get along just fine, Jenny.'

She allowed him to propel her through the throng. Although she was aware of the watching eyes and excited murmurs as they passed, her attention was fixed on the old man in the wheelchair.

Ethan's skin was the colour of putty, his nose hooked, eyes almost colourless beneath hooded lids. Gnarled and heavily veined hands lay lifeless on the plaid blanket which covered his knees. The gaze that swept over her was sharp, intelligent and knowing.

'You remind me of Matilda,' he said loudly into the expectant hush. 'I wonder if you're as fiery.'

'Only when roused, Mr Squires,' she retorted, exchanging look for look, tone for tone. The actress in her disguised her shock at his pronouncement with a veil of hauteur.

Ethan snorted and looked at Charlie. 'Wanna watch this one, son. If she's anything like her predecessor, she'll run you off Churinga with a bullet up your backside.' His laughter was scornful, interrupted by a fit of coughing.

A slim, elegant woman in her late fifties pushed her way through and helped the old man to drink from a glass of water. She shot Charlie a disapproving glare. 'I told you not to get him excited. You should know better than to provoke him.'

He grasped Jenny's elbow as if in self-defence. 'Dad doesn't need provoking. He's just enjoying himself in his usual way.'

The woman raised her eyes skyward and sighed. 'I'm sorry, Mrs Sanders. You must think us very rude.' She held out a manicured hand that glittered with diamonds. 'Helen Squires. I'm married to Charlie's brother James.'

'Jenny.' She returned the friendly smile and firm handshake, and gratefully allowed the older woman to lead her aside.

'He's been looking forward to having a go since he heard about your arrival,' Helen said conspiratorially. 'Charlie really should have warned you about his rudeness. I'm sorry if Dad offended you, but you can't shut him up once he get's going.'

'No worries.' Jenny smiled, but beneath that polite façade she was still quaking from the shock. 'Let's hope he calms down enough to talk to me about the history of Churinga.'

She saw a silent message transmitted between brother and sister-in-law, but before she could say anything was firmly led away by Charlie to meet the other guests. 'There'll be plenty of time to chat with Dad but for now I think it's best to let him simmer,' he murmured. 'Let's get on with the introductions.'

Jenny shook hands and smiled into faces. Tried to remember names and family ties as she answered the same questions and uttered the same banalities. She felt naked beneath their curious scrutiny and was grateful when Charlie finally drew her out on to the verandah for brunch. She sipped the chilled champagne and forced herself to relax as a maid placed a dish of fluffy scrambled eggs in front of her.

'Bit of an ordeal, eh? Sorry. I think you handled things rather well – especially Dad's outburst.'

Jenny looked across at him. 'That was a strange thing for him to say, Charlie. What on earth did he mean by it?'

He shrugged and sipped his champagne. 'An old man's ramblings. Don't take any notice.'

'It sounded more direct than that,' she said thoughtfully.

He concentrated for a long moment. 'I suppose he saw something of Matilda's independence in you. That gleam of stubbornness – the haughty glare that promises fire if crossed.' He smiled back at her. 'Your quick riposte merely emphasised the similarity. I knew her once, she was not easily forgotten. You should be flattered.'

Jenny thought about it. 'Yes, I am.' She was about to ask him about the abrupt ending of his friendship with Matilda then decided maybe it would be better to get to know him better before she said anything. He wouldn't know about the diaries, and it might be wise to keep their existence secret.

His tone was brighter as he threw the napkin aside and leaned against the cushions of the wicker chair. 'It feels like the whole of New South Wales has turned up this year. But of course you don't need me to remind you who they've come to see. Two months of gossip and speculation has whetted their appetites.'

'I'll be yesterday's news soon enough.' She looked towards the paddock where she could see Brett amongst a knot of men leaning against the fence. Two months. It hadn't seemed that long, she thought. But winter was almost here, and soon she would have to make a decision about Churinga.

'Dollar for 'em.'

'They're not worth that much,' Jenny said lightly. 'When does the parade begin?'

He looked at his watch. 'In about two hours. We'd better get everybody on the move. I hope you'll do me the honour of riding in my car?'

Jenny smiled at his old-fashioned courtesy and glanced across the yard. She'd have preferred to travel with Brett and the men from Churinga, but they seemed to have made their own arrangements. The knot of men moved to the utilities. 'Thanks, Charlie,' she said. 'It would be an honour.'

The cenotaph was at the end of a dusty street on the outskirts of Wallaby Flats. Jenny was sheltered from the billowing dust and debilitating heat by the air-conditioned interior of Charlie's car. She looked out of the window at the crowds that lined the street and wondered where they had come from. There were stockmen, drovers, shearers, jackaroos and shopkeepers. Squatters, rich and poor, in cars or on horseback. Overlanders and sundowners in their dusty wagons that clanged and banged with pots and pans. Women in bright cotton frocks and garish hats held on to small children; men lined up in their uniforms, medals proudly polished, slouch hats set at a jaunty angle over furrowed brows. Shifting and jostling against the backdrop of dark red earth and dappled sky, it was a kaleidoscope of colour, and Jenny wished she'd thought to bring her sketchbook.

Charlie parked the car next to the others from Kurrajong and they walked back slowly to mingle with the roadside crowd. She looked for Brett amongst the jostle and noise but couldn't find him. Then, with a strangled whine of a bagpipe, her attention was drawn to the start of the parade.

With a jingle of harness the horses trotted behind the Wallaby Flats brass and pipe band. The dust was lifted by many marching boots. The crowd lifted by a wave of patriotism as the band led more than three generations of servicemen to the cenotaph. There were faces she recognised, faces that passed by with eyes averted, chins lifted in pride as their medals glinted and swung – faces of men who rode out with sheep on Churinga, men she hadn't thought old enough to have gone to war.

Local dignitaries, resplendent in their finery, awaited their arrival. Then a priest, black cassock billowing in the breeze, began the service. The hymns were old favourites, sung with lusty enthusiasm, and Jenny was swept up in the patriotic fervour. And when the wreaths of blood red poppies were laid on the stone steps and the impossibly young soldier began to play the Last Post, she felt the tears well in her throat, and as the sad final note drifted off into silence over the land, she and the crowd gave a tremulous sigh.

'Now the fun begins,' said Charlie as he nodded towards the pub. There was already a crush of men at the door. 'There'll be more than a few sore heads by tonight.'

Jenny dragged her attention back to him, the sadness of the moment lost in his cheerful smile. 'What now?'

'Back to Kurrajong,' he said briskly. 'Before everybody grabs the best picnic spot.'

The Culgoa River rippled in the sunlit breeze. By the time Charlie and Jenny arrived there were already a great many blankets and picnic baskets laid out under the trees. Children splashed in the cold water and played football on the grass. Brightly coloured stalls had been set up and were busy. There were jugglers and fire-eaters, boxers, fat and bearded ladies, a carousel and swing boats.

'As host there are things I have to do, Jenny.' Charlie looked down at her solemnly. 'I could ask someone to keep you company if you'd prefer?'

She shook her head. 'You go on. I'm quite happy to explore on my own.'

He eyed her for a moment, then left. Although she'd enjoyed his company, Jenny was glad Charlie had other things to see to. She was looking forward to wandering on her own, and to a treat of candyfloss and toffee apple. The sounds and smells of the country fair had brought back memories of childhood at Waluna.

She picked her way around the picnic baskets and acknowledged cheerful greetings. It seemed everyone knew who she was, but thankfully only a few wanted to stop and chat. She walked past the beer tent. It was packed, and the pile of empties already stacked outside was growing by the minute. A heated argument was going on behind the tent, with a great deal of pushing and shoving, but within minutes the two protagonists were arm in arm, singing an old shearing song.

Jenny walked on, enjoying the taste of the sticky candy floss, and wondered if Brett was nearby.

She saw him finally, standing in a crowd that had gathered around the boxing ring. After pushing her way through, she came to a sudden halt. He was with Lorraine. Arm in arm, looking down at her as if quite at ease. They looked right together, as close as any couple enjoying a day out in each other's company.

Jenny turned swiftly before they caught sight of her. The day had somehow lost its promise.

# Chapter Fifteen

As Brett looked up, he caught sight of Jenny's stricken face before she turned away. His spirits plummeted as he realised how it must have looked, and he pulled himself free of Lorraine's grasp. She'd pounced minutes earlier, and rather than cause a scene he'd been waiting his moment to escape. 'I'd better get going,' he mumbled. 'The horses need seeing to.'

She pouted. 'I thought we could have our picnic together. I've set it out under the trees down by the water.'

'Can't eat before the races, Lorraine.' He saw the glint of obstinacy in her eyes. 'And I promised the Squires I would join them for a drink.'

'Promised that Sanders woman more like,' she sneered. 'You're making a fool of yourself, Brett Wilson. Her sort only go for money. I bet she's well in with that Charlie by now.'

'Don't judge others by your own standards, Lorraine,' he said grimly.

'Bastard,' she spat. 'I don't know what I ever saw in you. But if you think you've got it made with that Sanders woman, then you're mistaken. She's one of them. One of the rich – and you're just a hired hand.' She turned on her heel and flounced away, her high heels digging deep into the grassy earth.

Brett watched her retreat, stung by her words and reluctant to believe the truth of them. For the evidence of his eyes had reinforced that intuitive knowledge that Jenny was different to the Squires of this world. She would not be influenced by money and power, would make up her own mind about her future. He pushed his way through the jostling crowd and headed for the Kurrajong picnic area.

Yet as Brett caught sight of the large party, he hesitated. It was an interesting tableau – and one he felt reluctant to enter. Lorraine's words returned full force at the sight of Jenny so happily chatting to Charlie Squires. Her face was animated as he leaned towards her. She seemed at ease with his attentions, and with the lavish surroundings.

Blankets had been spread on the grass beneath the wilga trees. Tables and chairs set in the shade, glinting with silver and blinding white cloth. The Kurrajong women were coolly elegant in their summer dresses and large hats as they sipped champagne from crystal flutes and laughed and chatted to their guests. Old man Squires was holding court beneath a large umbrella, the smoke from his cigar lingering in a pall above his head as he barked orders and orchestrated his guests. Helen was, as usual, in attendance, dancing to his malevolent tune, while her husband James dispensed the drinks.

But it was to Charles and Jenny he turned. They looked comfortable together, he acknowledged. Although Charles was a good forty years older than Jenny, he was still a good-looking bastard who was known to have a way with women.

A rich bastard, too, Brett added in grim silence. One who could give her everything she'd ever wanted – but one whose only priority had to be the acquisition of land.

Brett turned away before they could catch sight of him. He had no part to play in this scene, would only have felt like the outsider he was. And yet his reluctance to leave was fuelled by the thought that Jenny was slipping away from him. Now she had tasted what life could bring a rich squatter, what could he ever offer her that she didn't already have?

Jenny had never seen a picnic like it. There were cold meats and salads, whole smoked salmon and roast chickens, and glossy caviar nestling on beds of ice. A pyramid of fruit graced the centre of the table which had been covered in white damask and glinted with silver and crystal. The masters of Kurrajong certainly knew how to entertain. And yet, for all the gracious hospitality and polite conversation, she felt there was something missing, and as she watched them interact with

280

each other over the weekend, she realised what it was.

This was a family of diverse characters who didn't much like one another. Ethan Squires was the indisputable patriarch who ruled his vast family of children and grandchildren by fear. The fear of being passed over. The fear of being cut out of a will. The fear that Kurrajong wealth would somehow be snatched away if his word was not instantly obeyed. Like many old people, it was within his power to hold them to ransom. And he wielded that power with relish.

James had had any fires of ambition in him burned out by the old man's relentless hand on the reins of Kurrajong. Charlie was pleasant enough company, but his own frustration was evident in the way he talked of plans for Kurrajong which could never be realised in his father's lifetime. Andrew was the only one who seemed comfortable with his life. But even though he'd escaped the old man's clutches to find a career in the city, the ties that bound him to Kurrajong were still strong. For all his sophistication, he was still at the mercy of Ethan's tyrannical rule. All Kurrajong business went through his office, and Jenny suspected Ethan kept tight control of everything.

Languid from too much food and wine and drowsy from the heat, she leaned back on the cushions and closed her eyes. The talk around her was desultory and as she was a stranger amongst these outback people she could take no part in the women's gossip.

'Strewth! Now that's what I call a bird of paradise.'

Jenny opened her eyes and sleepily wondered what Charlie was talking about. Her mouth dropped open. 'Diane,' she gasped.

Charlie tore his gaze from the vision in a scarlet caftan and eyed Jenny with interest. 'You know that exotic creature?'

She grinned and got to her feet. 'Too right I do,' she replied. 'And isn't she just a sight for sore eyes?' She didn't wait for a reply from the stunned Charlie. Diane always had that effect on men.

Jenny raced towards her friend and flung her arms around her. 'What the hell are you doing here?'

'That's a nice way to greet a mate who's come halfway across the country to see you,' Diane laughed and pulled away, her strong fingers gripped around Jenny's wrist. 'Jeez, you look good, girl. This outdoor life must be agreeing with you.'

Jenny eyed the vermillion caftan that somehow didn't clash with the orange scarf Diane had tied in a piratical swathe around her head. Gold earrings swung from her ears and bracelets clashed and jangled around her wrists. The make-up around her eyes was heavy as usual, despite the heat, and her perfume was reminiscent of the arab bazaars in Morocco. 'I see you decided to blend in with the locals,' she spluttered.

Diane looked around her, smiling at the audience that had gathered. 'Thought I'd give these wool growers something to talk about,' she said airily.

Jenny glimpsed Charlie making his way towards them. 'Let's get out of here so we can have a chance to talk,' she said quickly.

Diane followed her glance and stepped out of reach. 'No chance. Not until I've met everyone you wrote to me about.' She eyed Charlie. 'That's not Brett, is it? Nice-looking, but a bit old.'

'Behave yourself,' Jenny whispered hastily. 'That's Charlie Squires.'

The heavily kholed eyes widened. 'Not Squires of the dastardly deeds?'

'His son,' Jenny muttered as Charlie drew near.

Diane was like a bright parakeet amongst the sparrows as Charlie took possession of her and led her back to the picnic to introduce her to the others. Her bracelets clashed as she shook hands and accepted a glass of champagne. Her smile never faltered or dimmed as the other women looked on aghast.

Jenny watched her, knowing how much pleasure Diane was receiving from being the centre of attention. It had always been that way, and she supposed her friend's outrageous clothes and extrovert nature had a great deal to do with having been abandoned as a child. She was determined to be noticed, never to be ignored or sidelined again. It was her way of making a mark, a defence against the indifference and anonymity she'd suffered as an orphan.

Diane finally drifted away from the knot of admirers and,

linking arms with Jenny, they strolled down to the river. The sun was lower in the sky, and a welcome breeze cooled the heat.

'How the hell did you find me?' This was the first chance Jenny had had to speak to her alone.

'I bought an old camper from an artist friend who's just come back from the west coast. The exhibition went real well and I was exhausted. Needed to get away and find some space.' Diane laughed. 'And, boy, is there space out here! Miles and miles of it. I never thought I'd reach Wallaby Flats, let alone Churinga.'

Jenny eyed her. 'You drove all this way? You? Who hires a cab to go to the shops?'

Diane shrugged. 'We did it before, so why not now.'

'We were eighteen, Diane. And without an ounce of sense between us. When I think of the risks we took driving all over Europe and Africa, it makes my blood run cold.'

Diane pursed her lips, her eyes lighting up with mischief. 'But we had fun, though, didn't we?'

Jenny thought of the cold, damp room where they'd lived in Earl's Court, and the dark alleys they'd had to walk through when they'd finished working in the Soho bar. Thought of the dust and flies of Africa, and the dangerous, dark-eyed interest of the Arabs they'd met along the route to Marrakesh. She remembered the camaraderie of being poor and footloose amongst the other Australians who'd left home for adventure. Remembered how danger had only added spice to their travels. Sublimely ignorant and naive, they'd gone their merry way without a thought. But for all that, they'd made good friends during that year after art college, and the memories would always be with them.

'I still can't believe you're here,' she said finally. 'Jeez, it's good to see you again.'

Diane's gaze was direct. 'I was worried about you, that's why I had to come. Your letters were too few and far between. They weren't telling me anything, but I got the feeling something wasn't right.'

Jenny gave her a hug. 'Everything's fine. I just got caught up in the diaries and let my imagination get the better of me for a while. But I've had the time and space to come to terms with everything, and in a crazy way I reckon the diaries have helped me to see there is life after tragedy. Matilda's example has made me realise it's time I got on with my life and left the past behind.'

'So you're planning to come back to Sydney, then?'

'Not necessarily,' she replied carefully.

'This hesitation wouldn't have anything to do with a certain Brett Wilson, would it?'

Jenny felt the blush creep up her neck. 'Don't be daft. He's here with his girlfriend.'

Diane eyed her thoughtfully for a moment, then let it pass without comment. 'Looks like it's time for the next race,' she said as the crowds began to gather towards the marked out circuit. 'Anyone interesting riding in it?'

Jenny shrugged. 'I've got no idea,' she said truthfully. 'It's the veterans' race before the final.'

They pushed their way through the crowd and were soon caught up in the excitement as they stood by the railings and watched the men and horses prepare. The stock ponies seemed to sense something was about to happen, and they stamped and snorted and kicked out at one another, teeth gnashing, lips curled.

As in all the races over the weekend, the riders were a fair representation of the men who worked and inhabited the outback. Squatters, drovers, shearers, and station managers. Each dressed in the bright colours of their sponsor, with a bed roll or Bluey over their back.

Silence fell on the crowd. Horses and riders tensed. The starter's flag fluttered in the breeze. Then they were off in an explosion of dust and a roar of encouragement.

The course ran along a narrow straight, then up a hill to wind through trees and around termite mounds. The crowd lost sight of the leaders but even after two days of racing that did nothing to dampen their enthusiasm as they watched the trail of dust hovering over the bush. Long minutes passed until the leader was spotted emerging from the trees to begin the steep descent back into the valley. With hooves slipping on shale, breath fiery in their lungs, the stock horses swung left and right through the stand of tea trees and raced over the uneven ground. The men on their backs gripped the reins, heels thumping as they leaned against sweat-frothed necks and shouted into pricked ears. The finishing line was up ahead, and there could only be one winner.

Jenny and Diane yelled and cheered as loudly as everyone else when the Kurrajong drover won. 'Whew! This is more exciting than the Melbourne Cup,' said Diane. 'How about putting a bet on the next race?'

'What a splendid idea, ladies. Would you like me to place them for you?'

Charlie smiled down at them. 'I suppose you'll want an each-way bet on your manager, Jenny? His odds are short but you could do worse.'

She studiously avoided Diane's sharp eyes as she gave him five dollars. 'Why not? But let's make it to win, not each way. After all, he's wearing Churinga colours and I'm sure he knows what he's doing.'

'Why are the odds so short?' Diane said, handing over her money.

Charlie laughed. 'Because he's won for the last three years. But Kurrajong have a secret weapon this year and I reckon Brett's reign as King of the Hill is over.' His glance moved swiftly towards a skinny youth with a sly face who sat perched on a vicious little skewbald.

'Dingo Fowley's already won in Queensland and Victoria this year, and he showed up well in the heats. Reckon he's the best rider I've seen in a long while.'

Jenny watched him saunter away and turned to find Diane staring at her. 'So, which one is he then?' she said impatiently. 'I want to see what I've bought for my five dollars.'

Jenny looked across to the starting line. Brett was astride a chestnut gelding, the Churinga emblazoned in Aboriginal artwork on his green and gold shirt. He looked handsome and darkly powerful in the saddle, his capable hands soothing the excited horse and keeping him steady. Their eyes met and held. His lazy wink suggested an intimate conspiracy that isolated them both from the crowd and drew them together.

Diane made a sensuous growling noise in her throat. 'Now that's what I call a secret worth keeping. No wonder you didn't have the time to write.'

Jenny could feel the heat in her face as she looked away

from Brett. 'You've got a dirty mind, Diane,' she said firmly. 'Nothing could be further from the truth. This is the first time I've seen him all weekend.'

'Really?' her friend murmured thoughtfully.

The starter's flag was up and Brett took a firmer grip on the reins. Stroller was twitching beneath him, dancing on his toes in nervous anticipation. Dingo Fowley's skewbald nudged and baulked beside him but Brett kept his concentration on the track. He'd heard about Dingo and the tricks he'd played in the heats, and was determined to beat him. He had a reputation to keep and a trophy to win – and with Jenny watching him carry her colours, it was more important than ever to remain King of the Hill.

The flag dropped and Stroller burst from the line with the skewbald neck and neck. The narrow run was rutted and steep. Dingo's boot jarred against Brett's stirrup, kicking his boot loose, upsetting his balance. Stroller lengthened his stride and pulled away as they made the first turn at the top of the hill and began the tortuous run through the bush.

Adrenalin was pumping as trees lashed them to either side and hooves thudded against dry earth and scrub. Termite hills loomed as high as a man – solid barricades that had to be swung around with the sure-footed swiftness that came only from years of experience with rounding up sheep.

Man and horse were lathered in sweat and dust as they approached the tunnel of light at the end of the bush. Dingo was still with him lying almost flat to the skewbald's neck, his hands and legs pumping encouragement to go that bit faster as he kicked out again to dislodge Brett's foot from the stirrup.

Sunlight blinded them after the green shade as they thrust their way out of the bush and pounded along the ridge. The world was a kaleidoscope of heat and dust, of drumming hooves and the smell of sweat. As Brett turned Stroller's head to begin the steep descent, he knew Dingo was still with him.

Hooves slid on shale, muscles bunched and mighty lungs heaved as slender legs fought to keep their balance. Hands gripped reins, knees gripped horse flesh. Sweat and grime clung as closely as rider to mount as they reached the final plateau. The finishing line was up ahead, but the sound of the crowd was lost in the drum of hooves. Dingo was beside him still, the skewbald's neck stretching nose to nose with Stroller's.

The colour and roar of the crowd enveloped them as the flag went down and the horses plummeted to a slithering, skidding halt. Stroller's nose had just edged in front.

'Nice goin', mate,' Dingo shouted. 'But it won't be that easy next year.'

Brett brought Stroller round to face him. His temper was barely in check as he grabbed the skinny little man's shirt collar. 'Try that again and your teeth'll be so far down your throat, you'll be eating dirt with yer arse,' he growled.

Dingo's eyes widened in mock innocence. 'Try what?'

Brett resisted the urge to pull him off his horse and smash his face in. He could see the Squires party approaching with the trophy and didn't want to cause a scene. 'The old boot in the stirrup routine, Dingo,' he hissed into his face. 'At least try and be original.'

The little man's laughter was cynical as Brett released him. 'See you next year. That's if you've got the balls.' He swung away and was lost in a circle of admirers.

Brett slid from Stroller's back and as he gathered up the reins was almost knocked off his feet. He reached out to steady himself and found he was trapped between Stroller and Lorraine. Her arms were around him, her mouth as persistent as blow flies as she smothered him in kisses. 'Great,' she breathed. 'You were great. I just knew you'd win.'

He tried to pull away, but without being heavy-handed about it found it impossible to break her grip. 'Lorraine,' he said roughly. 'Leave off. You're making an exhibition of yourself.'

She glanced over his shoulder and Brett caught the sly glint in her eye before she laughed up into his face and planted a kiss on his mouth. 'My hero.' Her tone was sarcastic but tinged with something akin to triumph and when she finally pulled away he understood why.

Jenny was standing a few feet away. By the look on her face as she turned back into the crowd, she'd obviously witnessed the whole charade.

He held Lorraine at arm's length. 'Why are you doing this?

It's over between us, why make trouble?'

'Not until I say so,' she retorted. 'You don't get rid of me that easy, Brett Wilson.'

'Who's the tart?' Diane came straight to the point as usual.

'Lorraine,' Jenny replied flatly. 'She's Brett's girlfriend.'

Diane grunted. 'Don't think much of his taste.' She put a cool hand on Jenny's arm. 'I shouldn't worry too much, Jen. It won't last.'

'Who's worried?' she retorted carelessly, but her tone belied the rush of despondency that took the brightness out of the day. She wished she was back at Churinga.

'Jenny, Dad wants you to present the trophy.'

She looked at Charlie in horror. 'Why me?'

He smiled down at her. 'Because you're the owner of the winning station. Come on.'

With a helpless look back at Diane, Jenny walked reluctantly towards the crowd that surrounded Brett. She heard the murmurs as she passed, and was aware of their eyes following her, but all she could see was Lorraine's smug face as she stood beside Brett.

Ethan glared up at her from his wheelchair. 'Congratulations,' he barked. 'Beginner's luck of course. We'll have that trophy back next year.'

She took the ornate figure of the bucking horse and turned to Brett. He was scowling ferociously as he stepped away from Lorraine. 'Congratulations,' she said coldly, and turned her head in time to avoid the kiss he was about to plant on her cheek.

'Jenny,' he said softly into her hair. 'It isn't how it looks.'

She looked into his eyes, saw something there that made her pulse race, then caught sight of Lorraine's possessive hand on his arm, and knew she had to be mistaken. 'I'll see you back at Churinga, Mr Wilson.'

As she turned back to Diane and Charlie, she heard the soft snigger of Lorraine's laugh and had to force herself to make polite conversation and drink champagne as though nothing was wrong. And yet it was – it was. What game was Brett playing? And why did his eyes send messages that belied his actions?

288

The rest of the day petered out as the picnic hampers were put away for the last time and the fairground booths were dismantled. Jenny made her excuses to Charlie and the others, made arrangements for one of the drovers to take her utility home, and climbed into the garishly painted camper with Diane.

'Welcome to Trevor,' she said as she switched on the ignition. 'All mod cons, even got air conditioning.'

Jenny looked into the back. A makeshift bed had been spread over the floor, sarongs from Bali had been strung from the roof, and sketchbooks and easels were stacked in the side compartments next to spare tyres and water canisters.

'Reminds me of something,' she said with a smile.

Diane laughed. 'Too right. Trevor could be Allan's twin.'

Jenny sat back and watched the passing scenery. Allan had been their camper all those years ago in Europe. Bought in Earls Court, he was painted blue, with a tube of high surf on one side, a sun and moon and stars on the other. He'd had the Australian flag painted on his roof, and the back doors had been decorated with very yellow sunflowers. Trevor had orange flames licking at his sides, with death's head skulls on his doors and ban the bomb symbols emblazoned on his roof. A different generation, perhaps, but the messages were the same. 'I wonder what happened to poor old Allan?'

Diane negotiated the rough road as she followed the Squires' cars. 'Probably still going,' she said wistfully. 'He was a good old bus.'

They fell into companionable silence as the miles passed, and when they'd finally pulled up in front of Kurrajong, Jenny smiled at Diane's reaction. 'A gin palace. How wonderful,' she breathed.

'Wait until you see inside,' she said wryly.

Helen greeted them in the hall. 'I hope you don't mind sharing? It's just that the house is full.'

Jenny and Diane grinned at one another. 'It'll be like old times, Helen. No worries.'

Jenny led the way upstairs and stood back so her friend could get a proper impression of their room.

'Bloody hell. You are moving with the rich and famous. I've never seen anything like it.' Diane gathered up an excited

Ripper and moved around the room, picking up ornaments and perfume bottles and peeking into cupboards and drawers. When she stepped into the bathroom, she let out a shriek.

'Whoever did that needs shooting,' she laughed. 'Have you ever seen such a terrible sculpture? Poor old Venus.'

Jenny laughed with her. 'She does look horribly smug. But then so would you if you had nothing better to do than sit in here all day.'

Diane threw herself on the bed and stretched like a cat in the last few rays of the sun. 'Bit different from when we shared as kids, eh? I keep expecting Sister Michael to walk in.'

Jenny shuddered. 'Don't remind me. If I ever see that woman or place again, it will be too soon.'

Diane rested on one elbow, her expression suddenly sombre. 'It was better than some of the places we were fostered to.'

Jenny didn't want to remember the nightmare of her first foster home. Didn't want to remember how her foster father crept into her room at night or the terrible row when she'd screamed and run to his wife. She hadn't been believed, told she was a lying, vindictive, evil little girl, and sent back to Dajarra.

Reverend Mother had listened and been kind, but Sister Michael's snide whispers told her she should have kept quiet and stayed put – regardless of what could have happened to her. She'd had to wait another year before she'd been taken to the refuge of Waluna.

Jenny fixed on a bright, determined smile. 'Want to take the first bath? We have three hours until the barn dance.'

Jenny had taken her time to dress and was just finishing her make-up when Diane came back from the bathroom. She was dressed in a deep purple shift that was threaded with silver and showed a great deal of cleavage and long, tanned legs. Her dark hair was piled high, fastened with silver combs, ringlets framing her face. Amethysts sparkled in her ears and at her throat. 'A going away present from Rufus,' she giggled. 'Rather nice, aren't they?'

Jenny noticed and looked ruefully at her own simple hoops

and locket. 'You make me feel under dressed,' she said wearily.

'Rubbish. That dress is drop-dead gorgeous – all you need is my jade earrings to set it off and a decent pair of shoes.' Diane began to rummage in her over-sized holdall and emerged triumphant with the earrings.

Jenny was looking with pleasure at the way the green and silver set off the dress when there was a knock on the door and Helen came into the room.

'Are we late?' Jenny took in the elegant black gown that showed pale, slender shoulders, the discreet pearl studs and choker that had probably cost a fortune.

The older woman smiled. 'Not at all. I just wanted the chance to have a chat and make sure you have everything you need.' She eyed them both with unaffected pleasure. 'What pretty girls you are,' she sighed. 'You'll have all the men asking you to dance.'

Jenny felt absurdly gauche before this elegant, sophisticated woman, and glanced nervously across at Diane. 'You don't think we've overdone it a bit, do you?'

Helen laughed. 'Of course not. When else can you dress up and have fun in this place?' She reached out and touched the sea green dress. 'This is beautiful. The colour does something to your eyes.' She sighed. 'I could never wear that colour without it making me look washed out. I hate being so fair.'

Jenny eyed the silky swirl of platinum hair that had been coiled so intricately into the nape of her porcelain neck. 'I could never hope to look as cool and elegant. I've always envied blondes.'

Helen's hand was soft on her arm. 'We do seem to have formed a mutual admiration society, don't we?' She gave a girlish giggle. 'But would you be offended if I give you a little advice?'

Jenny swallowed and glanced across at Diane. What had she done wrong? What taboo had she broken?

'It's the shoes, darling. Much too informal. Wait here and I'll fetch a pair of mine.'

Jenny and Diane exchanged glances as the door closed behind Helen. 'What about my toe?' she said in an urgent whisper. 'I'll never get into her shoes if they're too narrow.'

'Don't ask me,' said Diane. 'Let's just hope they're not too old-fashioned, because come hell or high water, you're going to have to wear them if they do fit.'

Helen returned minutes later with a shoe box that had an impressive label. 'I reckon we're about the same size. Try them on.'

They were made of the palest, most delicate lace, and fitted as if made for her. The tapering heel was stiletto thin, the toes long and encrusted with seed pearls. Jenny heard Diane gasp, and looked up at Helen.

'They're beautiful,' she breathed. 'But I don't know if I dare wear them.'

'Nonsense,' she replied firmly. 'You keep them. The dress I had to match is hopelessly out of date, and I'm probably far too old to wear such things any more. Now come on. As the hostess I have to be early, and as you're both ready, you might as well come with me.'

The great barn was almost two miles away from the homestead, and to protect their finery the family drove there. The barn still smelled of hay but had been scrubbed clean for the occasion. Bales had been placed around the room for seating and a bar had been set up by the door. A group of men dressed in American cowboy outfits were tuning their instruments on a make-shift stage, and the rafters had been hung with flags and balloons.

'This all looks familiar,' said Diane. She nodded towards a cluster of young girls sitting eagerly in the corner. 'And so does that. Do you remember how awful it was waiting to be asked to dance?'

Jenny nodded. The memory was all too vivid but in truth she could never remember Diane being a wall flower. They took the glasses of champagne Andrew served and watched the flood of arrivals. 'He isn't here yet,' murmured Diane. 'But then neither is she.'

Jenny didn't need to be told who her friend was talking about but managed to avoid replying in the applause that greeted James and Helen as they took to the floor to get things under way. There was no time to wonder where Brett was as Charlie grabbed her and twirled her enthusiastically into a polka.

The barn was soon filled with energetic dancing. Jenny was swept away by men she'd never seen before, gripped tightly by youths with hot hands and beer-laden breath who whirled her round and round until she was giddy. Promenaded by grizzled drovers who trod on her feet and looked down her cleavage. She was sweating and exhausted when finally she managed to escape the chaos and collapse on a straw bale to catch her breath.

The attentive Charles was nowhere to be seen and Diane was still careering around the room in the arms of the very handsome drover who'd been the first to ask her to dance. She seemed to be enjoying herself immensely. Jenny envied her her energy but it was pleasant just sitting here watching the colour and movement of the room.

She was about to take a drink when the glass was plucked from her hand and she was pulled to her feet. 'Charlie, I can't.' Her protest died as Brett drew her into his arms.

'It's a slow one, but I can't guarantee not to step on your toes,' he yelled above the noise.

Jenny moved into his arms as if in a trance. She could feel the heat of him through his shirt, feel the palm of his hand, hot and steady, on her back. Somehow it enhanced the excitement of the moment – made Charlie's expert but clinical approach to dancing a distant memory. For despite all her denials, this was what she'd been waiting for. She relaxed into his arms and closed her eyes.

The band was very good and had begun a medley of country and western favourites. Broken dreams, broken hearts, broken promises – the lyrics might have been sad, but as she danced within his embrace, she realised she hadn't felt this happy in a long while.

'You look real nice, Jenny,' he said into her hair.

She looked up into his grey eyes and knew he meant the compliment. 'Thanks. And well done for winning King of the Hill.'

'Fourth year running,' he said proudly.' But I reckon this is better.'

'Do you?'

He nodded. 'I told you earlier – things weren't as they seemed. Lorraine and I are finished.'

She eyed him thoughtfully for a moment, decided not to let doubts spoil the evening, and let him sweep her into the fast polka that followed the waltz. Finally she had to plead with him to stop. 'I'm too hot and my feet hurt,' she said with a rueful laugh. 'Can we sit this one out?'

He took her back to the hay bale. 'I reckon we could both do with a drink,' he yelled above the noise. 'Promise you won't go away?'

Jenny felt childishly pleased that he wanted to be with her, and nodded. Then she watched him manoeuvre through the dancing couples to the bar and felt suddenly very alone.

'Reckon you must be the belle of the ball, Mrs Sanders.'

Jenny hadn't heard him approach but then his wheelchair was silent on the wooden floor. They eyed each other in silence – an oasis of mutual dislike and curiosity in a sea of colour and noise.

'Matilda was too grand for this sort of thing. Hid herself away with her black fellers and refused all invitations.'

'Perhaps she had more on her mind than country dances,' replied Jenny coolly. She had a sharp image of Matilda at her one and only dance, and shuddered. People could be so cruel.

Ethan leaned forward in his wheelchair, bony fingers gripping her wrist. 'Charlie wanted her to marry him, you know. But I didn't reckon she was good enough for him. What do you think of that?'

'Perhaps she was relieved. He probably wasn't in love with her anyway.'

He let her go and grimaced disdainfully. 'Love,' he spat. 'That's all you stupid women think about. It's the land that's king here, Mrs Sanders. It rules us all.'

'It seems to have made you very bitter, Mr Squires. Why is that, I wonder?'

The hooded eyes slid away as he pretended he hadn't heard. When he looked back, his face was as composed and shuttered as a house in a dust storm. 'You thinking of staying on at Churinga?' he asked abruptly.

She was cool as she looked back at him. 'I don't know. Why?'

'I'll give you a fair price for it. Kurrajong's expanding into the horse breeding business. Churinga would make a good stud farm.'

Brett had arrived with their drinks and Jenny stood up, glad of the excuse to be rid of the old man's company. 'Andrew has already approached me with an offer. I turned him down. Perhaps if you tell me the real reason it's so important for you to have Churinga, I might reconsider.'

He remained silent, eyes boring into hers for endless seconds before he turned away.

'You didn't mean that did you – about reconsidering?' Brett's smile had disappeared and there was a frown between his brows.

She smiled as she took the drink from him. 'No. But he doesn't know that.'

It was almost four in the morning and the party was still going strong. Diane had disappeared into the night with her drover, Brett had been dragged off protesting by his mates to join in a particularly energetic reel which seemed to go on forever, and Jenny was exhausted. Her feet hurt, she'd drunk too much champagne, and Charlie's relentless pursuit was beginning to pall. It didn't look as if Brett would be driving her back to the homestead as she'd hoped either. With a sigh, she took a last look at the swirling dancers and left the barn.

The night was cool, the sky a pale velvet lilac in the hour before dawn, and as the noise from the barn faded into the distance, she took off her shoes and enjoyed the feel of the dry earth between her toes. The long walk home would give her time to clear her head and to hoard the precious time she'd spent with Brett.

The house was almost deserted, the lights streaming from windows into the gloom like homing beacons. She danced up the stairs singing. It had been the most wonderful night – now she could look forward to tomorrow.

Jenny woke five hours later. Diane must have crept in sometime earlier for she was sprawled on the bed beside her, dress rucked up around her hips. Ripper wagged his tail hopefully.

'Let me wash and dress first then I'll take you out before we go home,' whispered Jenny. The thought of Churinga spurred her on. Churinga and Brett. They had become the two most important things in her new life and she was at last looking forward to a future.

Leaving Diane to sleep, she hurried downstairs and stepped out on to the verandah. The business of the day was already under way, with horses and men moving about the yard, and the smell of bacon wafting from the kitchen. She let Ripper off his leash to go rooting in the shrubbery and breathed in the heady mixture of dust and bougainvillaea. It was going to be another hot day, with no hint of the rain they all so badly needed.

Her gaze trawled the yard and drifted over to the bungalow that Brett and the foreman had shared for the last few days. She wondered if he was already on his way back to Churinga or if he was still somewhere on Kurrajong. Then she caught a glimpse of something moving in the deep shadows that surrounded the bungalow – and hope died.

For there was Lorraine. Shoes in hand, hair tangled and make-up smeared, creeping through the door.

Jenny hadn't realised she'd moved off the verandah until she found herself halfway across the yard. I mustn't jump to conclusions, she told herself firmly. Lorraine had probably been with the foreman or was even making her way back from one of the visitors' wagons that had been parked behind the shearer's bungalows. It could just have been a trick of the light.

'G'day. That was some party, eh?' Lorraine balanced on one foot as she struggled into her shoes. She tried to bring order to her mussed hair and finally gave up with a knowing grin. 'Don't expect Brett to show too early at Churinga. He's had a heavy night.' She winked, 'If you know what I mean.'

Jenny's breath was sharp, and she rammed her fists into her pockets before she was tempted to grab Lorraine's bed-bedraggled hair and give it a good tug. She would not let this tart see how painful her words had been. 'I have no idea what you're talking about,' she said haughtily. 'And what were you doing in the foreman's bungalow? It's out of bounds as you well know.'

Lorraine laughed. 'Bloody hell, you sound just like my old school teacher.' Her expression hardened and one bright red nail jabbed the air between them. 'Look here, Mrs High and

296

Mighty. This ain't your place and I'll flaming go where I flaming want.' She tossed her head and with one last defiant sneer delivered her departing blow. 'Brett said I could stay – so why don't you take it up with him?'

Jenny watched her climb into a battered utility and roar off the property before turning back to the house. She raced upstairs and slammed her way into the bedroom. 'Get up, Diane. We're going home.'

Diane's bleary eyes were smudged with make-up and her hair drifted over her face. 'What's going on?' she mumbled.

Jenny began to pack her bag with ruthless efficiency. 'It's that bloody, bloody man,' she swore as she fought to keep the tears at bay. 'You'll never guess what he's done now.'

Diane yawned and stretched. 'I couldn't even begin to try. Can't we at least have coffee before we go?' she whined. 'My mouth tastes horrible.'

'No, we can't,' hissed Jenny. 'The sooner I get back to Churinga the better. I've made a complete fool of myself. It's time I finished the diaries then got back to Sydney.'

She slammed drawers and crammed underwear into the bag. 'Lorraine's welcome to Brett, and Squires is welcome to Churinga,' she said gruffly. 'And you,' she said sternly to the little dog, 'will have to get used to lamp posts.'

# Chapter Sixteen

Diane remained silent as she drove towards Churinga. Jenny was obviously in no mood to talk, and experience told her it was best to let her friend stew for a while. She would explain everything eventually – she always did. Yet it was frustrating to have to wait, and the lack of sleep and coffee did nothing to ease this frustration.

Diane clung grimly to the steering wheel as she negotiated the barely discernible road and wished she was back in the city. Not that she couldn't appreciate the primitive beauty of the place, she admitted as she watched a lone hawk float effortlessly above the scrub, but she'd got used to proper roads and shops, and having neighbours that weren't several hundreds of miles away.

Lighting a cigarette, she glanced across at Jenny who was staring out of the window. If only she would explain why they had to make this mad dash for Churinga. What the hell had happened between her and Brett to make her so angry?

The silence was suddenly unbearable. 'I don't know how you can even think about living out here, Jen. There's nothing to see but earth and sky.'

Jenny turned her head, eyes wide with amazement. 'Nothing to see? Are you mad? Look at the colours, at the way the horizon shimmers and the grass ripples like molten silver.'

Diane felt a quiet satisfaction. She'd known Jenny couldn't resist defending the primal beauty of the place. 'I suppose it has a certain rugged charm,' she said nonchalantly. 'But all this space is claustrophobic.'

'You're talking in riddles, Diane.'

She smiled. 'Not really. Think about it, Jen. Here we have thousands of miles of nothing, and in the middle of that nothing a bunch of people isolated in small pockets. That's where the claustrophobia comes in.'

'Go on.'

Diane glanced at her. She could see Jenny was getting the point but there was no harm in expanding upon it. 'These people live and work in tiny communities. They stay in touch through the radio and now and again meet each other at the local dance, or parties, or picnic races. Always the same faces, the same topic of conversation, the same old rivalries.'

'It's like that everywhere,' Jenny interrupted.

'Not really. Sydney's a big place, with a lot of people who don't know each other. It's easy to move and start again, to change your job and make new friends. There are other things to occupy the mind, boredom doesn't set in quite so firmly. Out here there's nothing but sheep and land. The isolation brings people together because they need that human contact, but with that contact comes gossip and the fuelling of old rivalries. It must be almost impossible to escape. These people rarely move on – especially the squatters. They have an intimate knowledge of each other through gossip and intermarriage. Loyalties are cast iron. Make an enemy out here, and you make a dozen.'

Jenny stared out of the window. 'I think you're exaggerating, Diane. There's plenty of space for everyone, and if a person wants, they need never leave home.'

'Okay. But that home is filled with people who have their own set of loyalties, their own rivalries and grudges. What if you don't get on with them? Find their manners boorish, their habits repellent? It's almost guaranteed you'll see them at least once a week. There's nothing you can do to avoid it – they live and work on your land. Are part of the small community that makes up the station.'

Jenny was silent for a long moment, then turned to face her friend. 'I know what you're getting at and I realise you're only trying to help. But this is something I have to deal with, Diane. So drop it.'

Trevor whined up a steep slope as Diane crunched the

gears. 'What happened between you and Brett?'

'Nothing.'

'Don't give me that! I saw the way you looked at each other. You were positively blooming.'

'Then you're as blind as I am,' retorted Jenny. 'Brett may be charming company but he and Charlie are two of a kind – just out for what they can get.'

'Where does Charlie come into all this?'

'He doesn't. Not really. He's good company, that's all, but his charm can't hide the fact he's after Churinga. And so's Brett.'

Diane frowned. 'How do you know that?'

'Because he more or less said so,' Jenny replied with exasperation. 'It's all he's worried about since I arrived. Pestering me about my plans, following me around trying to convince me not to sell.'

'I think you're being a little harsh on him, Jen. He seemed genuine enough when I met him, and he obviously thinks a great deal of you.'

'Hmph. Cares so much that after whispering sweet nothings in my ear, he spends the night with Lorraine.'

Diane almost lost control of the camper as her concentration wavered, and the wheels jolted into a particularly steep rut. 'Do you know that for a fact?'

'I saw her leave his bungalow this morning. She was only too pleased to make it clear that she and Brett had spent a very energetic night together, and by the looks of her she wasn't lying.' Jenny's voice was sharp.

Diane was puzzled. Her instincts had failed her for once. She'd been so sure he was as smitten with Jenny as she obviously was with him. So sure Lorraine posed little or no threat. No wonder Jen had been upset this morning.

'I'm sorry it didn't work out,' she said softly. 'I thought . . .'

'Well, you thought wrong.' Jenny straightened in the seat, arms folded tightly around her as if to ward off further probing. 'I should have had more bloody sense than to fall for the first handsome man who strung me a line. I don't know what possessed me.'

'Loneliness? We all need someone in our lives, Jen. It's

been a year. Time to begin again.'

'That's rubbish and you know it,' she said firmly. 'I'm perfectly happy with my own company. The last thing I need is a man cluttering up my life.'

'That's what I thought,' said Diane wryly. 'But since Rufus went back to England, I've found I've missed him more than I'd have thought possible.' She was aware of Jenny's long stare and kept her eyes on the road ahead. 'That's not to say I won't get over him. We all do that eventually,' she said with a lightness she didn't feel.

Jenny was silent for a long moment. 'In my case, it's more a question of hurt pride,' she said finally. 'I suppose I was flattered, and in my vulnerable state easily fooled – and that's what makes me so mad.'

Diane nodded in sympathy. 'Better to get mad than skulk away and lick your wounds. But if you want to restore that pride, you'll have to face Brett again before you leave.'

'I know,' Jenny replied firmly. 'And the sooner the better.'

Diane wasn't fooled by the brittle veneer. She knew Jenny too well.

Brett was puzzled by Jenny's early disappearance from Kurrajong. He'd wanted to explain that he'd fully intended to take her home from the dance but by the time he'd managed to get away from his mates she'd already left the barn. Coupled with a blinding headache, his frustration that morning was heightened by the men's reluctance to leave their beds and head for Churinga.

His patience almost ran out when he discovered two of the Aboriginal boys had gone walkabout, and one of the horses had cast a shoe. He'd had to wait for the Kurrajong farrier to fit another one, and in the time it took to do that, the men had sloped off and it took a further half hour to round them all up again. Eventually he'd managed to get everyone loaded into the trucks, and now, as the sun began to set behind Tjuringa mountain, the ragged caravan was on the final leg of their journey.

He breathed a sigh of contentment as the homestead came into view. The hippy bus was parked by the front steps, Jenny was at home. Yet by the time he'd seen to the horses and dispensed the orders for the next day night had fallen and the lights had come on in the bedrooms. It was too late to visit, he realised, and although he longed to see her, he knew he would have to wait until morning.

He slept well, dreaming of violet eyes and a dress that reminded him of the ocean. As the first rays of light touched his face he leaped out of bed. Within half an hour he was walking across the flattened earth of the yard, his pulse racing as he caught sight of her on the verandah.

Jenny hadn't seen him yet, and he took those few moments to study her. She looked good, even in those old jeans and faded shirt. Her hair was the colour of his chestnut gelding, and as she strolled along the verandah, its copper light caught the early sun. The warm memory of her dancing in his arms made him smile, and brought a lightness to his step that had been missing for too long.

'G'day, Jen. Great party, eh?'

She was standing with her back to him at the top of the steps and at first he thought she hadn't heard him. He was about to speak again when finally she turned round, and what he saw made him go cold. Her eyes were focused on a distant point beyond his shoulder and her face could have been hewn from marble for all the emotion it showed.

'I suppose it was all right if you like that kind of thing. But then I'm used to less parochial entertainment.' She sounded cold and superior, quite unlike her usual self.

He frowned. This was not the woman who'd danced so enthusiastically in his arms. Not the woman who'd smiled and laughed and who'd seemed so at ease with him two nights before. His spirits tumbled. This distant creature was a world away from the Jenny he knew and loved. 'What's happened?' he said quietly.

She stared off into the distance – as remote and unreachable as the horizon. 'I realise I have nothing in common with the people out here,' she said coldly. 'Diane is going back to Sydney in a week's time. I plan to leave with her.'

He was appalled at her ruthlessness. 'But you can't,' he spluttered. 'What about us?'

She looked at him then, violet eyes as hard and bright as uncut amethyst. 'Us. Mr Wilson? There is no "us" as you put

302

it. I own Churinga. You are my manager. It's not your place to question my decisions.'

'Bitch,' he breathed, appalled that he'd been so easily taken in. She was no better than Marlene.

It was as if Jenny hadn't heard him. 'I'll have my lawyer inform you of my plans. Until then you may remain as manager.' She turned away, and before he could speak had slammed the front door behind her and was gone.

Brett stood there for a long moment, anguish and confusion fighting an inner battle as he waited for her to come back out. It had to be some kind of cruel joke she'd been playing. But why? Why? What had happened in the past twelve hours to bring about such a change in her? What had he done?

He took a step back, then another, and after a last, long look at the door, he turned and walked away. Logic told him he was better off without her, but his heart told him otherwise. Despite her denial, something must have happened to make her turn so nasty. As he leaned on the fence of the home pasture, he thought back over the previous night's dance. She'd been happy then, warm and compliant in his arms, her perfume making him giddy with pleasure. He'd almost told her how he'd felt but Charlie Squires had butted in and dragged her off to join the Kurrajong party in a reel. That had been the last time Brett had danced with her. Minutes later he too had been dragged into a hectic dance with his mates and by the time he could extricate himself she'd left the barn.

His eyes became slits as he looked into the horizon. He'd gone outside to look for her but he hadn't found her, and now, as he thought about it, he realised there had been no sign of Charlie's car either. His knuckles showed white as he gripped the railings. Charles and Jenny. Jenny and Charles. Of course. How could he have been so stupid as to think he had a chance with a woman like her when Charles Squires could offer so much more? Lorraine had been right all along. Jenny had tasted what life could be for the rich squatters, had been charmed by that womanising snake Charles Squires – and had decided she liked what she saw.

Memory brought snapshot images of them dancing together. Two heads close together as they talked and sipped champagne. They were two of a kind. Rich and educated, more at home in the city than on the land. It was only to be expected that Jenny wouldn't look twice at a man who could offer her nothing but the sweat of his brow.

Feeling sick with disappointment, Brett pushed himself away from the railings and headed for the barns. He no longer cared that Churinga would be swallowed up by Kurrajong for what good would it do him if he didn't have Jenny by his side to run it?

He squinted into the sun as he saddled up the gelding and turned towards the winter pastures. There was work to be done and if he concentrated on it hard enough it might just dull the pain.

Jenny leaned against the door, the tears hot as they rolled down her face. The break was final but she would never forget the look of contempt in Brett's eyes for the way she had done it. And yet it was the only course she could have taken. If she had relented she would have been lost.

'Strewth, Jen. That was harsh.'

She smeared away the tears and sniffed. 'Had to be done, Diane.'

'Maybe. But you came over as a real bitch and that's just not you.' Diane's expression was concerned. 'Are you sure you've done the right thing?'

'Too late for doubts.'

'Yes,' her friend replied slowly. 'I rather think you've burned all your boats there.'

Jenny pushed herself away from the door. 'There's no point in discussing this, Diane. What's done is done. I'm not proud of the way I treated him but he needed to be taught a lesson.' She shifted her gaze from Diane's direct stare. 'I'm a big girl now,' she said defiantly. 'I can take the consequences.'

'So you reckon you'll be able to face him in the coming week then?'

Jenny nodded. Yet shame and heart-ache were strange bedfellows, and to be asked to analyse how she would feel when she saw Brett again would take too much effort.

Diane folded her arms around herself. 'Rather you than me, girl. If it was me, I'd be out of here today. That claustrophobia thing has suddenly become horribly real.'

Jenny knew exactly what she meant but was damned if she was going to let Brett influence her decisions. 'I won't be forced out of my home until I'm ready,' she stated roundly. 'I want to finish the diaries first.'

'Why not take them with you? I don't mind leaving earlier than planned, and you can read them just as well in Sydney.'

'No, I can't. Matilda wants me to keep them here on Churinga.'

'Seems like a lot of fuss over a few mouldy old books. What does it matter?'

'It matters to me and to Matilda,' Jenny said quietly.

Diane's expression was scathing. 'You don't really believe that, do you?' Her expression changed to wonder as Jenny remained silent. 'Are you telling me you think Matilda's ghost lives on at Churinga?'

'Her spirit's here, yes,' Jenny replied defiantly. 'I feel her presence so clearly sometimes, it's as if she's with me in the room.'

Diane shook her head. 'It's definitely time you got out of this place, Jen. All this isolation has turned your brain to mush.'

Jenny eyed her for a moment, then went into the bedroom. When she returned, Diane was stacking canvases.

'These are wonderful. We could have an exhibition when we get back, and I wouldn't mind betting it'll be a sell out.'

'Leave those, Diane.' She had no heart to discuss her paintings. They were done when she was content to stay, now they were just a reminder of what she was about to lose. 'I want you to read Matilda's diaries. Then perhaps you'll understand why they have to stay here on Churinga.'

It was Sunday evening, 3 September 1938, and Matilda was visiting Tom and April. The news from Europe had steadily grown worse and since Hitler's invasion of Poland on Friday speculation was rife. There was silence in the little kitchen as they listened to the cut glass Pommy accent of the announcer introducing Prime Minister 'Pig Iron Bob' Menzies.

'Fellow Australians,' he began in his reassuring accent, 'it is my melancholy duty to inform you officially that in consequence of the persistence by Germany in her invasion of

305

Poland, Great Britain has declared war upon her, and that as a result, Australia is also at war.'

There was a gasp from April and Matilda, an excited murmur from the boys.

'Our staying power, and that of the Mother Country, will be best assisted by keeping our production going, continuing our avocations and business, maintaining employment, and with it, our strength. I know that in spite of the emotions we are feeling, Australia is ready to see it through.'

April reached for Tom's hand, hope bright in her eyes. 'You won't have to go, will you Tom? The Prime Minister said it was important to keep working the land.'

He put his arm around her shoulders. 'They won't want all of us, April. But it'll be hard work keeping the place going without the men.'

Matilda looked at him and saw the flare of excitement in his eyes. How long would it be before he succumbed to the war fever that was sweeping the outback? she wondered. The two-way radio at Churinga was a conduit for gossip and speculation, just as it was in every homestead in New South Wales. She had listened in to try and catch the mood, and had soon realised that the men were eager for war, and although their hearts were breaking, the women couldn't quite resist the opportunity to boast of their sacrifice to the cause.

'My drovers have already volunteered,' Matilda said quietly. 'They came on Friday, after the world news, and handed in their notice.'

She gave a mirthless smile. 'Said it was a chance to get out and show the rest of the world what tough men we breed out here.' Her tone was scathing. 'If you ask me, it's just an excuse for one glorious punch up. Better than anything in the pub on a Friday night – far more exciting than a bunch of shearers on the rampage.'

She fell silent as she caught the expression of bewildered fear on April's face, but she knew she spoke the truth. The Australian male would go to any length to prove his manliness, and they both knew Tom was no different.

April looked at her boys, who sat wide-eyed around the table. 'Thank God they're only babies,' she murmured.

'I'm not a baby, Ma. I'm nearly seventeen,' Sean protested,

scraping back his chair, his face alive with excitement. 'I just hope it goes on long enough for me to join in.'

April slapped him hard across the face. 'Don't you dare talk like that,' she screamed.

Sean stood tall in the ensuing, shocked silence, his bony wrists peeking from his cuffs, his shirt buttons straining over his expanding chest. His face bore the impression of his mother's fingers, but the brightness in his eyes had nothing to do with the pain she'd inflicted.

'I'm almost a man,' he said proudly. 'And an Australian. I'll be proud to fight.'

'I forbid it,' shrieked April.

He ran his work-roughened hand over his bruised cheek. 'I won't stay here hiding behind your skirts while my mates are fighting,' he said firmly. 'I'll join up as soon as they'll have me.' He looked around at them all then quietly left the room.

April broke down and sobbed into her hands. 'Oh, God. Tom, what's to become of us? Am I supposed to see my man and my child go off to war with no say at all?' There was no reply and she lifted her tear-streaked face to him. 'Tom? Tom?'

He made a helpless gesture with his hands. 'What can I say, April? The boy is old enough to make his own decisions, but I'll do my best to keep him home until he's called up.'

Her sobs came from deep within and Tom drew her into his arms. 'Don't fret yourself, luv. I'm not going anywheres until I have to – and neither's Sean.'

Matilda caught a glimpse of sixteen-year-old Davey's expression and went cold. He too had caught the battle fever and the influence of his older brother would make it hard to convince him he would be needed on the property.

She got up from the table and shepherded the younger boys out of the room. Tom and April needed time together and it wasn't fitting for them to see their mother so distressed. After answering the boys' many questions, and calming their excitement and bewilderment, she finally blew out the kerosene lamps and went out to the verandah.

Sean's outburst had shocked her as much as it had April. Matilda had watched the boys grow and like April still considered them to be children. And yet after tonight she could see there would be trouble, for Sean and Davey were indeed almost men. The outback life had made them tough. They could ride and shoot as well as Tom, and the sun had already baked their skin and threaded fine lines around eyes and mouth. Bushmen would be welcomed in the army ranks for their tenacity and strength – just as they had been in Gallopoli.

Over the following year Matilda and April clung to the hope they could keep Tom and Sean on the land, but the war news was a distant rumble that encroached on the outback world and finally demanded its men take up arms and leave the land to the women, the boys and the elderly.

Even in the good times manpower was short; now it was at crisis level. The drought was in its fifth year and rain was a distant memory, the price of feed was high, and because of the explosion in the rabbit population grass was scarce. Matilda and Gabriel patrolled the pastures, moving the mob constantly to conserve the brittle grass. They slept out, rolled up in blankets, alert for predators, knowing that any loss could spell disaster.

The battle of Dunkirk finally opened the flood-gates and Australians poured into the recruiting centres to sign up for the Second Australian Imperial Force. The outback seemed more deserted than ever and Matilda wondered how long she could hold on to Churinga. The past years of work had increased the mob ten-fold – but that increase meant more work, more expensive feed, and without the men to help her, she knew it would be far harder to survive.

It was the middle of June but not a cloud marred the blue of the sky as she rode into Wallaby Flats to say goodbye to Tom and Sean. The little town was bustling. A brass band played outside the hotel, cars, trucks and horses were lined up beside wagons, and children ran wild.

Matilda tied the horse to the hitching post and studied the faces around her. She recognised drovers, stockmen, shearers and squatters – and even one or two of the drifters who had occasionally worked for her. War fever had struck deep into the heart of the outback and she had a terrible feeling that it would never be the same again.

Ethan Squires stood beside his gleaming motor car. James, Billy, Andrew and Charles looked handsome in their officer's

308

uniforms as they drank champagne, but their laughter was too high-pitched, too loud, and she could tell that for all their youthful sophistication, they were as scared as everyone else.

The publican's boy looked far too young to have been called up and she suspected he must have lied about his age as so many others had done. The store-keeper's two sons stood quietly in the shade of the pub verandah, as alike as two fleas on a sheep's back, their yellow heads bent towards each other as they read a newspaper.

Yet it was the women who caught her attention and held it. Their faces were resolutely closed on all emotion. Heads high, they watched as their menfolk gathered in front of the pub. They were too proud to let their weakness show in tears but their eyes betrayed them. Glistening, following every move-ment of their loved ones as they shuffled past the table to show their letters. Hoping, always hoping, that their man would be turned away. Gone was the parrakeet chatter, the patriotism that had fired gossip and speculation. This was harsh reality, and nothing could have prepared them for it.

Matilda watched it all with growing anger. A line of army trucks stood outside the store in the sweltering heat, engines running, exhausts churning out black smoke as their drivers lounged against the bonnets. They would take away the men and some faceless, nameless soldier would train them to kill others. And if the men were lucky – very lucky – they might bring them back. But war would have changed them, would have killed their spirit, just as it had with Mervyn.

The drivers climbed into their trucks and revved the engines. Fathers shook hands awkwardly with sons, the bloody-minded image of the tough Australian male making them afraid to show the emotions that must have been sweep-ing through them. And yet the women were obviously finding it even harder.

Matilda could sense their longing to touch and hold loved ones just once more before the trucks took their men away, but their harsh lives had instilled in them an inner core of steel. They were mothers and wives, stalwarts of the outback stations who were expected to remain strong in adversity. Matilda could see how it hurt to keep the tears at bay, how agonising it was for the mothers not to kiss their sons just one last time, and gave up a silent prayer of thanks that she had no menfolk to send. The little silver brooches given to the women as a symbol of their sacrifice were no compensation for this heart-break.

Matilda stepped off the porch and slowly made her way through the crowds to Tom and April. She could see Sean, tall by his father's side, so grown up in his brown uniform and slouch hat, a mirror image of Tom. April was weeping. Slow, silent tears that rolled down her face as she clung to their hands and devoured them with her eyes. The younger boys were strangely still, as though in awe of this momentous occasion, not fully understanding what it might mean to them.

Tom looked over April's head and smiled as Matilda approached. His face was ashen and she could see he was fighting to keep control of his emotions.

She stepped into his embrace and stood on tip-toe to kiss his cheek. He was the brother she'd never had. His leaving would create an enormous void in her life.

'Take care of yourself, Tom,' she murmured. 'And don't worry about April and the boys, I'll watch out for them.'

'Thanks, Molly.' He cleared his throat. 'April's going to need you, and I know you'll never let her down.'

One by one he rested his hand on the heads of the other boys, stopping just a little longer over Davey. 'Look after the women, son. I'm depending on you.'

The sixteen-year-old nodded as he twisted his hat in his hands, but Matilda could see the longing in his eyes as Tom and Sean finally boarded the truck, and knew it wouldn't be long before he joined them.

She put her arm around April's waist as the truck pulled away and the boys chased after it, waving their hats and shouting. All around them women surged forward to get just one more glimpse, but all too soon there was only a cloud of dust and exhaust fumes on the horizon.

'You're coming back with me, April,' Matilda said firmly. 'No point in you and the boys going back to an empty house tonight.'

'What about the stock?' April's eyes were huge in her pinched little face. 'The rabbits have eaten most of the grass and I need to hand-feed the mob.'

310

'You've still got two stockmen to do that, April. They might be too old for war but they're strong and know what they're doing.'

Matilda thought of the two elderly men and thanked God for them. The two properties were suffering enough from the drought and the rabbits, it would have been impossible to keep a constant watch on the two mobs without them. April was going to need a good deal of shoring up if she was to be of any use. There was no point in letting her dwell on her sorrow.

'The rabbits can eat all the grass they want tonight,' Matilda said as she steered the family towards the horses. 'Come tomorrow, Davey and the boys can go back to Wilga then I'll teach you how to muster the mob and shoot the rabbits. God knows how long this war will last, but we have to make sure Wilga and Churinga keep going until the men get back.'

April looked at her, the tears once again threatening. 'They will come back, won't they?'

Matilda mounted her horse and gathered up the reins. 'Of course they will,' she said with more assurance than she felt.

'How can you be so strong, Matilda? So sure that everything will turn out right?'

'Because it's necessary,' she replied. 'To think anything else is defeatist.'

The days and weeks became months and the dividing fences between Churinga and Wilga were torn down. It was easier to keep an eye on the two mobs if they were kept together and would also ensure the grass wasn't over-grazed.

Like Gabriel and the two drovers, Matilda and April patrolled the fields with knives as well as rifles. The drought was taking its toll and dying beasts had to be quickly put out of their misery. A swift cut through the throat was the most humane way, but April found the whole business distressing and it was more often than not left to Matilda to make the final incision.

The land was hard-packed, baked into cracks. Dismal stands of trees drooped over the silver tendrils of grass the rabbits had left and dingos and hawks became more predatory. Mobs of 'roos, wombats and emus invaded the home pastures

311

and had to be shot at or chased off. Water was down to a trickle in the rivers and streams and only the sulphurous bore water could be used to keep the stock alive. Churinga tanks were holding out but every drop of water was jealously guarded for yet another year had passed and still no sign of a break in the drought.

The radio was their only link to the outside world, and it became a ritual that each night one of them would listen to the world news so it could be relayed to the others.

'Pig Iron' Bob stepped down and John Curtin formed a Labour government. The Japanese bombed Pearl Harbour and Hong Kong fell. Suddenly the war seemed very close and Matilda and April waited in dread. The great empty plains of Australia were too near to the Asian islands. If the Japanese invaded, there would be nothing to stop them. Australia was bereft of fighting men – they were all in Europe – and the yellow peril was suddenly a very real threat.

Matilda was struggling to crutch cut a squirming ram when she heard the sound of drumming hooves. Shielding her eyes with her arm, she looked up and saw April, hair flying, skirts flapping, her heels urging on the horse as she rode headlong across the pasture. Matilda's pulse thudded dully as she waited. Only bad news would make her ride so fiercely.

She brought the animal to a shuddering halt and slid from his back. 'It's Davey, Matilda! Oh, my God, it's Davey . . .'

Matilda unloosed the clutching fingers, grasped her arms and gave her a shake. 'What's happened to him?'

April was incoherent and Matilda slapped her face. 'Pull yourself together, April and tell me what the hell's happened to Davey?' she yelled.

The pinched little face froze as the mark of Matilda's hand bloomed on her cheek then she held out a scrap of paper and collapsed in a storm of tears.

Matilda knew what it was even before she read the boyish scrawl and her spirits sank. Davey had run off to war. She looked down at April, the pain of that loss echoing deep within herself, and understood that there were no words that could wipe out this pain. April had finally crumbled. It was, as usual, down to Matilda to be the practical one.

Putting a tight rein on her own fears, she pulled April to her

312

feet and held her until the weeping storm was over. When the sobs had turned to sniffles, and April pulled away to dry her face on her apron. Matilda had put their priorities in order. 'Have you rung through to the recruiting station?'

April nodded and blew her nose. 'I tried to get through but there's no one there any more except for a caretaker. The trucks left Dubbo real early this morning.'

'Did he give you a number to ring? The army can't take him. He's still too young, they must be told.'

April shook her head. 'The bloke at the recruiting station said that as he was nearly eighteen, it wouldn't much matter. And if he was on one of the trucks this morning, then he's on his way to the training camp and there's nothing anyone can do.'

Matilda's thoughts whirled but she kept them to herself. There was no point in raising April's hopes that a call to army headquarters would bring back her son, for she doubted the army would waste time looking for yet another underage recruit who had slipped through the net. There had been so many and Davey was only a couple of months short of his birthday, so why postpone the inevitable?

'You couldn't have stopped him, April. The boy's been on about this ever since Sean went off with his father.'

April's blue eyes were swimming with fresh tears. 'He's only a boy. I don't want him out there. Tom doesn't say much in his letters, and neither does Sean, but I can read between the lines and the censor's cut-outs. It's carnage, Molly. And I don't want any of my family out there – I want them home with me. Safe, and working the land the way they should be – the way we've always been.'

'All three of them are old enough to know their own minds, April,' Matilda said carefully. 'Davey might be young, but he's ridden the paddocks since he was knee high, and is as tough and strong and bloody-minded as all Australians.'

She held her friend close, cradling her head and stroking back her hair. 'He wanted to fight, you know that, and there was nothing any of us could do to stop him.'

The two women battled the elements and their own inner pain as the war dragged on. Tom and the boys wrote regularly, and Matilda was grateful to April for sharing their

313

letters with her. They were precious to both of them, and although the censor's scissors made them tattered and difficult to read, they were at least confirmation of the men's survival. Bit by bit the two women pieced together the clues and with the help of a very old atlas followed the men.

Tom and Sean were somewhere in North Africa, and Davey, poorly trained and quickly shipped out, was in New Guinea.

Matilda read his letters carefully, and because she had made a point of borrowing books from the travelling library, knew the realities behind the carefully worded scraps of paper to his mother. She kept her knowledge to herself. What was the point of telling April that jungle warfare meant days, maybe weeks, of darkness where a man could never get dry? Damp rotted the skin and mould bloomed on their clothes. Humidity weakened them and mosquitoes brought disease. Venomous snakes and spiders were as deadly as mantraps. The Australian bushmen would find the jungle a very different, far more deadly world than the hot dryness of the one they were used to. Better to let April think her boy was in a comfortable barracks getting three square meals a day.

The summer dragged on and Malaya and the Philippines were invaded. Now it was even more important that they stay in touch with the outside world and every evening they returned to one of the homesteads and listened to the news.

Singapore fell to the Japanese on 8 February 1942. In stunned silence the old men, the young boys and the work-weary women stared at each other in horror. It was only a short hop to mainland New Guinea and the Cape York Peninsula at the 'top end' in Queensland. Suddenly the war was closing in, their great empty plains an open target now Australia was bereft of her armed forces.

Prime Minister Curtin demanded that Churchill give the Australians the right to defend their country and finally two Australian divisions embarked from North Africa for the long journey home.

'They're coming back,' April said in wonderment. 'Tom and Sean are bound to be on that troop ship.'

'They won't be coming back to the land,' Matilda warned. 'They'll be needed up at the top end to defend us from the Japs.'

April's face was radiant. 'But they'll be allowed leave, Molly. Just think, to see them on Wilga again. To hear their voices.' Her spirits suddenly tumbled. 'But what about Davey? Why can't he come home too?'

Matilda caught the knowing glances that were exchanged between the two elderly drovers and knew what they were thinking. Davey was in the thick of things, his last letter had been weeks old before they'd got it. There was little hope of seeing him again until this was all over.

Matilda sighed and grasped April's hand. 'It won't be forever,' she said softly. 'They'll all come home soon.'

But it was not to be. Churchill and Curtin struck a deal, and instead of all the Aussie troops coming home, Australia was sent an American Division instead. Along with the rest of Australia, Matilda and April felt betrayed by the Mother Country. How could so few hope to defend such vast territories, and why should England refuse Aussie soldiers the right to defend their homeland after they had fought England's cause so bravely throughout Europe?

Sick at heart, the women struggled on over the next few months, deriving comfort from one another and the ceaseless round of work. Yet nobody strayed too far from the radio – its news was their only life-line to the outside.

Matilda had returned to Churinga to collect a delivery of feed that had come that morning by dray. The sheep were surviving but it was a never ending task to make sure they were fed properly. She and Gabriel were loading sacks on to the back of the utility she'd bought a few months previously when she heard the familiar bray of the priest's mule.

'Take these up to the east field, Gabe. I'll catch up with you later,' Matilda said quietly.

'Trouble, missus?'

She nodded. 'I think so, Gabe. Better to leave it with me.' She heard him rev up the engine and go but her concentration was on the priest.

Father Ryan was a thin, dark man who had refused to move with the times and still rode his vast parish on the creaking seat of a buck board. The war years had made him old and now there was silver in his Irish black hair, the weight of too much sad news bringing a stoop to his shoulders.

'It's bad news, isn't it?' Matilda asked as she waited for him to climb down and water the mule.

He nodded and she slipped her arm through his and led him into the house. Her heart thudded painfully as she thought of the inevitability of what she was about to hear. But not yet, she pleaded silently. I'm not ready.

'Let's have a cup of tea first. I've always found it's better to hear bad news when you're sitting down.' She bustled about the kitchen, avoiding his gaze, refusing to contemplate which one of the Finlay men wouldn't be coming back. Soon enough to find out – nothing could change it now.

Father Ryan sipped his tea and nibbled on a couple of biscuits she had made that morning. 'These are tragic times, Matilda,' he said mournfully. 'How are you coping out here on your own?'

'I have Gabe here at Churinga, and April has the boys and the two drovers. We've put the mobs together for the duration. It's easier that way.'

'She is going to need all the strength she can muster in the coming days, Matilda. But you already know that, don't you?' His gentle smile was weary as he took her hands and held them.

She nodded. 'Which one, Father?' she asked gruffly – although she didn't want to know, couldn't bear to face the reality of war out here in the land she loved so much.

Silence stretched between them into what felt like an eternity. The priest's hands were warm and comforting, an anchor in the stormy sea of emotion that was sweeping through her.

'All of them, Matilda.'

She stared at his ashen face and empty eyes. 'All of them?' she whispered. 'Oh, dear God,' she moaned as the full horror of his message sank in. 'Why, Father? In God's name, why? It's not fair.'

'War is never fair, Matilda,' he said gently. 'And you can't blame God for making it. Man did that, and it was man who killed them. Tom in a trench outside El Alamein, Sean in a rocket attack on the same battlefield, and Davey by a sniper's bullet in New Guinea.'

Tears blinded her as she thought of the two boys she had loved as dearly as her own, and of the man who'd been as close as a brother. She would never see them again. And that knowledge opened up a void so vast it encompassed her world. Nothing would ever be the same again.

Father Ryan gently prised her fingers from their stranglehold on his arm and came to sit beside her. Matilda leaned her head on his shoulder and breathed in the faint perfume of incense and dust as her tears dampened his shabby cassock.

'There are others who share your pain, Matilda. You are not alone.'

His voice was soothing and through the darkness of her sorrow she listened with that deadly calm that comes before the storm.

'Kurrajong has lost Billy,' he said softly. 'Sure, 'tis a terrible thing, this war.'

She pulled away from him, angrily smearing the tears from her face. 'Yeah. But it doesn't stop those bloody fools from going off with their guns and their ballyhoo to prove what great big brave men they are, does it?' she yelled. 'What about the mothers, the wives and sweethearts? They have a different war to fight, you know. The enemy might not be firing at them but the scars are real enough. What's April going to do without a husband? How's she going to face a future without her two eldest boys? Has your precious God got an answer for that one, Father?'

Glaring at the priest, her chest heaving, she was immediately sorry for her outburst. She'd been angry, yes. But it was anger born out of sorrow – out of the futility of war.

'I understand your feelings, Matilda. It's right you should be bitter. There have been too many telegrams over these past few years, and I'm not immune to the suffering they have caused.'

He paused as if to find the right words. 'But anger is what killed our men. An inability to find peaceful solutions is at the heart of all this. Anger, although good for the release of heartache, won't bring them back.'

'I'm sorry, Father.' She sniffed. 'It's just that the whole thing seems so pointless. Men killing men over a piece of land. Women fighting to survive droughts and bombing raids. What's it all for?'

The priest hung his head. 'I can't answer that, Matilda. I wish I could.'

317

The long ride to Wilga was passed in silence as each kept to their own thoughts. Matilda was dreading having to face April and tightened her grip on the reins as she saw they had been spotted from the homestead.

The look on her friend's face was enough to tell Matilda she already knew why they had come yet the full horror of their news would surely be enough to break the little woman who had struggled so hard to overcome her frailty – and Matilda dredged the last ounce of her own strength in readiness for what was to come.

April refused to let them into the house. Refused to let either of them near her, but stood on her front porch, features etched as though in stone as she listened to what the priest had to say.

Finally, after an unbearable silence, she took a deep trembling breath. 'Thank you for coming, Father, Molly, but I'd rather be alone right now.' Her voice was dull, lifeless, devoid of all emotion, and with her chin tilted defiantly, she turned her back on them and closed the door behind her.

Matilda wanted to go after her, but the priest stilled her. 'Let her be. We all have our own way of mourning and she needs to be with her children.'

She stared at the closed door and nodded reluctantly. April's reaction to the news had surprised and worried her, but she knew she would come to her when she needed help.

'I'll carry on with the work, then,' she said finally. 'At least I can do something useful to take my mind off things.'

Father Ryan patted her hand. 'You do that, Matilda. And remember, God will give you the strength to see you through.' He flicked the whip between the mule's ears and headed north. There were other telegrams to deliver – other families to comfort and pray for.

Matilda watched him go, and wondered where his God had been when Mervyn raped her. Where he had been when Davey and Sean and Tom needed protecting. What was the use of a god if it still meant a woman like April had to lose two sons and a husband to satisfy some nameless, faceless general's lust for battle?

She turned her horse and headed for the Wilga pastures. The shearing season was about to begin, and there was work to do – and even Father Ryan's all-knowing, all-seeing God couldn't shear thirty thousand sheep.

It was another three days before Matilda saw April again. She arrived late in the afternoon in Tom's old utility. The children were sitting beside her, and the flat-bed was loaded high with household possessions.

'I'm going back to Adelaide,' she announced as she climbed out of the truck. 'My parents are there and they've offered us a home.'

Her voice was controlled. Matilda could only guess what an effort it cost her not to break down in front of the children.

'What about Wilga? You can't just leave it behind. Not after all the work you and Tom have put in over the years.'

April's eyes were cold. 'What's the use of land when I have no man to help me work it?'

'You and I have managed pretty well so far. And the boys are getting real good with the sheep.' Matilda reached out to touch April's but she drew away. 'Wilga's been in Tom's family for three generations, April. You can't just walk away from it.'

'Then make me an offer,' she said implacably.

Matilda stared at her. 'You need time to think this through, April. A hasty decision now will rob your kids of their inheritance. And you know that's not what Tom worked so hard for.'

April shook her head as she took the youngest boy on her hip. 'I never want to see the place again,' she said bitterly. 'Every tree, every blade of grass, every bloody rabbit and sheep reminds me of what I've lost. It's yours Matilda. For whatever price you want to pay me.'

She saw the resolute little face and knew that in April's current frame of mind she could not be persuaded to take her time over such a momentous decision.

'I don't know how much Wilga is worth, April, but I know I probably don't have enough money in the bank to cover it. Perhaps you should wait a while and put it on the open market? You could get a good price and it would set you and the kids up good.'

'No.' Her tone was vehement. 'Tom and I discussed the possibility of his not returning and we agreed you should have it.' She riffled in her handbag and pulled out a sheaf of documents. 'Here are the deeds and the keys to the house. And here,' she dragged a pile of books from the utility's front seat, 'are the stock listings and the account books.'

She dumped them on the verandah table. 'Pay me what you think is fair, and send the money on when you can. Here's the address in Adelaide.'

'But, April . . .'

She waved away the protest. 'I'll be right, Molly. Mum and Dad have got a good little business in the city – I won't be short of a bob or two.'

'You can't . . .'

'Enough, Moll. You've been a bonzer mate. I don't know what I would have done without you these past few years. I know you must be grieving as much as me but . . .' Her eyes grew glossy and she cleared her throat and hitched the small boy higher on her hip. 'This is what Tom and I decided so don't make things harder than they already are. Goodbye, Molly. And good luck.'

Matilda put her arms around the frail little woman who had become her closest friend, and wanted desperately to beg her to stay. Yet she knew April would fare better in the city where she belonged. It would be selfish to try and change her mind.

'I'm going to miss you,' she said softly. 'You too,' she added, kissing each small boy in turn.

With a final hug, April herded the boys into the ute and fired up the engine. 'Goodbye, Molly,' she called, and with a wave of her hand, left Churinga for the last time.

Matilda stood alone in the yard that had suddenly become more deserted than ever, and wondered how to solve the problem of Wilga. The drought was in its ninth year and no one was buying property. The stock was starving, the wool was poor, and as her savings dwindled, the rabbits multiplied. It had been hard enough to cope with the two properties when she'd had April and the boys to rely on. Although the gift of Wilga would have been a godsend in better years, now it was just an added responsibility.

She saddled up her horse and headed for the pastures. Tom had put his faith in her and April needed the money. Somehow Matilda decided, she would have to repay that faith.

# Chapter Seventeen

Jenny closed the book and lay staring at the ceiling. She'd heard the war stories of old men as they reminisced in pubs but now she was learning from Matilda's diaries just how hard it must have been for the women who'd been left behind. Their hardships weren't trenches and bullets, their enemy wore a different uniform. Battles were fought against the very earth they depended upon as they struggled against the enemies of drought and voracious rabbits. Their bravery had been unconscious, yet they were as battle-hardened and heroic as the Diggers.

She yawned and stretched before climbing out of bed. Diane was already moving around in the kitchen and Jenny was interested to see what she thought of the early diaries.

'Morning, Jen. Here, grab some of this. I don't know about you but I was up reading most of the night.' She handed over a mug of strong tea and a slice of toast.

Jenny tasted the tea and grimaced. It had too much sugar in it. 'So what do you think of them? Strong stuff, eh?'

Diane swept back her dark hair and tucked it behind her ears. She looked tired.

'I can understand how you got hooked by it,' she said thoughtfully. 'It's an everyday tale of incest and poverty – all too familiar to people like you and me – but I admit I'm as eager as you to get to the end.'

She paused, staring into the steaming mug before her. 'I still can't see why you feel so strongly about keeping the diaries here, though. A publisher would snatch your arm off to get hold of them.'

'Exactly. And that's why they have to stay.' Jenny put down the mug and leaned across the table. 'How would you feel if your deepest, darkest secret was splashed all over the place? So far there have only been rumours about Churinga and the people who lived here – I would feel I'd betrayed Matilda if I let the truth be known.'

'She left those diaries to be found, Jen. She wanted someone to read them. Why have you taken this on as a personal crusade? Matilda was nothing to you.'

'Think about it, Diane. She might have been a stranger, might have lived in a time of terrible hardship that I couldn't begin to imagine if it hadn't been for those diaries – and yet our lives are linked by the things that have happened to both of us. They touch each other time and time again and I feel very strongly that it was I who was meant to find those books and decide what to do with them.'

Diane eyed her as she lit a cigarette. 'I still think none of this is doing you any good, Jen. Why dredge up the past, relive those years of abuse, isolation and loss, when you've only just come to terms with it all?'

'Because Matilda has become my inspiration. She's taught me that nothing can kill the human spirit if it's strong enough.'

Diane smiled. 'You've always had enough spirit to put two fingers up to the world, Jen. But I suppose if Matilda's diaries can help you see that, then it's a good thing you found them.'

Jenny stared at her friend. If she had been asked to describe herself, she would have used the word dogged, and as she had never seen herself as spirited or brave. Diane's words surprised her.

'Let's go out on to the verandah. It's already too hot in here,' she said distractedly.

Diane followed her as she pushed through the screen door. The yard was deserted but they could both hear the ring of the smithy's hammer. Despite the onset of winter, it was one of those days when the sky seemed to be closer to the earth than usual. The humidity had risen with the sun and not a breath of air lifted the dusty earth or rustled the trees. Even the birds seemed to have lost the energy to chatter.

Jenny stared out over the yard. A strange kind of silence

hung over everything. It was as if the great red heart of Australia had stopped beating.

'It's at times like this I wish I was back in Sydney,' muttered Diane. 'What I wouldn't give for the smell of salt and the sight of those great curling breakers crashing on the rocks of Coogee.'

Jenny remained silent. She wanted to commit all this to memory, to carry it with her back to the city, so that on cold, wintry nights when the seas thundered on the rocks she would be warmed by them.

'Looks like you've got a visitor.'

Jenny followed her line of sight and groaned. Charlie Squires was just riding through the last gate. 'What the hell does he want?'

Diane grinned. 'Probably coming courting. You know how this hot weather affects men.' She ground out her cigarette. 'I'll leave you to it.'

'Don't go,' hissed Jenny as Charlie got down from his horse. But she found she was talking to herself. Diane had already gone back into the house and it was too late for her to do the same.

'G'day, Jenny. I hope I'm not too early to call but I wanted to make sure everything was all right.' He took off his hat and smiled. The silver at his temples enhanced his handsome face, and his immaculate moleskins and crisp shirt were a refreshing change from the dusty, sweat-stained clothes of the men who worked Churinga.

She shook his hand and smiled back. He'd been pleasant company over the weekend. 'It's nice to see you again, Charles, but why should you think anything was wrong?'

'You left in such a hurry the other morning. I hope nothing happened at the dance to make you feel unwelcome at Kurrajong?'

She shook her head. 'Your hospitality was wonderful. I'm sorry I never got the chance to say goodbye properly but I had to get back here.'

'That's the problem with being a squatter. The work is never done.' He smiled again and lit a cheroot. 'I was hoping I could show you around Kurrajong. Still, there's always next time.'

323

Jenny saw no point in telling him she would be leaving in six days. 'That would be lovely,' she said politely. 'And it will give me a chance to see Helen again. She and I got along real well, and I promised her one of my paintings.'

'Helen asked me to send her best wishes. She enjoyed having you and Diane to stay. She so rarely leaves Kurrajong nowadays, what with Dad and everything, but your brief visit really cheered her up.'

'Come in and have a cuppa, Charlie. Diane's about the place somewhere, and I know she'd like to see you.'

His mouth twitched. 'Not so sure about that, Jenny. I saw her duck out when she saw me coming. Hope it wasn't something I said?'

Jenny laughed as she poured tea. 'Now what on earth could you have said to offend Diane?'

He laughed with her. 'I don't know,' he spluttered. 'But I can't afford to damage my reputation, you know.'

Jenny was still smiling when she caught sight of Brett in the doorway. Her pulse quickened and she was immediately on the defensive. 'What are you doing lurking out there, Mr Wilson? Can't you see I have a visitor?'

Brett glowered at Charlie and stepped into the kitchen. Ripper jumped up to be patted, but was ignored. 'I came to collect the last of my things. They're in the store-room.'

Jenny nodded her assent, furious with herself for not remembering the boxes and bags he'd left behind when he'd moved out. She was horribly aware of his presence in the house as his boot heels rang on the floorboards, and wished Diane would show her cowardly face and rescue her. She turned back to Charlie who was looking at her curiously, one brow raised.

'I didn't realise that was the way of things,' he said with relish.

'Brett moved out when I first came here,' retorted Jenny. 'There is absolutely nothing going on that couldn't be discussed at a vicar's tea party.'

'Methinks the lady doth protest too much,' he murmured with a sly arch of his brow. 'But then, who am I to cast the first stone?'

'Charlie, you're impossible,' she sighed.

Brett strode into the kitchen, his arms laden with boxes. He glared at them both then slammed through the screen door and out on to the verandah.

'Oh, dear,' sighed Charlie. 'Your Mr Wilson does seem to be out of sorts this morning. Obviously pining after that saucy little barmaid of his.' He turned very blue eyes on her. 'They make a good couple, don't you think?'

She looked away, afraid of what he might see in her eyes. 'I have no opinion on Mr Wilson's love life,' she said firmly.

His chuckle was soft and very telling. 'Well, I won't keep you, Jenny. I know you must be busy. Give my regards to Diane for me, and don't forget your promise to visit. Helen would love to see you both.'

He took her hand and held it a fraction longer than was necessary. 'I would like to see you too,' he said softly. 'You have brought colour and life to Churinga. It wouldn't be the same without you any more.'

'It's always rewarding to know one has made an impression,' she countered.

'I can see you aren't easily flattered, Jenny. And I admire that in a woman. I must try harder next time. Wouldn't like to think I'd lost my touch.' He smiled and kissed her hand.

Jenny eased away from him and led the way back out on to the verandah before he could say more. This conversation was getting out of hand and as the night of the dance was still crystal clear in her mind she felt uneasy. She could remember how closely he'd held her as they waltzed, and the way she'd had to tilt her chin and look into those mesmerising eyes. There was no doubt about it, Charles Squires was a rogue and a womaniser. Although she was not in the least bit fooled about the real reason behind his flirtation, he had a sense of humour and she liked him for that.

'Reckon you could be all right there, Jen. Might be worth hanging around here a bit longer.'

She whirled round to face Diane who was standing, arms akimbo, watching Charlie's dust disappear into the horizon. 'Just what the hell do you mean by that?'

'Temper, temper,' mocked Diane, one long painted fingernail wagging back and forth. 'I just meant that if you really have finished with Brett, then why not hang out for the really big fish? Old Charlie Squires must be worth a bob or two.'

Jenny's exasperation had reached boiling point. 'You have no taste, Diane, and you're a coward as well. You left me with Charlie when you knew I didn't want to be alone with him, and to cap it all Brett turned up as well.'

Her eyes widened. 'My, my. So many men – so little time. You have had a busy morning.'

Jenny laughed. It was impossible to stay angry with Diane for long. 'You should have seen Brett's face,' she spluttered. 'If looks could kill, I reckon Charlie and I would be stone dead by now.'

'You might be able to fool him but you can't fool me, Jen. You still care for Brett and I reckon you've made a big mistake letting him go the way you did. You gave him no chance to defend himself, and seeing you with Charles would only have made things worse.'

'I don't want to hear this, Diane.'

'Maybe not,' she retorted. 'But I have a right to my opinions too, you know.'

Jenny stared at Diane, then pushed past her. 'It's too hot to argue. I'm going back to my reading.'

Diane shrugged. 'That's up to you. But sooner or later, you're going to have to live with your decision to leave – and losing yourself in Matilda's diaries isn't going to make it any easier.'

Jenny reached her bedroom and stared out of the window. Diane was right, of course, but she would never admit she had made a mistake. She picked up the diary, found her place and began to read.

Matilda had spent the last month patrolling the Churinga pastures alone. Gabriel had gone walkabout a few days after April had left for Adelaide and the drovers were busy with the breeding programme they'd begun at Wilga. She was tired, hot and thirsty after her four-day stint and needed to get back to Churinga to refill her water bag.

As she rode over the dusty, rustling remains of the silver grass, Bluey trotted along beside her. He was getting old, she realised. Soon he would no longer be able to work the pastures. When the time came she would make sure he got his well-earned rest. Not for him the bullet, but a blanket in front of the fire.

Her thoughts strayed to that devious old scoundrel Gabriel. Trust him to disappear just when she needed him most. He was work-shy and cunning, and must have realised that April's leaving would mean more for him to do. She hadn't been surprised to find him gone from his gunyah – they had known each other too long to be able to surprise one another any more – but she was crestfallen that he should desert her when he knew how much she would need him now she had two properties to look after.

Something sharp on the warm breeze made her forget her problems with Gabriel and she froze in the saddle. She lifted her head and sniffed, pulling on the reins to still her horse.

Smoke. She could smell smoke.

Matilda's throat constricted with fear as she searched the horizon for sight of fire. It was the one enemy she was powerless to fight.

The grey tendrils that drifted into the clear blue looked too fragile to cause harm, yet she knew that this could become an inferno within seconds, sweeping everything before it in a rushing, roaring tide of destruction.

Her heart thundered as she kicked her horse into a gallop. The smoke was coming from the direction of the house. Churinga was on fire!

She spurred the horse to take the last fence and thundered towards the yard. The smoke was thicker now but still coming from the one place. There was a chance she could dowse it before it spread. Racing around the corner of the shearing shed, she saw the source of the fire and brought her horse to a skidding, dancing halt. Matilda slid from his back. She was trembling with rage.

'Gabriel,' she yelled. 'What the hell do you mean by starting a fire in the bloody yard?'

The old man unfurled his crossed legs and sauntered towards her with a cheerful grin. 'Gotta eat, missus.'

She eyed him crossly. He'd been away for a month and she could count his ribs. There was silver in that great bush of black hair and the last of his teeth had finally dropped out.

'Where the hell have you been? And who are all these people?'

He looked casually at the circle of men and women who squatted around the deeply dug bush-tucker fire and sucked his gums. 'Bring black fellers to help, missus. Work good for baccy, flour and sugar.'

She regarded him for a moment, then took in the wattle and twig humpies they'd built down by the dry river bed, and the ragged children playing in the dust. There must be nearly thirty people here, she thought in horror – and they expect me to feed them. She turned her attention back to Gabriel.

'No baccy, no flour, no sugar. I never met one of you lot who knew what a day's work was. I can't afford you.'

He eyed her soulfully. 'Womens and children hungry, missus. Work alonga good you.' He flexed a scrawny arm and grinned. 'Plenty muscle. Good worker me.'

Matilda had heard this before and was not impressed. She'd seen what Gabriel's idea of a day's work was. Yet, as she looked at the ragged assembly and the skinny children, she relented. If it was hard for her, it had to be worse for them. They lived in a hand-to-mouth existence even in the good times, and although she doubted she would get much work from Gabriel and his motley crew, it was the only help she was likely to get while the bloody war was on.

'You're on, Gabe. But everyone stays out of the house and barns unless I give the say so. I catch any of them near the chooks or pigs, I'll shoot first and ask questions later. You understand?'

He nodded.

She looked at the simmering billy-can and sniffed suspiciously. 'No stealing my vegetables either – and if you don't work, you won't get baccy.'

'Yes, missus. Most these black fellers from mission place along Dubbo. Good mens. Like baccy.'

'Right-oh. You can start by chopping wood for the stove. You know where the axe and the wood-pile are. One of the boys can take care of the horses, and he can start by rubbing this one down and giving it feed. Get some of the men to clear the dead trees and make a start on a much wide fire break. Don't want to take chances in this drought. And tell one of your women I need her to help me in the house. The place is filthy now I hardly ever live in it.'

Gabriel's dark eyes held a cunning glint, but his smile was innocent enough. 'Plenty womens, missus. Gabe got new lubra.'

She looked at him in amazement. Gabriel's wife had died five years ago, and he'd seemed perfectly content to let the other women bring up his children and give him comfort.

'Right-oh,' she said, trying to hide her surprise. 'Which one is she, and what's her name?'

There were several women standing around, dressed in the tattered remnants of what she guessed were mission hand-me-downs. They were shyly watching her and giggling behind their hands as Gabriel pulled three of them out of the circle.

'Daisy, Dora, Edna,' he said proudly.

What ridiculous names, Matilda thought. The mission at Dubbo had a lot to answer for. She eyed the three women for a moment. It was very unusual for an Aborigine to take more than one wife – they were a monogamous race, and had strict rules about promiscuity. Perhaps the three women were sisters and he'd taken them in, as was the way.

'Which one's your wife, Gabe. I don't need all three.'

'Edna,' he replied. 'But all three womens good.'

'I'll take the one who won't go walkabout the minute my back's turned,' Matilda replied tartly.

Gabriel shrugged, his grin slipping just a little as he eyed the three women thoughtfully. 'Edna,' he said finally.

'Fair enough.' She tried to keep a straight face, but it was difficult when he looked at her with such obvious guile. 'Remember now, Gabe. No work, no baccy. And that includes your lubra. Understood?'

He nodded sagely. 'Oh, yes, missus. Gabe know.'

'Come on, Edna. Let's get cleaning.' Matilda began to walk towards the house, then realised all three women were behind her. 'I only need Edna,' she explained. 'You two can clean out the shearer's quarters.'

Edna shook her head emphatically. 'Daisy, Dora alonga me, missus, eh? Do other house later.'

Matilda eyed each of them in turn. They were no beauties, and definitely past their prime, but there was the dignity about them that was in all these bush Aborigines, and she admired them for that. With a sigh, she gave in.

'Right-oh. But I need you to work, not stand around gossiping all day.'

Life went on at Churinga much as it had done for years, but Gabriel's idea of bringing in the rest of his tribe had proved to be a godsend. He was a wise if cunning old bastard, and managed to get his men and women to work far harder than she'd expected.

Of course, as befitted the leader of the tribe, Gabriel never did very much himself, but sat dreamily by his gunyah and threw orders around, making a show of being in charge.

Matilda had never approved of the way he treated his women but had realised long ago that she couldn't interfere. The lubras accepted their beatings with stoicism and then paraded their bruises like trophies. Their sense of hygiene and the way they cooked and looked after one another would have appalled a so-called civilised society, but the Aborigines had their own way of dealing with things and she had no intention of changing thousands of years of tradition.

She trained the younger men to be jackaroos, and the women in how she wanted things done in the house and the station kitchen. She even got the children helping in the vegetable garden.

They were impossibly easy to spoil, she found, with their limpid eyes, their cheeky smiles and ragged hair, and she would often make them sugary sweets to suck as a treat. She had to watch them though, they were as cunning and quick as Murray magpies. A chook went missing occasionally and vegetables had a habit of disappearing before they reached the kitchen table, but Matilda didn't really mind so long as it didn't go too far. Gabriel and his tribe had rescued her from extinction. The future suddenly didn't look quite so bleak. News of a turning point in the war meant that for the first time in six years there was real hope it would soon be all over.

Bluey died in the winter of 1943. He had slowly wound down like an old and very tired clock. One night he fell asleep on his blanket and never woke up. Matilda was heartbroken as she buried him under his favourite wilga tree. He'd been with her for so long and was her closest companion. Even though she knew his spirit and tenacity lived on in his pups, she would miss him.

Now she had Wilga to manage as well, she was rarely at home. The two drovers were finding it hard to keep up with the work, and she'd had to teach a couple of Gabriel's younger boys how to look after Tom's cattle. There were only about a hundred head, but they provided milk and cheese, which she sold, and the occasional steak. Matilda hoped that by the time the war was over, she could begin to see the fruits of her breeding programme, for cattle could do well out here.

The bulls and rams had been penned throughout the drought and hand fed, they were the life blood of the properties. But the bills from the feed store were high, and she didn't know how long she could manage to pay them. The wool cheques had been meagre, mirroring the fall in quality in the wool, and as she pored over the books every night, she realised they still had to live from day to day despite the intense labour over the past few years.

The Australians and Americans fought fiercely to drive the Japanese out of Indonesia, but hundreds died there from the bitter cold and the jungle fevers which could rage through an army division faster than a sniper's bullet.

Matilda listened to the news reports when she could, and tried to imagine the hell of fighting in a jungle that glowed with phosphorescent fungi and steamed in tropical rain. The Australians and Americans were being slaughtered not by the enemy but by the conditions in which they had to fight. Beriberi, foot rot, open sores which attracted creeping, stinging things, malaria and cholera – all unavoidable in jungle warfare. It made her feel lucky to be in the middle of a drought. How the diggers must be longing to smell the baked earth of home and to feel the sun warm and dry on their faces after the leeches and humidity of the jungle.

Gabriel had been afraid of the radio at first, shaking his fist at it and murmuring his heathen curses, but Matilda had shown him it presented no threat by sitting on it and switching it on and off. Now he came to the house, surrounded by his large tribe, and took up his place in the doorway, one foot resting on a knobbly knee as he listened. She doubted very much if any of them understood what was being said, but they

331

liked to hear the concerts that always came after the news.

She and Gabriel had become friends over the years and Matilda had even learned enough of his language to understand the story-telling that was so much a part of his tribal tradition. He was exasperating at times, and work-shy, but she looked forward to his company on the few evenings she took off to sit on her verandah.

She was sitting that evening in the rocking chair her mother had once used, her mind drifting with Gabriel's sing-song voice as he sat on the top step, surrounded by his tribe, and began to tell the story of the creation.

'A great darkness was in the beginning,' he said as he looked down at the spell-bound faces of the children. 'It was cold and still and covered the mountains and the plains, the hills and the valleys, and even went down into the caves. There was no wind, not even a breeze, and deep inside this terrible darkness slept a beautiful goddess.'

There was a murmur amongst the tribe. They loved this story. Gabriel settled himself on the step.

'One day the great Father Spirit whispered to the beautiful goddess: "Awake and give life to the world. Begin with the grass, then the plants and trees. Once you have done this, then you will bring forth the insects, reptiles, fishes, birds and animals. Then you may rest until these things you have created can fulfil their purpose on the earth."

'The Sun Goddess took a great breath and opened her eyes. The darkness disappeared and she saw how empty the earth was. She flew down and made her home in the Nullarbor Plain then set out on a western course until she returned to her home in the east. The grass, the shrubs and trees sprang up in her footsteps. Then she travelled north and kept going until she passed to the south, repeating her journeys until the earth was covered with vegetation. Then she rested on the Nullarbor Plain, in peace with the great trees and the grass she had given birth to.'

Nods of recognition went round the circle and Matilda looked at the faces and felt she was privileged to be a part of such an ancient ritual.

'The great Father Spirit came to her again, telling her to go to the caves and caverns, and to bring life to those beings that had dwelled there for so long. She obeyed the Father Spirit, and soon her brightness and warmth brought forth swarms of beautiful insects. They were all colours, all sizes and shapes, and as they flew from bush to bush they painted their colours on everything and made the earth glorious. After a long rest, in which she shone continuously, she rode her chariot of light up into the mountains to see what glory she had created. Then she visited the bowels of the earth and drove the darkness away. From this abyss came snakes and lizard forms which crawled on their bellies. A river came from the ice she had melted and ran into the valley. Its waters held fish of all kinds.

'The Sun Goddess saw that her creation was good, and she commanded that the new life live in harmony. After returning to rest on the Nullarbor Plain, she again went into the caverns, and with her light and warmth brought forth birds in great numbers and colours, and animals of all shapes and sizes. All the creatures looked upon her with love, and were glad to be alive. The Father of the Spirits was content with what she had done.

'It was then that she created the seasons, and at the beginning of spring she called the creatures together. They came in great numbers from the home of the north wind. Others came from the home of the south wind and the west wind, but the greatest number came from the east, the royal palace of sunshine and sunbeams. Mother Sun told them her work was complete, and that she was now going to a higher sphere where she would become their light and life. But she promised to give them another being who would govern them during their time on the earth. For they would change, their bodies returning into the earth, and the life the great Father Spirit had given them would no longer dwell in form on the earth, but would be taken up into the Spirit Land where they would shine and be a guide to those who would come after them.

'Sun Mother flew up and up into the great heights and all the animals and birds and reptiles watched in fear. As they stood there, the earth became dark and they thought Mother Sun had deserted them. But then they saw dawn in the east and talked amongst themselves – for had they not seen Mother Sun go to the west? What was this they could see coming from the east? They watched her travel across the sky and finally

understood that Mother Sun's radiant smile would always be
followed by darkness, and that darkness was the time for them
to rest. So they burrowed in the ground and roosted on tree
boughs. The flowers that had opened to the bright sun, closed
up and slept. The Wanjina of the river wept and wept as it
rose and rose in search of brightness that it became exhausted
and fell back to earth, resting upon the trees and bushes and
grass in sparkling dewdrops.

'When dawn appeared the birds were so excited that some
of them began to twitter and chirp, others laughed and laughed
while some sang with their joy. The dewdrops rose to meet
Mother Sun, and this was the beginning of night and day.'

The tribe began to move away from the verandah, murmuring amongst themselves, sleepy children dangling from hips,
as they headed for their gunyahs. Matilda carefully rolled a
cigarette and handed it to Gabriel. 'Your story is very like the
one I was told as a little girl,' she said softly. 'But somehow it
feels more real when told by you.'

'Elders must teach the children. Dreamtime important.
Walkabout part of that.'

'Tell me why it's so important, Gabriel? Why do you keep
going walkabout? What is it out there you have to find when
there's food and shelter here?'

He eyed her solemnly. 'This Mother Earth. I am part of
earth. Walkabout give black fella his spirit back. Take 'im to
hunting grounds, Uluru, meeting places and sacred caves.
Speak with ancestors. Learn.'

Matilda smoked her cigarette in silence. She knew by his
expression that he would tell her no more. He was a part of an
ancient people, almost the same now as they must have been
in the Stone Age. He was, and always would be, the nomadic
hunter who knew the land and the habits of the creatures and
plants that inhabited it with a skill that few white men could
emulate.

She had seen one of the younger men bring down a kangaroo with a boomerang, had watched the children trap
scorpions in a ring of fire. The blocking of the wombat's hole
several feet from the entrance meant that when the hunter
approached with his nulla nulla, the animal found itself to be
trapped as it tried to get into its burrow. The tug of war that

followed was always fierce for the wombat is extremely obstinate.

Gabriel had shown her where a few scratches on a gum tree showed where the opossum was resting in the hollow trunk or amongst the thick boughs. How a few hairs among the rocks leading to a hole with a smooth surface to the entrance indicated the presence of sleeping opossums. She had been entranced by the cleverness of his honey collecting. She had watched in awe as he attached a feather to a spider web then dropped it on to the back of a bee as it sucked nectar from the wattle blossom. For over an hour, she and Gabriel had followed that bee as it went from flower to flower, then, with the white feather trailing behind it, returned to its hive. Gabriel climbed up the tree and carefully plunged his naked arm into the hive to steal the honey. The bees seemed unaware of his presence and he wasn't stung. Matilda felt foolish as she hid behind the tree.

She sighed and stubbed out the last of her cigarette. She knew the other squatters thought her strange, and had overheard their speculation about her relationship with Gabriel, but she ignored them in their ignorance. Gabriel and his tribe could teach her far more than any gossiping, small-minded squatter's wife.

'Why you got no man, missus?' Gabriel's voice dragged her back from her thoughts.

'I don't need one, Gabe. I've got you and your tribe.'

He shook his grizzled head. 'Gabriel soon go on last walkabout.'

Matilda's spirits fell as she looked at him. He'd seemed old when she was a child, but had become such a part of the surroundings she hadn't really taken much notice of how much he'd aged recently.

Yet, as she regarded him now, she could see his skin had lost its healthy black sheen and was the colour of dust. But then age was catching up with all of them, she thought as she did a rapid calculation and realised with a sense of shock that she was almost thirty-six. How the years had flown. She was older now than her mother had been when she died.

Dragging herself back to the present, Matilda touched Gabriel on his bony shoulder. 'Don't talk nonsense,' she said

335

firmly. 'The earth can do without your old carcass for a few years yet. I need you more than the Spirit World.'

He shook his head. 'Sleep come soon. Gabriel must go back to the earth, meet his ancestors, throw stars into sky.' He grinned toothlessly. 'You look, missus. One day you see new star.'

'Shut up, Gabe,' she said sharply. If he left, then so would the rest of the tribe probably. He'd become a part of Churinga, and it wouldn't be the same without him.

'You're talking nonsense. You still have years ahead of you. Don't wish your life away.'

He seemed not to hear her. 'Churinga lucky place, missus,' he murmured as he looked out over the parched earth and wilting trees. 'Rain come soon. Men come home. You need a man, missus. Man and woman need to be together.'

Matilda smiled. Gabe was a past master at changing the subject, but she did wish he'd change his tune now and again.

His eyes were misty as he looked into the distant horizon. 'In Dreamtime black fella meet black woman. Black fella say, "Where you from?"

'Woman say, "From the south. Where you from?"

'Black fella say, "From the north. You travel alone?"

'Woman say, "Yes."

'Black fella say, "You my woman."

'Woman say, "Yes, I your woman."'

Gabriel turned his solemn face towards her. 'Man need woman. Woman need man. You need man, missus.'

Matilda looked deep into his wise old eyes and knew he spoke the truth as he saw it. There was nothing she could do to stop Gabriel from leaving her, and he was trying to make sure she had someone to look after her once he was gone.

'Fight it, Gabe. Don't leave me now. I need you. Churinga needs you.'

'The spirits sing me, missus. Can't fight the singing.' He stood and looked down at her for a long moment, then stepped away.

Matilda watched him crawl into his gunyah and take the youngest of his dozen children into his arms. He sat very still, staring out over the land of the Never Never, and the child lay quietly looking up at him as if communing with his silence and understanding the portents.

Emperor Hirohito's delegate signed Japan's surrender and on Sunday 2 September 1945, the world was finally at peace. For the Australian squatters it had been six long, gruelling years. Afterwards, while Europe laboured over her devastated cities, Australia looked to her land.

For almost ten years not a drop of useful rain had fallen but on the morning peace was declared the skies rolled black and laden over the parched earth. The clouds split and the first heavy drops began to fall.

To Matilda, it was as if Father Ryan's God had held back his gift while the world was at war to punish man for his violence and hatred. But the rain was surely a sign of his forgiveness and the promise of better things to come.

She and the tribe stood out in it and let it drench them in its refreshing coolness. The earth swallowed the downpour and the streams and lakes began to fill. For hours rain soaked into the land, darkening it, turning it into swirling, raging rivers of mud. The animals spread their legs as they stood in the fields and let the cooling water run down their backs and wash away the lice and ticks. Trees bent beneath the deluge, galahs hung upside down from their branches, opening their dusty, mite-ridden wings to the water. As it thundered on the galvanised roof she thought it was the sweetest sound she would ever hear.

Matilda stood on the verandah. She was soaked to the skin but it didn't matter. How sweet the air was, cool and perfumed by the smell of water on parched earth. How willingly the gums bent under the weight of water, their leaves touching the ground, their branches glistening like silver in the gloom. Life was suddenly good. The war was over, the men would return, and the land would yield wonderful, life-giving grass. Churinga's water tanks had just held out. They had survived. Gabriel had been right. This was a lucky place.

The rain fell for three days and nights. Rivers broke banks and the earth turned to mud, but the sheep were safe on high ground, the cattle well away from the creeks. Ten inches of rain meant new, strong grass. Ten inches of rain meant survival.

On the fourth day the rain petered out and a weak sun peeked from behind dark clouds. A green fuzz could already be seen over the paddocks, and within a couple of weeks, the first plump plumes of grass began to rustle in the breeze. Life had begun again.

'Where's Gabe, Edna?' Matilda had just ridden into the yard after a long stint in the pastures. 'I need him to take a work party up to the north field and mend the fences. The river's run a banker, and about three miles of posts have been ripped out.'

Edna looked up at her from the top step of the verandah. Her eyes were wide and untroubled as she rocked her baby. 'Walkabout, missus. Singing take him.'

A jolt of dread made Matilda unsteady as she climbed off the horse. Although she was desperate to know Gabe's whereabouts, she knew Edna would only become mulish and tight-lipped if she shouted at her. Sick with worry, she tried to keep her voice calm.

'Where's he gone, Edna? We got to find him quick.'

'Out there, missus.' She pointed at some vague spot in the distance before climbing down from the verandah and ambling back to the camp fire which always seemed to be burning.

'Bugger it.' Matilda rarely swore, but she'd been around men long enough to have quite a colourful vocabulary. 'Damn and blast the lot of you,' she yelled into the faces of the men and women who seemed unfazed by the fact their leader was dying out in the middle of nowhere. 'Well, if you won't do anything about Gabe, then I bloody well will.'

Leaping back into the saddle, she galloped out of the home paddock and began the long trek towards the water hole. The knot of trees stood at the foot of Tjuringa mountain where the water trickled into a pool from out of the rocks. Ancient paintings marked it as a place sacred to the Bitjarra. She hoped Gabriel hadn't chosen somewhere else to die. If he had, then she would have to return to the homestead and get the men together for a more concentrated search further afield.

For twelve long hours she searched all the ancient sites she could think of, but without help from the other tribesmen knew she could go no further. The caves were empty, the rock pools deserted, there was no sign of Gabriel.

She turned her horse towards home where there was no word of him, and finally, reluctantly acknowledged she couldn't spare the time or the men for another search party. If Gabriel didn't wish to be discovered, she knew no white man – or woman – would ever find him.

The Bitjarras were stoic in their acceptance of his disappearance. She would find no help there. It wasn't laziness on their part, they cared for the old man and respected him, but it was a part of their tradition that when the time came, death was for the person who had been sung – it didn't concern the rest of the tribe.

And as Gabriel had said, you couldn't fight the singing.

Three days later one of the boys, who had been out in the bush as part of his initiation into manhood, returned to Churinga. Matilda had seen him come back and had watched with suspicion as he headed straight for the elder. She couldn't hear what he was saying but recognised the bull roarer he had tucked in the kangaroo hide around his waist.

'Come here, boy,' she called from the verandah. 'I want to speak to you.'

He looked at the elder, who nodded, then came reluctantly to the foot of the steps.

'You've found Gabriel, haven't you? Where is he?'

'Over Yantabulla way, missus. Gone to spirits.'

Matilda looked at him in amazement. 'Yantabulla's over a hundred and fifty miles away. How on earth did Gabe manage to walk that far?'

He grinned. 'Take three or four turns of the moon, missus. Gabe good runner.'

Matilda doubted Gabe had been capable of running anywhere, but the fact that he'd died so far from Churinga lent credence to this statement.

She started as a terrible wail began outside the gunyahs and they both turned to watch the extraordinary sight of Edna on her knees by the side of a long-dead camp fire, beating her head with a nulla nulla and slashing at her arms with a knife.

'Why did you leave me, husband?' she wailed. 'Why did you leave me, husband of mine?' She bent and took the dead ashes from the fire and smeared them over her head and body.

'What's going to happen to her?' Matilda whispered to the boy.

'One full turn of the moon and she will make a clay cap. After four seasons of wearing this, she will take it off and wash the clay from her face and body then put the cap on the burial place of her husband. Then she will look to her husband's brothers for protection.'

The news of Gabriel's passing spread quickly through the tribe and the men began to paint white circles and lines on their faces and bodies. The women gathered feathers and bone necklaces and draped them around their men's necks. Spears were taken out and sharpened, shields of stretched kangaroo hide were painted in bright tribal emblems, and heads of all but the widow were coloured with red dye.

The men moved slowly in regal procession away from their camp and Matilda and the women followed them out into the plains. After many hours they came to a place where the grass grew around ancient stones that were adorned with totem symbols.

Matilda and the women sat in a circle a mile or two away, forbidden to take part in the ceremony. As they listened, they heard the mournful sound of the didgeridoo. Bull roarers sang as they were spun through the air, and the dust began to rise as the men began their ritual dance.

'I wish I could see what was happening, Dora. Why aren't we allowed any nearer?'

She shook her head. 'Forbidden for womens, missus.' She leaned closer and whispered, 'But I tell you what's happening.'

'How come you know if it's forbidden?'

Dora grinned. 'I hide when little, missus. See what mens do.' She shrugged. 'Not really interesting.'

'Never mind that,' Matilda said impatiently. 'Tell me what's going on over there?'

'Mens dress up in feathers and paint, carry spears and bull roarers. They make music and dance and dance. Each man has spirit animal inside him. He do the dance of his spirit, make same dance as kangaroo or bird, dingo or snake. But in silence. He must not speak so that spirit can come out and carry Gabe long and long to Dreamtime.'

Matilda stayed with the women until the light was gone from the sky then she returned to the homestead. The ceremony would go on for days and she had work to do, but at least she had been able to mourn Gabe, she thought wearily. The Aborigines might be considered heathens but their ceremony today was very like an Irish wake she'd once attended years ago – only there was no drinking, and the whole thing had been performed with dignity.

She climbed the steps to the verandah and came to a halt. There, on the floor was a stone amulet – a churinga. Who had put it there was a mystery but as she picked it up she knew she would always treasure it as a reminder of Gabriel.

The men began to return from war but too many would never see the grasslands of home again. Apart from Billy Squires and Tom Finlay and his sons, there were other casualties. The local policeman would never leave hospital in Sydney. Shrapnel had severed his spinal cord and he lay in a coma that would finally finish what the enemy fire had started. The publican's boy had survived, but he would always walk with a limp and have terrible nightmares. The storekeeper's two boys had died at Guadacanal, and their parents moved back to the city where the memories were not quite so sharp.

The face of Wallaby Flats was changing. New people came to take over the pub and the store, the old church was restored, the streets metalled and a commemorative garden planted. There was a bustle about the place that had been missing for too long, and along with this bustle came the rush for cheap land.

Curtin's Labour Party looked at the great tracts of land inhabited by a minority of people and decided that the thousands of men who had come home should be given the chance to work their own stations.

It was an old solution to the problem of what to do with the sudden influx of war-weary men – one that had been tried after the Great War and had proved to be a failure. For what did these men know of the hardships of the squatters life, or of the endless battle to survive? Men and women had struggled for months, sometimes years, at their new lives, but had mostly given in and moved back to the cities. The outback had a way of separating the men from the boys, and only the strong survived.

Howls of protest and argument could be heard from the Gulf of Carpentaria to the shores of Sydney, but the government went ahead and put compulsory purchase orders on thousands of acres of prime grazing.

The biggest land owners were the ones to feel the pinch. Squires lost sixty thousand acres of his one hundred and twenty. Willa Willa forty thousand, and Nulla Nulla forty-five.

Matilda had moved quickly once peace was announced. She remembered what it had been like when her father came back from the Great War, and knew that if the government forced her to sell Wilga, they would pay far less than it was worth on the open market.

She needed to get the best price possible. For despite the money Matilda had already sent her, April was having a hard time of it in Adelaide and the responsibility of overseeing so many thousands of acres had become too much for Matilda on her own.

The new owner had written from Melbourne to say he didn't want the cattle as he was planning to breed stock horses on Wilga. He agreed she could keep half of Wilga's mob. Matilda knew she had enough grass to accommodate so many sheep and needed the rams to bring a stronger element into her mob. The wool was good this year but next year it would be even better.

It was the cows that proved to be the problem. Until now she had had very little to do with them but the old drovers had retired and she soon found that cattle had very different needs to sheep. She pored over books every night, learning about prices, breeding, slaughtering and the countless infections she would have to deal with. No wonder the new owner didn't want to take them on, she realised. They would be expensive in the drought, and would churn up the grassland with their hooves.

The fences dividing Wilga and Churinga had been replaced but still she hadn't met the new owner. Although gossip over the radio said he was young and handsome and a good catch for some lucky girl, Matilda wondered what he was really like, and how long he would survive.

She had little time for the city men who thought living out

here would be easy, and doubted he was any different from any of the others who'd taken over the acquisitioned land since the war.

She hired three more drovers, a cowman and two boys. Three of her stockmen returned from the war looking for their old jobs, and she took them on willingly. She had a new barn raised, a cowshed and stalls, and set aside a thousand acres just for the cattle. The grass was high, the price of wool, mutton, beef and milk soared. Europe was starving and the great open grazing of the outback provided the world with its meat. At last there was money in the bank and new hope for a prosperous future.

Thrift was a way of life Matilda couldn't easily abandon, but she knew she had to move with the times and over the next year began to modernise. She bought a new cooking range, a gas fridge and a slightly less battered utility. The luxury of electricity came in the form of two generators, one for the house and one for the shearing shed which had been repaired and extended. New curtains and comfortable chairs, sheets, crockery and cooking pots all made Churinga a more comfortable home. The drover's bungalow was extended and a new cookhouse and bunk house added.

She invested in good breeding ewes, a ram and half a dozen pigs. She reckoned that if things went on as they were, she could afford to build a forge and a slaughter house in a couple of years. That way Churinga would become almost self-sufficient and would save money in the end. Shop-bought horseshoes were expensive, and so was the cost of having her animals slaughtered by the butcher in Wallaby Flats.

Despite her new-found wealth, Matilda still patrolled the pastures and kept an eye on how Churinga was being run. Old habits died hard, and she grew bored around the house now that Edna, Dora and Daisy had finally learned to do things properly. Matilda still rode out in the shabby trousers and loose shirt she'd always worn, with the old, sweat-stained felt hat squashed over her thick tangle of hair.

The humidity was high that afternoon, the rain of the previous night steaming in the lush grass and glinting in the shade of the stand of trees at the foot of Churinga mountain. She took off her hat and smeared her shirt sleeve across her forehead.

343

The blurred outline of a horse and rider emerged out of the shimmering horizon, and as she drank from her water pouch, she watched the almost dreamlike figure sharpen into focus.

At first she thought it was one of her drovers, but as he drew nearer, she realised he was a stranger. With the water pouch stowed away, she reached for her rifle. It had been many years since the Depression and its wandering vagrants but it was better to be safe. Her drovers were spread throughout the thousands of acres of Churinga and she was alone.

She sat very still in the saddle and watched him approach. It was difficult to tell how tall a man was when he was in the saddle but she guessed he was above average height and by the way he rode, obviously at home on a horse.

'G'day,' he called when he was within earshot.

Matilda acknowledged his greeting by lifting one hand in a wave and the other to take a firmer grip on the rifle. She could see now that he was broad-shouldered and slim-hipped. His shirt was open at the neck and his moleskins and boots covered in dust. She couldn't see his face, it was in the shadows beneath his wide-brimmed hat, but as he drew nearer, she saw it was friendly.

He brought his mean-mouthed stock horse to a dancing halt and took off his hat. 'You must be Miss Thomas,' he drawled. 'Glad to meet you at last. Finn McCauley's the name.'

His hair was black and curly, his smile warm and his eyes the most extraordinary blue. It was difficult to tell how old he was, the elements out here aged a man's skin and drew lines around eyes and mouth much sooner than in the cities – but the gossip over the two-way radio and bush telephone had not done him justice, she acknowledged. He had to be the most handsome man she'd ever seen.

'Pleased to meet you,' stuttered Matilda. She still felt awkward with strangers and he'd caught her off guard. 'How you settling in over at Wilga?'

His hand was warm and firm as it swamped hers. 'Good,' he said with a grin. 'It's a bonzer place, Miss Thomas. Just right for horses.'

She stuffed the rifle back into its saddle pouch and caught him watching her. 'Can never be too safe out here,' she said quickly. 'How was I to know who you were?'

'Too right,' he said solemnly. 'Must be crook for a woman out here on her own.' His amazing eyes were looking at her closely. 'But then, I suppose that doesn't worry you very much, Miss Thomas. I heard about how you managed through the war.'

'I just bet you did,' she replied tartly.

His laughter was deep and melodious. 'Fair go, Miss Thomas. A bloke's got to find out about his neighbours, and I know enough to believe only a third of what I hear over the bush telephone.'

She eyed him for a moment, not sure if he was teasing her. He only needs an eye patch and an earring, she thought, and he would make a perfect pirate.

She drew up the reins and smiled, prepared to give him the benefit of the doubt. 'Good thing too,' she said lightly. 'If half the things were true, this place would grind to a halt. No one would have any time for work.'

He looked at her for a long moment, his extraordinary eyes dancing over her before returning to her face. 'Reckon you're right,' he said softly.

He'd caught her off guard again, and she didn't like it. There was something in his eyes and in the way he spoke that did strange things to her insides, and as she had never experienced such feelings before, she wasn't sure how to handle them.

'I was about to stop for a drink and some tucker,' she said gruffly. 'Care to join me, Mr McCauley?'

One dark brow lifted and he smiled. 'Only if you call me Finn,' he drawled. 'Had too much formality in the army and a man kinda loses something of himself when he isn't called by his Christian name.'

'Then you must call me Molly,' she said before she had time to think.

She didn't wait for his reply but led the way through the green canopy of the Tjuringa mountain bush to the rock pools. He confused her, and it irritated her not to be fully in control of her thoughts. She needed these few moments to catch her breath.

Sliding down from her horse, she let the reins drop to the ground. A good stock horse was trained to stand still once the reins were released, and she had no fear of its wandering off.

'This is ripper,' breathed Finn. 'I didn't even realise it was here.' He took off his hat and dipped it in the pool, tipping the water over his head.

Matilda was mesmerised by the way the droplets glistened in his dark tangle of curls and hurriedly dragged her attention back to her saddlebag.

'I try and come here once a week,' she said, pulling the bag down and carrying it to a flat rock. 'The water's so clean and cold after the sludge back at the homestead, and it's usually cool under the trees.'

She knew she was chattering like a galah, and tailed off. 'But it's a bit sticky today after the rain.'

He filled his water bag and drank deeply before wiping his mouth on his sleeve. 'Tastes wonderful after the tank water. No wonder you visit here as much as you can.'

His face was suddenly serious as he took in the broad flat stones and the deep pool that was so obviously just right for a swim. 'I hope I haven't spoiled your plans by turning up like this? If you want to swim, I'll leave you to it.'

Matilda blushed at the thought of how she'd planned to strip off and plunge right in as usual. 'Of course not,' she said quickly. 'Too cold for a swim. I usually just paddle,' she lied.

He eyed her for a long moment, and if he disbelieved her, he wasn't saying.

Matilda took the sandwiches out of the saddle-bag and put them on the stone between them. 'Help yourself, Finn. They're probably a bit warm and soggy by now but I made them this morning so they're quite fresh.' She was gabbling again. What was it about this man that made her as senseless as a headless chook? she wondered.

He bit into the ham sandwich with strong white teeth and chewed contentedly as he stretched out on the rock and watched the waterfall. There was a stillness about him, she realised, a contentment with his life and who he was. Perhaps that was what made him so attractive.

He broke the silence, his slow, southern drawl a bass accompaniment to the orchestra of the bush birdsong. 'How long have you been at Churinga, Molly?'

'All my life,' she replied. 'My grandparents were pioneers,' she added with pride.

'I envy you. You must have a real sense of where you belong.' He looked around him. 'My parents moved around a lot when I was a kid and I never felt settled. Then the war came along and I was on the move again.'

'Where did you serve?'

'Africa and New Guinea.'

He'd spoken lightly, but she'd noticed the shadow in his eyes and decided to move away from what was obviously a painful subject.

'I've never heard the name Finn before. Where does it come from?'

He lifted himself on to an elbow, his head cradled in his hand, and smiled. 'It's short for Finbar. My parents were Irish.'

She grinned back at him. 'So were my grandparents.'

'So,' he said thoughtfully. 'We have something else in common other than Wilga.'

She looked down at her hands. 'So you reckon you'll stay, then?' It was absurd to feel her pulse race as she waited for his reply.

'I'm not new to this way of life. I come from Tasmania, Molly, and although I haven't had much to do with sheep, the drought and heat there are much the same. I'm not planning on moving anywhere for a very long time.'

She looked at him in surprise. 'I thought Tassie was supposed to be like England? All green, with lots of rain and cold winters.'

He laughed. 'Common fallacy, Molly. The coastline is cooler than here, but the plains in the middle can get just as brown and dusty. We suffered as much as you in that last long drought.'

'So why choose to come here and not return to Tassie?'

His easy smile vanished. 'I wanted a new start and the government were willing to teach me about sheep farming.' He threw a pebble into the water and watched the ripples spread. 'Horses are my real passion, but I knew I would have to have another source of income until my breeding programme was up and running. These wonderful rich pastures give me room to breathe, Molly. I needed to get away from small-town gossip where everyone knows your business.'

347

It was her turn to laugh, and it held a sharp edge of scorn. 'Then you've come to the wrong place. Gossip out here is what keeps everyone going. And I wouldn't mind betting you've already heard a good deal of tittle-tattle about the strange Matilda Thomas who lived alone with her Bitjarras for almost twenty-five years.'

His grin was mischievous. 'I heard Matilda Thomas kept herself to herself and was thought to be stand-offish. But I see no evidence of that.'

She looked at him and smiled. 'Welcome to New South Wales, Finn. I hope your new life gives you what you've been searching for.'

His eyes were so darkly blue they were almost violet. 'I think there's every chance of that,' he said softly.

Jenny brushed away the tears and sighed. At last things seemed to be coming right for Matilda – and although it was early days, she had a feeling the last diary would bring about a happy ending.

She leaned back on the pillows and stared out at the paddocks, surprised to find the day had dwindled and time had lost its meaning while she'd been reading. She thought of Diane and felt guilty. Poor Diane. She was only trying to make light of the situation with Brett and Charlie – she didn't deserve to be shunned.

With a yawn and a stretch, Jenny climbed off the bed and padded into the kitchen. There was no sign of Diane but a note on the table said she'd gone for a ride. It was signed with a flourish and two kisses. Diane must have forgiven her.

Feeling better, Jenny let Ripper out for a run in the home pasture, and while she waited for him, leaned on the fence post and watched the dozing horses. The temperature was high, the sky a clear denim blue and almost impossibly wide. She breathed in the smell of hot earth and could hear the rustle of dry leaves on the gum trees. The grass was thinning in the paddock, soon the horses would have to be moved.

She snapped out of her rambling thoughts and turned away. It didn't matter to her that the horses would have to be moved or that it hadn't rained for months. Churinga wouldn't be her concern in another few days.

# Chapter Eighteen

The storm clouds gathered overhead and as the next two days wore on the heat intensified. The air crackled with electricity as rolls of thunder swept across the sky and Ripper sought shelter beneath the kitchen table, trembling.

Diane stared out at the looming sky. 'Gonna be a fair cow when she breaks,' she said as she towelled her hair after her shower. 'I hate these dry storms.'

Jenny looked up from the rocking chair on the porch. 'So do I. There isn't a breath of wind and I'm positively drained by this awful heat.'

Diane grimaced. 'At least we have air con in Sydney, and as much as I hate the way it dries you out, it's a godsend at times like this.'

Jenny ran her fingers over the tooled leather of the diary in her lap. She wanted to get back to it, to escape the ferocity of the impending storm and return to Matilda's world. But reluctance had made her hesitate over these past two days.

'That the last tone?'

Jenny nodded. 'It's the final chapter,' she murmured. 'And I almost don't want to read it.'

'Why?' Diane shook out her dark curls and flopped into the chair next to her. 'I thought you said it was bound to have a happy ending?'

Jenny thought deeply for a moment. 'It's not that so much. It's just that when I've finished the last page, it will be like saying goodbye to a close friend I'll never see again.'

Diane's dark eyes stared back at her. 'You can't just leave things unfinished, Jen. Not when it obviously means so much

349

to you. Besides,' she added practically, 'you'll always wonder how things turned out.'

'I know. I'm being silly, aren't I?'

Diane's curls bounced. 'Not at all. I always feel sad when I come to the end of a good story – but you soon get over it.'

Jenny opened the fly-leaf and rifled the pages. There weren't many more to read, for the book was only half used. She smoothed back the first page and settled deeper into the chair. Perhaps her reluctance to finish the diaries had more to do with that strange headstone in the family cemetery than with unwillingness to break contact with Matilda. For the mystery of that enigmatic epitaph was bound to be explained in these last few pages – and she was almost afraid of what she might learn.

She hadn't read more than a few words when the telephone rang.

'Who the hell is that?'

'Not being blessed with telepathy, I wouldn't know,' answered Diane dryly. She returned moments later. 'It's Helen for you.'

Jenny frowned as she looked up from the diary, but Diane merely shrugged. 'I know as much as you.'

'Hello, Jennifer.' The cultured voice drifted above the click and hiss of many party lines. 'I'm so glad to have caught you.'

Aware that Doreen at the exchange and probably most of the stations in New South Wales were listening in, Jenny chose her reply carefully. 'With this storm looming, it didn't seem wise to venture far.'

There was a moment's hesitation at the other end of the line before Helen spoke again. 'I was wondering if I could come over?'

Jenny frowned. 'Of course,' she said quickly. 'When?'

'Today, if that's not too inconvenient.'

Jenny heard the note of urgency and wondered if it had been transmitted halfway across the outback to the other stations. 'Fine by me. I'll do lunch.'

There was that hesitancy again and Jenny hoped Helen hadn't been drawn into the protracted tussle over Churinga – for she liked her, and the thought of a girls' lunch had lifted her spirits.

It was as if Helen had read her thoughts. 'I think I should warn you,' said the older woman carefully, 'I do have an ulterior motive for my visit – but it has very little to do with what you and Andrew discussed the other week.'

'Then you've probably saved me a journey to Kurrajong,' Jenny said with relief. 'There are things we need to talk about.'

'I agree,' Helen said firmly. 'But not with half the state listening in. I'll see you in about three hours.'

The click at the other end echoed through the wilderness. As Jenny replaced the handset she stared at it thoughtfully. Helen had made it clear that Ethan's hostility was not an influence, but would her impending visit explain the vendetta that had been going on for so long or merely muddy the waters?

Jenny chewed her lip as she went back out to the verandah. The sky was pregnant with storm – perhaps a portent of things to come?

Diane took the news of Helen's visit with surprise then delight. 'Nothing like a girly lunch to blow away the blues,' she said cheerfully.

Jenny smiled but felt uneasy as she took the diary back to the bedroom and changed into clean clothes. Something was obviously bothering Helen, and as she was part of the family who had waged a vendetta against Matilda and Churinga, she wondered if it could be connected with that.

'We'll have salad,' Diane declared. 'Too hot for anything else.'

Jenny took the steaks from the freezer and put them in the meat safe away from Ripper's inquisitive nose and the ever-present flies. As Diane mixed up a jug of lemonade and laid the table, Jenny whipped up an apple fool then set to preparing a salad from vegetables she'd just cut from the garden. With a dressing of oil and garlic, lunch was almost ready.

The house was as clean and dusted as it could be, the great vases of wild flowers Diane had placed strategically around the room bringing a welcome touch of colour to the gloomy morning. Jenny and Diane stood back and admired the effect, but the thought that this was probably the last time she would entertain here made Jenny restless.

'I'll take Ripper for a walk while you get changed,' she said finally.

An oppressive heat lay over the pastures as she and Ripper followed the line of trees which stood sentinel by the dry creek. Birdsong was lethargic, black hairy spiders hung drowsily on giant, silken webs, and a mob of 'roos lay supine in the shadows of the tea trees.

Ripper found a basking goanna and gave chase as it whipped away in fright. Jenny called him repeatedly but he was obviously on a mission and chose to ignore her.

With a sigh, she leaned against a tree and watched a colony of termites repair their damaged hill grain by grain. The similarity between their lives and those of the squatters was not lost on her. For inch by inch they had carved out a life in this wilderness – a fragile life that could be destroyed in seconds, by fire, flood and drought – and yet it was their spirit for survival that gave them the will to begin again.

A stealthy rustle at her feet tore her from her thoughts. The snake paused, inches from the toe of her boot, and Jenny froze. It was the deadliest of them all – one bite, and it would all be over. Her pulse raced as her heart hammered against her ribs. The moment stretched into endless seconds before the snake finally moved away and she could breathe again.

Ripper came bouncing out of the undergrowth, caught sight of the snake and pounced. Jenny didn't have time to think as she grabbed him by the scruff and hauled him off.

'You stupid bugger,' she rasped as he struggled to get back to his quarry. 'You'll get yourself killed, carrying on like that.' Jenny held him close as the snake went on its sinuous way. Then, with a sigh of relief, she headed back to the house.

'What was all the barking about?' Diane was standing on the porch, resplendent in a peacock blue caftan.

'Tiger snake. Ripper thought it was a toy,' she said grimly. 'I'd better shut him indoors for the afternoon.'

Helen arrived minutes later, the gleaming Holden lifting the dust in the yard as she drove up to the house and killed the engine. She looked cool and elegant in a cotton dress, her platinum hair softly gleaming in the dull sunlight.

'Thanks for agreeing to see me,' she said as they shook hands and settled on the verandah. 'I wasn't at all sure if you would.'

'Why ever not? After all, I've sampled your hospitality, and there are so few women out here it seems silly to ignore each other because of something that happened years ago,' replied Jenny lightly as she poured lemonade for each of them.

Helen lifted her glass. 'Cheers. Here's to common sense.'

Jenny glanced across at Diane then back to Helen. She was puzzled by the older woman's vehemence.

'Don't mind me, girls,' she laughed. 'I've lived too long in this place not to realise men really are the most incredibly stupid creatures. They strut about like cocks of the walks, trying to prove their machismo by out-shooting, out-riding and out-drinking each other, when all the time the women are the ones who put things to rights.'

She grinned as she eyed each of their puzzled faces. 'Don't worry, I'm not the Kurrajong version of the Trojan horse. I'm here as a mate, because I think it's about time all this nonsense between Kurrajong and Churinga came to an end.'

Taking a long drink of the home-made lemonade, she set her glass down. 'But let's forget all that for the moment and have lunch. It's been ages since I've been able to relax with a couple of friends.'

They ate on the verandah where it was cool and as the meal progressed, Jenny found herself strangely drawn to this woman who had to be old enough to be her mother, but young enough in spirit to be able knowledgeably to discuss the latest pop music, the Bay of Pigs incident, and the current fashions in London's Carnaby Street.

'We do get newspapers out here, you know,' laughed Helen. 'And I make sure I get down to Sydney as often as possible. Without my little forays into civilisation, I would shrivel up like most of the other women out here.'

'You aren't from the outback originally, then?' Jenny had cleared away the dishes and they were sipping the wine Helen had brought with her.

She shook her head. 'Good heavens, no. James and I met at one of my father's business parties in Sydney. He runs a meat exporting company and we were always entertaining squatters and graziers.'

She smiled softly. 'James was so handsome – and charming – and when he proposed I accepted right away. I thought living out here would be an adventure, and in a way I was right. But I still need to go back now and again to recharge my batteries.'

'I know what you mean,' said Diane, grimacing at the horizon. 'It's okay to visit but I certainly wouldn't want to live out here.'

Helen smiled. 'Don't get me wrong, girls, I'm very happy. James and I have a good, rich life, but I think you have to be born to this to be able to stay permanently. Andrew's the only one who seems to prefer the city, the rest of the family never leave Kurrajong unless they absolutely have to. He's a lawyer, you know, and a very good one too.'

Jenny nodded. 'I'm sure he's very powerful in court. He certainly seems out of place here, too clean and gentrified.' She came to an abrupt halt, realising too late how rude she must have sounded.

Helen laughed and finished her glass of wine. 'I know just what you mean. I sometimes have the strongest urge to roll him in the dirt or ruffle his hair. But James says he's been like that all his life, and he's far too old to change now.'

Silence fell over them as they looked out towards Kurrajong.

'You've been very patient, Jennifer,' Helen said eventually. 'And I have rambled on, but there is a reason for my visit, as I explained on the phone.'

'Is it to do with the persistent haggling over Churinga?' Jenny asked.

Helen eyed her for a long moment then nodded. 'In a way, I suppose it is – although that's only the result of one old man's refusal to see that the past is long gone and there's no profit in keeping it alive.'

Jenny tried to hide her mounting excitement by resting her chin in her hands and her elbows on the table. At last she was to learn the secrets that had been kept from the diaries – secrets perhaps even Matilda didn't know.

'It all started way back in the middle of the last century when the two families came to this part of New South Wales. They were pioneers, the Squires family arriving from England, the O'Connors from Ireland. But it was the O'Connors who got here first and took over the land we now

354

know as Churinga. It was good land, the best in these parts, with plenty of artesian water and mountain rivers.'

Helen fell silent for a moment, eyes misty as she looked out over the landscape.

'Despite the enmity between the English and Irish at that time, this place has a way of levelling people and the families got on well. The O'Connors had a daughter, Mary. She was to be their only surviving child. Life was even tougher back then and the infant mortality rate was high. Jeremiah Squires had three sons, Ethan, Jacob and Elijah.'

Helen smiled. 'In those days the Squires family was very religious, and although the names seem strange now, they were quite common then.'

Diane took a cigarette and offered one to Helen who fitted it into an ivory holder before she lit it. Jenny's mind was back in the past, trying to picture the people who'd lived and worked here all those years ago.

'Ethan was seventeen when he began to court the fifteen-year-old Mary. She had grown into a fiery beauty, by all accounts, and was considered to be far ahead of her time.'

Helen smiled. 'She was quite a handful, evidently, but then she'd have needed to be if she was to marry Ethan.'

'But she didn't,' said Jenny quietly. 'What happened?'

'Something no one expected, and it's this part of the story that's been kept a secret within the family ever since.' Helen watched the smoke curl up from her cigarette and dissipate in the hot air. 'So secret that I'm probably the only one who knows it.'

The silence was tangible and weighed heavily between them.

'How did . . .' Jenny began.

'I'm coming to that. But you have to understand this is a confidence that cannot be shared outside this place.'

She eyed each of them solemnly, then carried on. 'A few years back Ethan had a stroke and we all thought he was going to die. It was during one of his depressive stages that he confided in me.' She sighed and looked out over the land. 'He swore me to secrecy, not thinking he would survive for long, but of course he recovered and now he hates me because I know too much and he can't do without me.'

355

She gave a sad smile. 'At least it means I have some kind of authority over him for a change. He's an almost perfect patient – and as he loathes everyone, I don't feel insulted by his rudeness.'

'I don't know how you put up with him,' muttered Diane. 'If I was in charge, I'd have probably put something in his tea by now.'

Helen grinned. 'Don't think I haven't considered it. But he's James' father, and I don't feel so strongly I'd bump him off.'

The glasses were refilled and the three women settled back in their cane chairs. The heat was pervasive, the sky leaden. It was as if, like Jenny, the outback was holding its breath.

'Ethan and Mary were engaged for almost two years when he decided he couldn't wait for the wedding night. He was persuasive and because Mary loved him she turned her back on convention and gave in. Two months later she rode over to Kurrajong to find her father. He'd gone there to help with the shearing and as there was a minor crisis at home, her mother needed him. It was as Mary was walking past the drawing-room window that she heard something she shouldn't have, and that's when the trouble began.'

Helen sighed and turned the glittering rings on her fingers. 'Jeremiah Squire and Patrick O'Connor were having a furious row. Jeremiah was threatening to call the wedding off if Patrick didn't sign over several thousand prime acres of Churinga as a dowry. Patrick accused him of blackmail amongst other things. His daughter had been made promises, the wedding was due to take place in a week's time, and there had been no mention of a dowry two years before when the engagement was announced. He was a man caught in a terrible dilemma. His daughter would be disgraced if she was jilted, but the loss of so much prime land would drain Churinga. He refused Jeremiah's demands.'

Helen's eyes glittered as she stared across at Jenny and Diane. 'It was then that Jeremiah sneered at Patrick and told him his son had never wanted to marry Mary, had never even loved her. He was just doing as Jeremiah ordered, and if the land was not a part of her marriage settlement, then Jeremiah would marry him off to a widow, Abigail Harmer, whose father owned the big station to the north of Kurrajong, and was willing to hand over a large parcel of land as a dowry to get his daughter off his hands a second time.'

'Patrick pleaded with Jeremiah to see reason, but the old man would not be swayed. Mary was distraught and went to find Ethan. She confronted him with what she'd overheard, and after a long, heated argument, threw back his ring and returned to Churinga with her father. Within a matter of weeks she was married to Mervyn Thomas who'd been working on Churinga station as a stockman, and they moved out of the district.'

Jenny shivered despite the heat. 'She didn't have such a lucky escape,' she murmured.

Helen tilted her head in enquiry. 'I'll explain later,' Jenny said. 'Please go on with the story.'

'Ethan was distraught. He'd found that although it had begun as a ploy to get Churinga land, his courtship of Mary had turned into something more akin to love, and the thought of her married to someone else was impossible to come to terms with.'

'That's typical of a man,' snorted Diane. 'Never know what they want until someone else takes it away.'

Helen nodded. 'Exactly, but that wasn't the only reason. Months later Mary and Mervyn returned to Churinga. Patrick had died of a fever and they were needed to help her mother run the place. But they didn't come alone. Mary had given birth to a little girl whom she called Matilda. Although the child could just possibly have been Mervyn's, Ethan was convinced she was his. He decided to get both of them back, along with the land Mary had inherited from her mother.'

'So Matilda Thomas was Ethan's daughter?' gasped Jenny.

Helen nodded. 'Mary denied it vehemently and refused to discuss it until many years later when she knew she was dying. Ethan was furious. He wasn't the sort of man who took defeat lightly. Still isn't, miserable old bastard,' she added with a grim smile.

Jenny opened another bottle of wine. 'So what did Ethan do? Was this the start of his campaign to get his hands on Churinga?'

'In a way. You see, he felt he'd been cheated not only out of the land but also of the woman he loved and the child he'd sired. He married Abigail eventually, gave her a son, Andrew, his name, and Kurrajong gained thirty thousand acres, making it the biggest station in this part of New South Wales.'

Helen took a sip of wine and stared out over the home paddock. 'His two brothers were only too willing to hand over their share of the station once old man Jeremiah died, and with the money Ethan paid them, set up a wool shipping business in Melbourne. Now he was rich and powerful, a man with a great deal of influence. But he never forgot the one thing he'd been denied.'

Her tone was bitter as her eyes returned to Jenny. 'When the first world war began he used his influence as an officer to put Mervyn into the thick of the fighting. His plan was to get his rival killed. Then, with no man to look after her and the land, Mary would sell him Churinga.'

'But his plan backfired. Mervyn came back.'

Helen nodded. 'Not only that, Mary kept the place running and made a better job of it than Mervyn had ever done. Their paths crossed frequently over the years immediately after the war, and there was an uneasy truce between them, possibly even friendship. The real killer stroke came when Ethan got a private detective to look into the deeds and discovered Mary had full ownership rights to the land that were held in trust for Matilda. No one else could touch the land. Not him. Not Mervyn. Shortly after Mary died, Mervyn turned up at Kurrajong and asked Ethan to buy him out. It was a small victory to refuse the man who'd taken everything he'd once cherished, but the irony of the situation he found himself in wasn't lost on Ethan.'

'Knowing Mervyn, he'd have been furious,' muttered Jenny.

Helen shot her a curious look. 'How do you know so much about Mervyn Thomas?'

'I only know he was a bully and a drunk,' Jenny replied. There was no point in saying more. Some skeletons were best left in cupboards.

Helen nodded. 'That's what I heard. So did Ethan. But Mary couldn't be persuaded to leave him, even when he began to beat her and the child. Divorce was rare, and after the scandal of her broken engagement, she just wanted to remain anonymous.'

Helen gave a sigh. 'Ethan knew what was happening, but could do nothing. When Mary died he was heartbroken. I honestly believe he truly loved her. But after her death the need to reclaim what he considered his became an obsession with him. He began to hate Churinga and all it stood for. After Mervyn was killed in a flash flood he tried to make his peace with Matilda. But she was too like her mother and would have nothing to do with him.'

'So he never told her she was his daughter?'

Helen shook her head. 'He was either too proud or too stubborn to tell her the truth. Perhaps if he had things would have been different.'

The silence was heavy as they each considered their own thoughts.

'Sad, isn't it, when men are too proud to show their feelings and have to bury them in hatred and revenge?' Diane's voice was thoughtful.

'Even sadder when you think it was Jeremiah who triggered the whole thing off with his greed. How different all their lives would have been if only one of them could have faced the truth and spoken out.'

Jenny thought of the terrible life Matilda had had, and could have cried. Life was unfair – especially when it was blighted by an evil, greedy man like Jeremiah Squires.

'That was when things got out of hand. Ethan began to steal her sheep and block the creeks. He used Andrew as bait, trying to marry him off in return for ownership of Churinga, and got Billy, the youngest of the brothers, to do his dirty work out in Churinga pastures.'

She gave the two younger women a soft, sad smile. 'Things started to go wrong for him when Charlie made it obvious he was interested in Matilda. The old man blew a fuse, and without telling the boy why, threatened to cut him out of his will if he so much as looked at her again.'

'That would explain it,' muttered Jenny. 'I wondered why, when Ethan was so keen on getting his hands on Churinga.'

Helen frowned. 'You seem to know an awful lot for someone who's only just moved here?'

359

Jenny looked away. 'People talk. You know that, Helen.'

The older woman was silent for a long moment then she resumed her story.

'Matilda beat him at every turn, and I think in the end Ethan had a grudging respect for her. It became a battle which I think they both almost came to enjoy. But when Abigail died and his son Billy was killed in the second world war, the bitterness grew deeper. He found it easier to blame everything on Mary, Matilda and Churinga.'

Helen lit another cigarette and stared through the smoke. 'I don't pretend to understand the way his mind was working. Maybe he thought that if he and Mary had married he wouldn't have had a loveless marriage, or lost a son. He would have had the land his father had promised him and a daughter he'd never held. The bitterness was corrosive, that's all I know, and he began to look to Churinga again to exact his revenge.'

'And that's where I came in,' said Jenny bitterly. 'But I have nothing to do with this age-old feud. The people who once lived here are dead and gone.'

Helen looked at her for a long minute, eyes steady, fingers not quite still on her cigarette. Then she picked up the glass and took a drink. 'As you say,' she murmured, 'there's no one left.'

Jenny wondered what it was Helen was holding back but decided not to probe. She had come here willingly, and told her so much more than she could have hoped for, it would have to be enough.

'I almost feel sorry for Ethan. Poor old man. He must have loved Mary very much. What a waste of life – and all because of Jeremiah's greed.'

Helen's delicate fingers covered Jenny's hand on top of the table. 'I shouldn't waste your time feeling sorry for the old coot if I were you, Jennifer. If he'd loved Mary enough, he'd have defied his father and married her. He's a mean-minded, hateful man. If he ever did get his hands on Churinga, he'd probably raze it to the ground.'

'Thanks for coming over and telling me all this. It's put things into perspective, and I know now that if I do sell, it will never go to Ethan.'

'Old men have to be humoured, but the rest of the family

want nothing to do with the vendetta. Andrew is sick of doing his father's bidding and only the bribe of three hundred thousand dollars sent him here to make an offer for Churinga. As for Charlie . . .'

She shrugged, a soft smile playing on her lips. 'He'll never change. He loves Kurrajong and women, not necessarily in that order, and despite two marriages, will never settle down. Enjoy his flirting but don't take it seriously.'

Jenny laughed. 'I never intended to! Charlie is about as transparent as glass.'

Helen pleated the linen napkin on her lap. 'Kurrajong will be run by my daughter and her husband when it's time for us to hand over the reins and if you decide to stay I can guarantee nothing more will be said. My husband is quite taken with you, you know. He's pleased to see someone young on Churinga again. What happened all those years ago was unfortunate but the past is dead and so are most of the people involved. It's up to us to make the best of what we have.'

Jenny smiled. 'Someone else said that to me only a few weeks ago.' At the memory of that conversation with Brett, her smile slipped and she stood up. 'What about a real drink before you go? I've got a bottle of gin somewhere.'

Helen followed her into the kitchen. 'This person wouldn't happen to be the delicious Brett Wilson, would it?'

Jenny's hands faltered as she poured the drinks. 'What makes you say that?'

Helen smiled. 'Just the way you looked at each other when you were dancing. You're obviously both smitten.'

The retort was never uttered. Jenny stayed busy with the drinks.

'I'm sorry, Jennifer. I hope I didn't say anything out of place. It's just that here in the outback we have so little to occupy our minds that it makes us observant. The gossip over the telephone and the two-way is fair enough, but the only real chance of sniffing out the juicy bits are when everyone's gathered for a social event. You'd be surprised how much you can find out about people just by standing back and observing.'

'Well, you got it wrong this time, Helen.' Jenny laughed, but it sounded high and false.

'Plenty of fish in the sea,' she murmured with a frown.

361

Then she brightened. 'Let's drink to the future – whatever it may be.'

The three women chatted over their drinks as the sky darkened and the bustle of Churinga went on around them. Eventually Helen stood up. 'Time I was out of here.'

Jenny and Diane leaned into the car window and watched her kick off her delicate sandals.

'Can't feel the bloody pedals in these things,' she explained with a hiccup.

'Are you all right to drive? You look fairly tanked.' Diane turned to Jenny. 'Perhaps she'd better stay the night.'

'No worries, girls,' laughed Helen. 'What can I hit out here?' She patted Jenny's hand. 'Good talking to you, Jen. I feel much better now it's all out in the open.' She smiled. 'Stay in touch, and if you decide to go back to Sydney look me up. Here's my address in Paramatta.'

Jenny and Diane watched the car speed off in a cloud of dust. When it was merely a blur on the horizon they went indoors. The light was fading fast, thunder was rumbling in the distance and flies swarmed in black clouds around the horses in the paddocks.

'That was some story,' muttered Diane.

Jenny nodded. 'It explains a lot. Mervyn must have suspected Matilda wasn't his child – that was why he did what he did. Out of spite.'

Diane yawned. 'I don't know about you, Jen, but I've got a headache. Time for bed.'

Jenny agreed. The storm and the gin were having the same effect on her. The last of the diaries would have to wait until morning.


Brett had not been surprised to see Helen drive into Churinga. After all, he reasoned, if there was to be a wedding, she would be the one to make all the arrangements. But he was surprised she had come alone. Ethan might be an old man and confined to a wheelchair, but this wedding was the culmination of years of plotting and Brett was puzzled that he hadn't made sure he was in at the death. How he must be rubbing his hands at the thought of finally getting Churinga into the family.

The day had dragged on, the work around the station making it necessary for Brett to remain close to the homestead. He watched the women surreptitiously as they ate on the verandah, and although he could hear their laughter and chatter, was never close enough to overhear what they were discussing so earnestly. Yet he suspected a plot was being hatched, a wedding being planned. As soon as Helen left he would face Jenny and hand in his notice. There was no point in staying once Squires owned the place.

He found it almost unbearable to be around the homestead and finally managed to escape to the paddocks, but his mind wasn't really on what he was meant to do. Jennifer was different from any other girl he had met and Brett acknowledged sadly that even after three months she was still a mystery to him. They had sparred with words and gestures to begin with but he'd sensed a gradual change in her and in himself. The night of the dance had been his chance to make his feelings known.

Yet he'd blown it because he'd lacked the courage to speak to her. He'd been afraid of rejection. Afraid that his mates' taunting gibes of making up to the boss had reached her, and she would think the same.

His smile was bitter as he turned the horse towards home. The rejection had still come – had been far more painful because of the distance she had put between them. Lorraine wasn't helping either, and her recent behaviour did nothing to ease his conscience. She'd made herself look cheap by sleeping with one of the stockmen in the bungalow he'd shared on the night of the dance. It had been impossible to stay there with all that noise coming from the other man's room and Brett had been made all too aware the next morning that she'd done it out of spite.

He thought of how he'd taken a bed-roll and bunked in with the horses. Of how she'd come creeping into the stall at first light and told him what a great time she'd had. Then how she'd cursed and reproached him before tottering back out.

His sigh was deep. It was time to move on. Jenny would soon be married and Squires would put his own men on Churinga. The little sheep station in Queensland was beginning to look an attractive alternative.

363

He looked up at the looming sky and watched the heavy clouds roll. There was one hell of a storm brewing, he'd better make sure the mob was secure and that the penned animals couldn't break loose. One bolt of lightning and he'd have bloody woollies everywhere.

It was dark when he finally returned to the homestead. The Holden was gone, and the lights were out. The thought of handing in his notice depressed him.

'Jeez, Brett,' he muttered. 'You're getting to be a bloody old whinge. For Christ's sake, pull yourself together,' he muttered crossly as he rubbed down the horse and headed for his bungalow.

Slamming the door behind him, he threw himself on to the bed and stared at the ceiling. If the storm hit in the night there wouldn't be much sleep for anyone, but he doubted he would sleep anyway. All he could see was Jenny's face, and no matter how much he tossed and turned, the image refused to fade.

# Chapter Nineteen

The deep, menacing growl of thunder finally woke Jenny up. Her sleep had already been disturbed by dreams and images from the past. They paraded before her, faces indistinct and voices unintelligible.

She lay there for a while, hoping the images would fade. Yet even as they drifted away with the final tendrils of sleep, she could still feel their presence. They seemed to be all around her. Hiding in the shadows. Hovering close to her bed. Entwined in the very fabric of the old building.

Jenny swung her legs out of bed and padded into the kitchen. Her nightshirt was soaked with perspiration. The temperature was high even though it was a winter midnight and the thunder rolled mercilessly on over the land as if in search of a place to rest.

Lightning forked in yellow veins across the black sky. She shivered. She had always hated storms ever since her first foster father had locked her in a barn and left her there for the night. She'd been terrified as the storm gathered overhead and shook the earth and had screamed to be let out. It was only the threat of fire that had sent his wife to rescue her, and ever since then storms had a way of bringing back that terror.

Reaching for the remains of the lemonade, she took a long drink. Yet it couldn't quench her thirst, or cool her, for the heat seemed to have lodged deep within and nothing could touch it. With restless energy, she wandered through the house.

She could feel Matilda walking beside her but her presence neither soothed nor unsettled Jenny. The memories of the past were too vivid for that – the haunting refrain of the waltz too familiar.

The storm seemed to be growing nearer, the heat pressing down like a great weight, and after a sluice in tepid, murky water, Jenny returned to the bedroom and lay exhausted on top of the covers. The windows were open, only the screens keeping out the bugs, and the night sounds of the outback drifted in beneath the rumble of thunder.

She lay there thinking about what Helen had told her, and finally reached for the last of the diaries. The pieces of the jigsaw of Matilda's life and times were almost in place and, although she doubted she could concentrate with the elements fighting overhead, Jenny was ready to finish the story.

Churinga was at last making a profit. After discussing it with Finn, Matilda decided to seek help in investing that profit for the future. Life out here was uncertain, feast or famine, and after the drudgery of the war years she was determined not to return to grinding poverty.

After a series of letters to and from the business adviser at the Bank of Australia in Broken Hill, Matilda decided to make the long journey and discuss her business face to face with him. She was used to dealing with men who understood the pitfalls of life in the outback and had no idea how the city folk conducted their business.

The thought of having to deal with such an important issue as the future of Churinga with a stranger made her uneasy.

This was the first time she'd left the familiar surroundings of Wallaby Flats and Churinga. Although Finn had offered to come with her, Matilda had declined. She had managed alone this far, she was damned if she was going to let a little thing like this beat her.

It took several days of careful driving on the new highway to reach Broken Hill. At night, as she lay rolled in a blanket on the flat-bed, she rehearsed what she would say to the adviser, Geoffrey Banks.

His office was on the second floor of an elegant Victorian building that Matilda guessed had once been a private house. Fronted by a white colonnade, it was surrounded by well-tended gardens where smartly dressed women sat on benches under the shade of flowering gum trees.

Feeling a little awkward in her new shoes and summer dress, she squashed her hat firmly over her recalcitrant hair and climbed the steps.

Geoffrey Banks was young, with a firm handshake and a pleasant smile. Matilda watched him for signs of duplicity as he told her he understood her problems at Churinga, but when he mentioned that it was his brother who owned Nulla Nulla, her anxiety faded.

It took some time to settle upon a portfolio of investments but finally it was done and Geoffrey poured her a glass of sherry. He eyed her over his glass for a moment then said thoughtfully. 'Have you considered drawing up a will, Miss Thomas?'

Matilda was startled. It was something which had never occurred to her. 'Not much point,' she said. 'No one to leave the property to when I've gone.'

He leaned his elbows on the desk. There was a twinkle in his eye that might have been interpreted as flirtation if Matilda hadn't known better. 'You're still a young and, may I say, attractive woman, Miss Thomas. Who knows what the future might bring? I suggest that unless you want the government to take over your property when you pass on, you put the whole estate into trust for your heirs – just as your mother and grandmother did before you.'

Matilda eyed him sternly. Who did he think he was, getting fresh with a woman old enough to be his mother? 'There are no heirs,' she said firmly. 'And I don't see my life changing.'

'I understand, Miss Thomas,' he said carefully. 'But I really do advise you to reconsider. Life has a habit of catching us out, and who knows? You might yet wish to get married, even have a family. If you die intestate, then that family will have to fight in the courts to attain what is their rightful inheritance. Now you wouldn't want that, would you?'

Matilda thought of Ethan and Andrew, and of the way the Squires family had always wanted to get their hands on Churinga. If what he said was true, then the minute she died, they would pounce. She looked back at Geoffrey Banks. He had the cheek of the devil but even though she was likely to remain a spinster, Matilda could see what he was getting at.

'It probably won't make much difference one way or another but I suppose it wouldn't hurt,' she said finally. 'What do I have to do?'

Geoffrey Banks smiled. 'First, we have to decide who you want to inherit Churinga. Do you have anyone in mind?'

She stared off into the distance. Her way of life had left her with few friends and no relatives. She and April wrote to each other but somehow Matilda could feel a distancing between them and as the years passed it had become harder to find things to write about. Their lives were different now, with April living in the city and working in an office among smart, sophisticated people who sounded so interesting after the parochial blinkered people of the outback. April's children would be well taken care of when their grandparents passed on and Matilda doubted they would want to return to the outback anyway.

If she was to keep Churinga out of Squires' hands, then she had to find someone she could trust.

She thought for a moment then came to a decision that surprised her. Yet, as she examined the idea more closely, she realised it made perfect sense. She had been very wary of Finn McCauley when he'd first arrived, but as the months passed realised she had grown to like him and to value his friendship. Despite his youth and his handsome appearance, he was a quiet, almost shy man, who loved the land and was reticent with strangers. Yet he seemed at ease with her, making the three-hour drive to Churinga from Wilga at least once a week, and Matilda had fallen into the habit of cooking a special dinner for them both every Saturday night. After the meal they would listen to the wireless or talk about the week's work then he would leave as quietly as he'd come.

She smiled to herself as she thought of their deepening friendship and the trust which had been forged through it. He was bound to find himself a wife eventually but it would be nice to think she could leave Churinga to someone who would take care of it.

But he must never know what I've done, she told herself silently. I don't want our friendship tainted.

'I want Churinga to go to Finbar McCauley of Wilga station,' she said finally. 'And to be held in trust for his heirs.'

Geoffrey didn't question her decision and soon they were shaking hands. 'The papers will be typed and ready for you to sign in a couple of hours, Miss Thomas. It has been a pleasure to meet you at last.'

Matilda smiled up at him and left the office. She was pleased with the way things had turned out and those two hours would give her time to look around Broken Hill.

She walked along the parade of shops and stared in awe at their windows. Everything was so sophisticated here compared to the ramshackle ordinariness of the shops in Wallaby Flats. Her cotton dress looked drab beside the gowns that hung upon the plaster manequins, and although she knew she would probably regret it, she couldn't resist buying three new dresses, a pair of trousers, a jacket and some new ready-made curtains for the bedroom.

But it was the underwear that astounded her. She had never imagined women wore such fine things next to their skin. The cloth was soft and slippery and melted between her fingers like butter. And the colours . . . So many to choose from after the plain white cotton of the catalogue underwear she usually bought.

Her spirits rose as for the first time in many years Matilda began to have fun.

Loaded with parcels, she finally retraced her steps back to the utility. As she passed the broad, inviting window of the art gallery, she hesitated, intrigued by the bright posters advertising an exhibition.

The only paintings she had seen since she was a child, were in books and magazines she'd borrowed from the travelling library. This was a chance she might never have again.

She paid her sixpence and stepped into a world of outback colour and Aboriginal folklore. The sight of so many paintings took her breath away. The richness of their colour and the clarity with which the artists conveyed the world she knew pricked something deep inside and she recognised it as a longing to be able to create such beauty for herself.

There had been a time, long ago, when she had spent hours watching her mother paint. Watercolours of the landscape of Churinga, and the birds and animals which inhabited it,

369

seemed to appear like magic on Mary's paper and Matilda had been fascinated. It was a gift her mother had passed down to her, but since her death there had been no time for child's play – and her need for beauty had been fulfilled by the sight of her sheep, fat and healthy in the fields.

Yet, as she stood there in front of a particularly fine oil painting of an isolated cattle station, she felt that surge of longing return. Life had changed for her since the war. With money in the bank and men to do the hard work, there was time for the things she had neglected. With rising excitement, she walked through the gallery until she came to the counter.

There was such a confusing array of artist's materials set out that it took her a long time to decide but finally she chose a box of watercolours, some fine brushes, pencils, paper and a light easel. Guilt surged through her as she handed over the money and waited for them to be wrapped. This journey was proving to be expensive and self-indulgent.

It took a few minutes to sign the papers and lodge them with the bank for safe-keeping. When she eventually returned to the street, she realised she'd had enough of Broken Hill. The hotel was expensive, the people were strangers, and she missed Churinga. Climbing back into the utility, her shopping loaded up beside her, she headed for home.

At Churinga Matilda settled down to doing the things she had always wanted to do but never had the time for. There were books to be read, clothes to be made on the treadle machine she'd unearthed from one of the barns. A dollop of oil and new needles and it worked like a charm.

Then there was the joy of painting. The pleasure of fine, new paper beneath a brush. The soft sweep of colour that took her away from her day-to-day problems and completely absorbed her.

Matilda eyed her latest effort critically. It was better than she could have hoped she realised, as she studied her impression of how Churinga had once been before the improvements. Who would have guessed that these stubby, work-worn hands could manipulate brush and colour to create such delicate beauty? She grinned with pleasure but knew she had a long way to go to even being to compare her work with that in the gallery.

The clash of gears startled her and she glanced at her

watch. The time had flown while she'd been painting. Now Finn was here and she hadn't even started on dinner. She hastily stuffed her brushes in a jam jar of water and took off her apron. The new cotton frock was mercifully clean of paint but her hair was as usual flying in all directions. She pinned it back with clips and grimly eyed herself in the scrap of mirror she'd hung on the wall.

What a sight, she thought. Baked by the sun, freckled and wild-haired, you're beginning to look your age.

Yet, without really knowing why, she'd begun to take care of her appearance since Finn began his visits, making sure her dress was clean and pressed and her shoes polished. Gone were the old moleskins and boots, the felt hat and unbrushed hair. She told herself it was because she was the owner of a wealthy station, and as such, it was only proper for her to appear a lady and not a hoyden. But deep inside she wondered if perhaps it had more to do with Finn's visits than anything else.

He knocked on the door and she called out to him to come in. She looked forward to their evenings together and had meant to try the new recipe she'd found in a magazine but now it was too late. They would have to do with the left-overs of last night's roast.

'G'day, Finn,' she said as she walked into the room. 'Caught me on the hop. Time sort of runs out on me when I'm painting.'

'If that's the reasons, then it's good enough for me. You've really caught the spirit of the old place in this one. I didn't realise how clever you were.'

He turned from the watercolour on the easel and smiled at her. For the first time Matilda noticed the subtle changes in him. His shirts were crisply laundered, his trousers pressed. He'd shaved and cleaned his nails, cut his hair. His efforts to tame the wild Irish curls by plastering them with water were commendable but not particularly successful. But that was all a part of his charm.

She blushed and turned away. 'Dinner will have to be make-do and mend tonight. I hope you aren't too hungry?'

'No worries,' he said in his mellow voice, 'Give me a beer and I'll do the spuds.'

They worked together in silence, and when the meal of cold

meat, potatoes and pickles was ready, they ate it in the glow of a kerosene lamp on the verandah. Matilda found herself responding to his gentleness as he described his day with his beloved horses. He was a man in tune with his life and land. As she listened to the deep, melodious voice, she knew these moments were precious. For he was young and handsome and soon he would meet a girl and fall in love, and their friendship would necessarily take a back seat.

She pushed the thought away and took a sip of beer. Perhaps it was time to make him aware of how their innocent friendship was being discussed, give him the chance to back off before it was too late. 'The gossips are having a field day, you know,' she remarked quietly.

His eyes were dark jewels in the flicker of the lamp light as he ran his fingers through his hair. 'What about?'

'Your visits here, Finn. Don't tell me you haven't heard them?'

He smiled and shook his head. 'Never listen to gossip, Molly. Got better things to do with my time.' He paused as he took a drink. 'Anyway, what business is it of anyone's if I decide to spend my free time on Churinga?'

She laughed. 'None. But that doesn't stop them. The mothers of the outback are sharpening their claws, Finn. You don't seem to realise you're the object of fevered speculation. The natives are getting restless, they have daughters to marry off.'

Finn laughed and returned to his dinner. 'Let them fuss and bother, Molly. Gives them something to keep their tiny minds occupied. Besides,' he added, looking into her face, 'I think I'm old enough to choose who I want to spend my time with – don't you?'

Matilda studied him. It was pleasant to have him here, sharing dinner and the wireless concerts. His company meant a great deal to her after all the years of loneliness, but she could understand why the gossip had started. She was much too old to be keeping company with Finn. He should be out looking for a companion of his own age – a wife.

The thought made her lose her appetite, and the swift, almost painful realisation made her pulse race. How foolish she'd been to encourage his visits! One day he would bring a wife to Wilga and then their close friendship would fade to polite conversation as they passed one another in the fields or in town – and with a sickening jolt of horror she realised she was jealous of this future wife, couldn't bear the thought of his being with someone else, sharing dinners and quiet confidences that up until now had been hers alone.

Matilda sat there in silence, her dinner forgotten as the appalling truth dawned. She had begun to see Finn through the eyes of a woman – and one who was old enough to know better. For what would this young, handsome man ever want with a dried up, middle-aged old maid?

'Molly? You feeling crook?'

His voice made her jump even though the words had been softly spoken. She looked away, afraid he could read her thoughts in her eyes. The muscles were tight in her face as she forced a smile. 'Just a bit of indigestion,' she muttered. 'I'll be right.'

He eyed her for a long moment as she fiddled with her napkin and cutlery. 'Gossip doesn't worry me, you know, and you shouldn't let it worry you either. Live in Tassie long enough and you'd soon get used to it.'

'I keep forgetting you don't come from around here,' she said with a lightness she didn't feel. 'Somehow I think of you as part of this place. You seem so at home here.' Her newfound emotions were troubling and she dropped her gaze swiftly to her glass of beer.

Finn pushed back his chair and crossed his booted feet as he lit a cheroot. 'I've never really told you much about myself,' have I?' he said finally. 'We always seem to be discussing the land and the properties, not what really brought us both to this place.'

'You know most of my history,' she said quietly. 'But I'd like to know about your life before Wilga.'

He puffed on his cheroot as he stuck his thumbs in his trouser pockets and stared out over the paddocks. 'Mum and Dad had a small place in the centre of Tassie, called Meander. It's in a vast plain surrounded by mountains and it gets very hot and very cold. We raised horses. I can't remember a time where there weren't horses in my life. That's why, after the war, I decided to take the government's offer to start my own place here.'

She studied him in the lamplight and saw something shadowing his eyes. 'Why didn't you go back to Tassie and begin again there?'

Finn shifted in his chair, took the cheroot out of his mouth and inspected it closely before flicking the ash into a saucer. 'Dad died several years back and I kept the place going until Mum passed on. The war came then and I was soon old enough to be called up so I sold everything and put the money into the bank for when I returned. Somehow the place just wasn't the same without Ma.'

Matilda sighed. 'I know what you mean. I'm sorry if I've pried into things you'd rather not talk about.'

He shrugged. 'No worries, Molly. The old man was a bit of a bastard, and to be honest it was almost a relief when he went. But Ma . . . Well, that was different.'

Matilda watched the conflicting emotions flit across his face and in his eyes. Finn rarely talked about his past but tonight he seemed to want to unburden himself of whatever it was that troubled him and she was loath to disturb the thread of his thoughts.

'You might think that a poor way to think about my dad but, you see, he hated me. I was his only son and wanted to please him, but from the very first I can't remember him ever showing me any affection. It was Ma who encouraged me, made me the man I am now,' he finished quietly.

Silence filled the room as he sat there deep in thought and Matilda conjured up a sudden image of Mervyn. Parents had a lot to answer for – it was a wonder she and Finn had grown up at all.

'After Dad died, I understood the reason behind his coldness,' he began again. 'You see, I wasn't his son. It was only years later, when Ma was dying, that she told me. I was adopted. But somehow I think deep down I'd already suspected as much. Yet it no longer seemed to matter once it was just me and Ma. She was a good mother and I loved her very much.'

'What about your real parents? Were you never curious?'

'Nah. Ma died before she could tell me more and I never bothered to try and find out. Mum was Mum. The only one I had and the only one I wanted. She was a good woman. After she died, I thought about joining the priesthood. It was something she, as a Catholic, had always wanted and hoped for, but I loved the land too much and the freedom of working with horses.'

He grinned. 'I reckoned I'd be doing the Lord's work better by devoting my life to that rather than being cloistered in a brotherhood.'

Matilda saw the light in his eyes and realised this was a new side to Finn she would never have suspected and it made her uneasy. 'Religion's not for me,' she said carefully. 'Too many things have happened in this world for me to believe in an all-forgiving, all-loving God.'

After looking at her for a long moment, he sighed. 'I take your point. The war was an eye opener for me too. My faith was put to the ultimate test time after time. It's hard to believe in God when you're surrounded by carnage and the death of your closest mates.'

He stubbed out his cheroot. 'But my faith is a part of me. A very personal part. I'm not about to spout religion or try to convert you, I just want to live my life as best I can.' He grinned. 'I don't know why I'm telling you all this. You must think I'm some kind of religious nut or at best a whinger. Sorry.'

Matilda leaned across the table and took his hands. 'Thank you for trusting me enough to tell me how you feel,' she said gently.

He didn't pull away but began to stroke her fingers. 'You're easy to talk to, Molly. Somehow I knew you'd understand.'

She swallowed the lump in her throat and wished she could stroke back the dark curls that fell over his forehead. Wished she could take him in her arms and hold him until the shadows faded from his eyes. The war had a lot to answer for and she regretted not having his kind of faith.

Then reason took over and she snatched her hand away and busied herself with the dishes. What on earth was she doing? she thought furiously. Pull yourself together, woman, have you lost every grain of sense you ever possessed?

Dumping the dishes in the sink, she turned on the radio and waited for it to warm up. 'You mustn't bury yourself out on

Wilga, Finn,' she said gruffly. 'There's a good social life to be had out there, and it's time you had some fun.'

A beautiful Strauss waltz drifted from the wireless and filled the silence which had fallen between them.

'You're being very wise for someone who rarely leaves Churinga. Why have you never gone to the dances and parties? How come you never married?'

'I've been too busy,' she said shortly. 'Besides, I don't need a man to make my life complete.'

Finn was swiftly beside her, his warm hands covering hers as he turned her to face him. 'Why is there so much anger in you, Molly? Who hurt you so badly that you shut yourself away out here?'

Matilda tried to pull away, but he held her fast. She glanced up at him, the top of her head barely reaching his chest. They had never been this close before and it was doing strange things to her insides.

'I'm not angry,' she said breathlessly. 'Merely settled in my ways. You seem to forget, Finn, I'm an old woman and it's too late for me to change.'

'You didn't answer my question, Molly,' he said softly. He put a finger beneath her chin and forced her to look up at him. 'Something happened to make you hide. Why don't you trust me enough to tell me?'

Some things she couldn't tell him. Didn't have the courage. She swallowed, then after a hesitant start found the words began to flow in an almost never-ending stream as she related some of her past. It felt as if a great weight had been lifted from her shoulders. She looked up at him, a silent plea in her eyes for him to understand and not question her further.

His breath came in a long, deep sigh as he folded his arms around her and held her close. 'You're a beautiful woman, Molly. Brave too. You shouldn't have to shut yourself away out here because of what happened in the past. Any decent man would be proud to have you as his wife.'

'Nonsense,' she stuttered against the broad, warm chest. She could hardly breathe and her pulse was racing with the intensity of his nearness. How she longed to rest her head there, to breathe in the wonderful, crisp, outdoor smell of him, feel the steady drum of his pulse.

She resisted the primal urge to give in to her longings and looked up. 'I'm old, with skin like a freckled prune and hands like a drover. My hair's the colour of carrots and about as tough as fencing wire. I'm quite happy to stay single. The land might let you down now and again but at least it never lies to you.'

She tried to pull away from him but his grip was firm, his gaze unwavering as he led her into the slow, seductive waltz. She was a moth, trapped in the intense light of his eyes, and as he bent his head and kissed her, she flinched. For a fleeting second in that butterfly kiss she'd been burned as if by flame. It coursed through her and sent her thoughts spinning into space – shattering the tenets of her solitary life into dust. And yet it was wrong. He was too young. She was too old. Things like this shouldn't be happening. She should pull away now and put a stop to this.

But she was transfixed. It was as if she had no control. He was leading her in a dance that she wished would last forever – and despite all her misgivings, there was nothing she could do about it.

They moved slowly with the music, becoming part of its beauty until the last refrain hovered in the stillness of Churinga. Then Finn cupped her face in his hands. He was so close she could feel his breath on her eyelashes and see the violet chards in the blue of his eyes. This was wrong – every sense told her so – and yet she wanted him to kiss her again. Wanted to feel that soft mouth on hers. Wanted the shock of electricity that sparked such conflicting, delightful emotions within her.

His lips were closer now, almost touching hers, and then slowly, slowly they settled.

Matilda was swept up in a vortex of a desire such as she had never known – had never believed possible. She clung to him, ran her fingers through his hair as she leaned into him. She drowned in the sweetness of his touch as he kissed her throat and the pulse in her neck before returning to her lips. His tongue explored the soft inside of her mouth, swirling eddies of unbelievable delight through her. She was melting into him, fusing herself into his very being – and still it wasn't enough.

'I love you, Molly,' he groaned. 'I love you so much it hurts. Be my wife,' he pleaded as he traced fire down the column of her throat and into the hollow at its base. 'Marry me, Matilda. Marry me before I go crazy.'

She fought her way back to reality and staggered from his arms. 'I can't,' she gasped. 'This is madness. It wouldn't work.'

She evaded him as he reached for her. If he touched her again she would be lost, and she knew one of them had to come to their senses.

The confusion was clear on his face. 'Why, Molly? I love you, and after what's just happened between us, I know you love me. Why are you letting your stubbornness get in the way?'

He took a step closer to her but didn't try to touch her. 'Not all men are like Mervyn,' he said softly. 'I promise never to hurt you. You're too precious.'

Matilda burst into tears. It was something she hadn't done for a long time, but her emotions were so muddled that nothing could surprise her tonight. She loved him – there was no doubt about it – the miracle was that he should feel the same.

Yet as she looked at him through her tears and saw the hurt and bewilderment in his eyes, she tried to see their future together. What if it was purely loneliness that had driven them into each other's arms? What if one day he looked at her and saw how old she was? What if he should discover he didn't love her at all, and turned to a younger woman who could give him the children and the promise of growing old together? How could she ever bear the agony of seeing him with someone else after knowing him so intimately?

She felt the pain as though someone had plunged a sharp knife into her, and although the agony was all-consuming she knew what her answer must be and the consequences it would bring. She was about to lose him. Their friendship could never be the same after tonight – and she would never know him as a lover.

'I can't marry you, Finn, because I'm nearly thirty-seven and too old and worn out with working the land for so long. Find someone who can grow old with you, my love. Someone who will give you kids and a long future together.'

His hands were strong as they gripped her arm and twisted her to face him. He held her tightly against his chest, rocking her as if she was a baby.

'I am going to marry you, Matilda Thomas,' he said fiercely. 'We love each other and I want you for my wife. I won't take no for an answer. We have only one chance in this life and I won't throw away the best thing that's ever happened to me because you think you're too old.'

Her tears drenched his shirt as she thought of Gabriel's story of the first man and woman, and how they decided to travel life's journey together. She loved Finn and he loved her – why try and look into a future that held no guarantees for anyone? If they only had a short time of happiness then surely that was better than the bleak emptiness without him?

She looked into his eyes, saw the love he had for her and relaxed in his embrace. Drawing his head down, she felt the wonder of his mouth on hers and knew it was right. She would cherish each day, each moment, so that when their time together was over, she would have a store of memories to treasure.

'Yes, Finn. I'll marry you. I love you too much to let you go.'

'Then come waltz with me, Matilda. Waltz with me forever,' he cried jubilantly, sweeping her off her feet.

She clung to him, the tears of happiness rolling down her face. For as long as it lasts, she silently promised herself. For as long as it lasts.


Jenny wiped away the tears and put the diary aside. Matilda was an extraordinary woman. She had survived the kind of life that would have finished off strong men and had almost sacrificed her happiness because she doubted anyone as young and handsome as Finn should want her. And yet she'd had the courage to face that uncertain future, no matter how painful it might become – for she understood that life held no guarantees, and he was worth the gamble.

Jenny sighed and thought of Peter and Ben. Her own life had seemed so settled, so secure, and yet fate had stepped in and torn that life apart. Her memories were all she had left, but they were better than nothing.

The first rays of light were struggling against the storm clouds, and as she watched them drift into the room, she wondered if memories of Brett and Churinga would remain with her once she'd returned to Sydney.

Certainly she would always carry the memory of Matilda, for how could those diaries not affect the reader. But Brett? he was no Finn McCauley, that was for sure.

'One more day, Ripper. That's all we've got.' She pulled the pup from his hiding place under the bed and cuddled him. He licked her face and trembled at each growl of thunder, his tail tight between his legs. 'Come on, boy. A quick run in the yard then you can eat.'

She carried him out to the back porch, and after a hurried scuffle in the long grass, he was back at her side. Jenny looked up at the sky. Despite the heat, she shivered. The electricity was tangible in the air, the ominous scent of gathering forces bound the earth and sky together in a tight, breathless balance, waiting for the moment when all the furies would be unleashed.

She glanced across at the paddocks. The horses had been corralled in the far corner away from the trees that swayed and dipped in the hot wind, their long, supple branches sweeping the dry earth. Sheep huddled in woolly clumps against fences, their backs to the wind, their stupid bleating drifting across the pasture.

The scene was one Jenny knew had been repeated over the decades, and would probably be repeated for years to come. The outback didn't change and neither did the people who inhabited it. They were a strong, invincible breed, as tough as the land they worked and the elements they fought.

Turning back into the house, she put Ripper's dinner in a bowl. His appetite had obviously not been affected by his fright, she noticed. She left him to it and crossed the room to look once again at the watercolours that had fascinated her even since her arrival.

This was Churinga as Matilda had known it. Each detail lovingly recreated with delicate brushwork and soft colour. Jenny was glad she and Matilda shared this love of art. It made her feel even closer to the woman she had never met but whom she'd had the fortune to know intimately.

Taking the paintings down from the wall, she stacked them carefully into an apple crate then wedged them firmly with her own rolled up canvases. Adding her drawing pads, oils and brushes, she tied the whole thing up with string and brown paper. She would take them back to Sydney, she decided. Not only as a reminder of what might have been but as a tangible record of one woman's life and influence on a small corner of New South Wales.

One more day, she thought sadly as she looked around the silent house. Only one more day and all this will be just a memory. Annoyed with herself, and feeling the need for company, she checked on Diane.

She was lying on top of the sheets, the bedside light casting a pool of yellow into the gloom, the diaries spread across the bed. She was asleep, a frown puckering her brow, her lips moving in silent communion with her dreams.

Jenny closed the door and went back to her own room. There were only a few pages left then it would be over. The last day could be spent riding over the land she had come to love so she could say goodbye.

Matilda was swept along in the wake of Finn's enthusiasm. 'I think we should wait a while, Finn,' she protested. 'You might want to change your mind.'

'No, I won't,' he said firmly. 'And there's no reason for us to wait, Molly. God knows it took long enough for us to find one another.'

'Then let's just slip off to a register office in Broken Hill,' she said urgently. 'I don't know that I want to be the focus of so much attention and gossip, and I'd feel a hypocrite going through a church service.'

He held her then and kissed the top of her fiery head. 'I'm not ashamed of what we're doing, Molly. I don't see why we shouldn't have God's blessing, and the whole world can look on as far as I'm concerned. It's you and me and the vows we take that matters – no one else.'

Matilda looked at him, not totally convinced he was right. She had spent too many years trying to silence the chattering voices over the bush telephone, and yet in the wake of Finn's determination, she could do nothing to stem the crumbling of that veneer she had built up to protect herself.

Father Ryan had aged. His long, thin face was wreathed in lines of weariness and his once dark hair was now iron grey. The mule and buck board had been replaced with a car, but those long years of travelling through his vast parish had taken their toll.

He smiled as Matilda and Finn told them why they had come. 'I'm delighted for both of you,' he said in his soft Irish brogue that had hardly been touched by an Australian twang. 'I know life hasn't been easy for you Matilda, and I would be honoured to perform the wedding ceremony.'

She looked across at Finn as he took her hand and held it on his knee. He was doing his best to reassure her but she still felt uneasy in the presence of the priest.

Father Ryan was turning the pages of his diary. 'So many weddings now the war is over,' he sighed happily. 'I'll call the banns this Sunday and arrange the service for four weeks' time.' He looked up. 'How does that suit you?'

Matilda and Finn exchanged glances, and he held her fingers tightly. 'Can't come soon enough, Father,' he said.

The priest looked sternly over his half-moon glasses, and Matilda blushed. 'It's not like that, Father,' she said quickly. 'We just don't see the sense in waiting, that's all.'

Her hand was sweating and the room seemed to be closing in. It had been a mistake to come here. A mistake to think she could face the priest again after the things that had happened with her father.

'Your mother brought you up to be a good Catholic girl, Matilda,' he admonished. 'I wouldn't like to think you'd be entering into marriage with sin on your soul.'

There's more sin on my soul than you'd ever think possible, she thought, as she gripped Finn's hand for support.

He leaned forward. 'Matilda and I have done nothing wrong, Father. We are content to wait until our wedding day.'

The priest shut the book and leaned back in his chair. He pulled out a battered pocket watch and flicked it open. 'Would you like me to hear your confessions while you're here? I have time.'

'It's been too many years, Father,' Matilda said hurriedly. 'I doubt if I could remember all my sins.' She smiled, trying to make light of it and to avoid his penetrating stare. She wanted to get out of the office and into fresh air. Needed to be away from the smell of furniture polish and musty books. Why had she let Finn bring her here when she'd sinned so badly that she was too ashamed to tell a priest? Father Ryan would preach hell and damnation if he knew what she'd done with Mervyn, and the consequences of that terrible deed.

Finn held her hand, increasing the pressure in tacit encouragement for her to remain strong. But she knew this was one time she would fail him.

'I'm sorry, Father. It's been too long and it would be hypocritical of me to try and confess now,' she finished lamely.

Father Ryan took off his spectacles and massaged the bridge of his nose. 'I can't force you, Matilda, and I wouldn't want to. But confession is a part of the ceremony and I hope you will change your mind. If you need to talk, you know where I am. That goes for you too, young man.'

He stood up and shook hands, then led them out of the presbytery. 'I expect you both to come to mass on the next three Sundays to hear the reading of your banns. God bless you.'

Matilda hurried down the path past the dusty, leaning tombstones and out into the street. She wanted to get as far away as possible from the claustrophobic reach of the church. It had been too many years since she'd thought about God. Too much had happened, and her faith had not been strong enough to survive the onslaught.

Finn caught up with her and grasped her arm. 'Wait on, Matilda. What's the rush? What is it you're afraid of?'

She looked at him for a long moment, the dust of the graveyard swirling around her feet. 'I have something to tell you, Finn,' she said quietly. 'But not here. Please take me back to Churinga.'

His silence was deep and puzzled as they walked back to the utility. She was grateful for it nevertheless. She didn't look at the grandeur of the sweeping grasslands as they drove out of Wallaby Flats; she was busy working out in her mind what she would say to him. It wasn't right to keep that last secret from him – the secret of the child she'd buried so long ago.

And yet it was a secret she would have given almost anything to keep to herself. She still felt used and dirty. Soiled by Mervyn's lust and the lie she'd had to live ever since. How would Finn react? Would he still want her? Would he understand why she couldn't possibly have gone to confession?

She stared out unseeing. She had to have faith in him. Had to believe he would understand why she couldn't begin their new life with this on her conscience. Her Catholic upbringing had finally proved too strong to ignore.

Finn drove into the yard and Matilda climbed down. She turned to him and held him in silence for a long moment then walked into the house. Her fate was in his hands.

Some time later, she stopped talking. She was dry-eyed as she saw the horror creep over his face and the shadows darken his eyes but so far he had said nothing.

'Now you know it all, Finn,' she said quietly. 'If you want to call off the wedding, then I understand.'

He rose from his chair and knelt at her feet. He put his arms around her as he rested his head in her lap. 'My darling girl,' he groaned. 'Did you think my love for you was so fragile? It wasn't your fault – or your sin – you have nothing to be ashamed of.'

Matilda's breath escaped in a long sigh as she ran her fingers through his thick, dark curls. And when he looked up into her eyes, she knew words weren't necessary. With the tranquillity of knowing she had finally come home, she gave herself up to his embrace.

They were married three weeks later in the little wooden church in Wallaby Flats. Two of their drovers acted as witnesses and the only guests were the men they employed on Churinga and Wilga.

Matilda had decided not to wear white. It didn't seem fitting and would only have been another lie. So she'd driven back to Broken Hill, and after much indecision finally chose a dress of sea green. It fell from the tiny rose at the waist almost to the floor in a swirl of silk that shimmered in the sunlight like she imagined waves danced on a distant beach. She chose shoes that were dyed to match and made up her own bouquet with roses cut that morning from her garden.

The dress set off the fire of her hair, which she'd brushed to a gleaming copper and left hanging down her back in a cloud of curls. A coronet of pale cream roses took the place of a veil. For the first time in her life she felt beautiful.

As she stood alone in the entrance to the church, she looked down the narrow aisle to the altar. The organ was playing, Father Ryan was waiting for her, and there by his side was Finn.

Matilda felt a flutter of awe. He looked so handsome in his suit, his dark hair damply curling around his ears and over his forehead, and she loved him deeply – and yet that still, small voice reminded her of the promise she made herself when he proposed.

'For as long as it lasts,' she muttered. 'Please let it be forever.'

The creaking organ was being thumped enthusiastically and Matilda suddenly wished she'd asked one of the men to escort her down the aisle. But it was too late now. She had been on her own for so many years, what was a few steps more towards a much brighter future?

She took a firmer grasp of the bouquet and with a deep intake of breath, walked towards Finn.

The service passed in a kaleidoscope of incense and flowers, of Finn's deep baritone and mesmeric eyes. Finally the ring was on her finger and her new husband was looking down at her with such pride she felt like crying from sheer joy.

Finn had arranged for their wedding breakfast to be held in the hotel. As they left the church to cross the street, Matilda was bewildered by the size of the crowd who'd come to watch.

Don't mind them,' he whispered, taking her hand and nestling it in the crook of his arm. 'They haven't seen such a beauty before.'

She shot a glance at the curious faces, the mouths moving behind hands and the sly smiles – and knew their reason for coming was very different. But for Finn's sake she kept silent.

The hotel had been decorated especially for the occasion with banners and balloons and tables groaning with food. There was even a three-piece band of violin, piano and bass.

Finn held out his hand and led her on to the tiny square of dance floor.

'Come waltz with me, Matilda,' he said with a grin as the band struck up the Banjo Paterson tune.

She laughed and stepped into his arms. 'Forever,' she whispered.

Two hours later they had cut the cake, changed into their travelling clothes, and were sneaking out of the back door of the pub.

'No one will notice,' insisted Finn. 'I gave the landlord enough money to keep those blokes in beer for at least another hour or so, and by that time we'll be long gone.'

'Where are we going exactly?' laughed Matilda, as she climbed into the utility. 'You've been so secretive.'

He tapped his nose. 'It's a surprise,' was all he would say.

She didn't mind where they ended up so long as they were together. She sat beside him in the ute, her head resting against his arm as he drove towards Dubbo.

The light was fading as they reached the airfield but still Finn refused to tell her his secret destination as he helped her up the steps of the light aircraft and buckled her into her seat.

'What's going on, Finn?' she laughed uneasily. She had never seen a plane this close before, let alone been in one. 'You aren't kidnapping me, are you?'

He rained kisses on her face. 'Too right, Mrs McCauley. Just you wait and see.'

The propellers whined, the plane rocked and they were tearing down the runway. Matilda gripped the arms of the seat as they took off into the sky. Then she let the breath escape and stared in wonder at the earth beneath them.

'I always knew it was beautiful, Finn, but I never realised how grand it was. Look at that mountain, and that stand of trees by the lake.'

He smiled as he took her hand and folded it between his own. 'From now on, Mrs McCauley, you will see things and visit places you have only dreamed about. I want you to enjoy life again, to have all the things you ever wanted.'

She stared at him. Where was the woman who was tough and rough and could swear and shout as well as any man? Where was that hard little woman who'd ridden out with the mob and kept Churinga going through the war years? She had melted away, Matilda realised. Grown soft and feminine. And all because of this man who'd shown her what love could be.

She sighed happily. Life was taking on a new meaning, and she meant to experience every last wonderful second of it.

They landed in Melbourne. After a snatched evening meal, he took the cases and dragged them out to catch a taxi. 'We aren't staying here, Molly. But I promise you that before tomorrow morning, we can begin our honeymoon.'

'Enough, Finn McCauley,' she said, trying to keep a straight face. 'I'm not going any further until you explain just where we're going.'

He slammed the taxi door and waved the tickets in her face. 'We're off to Tassie,' he said with a grin.

She couldn't find the words to express her surprise.

Finn hugged her, and as she leaned into him, kissed the top of her head. 'You let me into your past. Now it's my turn. I want to show you what a beautiful place Tassie is, and share it with you.'

The Melbourne docks were bustling as the taxi weaved its way around the giant stacks of freight, and the heavy machinery. The *Tasmanian Princess* was gently tugging against her moorings. As Finn took her elbow and steered her through the passenger terminal, Matilda looked up and up in awe. Painted blue and white, with a vast funnel emblazoned with the Australian flag, the ship's decks were alive with the colour and jostle of her many passengers.

'I booked one of their largest cabins,' Finn murmured as they followed a seaman along the narrow corridors. 'I just hope you like it.'

Matilda waited as the seaman unlocked the door and dropped their cases inside. The man smiled, touched his hat and pocketed his tip. Then Finn turned to her and swept her off her feet.

'This might not be the threshold of Churinga or Wilga, but it's our home for the next twelve hours.'

She put her arms around his neck and nuzzled close as other passengers eyed them with knowing looks. She was nervous and excited and knew she was blushing furiously – but how safe she felt in his arms, how certain she had done the right thing.

Finn carried her into the cabin and kicked the door shut behind him. He held her close, the rapid thud of his heart echoing her own. His eyes were dark as he bent his head and his mouth was soft but urgent against her lips.

Matilda clung to him, half afraid of what was to come, half impatient, and when he slowly set her back on her feet, she felt an ache of disappointment.

'I'll leave you to freshen up, Matilda,' he said softly. 'The bar's not too far away, and I won't be long.'

She wanted him to stay, wanted to tell him she didn't care about wedding night convention – but a tremor of doubt forbade it. When the door clicked behind him, she stood there for a long moment staring at it. The memory of Mervyn was suddenly very powerful in that flower-filled room. She thought she could feel the rasp of his hands and hear his breath.

She shivered, wrapping her arms around herself to ward off his presence. What if sex with Finn should bring back the horror of that time? What if she didn't please her new husband and found she couldn't give him what he wanted?

'Oh, Finn,' she sobbed into her hands. 'What have I done?'

'Molly?' His voice was soft as his arms held her close. 'I should never have left you. I'm sorry.'

She hadn't heard him come back. She looked up at him through her tears. He put a finger against her lips.

'Shhh, my darling, I know. And I understand.' He kissed her, softly, fleetingly, and as her arms curled around his neck, the kiss became deeper.

Matilda felt the presence of Mervyn fade into obscurity as Finn's gentle hands cupped her face and stroked the column of her neck. Now she understood how the wild colts must feel as he gentled them. How could she ever compare this languorous love-making to the violence of her first experience?

Finn kissed her neck and the hollow at her throat, tracing liquid fire with his tongue. His hands moved over her, arousing a tidal wave of yearning that seemed to have an endless height and depth that was beyond her reach – and when her dress fell in a slither of silk at her feet, she arched her back and gave herself up to the electricity of his hands on her skin.

His flesh was taut, the clean, firm lines running beneath her fingers like the softest of leather. She tasted the salt of his sweat, breathed in the earthy, manly smell of him, and buried her fingers in the tight curls on his broad chest.

Dark hair feathered her breasts as he softly kissed her belly and caressed her hips. She cried out as his tongue scorched a trail of fire along the inside of her thighs.

The outside world ceased to exist as she was swept up in a whirlwind of sensations. She wanted to consume him, to be consumed by him. As he moved over her and slowly entered her, she wrapped her legs around his waist and drew him deeper until they were fused in joyous communion. Flesh against flesh, sweat mingling, breath shared, they rode the riptide until it broke.

Matilda lay in the curve of his arm, as sensuous and languorous as a cat in the sunshine. She arched into him as he ran his hand down her spine and followed the valley of her waist and the hill of her hip. Even now, in the afterglow of his lovemaking, his hands could arouse her.

'I love you, Mrs McCauley,' he whispered.

Matilda's first sight of Tasmania astounded her. She hadn't really given much thought to this seventh state, and had only looked it up in an old atlas after Finn's arrival on Wilga, but now, as she stood on the deck, she realised that the tiny dot on the atlas had no bearing on the mountainous sprawl on the horizon.

Devonport was a sleepy port with a town that nestled between the Mersey River and the Bass Strait. Black rocks and yellow sand fringed the shores where green swathes of grass were sheltered by leafy trees, and little wooden houses perched on the hillside and in the valleys.

There was colour everywhere in the bright flowers, the shingled roofs and verdant lawns, and Matilda would quite happily have stayed here. But Finn had his own agenda, and she too was keen to see the place where he'd been brought up, so they hired a car and headed south.

Meander was in the middle of nowhere and reminded her of home. And yet the distances between properties were much less, the grass a little greener, the colours softer. What she missed were the flocks of birds, the jarring calls of the parra-keets and galahs, the laughter of the kookaburra.

Finn showed her the little wooden house that sat perched on a low hill surrounded by acres of grassland. It seemed too small for the large family that lived there now and she wondered why they didn't build on to it.

'Probably got no money,' Finn explained. 'Most of Tassie's landowners are money poor and land rich. They have no idea of the worth of some of their handed down heirlooms because all they care about is the land.'

He smiled down at her. 'Rather like their counterparts in New South Wales.'

'Not all of them,' she said in mock severity. 'I know exactly what I'm worth, and I don't plan on ever being poor again.'

He laughed and held her for a moment. 'Come on. I'll show you my old school.'

They visited the one-room school house, the secret hide-aways that all boys seemed to have when they were small, and the little town twenty miles away where he showed her the cinema and the ice-cream parlour and the long sandy cove where he remembered swimming in the icy sea.

Parts of Tasmania were very different from the parched outback and Matilda sometimes found it hard to remember this was all part of the same country. Here the grass was lush and mostly green. Great mountains soared on all sides, and lakes as big as the ocean sprawled in majestic swathes in the valleys. Trees grew crisp red apples and soft fruit, and fields of lavender and poppies swayed in the warm wind.

Rocky crags guarded the south-eastern coast, with perilous cliffs overshadowing stretches of sand so white they hurt the eyes. Waterfalls plummeted hundreds of feet into jungle valleys. Quiet secluded bays buzzing with insects, drowsy with heat, were the perfect hideaway for lovers to swim and lie in the sun. Pine and eucalyptus forests spread as far as the eye could see. The curious Tasmanian devil, platypus and wombat were shy creatures, only seen if the watcher had endless patience and knew where to look.

Matilda and Finn spent two weeks exploring the island, taking the time to laze in the sun and swim in the chill waters.

They visited Hobart and climbed Mount Wellington, toured the market on the waterfront and went sailing around the tiny islands. In the evenings they ate delicious crayfish or rainbow trout, washed down with glasses of fine wine that had come from the fledgling vineyards at Moorilla.

At night she lay in his arms, drowsy with their lovemaking, sated and content. Never, in her wildest dreams, could she have imagined a more perfect honeymoon.

'I wish we could stay longer,' Matilda said wistfully as the plane swept from the tiny runway.

Finn took her hand and squeezed it. 'I promise to bring you back before we're both old and grey.' he said, then smiled. 'It will be our own special place.'

They finally arrived back at Churinga to find the Bitjarra gone. They had been drifting away over the past year but now their gunyahs were empty, their cooking fire cold.

Matilda looked at it sadly. It was the end of an era but the beginning of something very much better. Perhaps, in their own mysterious way, they had realised she no longer needed them.

Life fell into an easy pattern. Finn moved his things into the house and arranged for a manager to live at Wilga. He would still breed droving horses but needed someone on the property to look after things. In six months they travelled to Broken Hill and, after one or two other important calls, went to see Geoffrey Banks and signed an agreement to make Wilga and Churinga one property.

Matilda adjusted her will, encompassing both properties, and couldn't help but smile at Geoffrey Banks as she did so. How right he'd been with his advice. Life was indeed full of surprises.

They had returned to Churinga, and Matilda waited until they had finished their evening meal and were sitting on the verandah. Finn pulled her on to his lap and they watched the moon sail above the trees.

'I've got something to tell you, Finn,' she said finally. 'It's to do with that visit I made while you were ordering your new riding boots.'

He was nuzzling her neck, his scratchy chin causing her to tingle with delight. 'Mmmm?'

She pulled away from him, laughing. 'How can I concentrate when you do that, Finn? Stop a minute and listen.'

He softly bit her neck. 'I'm still hungry,' he growled.

'Finn,' she said firmly. 'I've got something to tell you – and it's important.'

He looked at her, his face suddenly serious. 'What is it Molly?'

'We're going to have a baby,' she said quietly, waiting for his reaction.

He stared at her for a long moment and then his awe and delight appeared in a wide grin. He picked her up and whirled her around the room. 'You clever, clever girl! Why didn't you tell me?'

She laughed and begged to be put down. 'Because I wanted to be sure,' she said breathlessly. 'At my age it just seemed so daft.'

He kissed her then with aching tenderness. 'Precious, precious girl,' he murmured against her lips. 'I promise you, our child will have the finest property in New South Wales and the most loving parents. Oh, Molly, Molly. This is the greatest gift you could have given me.'

Matilda hugged her own contentment and joy. She still couldn't believe it, and as the months slid by had to keep putting her hands on her belly to confirm she wasn't dreaming. She yearned for the time to pass quickly and yet was almost jealous of sharing such a miracle.

How lucky she was, she told herself repeatedly. How loved and wanted after all the years of isolation. This child would want for nothing. She and Finn would love and cherish it, and he or she would grow up strong and healthy in the good air of Churinga and Wilga.

The baby was due to be born in the winter. The shearing season was over and as she went into the last six weeks of her pregnancy, Matilda began to feel her energy decline in the humidity. It was already raining and the creek threatened to run a banker. Finn had gone with the men to round up the mob and take them to the higher pastures, and from there he would visit Wilga and make sure it was prepared for the winter.

Matilda moved slowly around the house, the weight of the child making the heat seem more intense. She had planned to finish decorating the nursery Finn had built on to the side of the house, and despite his orders to leave it for him to do, she wanted to surprise him.

Besides, she told herself fiercely, you're getting too soft and lazy sitting around the house all day doing nothing. It's time you got on with something.

She gathered up a bucket of water, a penknife for scraping off old varnish, cleaning cloths and beeswax, and plodded into the nursery. It was small and bright with a large window overlooking the paddock. It smelled of newly cut timber. She had already whitewashed the walls and wanted to paint a mural of Churinga behind the small cot Finn had built several weeks before. The mural was to be a surprise and she was glad he would be gone long enough for her to finish it. He fusses too much, she thought indulgently, and will only get under my feet.

Finn had brought a chest of drawers and a wardrobe from Wilga. Matilda decided that before she could begin on the mural, she would clean them out. Everything had to be just right for when the baby came. She knew this almost obsessive need to clean and dust was all a part of her nesting instincts – much like the wild creatures of the outback.

With the warm water and cloths, she scrubbed away the dust from the bottom of the wardrobe and hummed to herself as she lined the shelves with paper. Then she polished the wood until it gleamed and stood back to admire the effect. The furniture Finn had brought with him had seen better days. Once the pieces had been put in here they'd almost been forgotten in the hurly-burly of the shearing season. Now she was pleased with how the wardrobe looked and turned to the chest of drawers.

As she opened the top drawer, she heard something rattle and then thud. Whatever it was, Finn had obviously forgotten about it. Now it had fallen down the back into the cavity behind the bottom drawer.

One by one she pulled the drawers out and set them in a stack on the floor. Then, puffing and blowing, she got down on her knees and scrabbled about in the dusty darkness. With the bulk of the baby between her and the furniture, it was difficult to see what she was doing.

Her fingers found something slippery and cold. It felt like a tin box. She pulled it out. Catching her breath, she looked at it more closely. It was a long, thin biscuit tin with a faded picture of tartan and thistles on the lid. It had once been filled with shortbread.

She gave it a shake. Something slithered and rattled inside. Intrigued, she prised off the rusting lid with the penknife.

Instead of biscuits, she found a few letters, a couple of newspaper cuttings and some photographs. Putting the letters aside, she looked at the photos. There was the house in Meander, the beach at Coles Bay, and Finn, smiling and proud in his school uniform.

She smiled and kissed the photograph. How she would tease him when he got home. Those knees!

Moving on to the next photograph, her hand stilled and the child in her belly gave a vicious kick. Here was Finn standing between two people Matilda would have recognised anywhere.

'That's impossible,' she breathed.

But when she opened her eyes again and read the newspaper obituaries. She knew it to be true.

And yet it made no sense. No sense at all. For how had the schoolboy Finn ever known Peg and Albert Riley. The Sundowners had gone back to Queensland, hadn't they?

The faces blurred in and out of focus as her thoughts became more contorted. She remembered Peg's voice the last time she'd heard it. It echoed in her head and seemed to fill the room, the house, the paddocks, and the miles between the years.

She stared at the back of the picture, but couldn't read the words that had been written there – couldn't focus at all. Yet she was loath to read them – wanted to turn the clock back – forget the picture even existed. It couldn't exist. Not here on Churinga. Not in a chest of drawers Finn had brought from Wilga.

'No,' she breathed fiercely. 'No, no, no.'

But she couldn't ignore the writing on the back of the picture, and despite her reluctance found herself drawn to it.

*'Good luck, son. Ma and Dad.'*

Matilda swallowed hard and angrily, forced herself to think straight. It had to be a coincidence, she was just being over-dramatic. Peg and Albert had had their own child, changed their name and moved to Tasmania. Of course, that was it. Logical really.

Finn's voice echoed in her head.

*'Ma told me I was adopted. It explained why my dad never showed me any affection.'*

'That doesn't mean anything,' Matilda said into the silence. 'They adopted him in Tassie. It's just a twist of fate he came here.'

She sat on the floor of the nursery, the photograph gripped to her chest as she tried to claw back the calm she knew she would need to recover. She had let her imagination run away with her, she told herself firmly. Women in her condition often went a little mad.

Her gaze fell on the tightly bound stack of letters. With a quick glance she realised most of them were from friends, men Finn had gone to war with, horse breeders and farmers. Matilda began to believe she really had been mistaken.

Then she found the one from Peg.

Mis-spelt, the writing almost illegible, it had obviously been meant to be read after her death. The words danced before Matilda, hammering their message home as surely as nails in a coffin.

*Dearest Son,*

*This has got to be the hardest letter I've ever had to write but you should know the truth, and now I'm gone, I hope you find it in you to forgive me for what I done. I take all the blame, yer dad didn't want nothing to do with it – but fate offered me a chance, and I took it.*

*Yer mum was only a kid herself when she brought you into the world, with not much of a future and no man to care for her. She was real crook after giving birth to you, and when I held you in my arms, I knew I couldn't let you go.*

*I stole you, Finn. Took you away from that poor wronged child and gave you the best I could give, 'cos I knew she wouldn't have been able to look after you even if she'd wanted to – which I doubt. We changed our names to McCauley years ago, but you won't find no papers proving anything, and it's better you don't know where you came from. She thinks you died at birth, Finn. God forgive me for the lie, but me and Bert couldn't have kids, and when I saw you, I knew it was meant to be.*

Matilda was almost numb with shock as the feeling of dread returned full force. Her clumsy fingers knocked the tin as she dropped her hands to her knees and something glinted as it fell to the floor.

She picked it up and let it swing like a pendulum in the sunlight. The gold and enamel glittered as she sat there mesmerised.

Catching the delicately engraved heart, she traced the initials entwined on the back and froze. With a deep breath, she forced herself to open the tiny catch and look at the two faces set in their ornately worked frames – and knew there could be no mistake.

The loss of her mother's locket had always been a mystery. Now it had been returned to Churinga to haunt her.

Her baby weighed heavy within her as she clambered to her feet.

'It's impossible,' she muttered. 'Impossible.'

Silence surrounded her. The day lost its brightness and she thought she could hear Peg's voice again.

'*Your baby died. Your baby died. Your baby died.*'

Matilda covered her ears and stumbled out of the room. Her feet led her on the inevitable journey she had no wish to take – but knew she must. Across the kitchen and out on to the verandah. The nightmare walk she had made once before and would have done anything to wake up from. Then into the yard and through the white wicket gate into the graveyard.

Sinking to her knees in the sodden grass, she looked at the small marble cross she'd bought with her first profits. Rain soaked her hair and trailed it across her face. Her dress clung to her like a second icy skin as she began to dig at the earth with her hands. But she was aware of nothing as she muttered the long-forgotten prayer from childhood.

'Holy Mother of God, blessed art thou amongst women.

Pray for my sins.'

Her hands moved faster, scooping out the heavy, rain-soaked earth, flinging it aside until she reached that rough little home-made coffin.

Finn was twenty-four. Finn was twenty-four.

The thought flew round and round in her head as her numb lips prayed. 'Holy Mother of God, pray for us. Forgive us. Please, God, forgive us.'

The rain and tears were blinding as she scrabbled desperately in the earth to uncover the box. She pushed her hands deeper, grasping the rough sides, coaxing it out of the clinging mud that seemed to want to keep it hidden.

She ignored the pain in her belly and the broken fingernails. Ignored the splinters and the rain. She had to see. Had to find out what Peg and Albert had buried in her graveyard twenty-four years ago.

The penknife slipped between the rusty nails, and with an angry squeal and a splintering of wood the lid came off. Matilda looked down.

The box was empty but for a large brick.

She sat in the rain with the crude coffin in her lap. She was numb. Dead to everything around her. If only the rain could wash away the terrible sin she had committed. If only she could melt into the earth and disappear. If only she could feel nothing for the rest of her life and simply drift into oblivion.

But it was not to be for the deep, persistent vice of pain that came in great, sweeping waves finally broke through her trance, forcing her to move. With the little coffin held tightly to her chest, she began to crawl towards the house. Her innocent child was coming into the world and there was nothing she could do to stop it.

Matilda dragged herself up the steps, over the porch and into her bedroom. The pain was all-consuming, driving its way into her chest, making it hard to breathe, to move, to think. She knew she was about to die, and fate would decide whether her unborn baby would survive – but as all her childhood fears of the Catholic hellfires returned, she knew this was fitting punishment for such wickedness as hers.

'Finn?' she called into the silent house. 'Finn, where are you?' She lay slumped on the bed, mindless of the mud and filth clinging to her clothes and staining the covers. 'I have to tell you, Finn. Have to explain,' she gasped through the pain.

Time lost all meaning as she closed her eyes. When she opened them again she could feel the sticky wetness between her legs. Almost bankrupt of strength, she reached for the diary and began to write. Finn had to know. But if the child survived, it must be cared for and loved somewhere far away where it would never discover the awful truth. There had been enough sin in this house.

The pen finally dropped from Matilda's fingers. She had written all she could, and her child wouldn't wait to be born. The end was near.

# Chapter Twenty

Jenny let the diary fall to the floor as the tears ran unchecked. She'd been right all along, Churinga was cursed. No wonder Matilda haunted the place. No wonder that waltz echoed each time her dress was worn.

She sat on the bed and grieved for Matilda and Finn as she grasped the locket around her neck. Matilda must have died, but what had happened to Finn? The sobs came to an abrupt halt. And what had become of the child? The true inheritor of Churinga.

She dashed away the tears as the questions in her head demanded to be answered. Finn had left Matilda's diaries behind for a reason. He had meant them to be read.

'But by whom?' she whispered. 'Did you hope your child would somehow find its way here to uncover the truth?'

'Talking to yourself, now, eh? Strewth, things must be bad.'

Diane's voice broke into her thoughts, and with a start Jenny blew her nose and tried to compose herself. She knew her face was ashen and her eyelids swollen.

'Whatever's the matter?' Diane sank on the bed beside her, a comforting arm around Jenny's shoulders.

'Matilda married Finn,' she croaked, the onset of more tears threatening.

Diane shrugged. 'So?' She eyed Jenny sharply, then grinned. 'Don't tell me the great cynic has finally gone all romantic and soppy? Jen, you surprise me.'

Jenny pulled away from her. 'You don't understand,' she rasped as she tried to clean up the tears. 'Finn was Matilda's son.'

Dark brown eyes stared back at her. Then Diane gave a low whistle. 'Well, that's a turn up,' she breathed.

Jenny picked up the diary and thrust it at her friend. 'And that's not all, Diane. They had a baby. Peter had no right to this place. Neither do I.' She screwed the handkerchief into a ball then wrestled to take off the locket. 'Even this isn't mine. It was Matilda's, and her mother's before her. No wonder I've been haunted ever since I picked up the diaries.'

Diane ignored the diary and stared back at her. 'That's nonsense, Jen. Peter had every right to buy the place if it was on the market. Perhaps the kid didn't want it. And who could blame it with a history like that to follow on?' Her shoulders slumped. 'Come on, girl. You're just letting things get to you. You've got all worked up over these damn' diaries and let your rather vivid imagination run away with you.'

Jenny slowly shook her head as she thought deeply about Diane's argument. Something didn't feel right. There were still too many questions that hadn't been answered, and having come so far with Matilda, she felt she had to continue until she knew it all.

She snatched back the diary, found the last few pages and held it out to Diane. 'Read this and tell me what you think.'

Her expression must have made Diane realise there would be no point in refusing. After a moment of silence she began to read. When she'd finished, she closed the book and sat for a long moment in a silence which stretched Jenny's patience.

'I think the whole thing's tragic and should be put to rest,' she said finally. 'The child either didn't survive or decided to sell up. No drama. Plain fact. As for the locket . . .' She took it from Jenny and fingered the delicate filigree. 'Peter probably found it here when he first decided to buy Churinga and thought it would make a nice present for you.'

Jenny felt her impatience with Diane grow. 'But don't you see?' she exploded. 'The diaries were left here for a reason. They had to be.' She took a deep breath. 'If the child survived, then why leave them here for anybody to read? Why not destroy them?'

'Jen,' warned Diane. 'Don't go off on that tack again.'

She clasped Diane's hands between her own, willing her to see things as she did. 'But what if that child is alive and doesn't know the truth? What if Finn left the diaries here because he knew the child would return one day? What then?'

'Pure supposition,' Diane retorted.

Jenny snatched up the locket and headed for the door. 'We'll see about that.'

'Where are you going?' Her friend's alarmed voice followed her out of the room.

'To phone John Wainwright,' she called over her shoulder.

Diane hurried after her, pulling her up sharply as she reached for the receiver. 'What good's that going to do? Let it rest, Jen. Enjoy Churinga, the locket, the story you've been privileged to read and live your own life. All second-hand jewellery has a history. That's what makes it so interesting. But old diaries should be returned where they belong. In the past. Nothing you can say or do will alter facts, Jen. What's done is done.'

'But I have to find out what became of them all, Diane. Have to know why Peter was able to buy Churinga. I owe Matilda that much.'

She turned away and as she waited for her call to go through, heard Diane say stubbornly, 'If I can't make you see sense then John Wainwright will.'

Jenny gripped the receiver as the familiar pommy accent drawled at the other end of the line. 'John? Jennifer.'

'Hello, my dear. What can I do for you?'

'How and why did Peter buy Churinga?'

'I explained that before,' he said smoothly.

'John,' she said firmly, 'I know about Matilda and Finn McCauley, and I'm wearing her locket. The locket Peter gave me last Christmas. The locket he said had something to do with my surprise birthday present. Now I want to know how he came by Churinga and the locket, and what happened to the person who should have inherited.'

'Ah.' There was a long silence.

Jenny shot Diane a glance as they both huddled close to the telephone. She had gone cold despite the heat in the kitchen, and although she was eager to find out more, something almost made her disconnect the call.

'What is it, John? What are you so reluctant to tell me?'

401

There was a sigh at the other end of the telephone and the rustling of paper. 'It's a long, involved story, Jennifer. Perhaps it would be better to come back to Sydney so I can explain?'

She almost smiled at the hopeful note in his voice. 'I'd prefer it if you'd tell me now, John. After all, it can't be that complicated.'

Another sigh and more rustling of paper. 'Peter came to me a few years before he died. He'd found a property, Churinga, and wanted me to handle the paperwork. It seemed there was an intriguing history behind the property and he'd spent a long time researching into it before coming to me. Once all the legal work was done, he begged me to keep his new acquisition secret until he'd had time to explain everything to you.'

Jenny frowned. 'Why keep it a secret if the history was that intriguing? I don't understand.'

There was a long pause. 'He knew you'd be upset,' was the quiet reply.

'Then why did he buy the damn' place if he knew that?' She took a deep breath. 'You're not making much sense, John. Is there something you're not telling me?'

Another long silence. 'How did you find out about the McCauleys?'

Two could play at that game. She returned his question with another. 'Did Peter ever come out here, John?'

'Not as far as I know. He was planning to make his first visit with you on your wedding anniversary. That's when he was going to tell you the history of the place.'

'But instead of that he died.'

John Wainwright cleared his throat. 'Peter's death meant I was to oversee the legal handover of Churinga in a particular way. He wanted you to visit the place, see what it was like and get used to the idea before you were told any more.'

'Yeah, I can see why he'd have wanted me to fall in love with the place first.' Jenny looked down at her hand. The locket was coiled in the palm snake-like – waiting to strike. 'If Peter never came to Churinga, how come he gave me Matilda's locket?'

'He came across it during his research into the history of Churinga. But from where, he didn't say,' replied the lawyer quickly. 'But to get on with the question of your inheritance: Peter was the most careful man I've ever met. He always took every contingency into account and insisted upon making his will and stipulating the order in which things should be done if the unthinkable happened. That's why you've rather caught me on the hop. How did you find out about the McCauleys?'

'Peter made a mistake. Missed a vital contingency. He didn't come out here first.' Jenny took a deep breath as she thought of the diaries. 'How much do you know about the McCauleys, John?'

'Nothing much.' His tone changed, sharpened, and she had a fleeting suspicion that she'd missed something.

'They were squatters. Some tragedy occurred and the property was put in trust for their child. The trust was being handled by one of our senior partners who's since retired but evidently there had been some communication between the orphanage and this firm over the years because of the way the trust had been set up.'

'So how did Peter get hold of Churinga? And what happened to the child?'

John's silence stretched for so long Jenny thought the line had been disconnected. 'John? You still there?'

In a deeply reluctant voice, he answered her. 'Peter had done a great deal of research before coming to me. I told him all I knew, which wasn't much. The child had disappeared and the convent was no help. The search was extensive, believe me. Peter was very thorough. But I must stress that everything has been handled according to the best legal practice. The deeds are yours and yours alone.'

'So the trust was revoked?'

'Something like that, yes. I'm sorry I can't be of more help,' he said lamely. 'But Peter kept most of the story to himself.'

Jenny thought for a moment. 'After all his careful planning, I'm surprised he didn't leave a letter or something to explain,' she said hopefully.

'There was a letter originally,' John Wainwright said slowly. 'But he destroyed it, saying it was best if the history behind Churinga came from him. I suppose that despite all his carefully laid plans he never believed he wouldn't be around to tell you.'

Frustration lodged like a lump in her throat and she quickly swallowed it. 'So you never read this letter or knew its contents?'

'No. It was a sealed letter he left in my safe-keeping to be opened only in the event of his death and after you had visited Churinga. I'm sorry, Jennifer. I can't tell you anything more.'

'Then it's up to me to find out the rest,' she said firmly. 'Thanks, John. I'll be in touch.' She put down the receiver, cutting him off in mid-sentence, then turned to Diane. 'Come on. We're going to see Helen.'

Diane looked at her with wide eyes. 'Why? What's she got to do with all this?'

'She'll know where I can find the priest,' Jenny said excitedly as she pulled on jeans and a shirt. 'Finn would have turned to him, I'm sure of that.'

She rammed her feet into boots and stood up. 'I have to know what happened after Matilda died. Where was Finn? And why couldn't anyone find the child?'

Diane grabbed her arm. 'Think about this, Jen. I know you. You get an idea in your head and then rush off where angels fear to tread. Do you really want to dig any deeper?'

She snatched her arm away and thrust through the screen door. 'I can't leave it unfinished, Diane. My conscience won't let me. Besides,' she added as she clambered into the utility and turned the key, 'don't you want to know the rest of the story? Aren't you just a little bit curious?'

Diane was still standing on the verandah in her nightshirt. Uncertainty made her bite her lip, but curiosity shone in her eyes.

'Are you coming or not?'

'Give me a minute.' Diane raced back into the house, slamming the screen door behind her.

Jenny drummed her fingers on the steering wheel as the moments ticked by and her thoughts raced. Father Ryan had to be very old by now. He could be dead or senile or shut away in some monastery where he couldn't be reached. Helen was probably her only chance of finding him.

Diane yanked the utility door open and clambered in. 'Ready when you are,' she said breathlessly. 'But I still think you're playing with fire.'

'Been burned before,' Jenny said grimly as they went through the first of the automatic gates.

She concentrated hard as she steered around potholes and cracks and manoeuvred through gates. The hot wind was whipping up the dust, making the trees dip and sway, sifting the dry earth across their path, masking the makeshift road. Thoughts came unbidden to be instantly dismissed. Matilda's child had been brought up in an orphanage, never knowing the truth of its birth. She knew how that felt. Empathised with the child, feeling its pain, knowing how lost and alone it must have been. It made her even more determined to uncover the truth. If her research led to the unknown child of Churinga, she could live the rest of her life in peace.

As they reached Kurrajong land she saw the men out mustering the last of the mob into the home pastures. There was no sign of Andrew or Charles, no wheelchair parked on the verandah, and Jenny breathed a sigh of relief. Ethan was the last person she wanted to see. Although he probably had most of the answers, she knew he wouldn't tell her.

They wrestled with the utility doors and began to climb the steps to the verandah. With a last glance at Diane, Jenny reached for the bell pull. It seemed an eternity before it was opened.

'Jennifer? Diane? How lovely to see you.' Helen, as elegant as always in pressed slacks and crisp shirt, greeted them with a smile.

Jenny had no time for polite conversation. She pushed her way into the hall and grabbed Helen's arm. 'I have to find Father Ryan,' she said fiercely. 'He has the answers, you see, and you're the only one I could think of who might know where he is.'

'Wait on, Jenny. Calm down and tell me what's happened? You're not making sense.'

Jenny noticed how startled Helen was before she pulled away from her grip and realised her windswept appearance and wild behaviour were making things worse. Helen had no idea about the diaries or about the terrible secret that had been buried for so long at Churinga. She took a deep breath and swept her tangled hair out of her eyes.

'I have to find Father Ryan,' she repeated firmly. 'And

405

you're the only one who can help.'

Helen's troubled gaze dwelt on her face. 'Why, Jenny? What's happened?'

She glanced across at Diane, and bit her lip. There just wasn't time to explain everything now. She was too impatient to get to the truth.

'It's complicated,' she muttered, shifting her feet. 'But it's also very important I find the priest.'

Helen regarded her for a long moment, her cool expression masking what Jenny knew were troubled thoughts. 'Come into my study,' she said finally with a quick glance at Diane. 'We can talk in there.'

Jenny turned swiftly at the sound of heavy footsteps and breathed a quick sigh of relief. It was only the station manager.

'The old man's sleeping and all the others are out mustering,' said Helen gently, as if reading her mind. 'We won't be disturbed.'

Jenny and Diane followed her into the book-lined office and perched side by side on the edge of a leather couch. A dull pain had begun to pulse behind Jenny's eyes and the awful events of Matilda's last few hours were neon bright in her head. She took one of the glasses of neat whisky Helen offered and tossed it back in one. It burned her throat and made her eyes water. She hated whisky but on this occasion it was what she'd needed to clear her head and make her think straight.

'You'd better start from the beginning,' said Helen. She had made herself comfortable in the leather chair behind the ledger-strewn desk. 'This hasn't anything to do with what I told you the other day, has it?' Her voice was soothing in the peaceful room.

Jenny twisted her fingers on her knees. Her impatience had gone and in its place had come a composure she'd never felt before. 'It's probably the last chapter,' she said quietly.

Diane squeezed her hand in encouragement. After a hesitant start, she grew more eloquent. As the final words dropped like cold water into the pool of silence, she waited for a reaction.

Helen came from behind her desk and sat beside the two friends. 'I never realised Matilda had kept a diary or that there was a baby involved.'

Jenny pulled the locket from her jeans. 'I was given this by my husband, and I always wondered who'd owned it,' she said. There was a tremor of something akin to excitement in her fingers as she opened it. 'Do you recognise either of these two people?'

Helen stared down at it. 'I don't know who the woman is,' she said finally. 'But I would guess by the hairstyle and dress that it's Mary, Matilda's mother. The young man is Ethan. I've seen similar photographs in the family albums. He must have been about eighteen or nineteen when this was taken.'

Diane and Jenny looked at each other in amazement. 'I have to find Father Ryan,' Jenny said breathlessly. 'Finn felt deeply about his religion, so it's logical he would have turned to the priest after Matilda died. He's the only link with the past, Helen. The only one who might know what happened to the child.'

Helen chewed her lip. 'There's always Ethan, of course,' she said doubtfully.

Jenny thought about that evil old man in the wheelchair and shook her head. 'Only if there's no one else.'

'I'll ring the presbytery,' Helen said. 'We give enough to the church, it's about time they did something for us.' She smiled at Jenny and Diane. 'As good Catholics we like to ease our way to the pearly gates, and the church always has its hand out.'

'Why not try the old bloke, Jen?' Diane hissed through cigarette smoke. 'Jeez, he was right in the middle of it all. He must know what happened.'

Helen put her hand over the mouthpiece. 'I wouldn't believe him if he told me what time of day it was,' she said grimly. 'Let's try this first.'

Jenny nodded in agreement.

Helen finally got through to someone called Father Duncan but the one-sided conversation shed little light on what was being said at the other end and Jenny and Diane had to wait until she'd finished.

'I see. Well, thank you, Father. By the way, how's the new jeep? Bet it's easier to get about in, eh?' She smiled as she put down the receiver.

'Well?' Jenny stood up.

'Father Ryan's still alive and living in a home for retired priests in Broken Hill. Father Duncan says he writes to him regularly to keep him up with local gossip, and although his sight's failing, most of his other faculties seem to be in good working order.'

She tore off a page from the writing pad. 'Here's his address.'

Jenny took the scrap of paper. Although the address meant nothing to her, she began to feel a tremor of excitement. 'Let's just hope this isn't all for nothing,' she murmured.

Diane came to stand beside her. 'We won't know until we get there, Jen. And seeing as how you're hell-bent on finding out everything all at once, I suppose we'd better make a start. How long will it take to drive to Broken Hill, Helen?'

'We normally use the plane, but with this wind and a storm brewing, it wouldn't be wise.'

'You have a plane?' Diane sounded suitably impressed.

Helen grinned. 'Bit over the top, isn't it? But it gets me out of here in a hurry when the going gets tough.'

She eyed them both, then seemed to come to a decision. 'It's a long way to Broken Hill by car, and if you don't know the roads you could easily get lost if the dust storm gets any worse. Why don't I drive you?'

Jenny glanced at Diane and they both nodded.

'No time like the present. I'll throw a few things in a bag, leave a note for James and we'll be on our way.'

Minutes later, with a bag packed and a note left on the hall table, the three women were in the vast kitchen which smelled of freshly baked bread and roasting meat.

Helen filled two thermos flasks with coffee and ordered the cook to make a mound of sandwiches. 'We'll have to use your ute,' she said. 'James has got ours and the spare is in the repair shed. Go fetch it, Diane, and bring it round to the garages at the side of the house.'

Jenny followed Helen out of the house and once Diane had brought the utility to a halt outside the garages, helped them load the four-gallon drums of petrol into the flat-bed. Two drums of water followed a couple of spare tyres, a jack, a rifle and spade, and a first aid kit. A hessian bag of tools and a collection of spare parts were slung in after them.

408

'Why do we need to take all this?' she asked in amazement. 'Surely Broken Hill isn't that far away?'

'Any travelling out here means always taking this lot with you. We could break down, get a puncture or be bogged down in sand – and we could be stuck out there for days before anyone found us. With this storm brewing, it's more important than ever to be prepared.' Helen climbed in and took Diane's place behind the wheel. 'Come on. Let's get going.'

Jenny and Diane squeezed in beside her and they set off. 'You might look as if you were more at home at a garden party,' asserted Diane thoughtfully. 'But, Helen, you're one tough sheila.'

Helen's polished nails glimmered as she swung the utility from one almost indistinct road to another. 'This is no place for shrinking violets,' she said. 'I learned that pretty damn' quick when I first came here to live.'

She shot a glance at the two young women beside her and grinned. 'But it's fun to pit your wits against the elements and the bloody sheep. They're not much different from women at cocktail parties, you know. All herding together, bleating brainlessly.'

'So how far is it exactly to Broken Hill?' asked Diane after about two hours.

'About four hundred or so miles. Once we reach Bourke, it's almost a straight run along the road which follows the Darling River to Wilcannia and Highway 32. The highway runs through Broken Hill and on to Adelaide.'

Jenny stared out of the window. It was almost midday but the sky was dark with fat, heavy clouds. Thunder rolled in the distance and forks of jagged lightning stabbed the pinnacles of the Moriarty Range. It was strange how life was going on around her, the earth still spinning – and she apart from it all, lost in the world of Matilda McCauley where everything was suddenly too real.

'I wish the storm would break and we could have rain,' said Helen as they reached the metalled road leading to Wilcannia. 'The grass is too dry for an electric storm and there's a real beaut building up over there.' She nodded towards the distant mountains where the clouds were at their most thunderous.

'If you're worried and want to turn back, tell us. We can do this journey another day.' Jenny hauled her thoughts back to the present. She felt guilty at having dragged Helen off on this wild chase but didn't relish the thought of having to turn back – not after they'd come so far.

Helen took her eyes off the road and grinned. 'She'll be right. We've had worse, and goodness knows there's enough blokes back on Kurrajong to take care of things.'

Yet Jenny heard the note of worry behind the bright declaration. Just because she didn't care a damn what happened to Churinga, was it fair to expect Helen to leave her beloved Kurrajong with a storm closing in?

'Are you sure? It's not too late to turn around.'

'Positive. I'm too intrigued. I just hope Father Ryan's got the answers you need. But I wonder if perhaps you should leave it to me to question the old boy?'

Jenny looked at the older woman. Did Helen know more than she was letting on? She decided she was letting her imagination work overtime again and shook her head. 'I know what questions to ask, Helen. Better that I do it.'

She sounded so calm and in control, she thought with surprise, and yet deep down she was excited and fearful of what she might learn. The last few hours had been crazy, and if she hadn't been bouncing about in the middle of the outback with Helen and Diane in the middle of the afternoon, she would have thought she was dreaming. But the questions posed by the omissions in Matilda's diary were clamouring to be answered – and she had no other choice but to pursue them,

They shared the driving and reached Broken Hill as the moon peered through scudding clouds. Realising it was too late to visit the priest, they took rooms in a motel where they had a late meal and fell into bed. All three of them were exhausted.

The next morning was dismal with a weak sun struggling through thick cloud. The wind had dropped but the humidity was high. Before they had finished breakfast, they all felt in need of another shower.

St Joseph's Rest Home was a long white building set in a large shady garden at the far edge of town. Helen pulled on the hand-brake and switched off the engine.

'We could always turn round and forget the whole thing?'

'No fear, not after having come all this way.'

'Okay. No worries.' Helen's smile was bright. 'Come on then. Let's see if the old boy has anything interesting to tell us.'

Brett woke to an all too familiar silence that didn't bode well. He clambered out of bed and looked outside. It was half-light and gloomy, which matched his mood. The heat was intense despite the earliness of the day and threatening clouds loomed low over Churinga. Not a breath of air stirred the trees or ruffled the crisp, dry grass. The storm was about to break.

He looked at the letter he'd taken so long to write the night before, and stuffed it in his pocket. It could wait. The stock needed seeing to, the fences checking just once more, for although they were already mustered in the two nearest paddocks, they would soon panic once the storm hit.

Lighting a cigarette, he looked towards the main house and frowned. There was something wrong, something missing. Then he realised that although the hippy van was still there, the utility was gone.

'Any you blokes moved the ute?' he shouted into the drovers' barracks.

They shook their heads and turned over in their bunks.

He looked back at the house. The lights were on and the curtains were drawn, nothing much looked out of place, but still he had the feeling something was wrong.

'Bill, you and Clem ride the paddocks today. Jake, Thomas, get the others and see to the stock. Batten down all the buildings and make sure the machinery's in the barns. Get the boys to check the dogs and pigs are penned safely, and while you're at it, make them clean up the bloody yard. There's tools and stuff out there which'll be blown into the next state when the wind gets up.'

He left the men grumbling and strode out of the barracks towards the house. Delivering the letter to Jenny would be a good excuse to make sure everything was all right. He knocked on the screen door and waited.

Ripper barked and Brett could hear the frantic scratch of his claws on the front door. He knocked again. She should have come to the door by now. Even if she and her friend were

411

asleep, Ripper was making enough racket to waken the dead.

'Mrs Sanders? Jenny? It's Brett.'

There was still no reply and he decided enough was enough. The feeling that something was wrong could no longer be ignored. He opened the door and was bombarded by Ripper.

'What's the matter, boy?' Brett squatted down and stroked the pup's head as he looked around the silent home. The lights were on, the bedroom doors were open, there was obviously no one at home. Several puddles on the floor were evidence that Ripper had been alone for some time and, from the way he was whining, Brett suspected he hadn't been fed either.

He walked into the kitchen and quickly opened a tin of dog food. He stood thoughtfully watching the pup gobble it down.

'Poor little bugger,' he muttered. 'But I wish you could tell me what's going on here.'

Leaving the pup to his meal, Brett made a hurried search through the deserted house. He stood in the doorway of Jenny's room and looked at the mess. The diaries were scattered across the unmade bed, clothes dropped on the floor or flung over the chair.

'Jenny,' he yelled. 'Where the hell are you? Answer me, dammit!'

He stood in the middle of the kitchen and ran his hand over his chin. He'd forgotten to shave, but that was the least of his worries. There was no sign of either woman outside and all the horses were still in the paddock so it stood to reason they must have taken the utility.

Slamming through the screen door he ran from barn to shed, from pen to slaughter house. None of the men had borrowed the ute and no one had seen the women leave.

'There's nothing else for it,' he muttered. 'I'll have to get on the two-way and try to track them down.' He marched back to the main house, temper rising with each stride. 'Silly bitches,' he hissed. 'Fancy going off for a bloody drive when this storm's about to break. Jeeezus!'

He stormed into the house and picked up the receiver. She's probably gone chasing after Charlie, he thought grimly. The sooner I leave the better. I'm far too old to be wet nursing a bloody townie.

'Kurrajong. This is James. Over.'

412

'Brett Wilson,' he replied curtly. This was no time for civilities. 'Is Mrs Sanders there?'

'Sorry, mate. She and my wife have gone to Broken Hill on some errand. I only found the note last night. Been out mustering the mob. Over.'

Brett gripped the mike. Of all the stupid, inconsiderate, hare-brained, bloody silly things to do! He took a deep breath and tried to remain calm. 'Any idea when they plan to get back? Over.'

'You know women, mate. When they go shopping they could be gone for weeks. How's things over there, by the way? Storm's building up here. Over.'

Brett thrust his uncharitable thoughts to one side. 'Same here, mate. Reckon it'll hit soon – been too long in coming. Over.'

'Gonna be a fair cow when she does. Good thing the women are out of it. I'll get Jenny to call you when she gets back. Over.'

'Yeah, right. Good luck, mate. Over and out.' Brett hooked up the mike and tuned in the radio to the weather station. None of the news was good. The storm was dry and ferocious and had already hit the south-east. Now it was heading their way fast. There was nothing they could do but batten everything down and wait for it.

He called Ripper and left the house. James was right about one thing, he acknowledged. The women were best off out of it. The last thing he needed was a couple of terrified females clinging to him when he was needed elsewhere. Yet he couldn't quite bury the thought that he wouldn't mind Jenny clinging to him – in fact, would rather like it.

'Get your brain in gear, Brett Wilson,' he muttered crossly. 'Stop mooning about and get to work.'

Ripper followed him everywhere in the next three hours as he organised the men into working parties and made sure everything was stowed away. The pup seemed lost without Jenny, and Brett knew how he felt.

With frequent returns to the house to check on the weather reports and listen in to the other squatters report their damage, he plotted the storm's path. Then he heard the words he'd been dreading.

413

'We got fire heading our way. It's about fifty miles south of Nulla Nulla and moving fast. We need every man we can get.'

Jenny clambered down after Diane and looked at the line of elderly men sitting in the shade of the verandah. 'I wonder if one of them is Father Ryan?'

Diane shrugged. 'Maybe. All I know is they look horribly lonely and forgotten sitting there in their rocking chairs. I reckon we're probably the first visitors any of them have had for years.'

As they trooped through the front door and into the reception hall, Jenny glanced at Diane. She had the unnerving sensation of having been here before. Then she realised it was the smell of furniture polish and antiseptic which had reminded her of the orphanage and Waluna. The crucifix on the wall and the small statuette of the Madonna and child brought all those memories back – and she could see by the pallor of Diane's face that it was the same for her.

The click and rustle of rosary beads against habit made her turn to face the nun who'd appeared from behind a highly polished door. Her courage almost failed her and she grasped Diane's hand for support.

As she looked into the face she realised it wasn't Sister Michael – but she could have been a close relative. Tall and austere, her white wimple cruelly pinched her thin face. With her hands clasped beneath the wide sleeves of her robe, the nun regarded them with unblinking hostility.

Helen seemed unperturbed. 'We've come to visit Father Ryan,' she said coolly. 'I understand Father Duncan telephoned to inform you of our arrival.'

The nun ignored her and cold, sharp eyes rested on Jenny and Diane. 'I can't have Father disturbed by visitors,' she said forcefully. 'He needs to rest.' She eyed each of them imperiously. 'Five minutes. That's all I'll allow.' She turned on her heel and strode down the long corridor.

Jenny and Diane exchanged horrified glances before they followed her. This was Sister Michael incarnate and they had been reduced all too swiftly to two little girls who had lived in terror of her cruelty.

Jenny followed the swishing habit and remembered how it

414

had been when she was just five years old. She had wondered then if nuns had legs and feet at all or if they were propelled by wheels for they'd seemed to glide everywhere on those highly polished floors. But when she'd asked, she'd been smacked hard across the face and told to make a penance of two rosaries and three Hail Mary's.

It wasn't until much later that her question was answered by a gust of wind which had whipped up Sister Michael's skirts. And as she'd gazed in astonishment at the marbled columns of flesh encased in heavy, gartered stockings, she'd received a well-aimed box around the ears for her newly found knowledge.

Nasty, vicious old bitch, she thought. Sister Michael had only succeeded in beating any love of religion out of her. Now she couldn't even go into a church without cringing.

'You have visitors, Father. Don't let them tire you,' said the nun as she yanked at his pillows and punched them into place. 'I'll come back in five minutes,' she warned, giving all three women a frosty glance before leaving the room.

Diane and Helen held back as Jenny hesitantly approached the old man. He looked so frail against the white cotton sheets and pillowcases, and now she was here, she wasn't at all sure she was doing the right thing.

She took his blue-veined hand gently in her own and held it. She'd thought long and hard during the drive of how she would approach this most delicate of situations, and had decided to come straight to the point.

'I'm Jennifer Sanders, Father. And this is Helen and Diane.'

The priest lifted his head and Jenny saw the milky clouds that blinded him. She experienced a pang of uncertainty. What could this old man tell her that she didn't already know, or at least suspect? He was old and should be left in peace.

'Jennifer, is it? Well now, there's a thing.' He fell silent for a moment then twisted awkwardly. 'Would you be moving these darn' pillows for me?' They're the very divil and give me a crook in the neck.'

Jenny smiled. Father Ryan might be old but his Irish outspokenness hadn't left him. She quickly adjusted the pillows. There wasn't much time. Sister would be back soon.

'I need to talk to you, Father,' she began. 'About what happened to Finn McCauley. Do you remember him?'

The priest lay still for a long time then turned his rheumy eyes on her. 'What did you say your name was?'

Jenny swallowed her impatience. 'Jennifer Sanders, Father.'

'Would that be your maiden name, child?' he asked softly.

With a puzzled frown to Diane and Helen, she shook her head. 'No, Father. I was christened Jennifer White. Evidently the list was down to W by the time I reached the orphanage.'

The old man nodded, his long sigh whispering like dry leaves on rough ground.

''Tis God's will you came in time, my dear. You have been on my conscience for many a long year.'

Jenny drew back from him. This was not what she'd been expecting. 'Why should I be on your conscience, Father?'

The old man closed his eyes and sighed. 'It was all so long ago. So many years of torment for your poor mother. But it started long before then . . . long before.'

Jenny froze. His words had dripped like ice into her heart and buried themselves deep. 'My mother?' she whispered. 'What about my mother?'

He was silent for so long Jenny wondered if he'd either fallen asleep or merely forgotten they were there. Either way, he'd muddled her up with someone else, that was for sure.

'Old boy's lost the plot, Jen. I knew this was a mistake.' Diane reached over and clasped her hand. 'Come on. Best leave him to it.'

Jenny was about to stand up when his frail voice stilled her. 'I first realised all was not well when I heard Mary Thomas' dying confession. She had married one man but loved another. Her child was not her husband's.'

'Then there was no doubt Matilda was Ethan Squires' daughter?' Helen interrupted.

The old priest lifted his milky gaze at the sound of her voice. 'None whatsoever. But she kept her secret right until the end. Mary was very strong, you know. Like her daughter.'

Jenny relaxed. Muddled he might be but at last she was finding out about Matilda and her family. What did it matter if he thought he was talking to someone else?

416

'I remember Matilda and Finbar coming to see me about their wedding. They were so happy then. So full of joy and looking forward to the future. It was a cruel thing that happened. Cruel and unjust after all Matilda had gone through.' He fell silent.

'I know what happened, Father. I found her diaries. Tell me what Finn did after Matilda died!' She took his frail hand and felt his pulse. It was thready, but his grip was firm.

'Your father called me out to Churinga to give your mother a decent burial. 'Twas a miracle she lasted long enough to give you life, Jennifer.'

'My fa—?' Her breath was trapped in her chest, making her head spin and the floor heave beneath her. This was crazy. The old boy must be rambling. 'Father, you're mistaken,' she manager to stutter. 'My name is Jennifer White. I am not related to Matilda or Finn.'

He sighed again and gripped her hand a little tighter. 'Jennifer White was the name they gave you. Jennifer McCauley is the one you were born with.'

He didn't seem to notice the electricity in the air. The stunned silence. The look of horror on Jenny's face as she sat there frozen, pulse drumming so loud and hard she thought it would burst from her chest.

'You were a poor little scrap. Yelling for your mother's breast and filling the house with your noise. Your poor father was heartbroken and at his wit's end.'

The silence was almost tangible as he paused for breath. Jenny was only half aware of Diane's hand gripping hers. Images from the diary were coming alive, parading before her, tearing her apart. And yet his voice would not be stilled.

'We buried your mother in the little cemetery on Churinga. And it was right she should be laid to rest with prayers and holy water. She had not knowingly sinned – was more sinned against. I stayed on for a few days to help Finn. He needed someone to see him through that most terrible of times.'

The priest fell silent as if lost in his memories. The only sound in the room was the rattle of air in his lungs as he breathed.

The tears were hot against Jenny's chilled face but the

compulsion to know everything had grown even stronger. 'Go on, Father,' she urged. 'Tell me the rest.'

'Finn read the diaries.' He turned his blind gaze towards her and tried to sit up. 'Finn was a God-fearing man. A good man. But reading those diaries so close after her death turned his mind. It was his darkest hour. Far darker than any battle-field. He told me everything. 'Tis a terrible sight to see a man destroyed and to have to watch as his spirit's crushed. There was nothing I could do but pray for him.'

The image this conjured up was too painful to bear. Jenny fought hard to maintain control. Give in now and she would be lost.

The old priest rested back on his pillows, his voice cracking with emotion. 'I've never felt so helpless in my life. You see, Finn couldn't believe that God would forgive him. And that's what finally destroyed him.'

The door opened and the nun stood on the threshold, arms folded, face grim. Jenny glared at her – wanting her gone – needing to hear the rest of the old man's story, knowing it could only bring pain.

'It's time for you to leave. I won't have Father upset.'

Father Ryan seemed to have found an inner strength. He raised himself on his pillows and shouted, 'You'll shut that door and leave me with my visitors.'

The austere expression faltered into confusion. 'But Father . . .'

'But nothing, woman. I have important things to discuss. Now go. Go.'

The nun eyed each of them with cold fury, then sniffed and shut the door rather too firmly on her way out.

'That one will never learn humility,' he muttered as he reached for Jenny's hand. 'Now, where was I?' His breath wheezed in his chest as he collected his thoughts.

Jenny couldn't answer him. She was in an agony of bewil-derment and disbelief.

'Finbar sat for hours holding you. I hoped it would bring him some kind of peace. But Matilda had left him a letter telling him to take you away from Churinga and he desper-ately wanted to do the right thing.'

The priest patted her hand and smiled. 'He loved you very

much, Jennifer. I hope that's a comfort to you.'

She squeezed his hand. It was a gesture that helped them both, and with it came the realisation that his words had indeed brought a degree of comfort to the torment of the past few minutes. 'Yes, Father,' she murmured finally. 'I think it is.' She wiped away the tears and squared her shoulders. 'But I need to know what happened next!'

The priest sighed and a tear slowly trickled down his own sunken cheek. 'Your father drew up a will and I witnessed it. He spoke to the manager of the Bank of Australia in Sydney and arranged for Churinga to be held in trust for you until your twenty-fifth birthday. Then, against my advice, he called in the manager of Wilga and arranged for him to take over.'

He grasped Jenny's hand tightly and she leaned towards him – dreading what was to come, but knowing she must hear it all if she was to understand anything of what her father had wanted for her.

'I had no idea what was going through his mind, Jennifer. No idea at all. He wouldn't listen, you see, and not even prayer could make him see reason. I failed as a priest and as a man. There was nothing I could do but stand by and watch him destroy everything he and your mother had built between them.'

'Destroy? You mean he wanted to destroy Churinga?' Jenny leaned forward and stroked back the wisps of hair from the old forehead and wiped away his tears.

'No.' The priest's voice was bitter. 'He wanted to keep it for you. He destroyed himself. Destroyed your life and any hope he might have had of making a home for you.'

'How did he do that, Father?' she whispered, already suspecting the answer.

'He decided to take you to Waluna. To the orphanage of the Sisters of Mercy where your identity would be concealed by a new name. The only link with Churinga was your mother's locket which he gave to the nuns for safe-keeping until you came into your inheritance. I tried to stop him but no words could reach him by this time. I had to watch him drive away with you in a basket on the seat beside him.' Father Ryan sniffed and blew his nose. 'If only I'd known what he was planning to do, maybe I could have stopped him. But hindsight makes fools of us all.' He faded into silence.

So that was how Peter had come by the locket. His research had taken him to Waluna and the orphanage. Jenny looked at the priest through fresh tears. He was old and tired and the burden he'd carried for so long had exhausted him. She sat back in the chair, his frail hand still cradled in her own as she tried to imagine that last journey with her father. What terrible things had been going through his mind? How had he been able to hand her over, knowing he might never see her again?

The priest's voice startled her from her thoughts, bringing her back to the cheerless room.

'I went back to Wallaby Flats. My conscience was bothering me, and for the first time in my adult life, my faith deserted me. What good was I as a priest when I couldn't find the right words to help a man in torment? What good was I as a man when I'd never known what it was to love a woman – or have to make a decision about my child? I had failed on both counts. I spent many hours on my knees but the peace I had always found in prayer seemed to elude me.'

Jenny felt a sickening plunge in her stomach as she waited for the old priest to put into words what she dreaded hearing.

'I wrote to Waluna and they told me you'd arrived, and that your father had arranged for money to be paid regularly into their account for your keep and well-being. I asked after you but all they would say was you were thriving. I kept up a regular correspondence with them over the years but they never told me much. You see, my child, I felt responsible for you. If I'd been strong enough in my faith, I could have stopped your father from committing the greatest sin of all.'

Here it comes, she thought. I don't want to hear. I don't want to believe it – yet it's inevitable.

'Finn went missing shortly after you were left at Waluna. I thought perhaps he'd gone walkabout to try and recapture some sense of peace in isolation. In a way it was a relief because I'd feared something far worse . . .'

The spark of hope died in the cold reality of his next words.

'A couple of drovers found him out in the bush and called the police. Luckily I had some influence. After they'd established his identity, I managed to persuade the police to keep it hushed up. It wasn't difficult. The drovers were only passing through, and the police didn't care one way or the other – they weren't local, you see.'

He patted her hand, his old face creased with concern. 'I knew you'd come back one day, Jennifer, and I didn't want your future tainted by what happened. But I suppose you've already guessed, haven't you?'

'Yes,' she said softly. 'But I'd like you to tell me anyway. It's better to know it all, then there's no room for doubt.'

He rolled his head against the pillow. ''Twas a terrible thing that he did, Jennifer. A mortal sin in the eyes of the church – and yet, as a man, I could understand why he did it. He had driven into the bush and turned his own gun on himself. The coroner said he must have been there for six months or more before the drovers found him. But I knew when he'd done it. It must have been the day he left you at Waluna. He'd planned it all along.'

Jenny thought about the loneliness of her father's death. Of the torment and pain such a gentle, religious man must have gone through to drive out into the middle of nowhere and put a gun to his own head. She dropped her face into her hands and gave in to the anguish.

Yet the tears weren't for herself alone, but for her parents who'd paid such a terrible price for falling in love, and for the priest who'd carried the burden of his loss of faith to this cheerless place where he would end his days, never knowing what he could have done to prevent such a tragedy.

When the tears finally ran dry and Jenny felt more in control, she looked once again at the old priest. He seemed very grey against the whiteness of the sheets and pillows – as if his life-force had been spent in the effort of relieving his burden.

'Father Ryan, I want you to believe you couldn't have done more. I've returned to Churinga strong and healthy, and because of my mother's diaries I now know my parents wanted only the best for me. I've come to love them through you, and the diaries, and to understand why my life began as it did. You have nothing to feel guilty about and I'm sure your God is waiting to welcome you with open arms. You're a good, kind man. I wish there were more like you. God bless you, and thank you.'

She leaned over the bed and kissed his cheek before

cradling him in her arms. Their tears intermingled as their heads rested together on the pillows. He was so frail and she wanted to find the right words to comfort him, but she knew his redemption could come only from the restoration of his faith.

'Is there anything I can do for you, Father? Anything you need?' she said finally.

'No, my child,' he whispered painfully. 'I can die peacefully now in the knowledge some good has come out of the tragedy. On your way out, would you ask Sister if Father Patrick could come and see me? I think it's time I made my last confession.'

Jennifer gripped his hand. 'Father, don't let go now. I'll stay here in Broken Hill and visit you every day. I'll bring you fruit and little treats, keep Sister off your back. Anything.'

The priest smiled. It was a gentle, sweet smile. ''Tis time, my child. Life is a circle and you have returned where you belong. As we all return eventually. Now go and get on with your life and leave an old man to his confessor.'

Jenny kissed the gnarled hand. 'Goodbye then, Father. God bless you.'

'God bless you, child,' he whispered as he lay back against the pillows. Then his eyes closed and his face became serene.

'He hasn't . . .?'

'No, Diane. He's just sleeping,' said Jenny softly.

'Come on, you two, let's get out of here,' hissed Helen. 'I'll look for the dragon lady, you wait for me in the ute.'

Jenny took the keys and she and Diane began the long walk down the silent corridors. She could hear their footsteps on the polished wood. They made a lonely sound, echoing the emptiness in her heart.

As they stepped out into the fragile sunlight, she looked up at the lowering sky. How she wished she could turn the clock back to the time of ignorance. What good was her inheritance when it had been forged in deception and betrayal? How was she supposed to live now, with the knowledge that her father had died by his own hand and her mother of a broken heart?

Sister Michael had been right all along. She was a freak. A bastard born from an unholy union, with the Devil's mark on

422

her foot to prove it.

Blindly she clambered into the utility. 'It's all so unfair,' she choked. 'Why, Diane? Why did it have to happen to them – to me?'

'I don't know, darling. For once in my life I can't find the words you need me to say. I'm so sorry.'

'I need to be alone, Diane. Please try and understand.'

Jenny stared out of the window as her friend went back into the rest home but saw nothing through the tears. John Wainwright had lied – he'd known all about the trust fund, known about her real identity. He just didn't have the balls to tell her. Peter must have known too. That was why Churinga had been kept such a secret. Why she hadn't been able to inherit until her birthday. Secrets and lies. What a tangled web they'd woven.

Pain turned to rage, then sorrow. She lost all sense of time and place as she stared through her tears out of the window. Then the faint, distant chords of an orchestra drifted back to her and she thought she could see a woman in a green dress, waltzing with her handsome husband. They were smiling at each other, lost in happiness.

Just before they faded into the great stretch of the outback, they turned towards her and Matilda whispered: 'This is my last waltz, darling. Just for you.'

Jenny collapsed over the steering wheel as her redemption came. It cleaned deep and began to heal the wounds.

When she finally dragged herself back to reality, she realised she'd been given a choice. Matilda and Finn had died in the hope the past would be buried so that she could take over the running of Churinga and bring new life and a brighter future to the land they had worked with such love. She could either fulfil their dream or turn her back and run away to Sydney.

The words of the old Aborigine came back to her.

'The first man said to the first woman, "Do you travel alone?"'

'And the first woman replied, "Yes."'

'The first man took her hand. "Then you will be my wife and we will travel together."'

Jenny sat very still. She finally understood what her decision must be. She loved Brett and couldn't imagine Churinga without him. Despite all that had happened between them, she would tell him how she felt. If he really didn't care for her, she would have to travel alone for a while. But if he did. Then . . .

'What's the matter, Jen? You've gone a very strange colour.'

Diane's voice brought her back. 'Get in, Di, We're going home. Going back to Churinga.'

# Chapter Twenty-One

Brett snatched up the mike. Nulla Nulla was only a couple of hundred miles south of Wilga.

'Churinga here. I'm sending over my men. Should be there in about five hours, Smokey. Can you hang on till then?'

Smokey Joe Longhorn's weary voice came back down the wire. 'Don't know, Brett. Already lost half me mob. It's a bastard. Moving faster than a freight train. Get out here as soon as. You'll be next if we don't stop it. Over.'

Brett slammed the receiver down and ran out the door. Ripper chased at his heels, ears flat, eyes wide. The heat was intense and lightning had begun to flash in the southernmost corner of Churinga. Thunder rolled and crashed overhead and the sky darkened with the threat of more to come as he pressed the fire bell.

Men poured out of the barns and buildings and in from the fields. They ran into the yard and milled around expectantly. Brett looked at each face and saw the same mixture of dread and excitement. There was nothing like fighting the elements. Nothing which pushed a man closer to the limits of his strength than a bush fire. 'There's fire at Nulla Nulla. I need volunteers.'

Hands went up and he chose the youngest and fittest to go with him. He put the others to work digging a wide trench on the southern side of the home paddock. Trees would have to be cut down and scrub cleared. The stock moved as far north as possible. Churinga had to be saved at all cost.

The men raced for axes and spades, picks and shovels. Brett shut Ripper in the house then drove the old four by four out of the shed. The jeep could travel fast over the rocky ground and the quickest way to Nulla Nulla was over the paddocks, through Wilga and then south. But it was a bloody nuisance not to have the utility. He'd give Mrs high and mighty Jenny Sanders a piece of his mind when she got back, that was for sure.

And if he was really pissed off, he'd put her over his bloody knee and give her a good thrashing.

The ten volunteers clambered into the back with sacking and spades, water bags and rifles. Their voices were high with excitement as they laughed and joked about what was ahead, but Brett knew that beneath the veneer of bravery, each man was terrified. He slammed his foot onto the accelerator and they tore out of the yard in a cloud of dust.

Lightning lit up the landscape in the gloom of the thunder clouds. As they careered over the paddocks, he saw it lick the tips of the ghost gums and jump from hill to valley, cloud to cloud.

Smokey Joe was right, he thought. It was a bastard. And as this was only the edge of it, it was sure to get worse the further south they travelled.

There was a two-way radio in the jeep and Brett kept in touch with the fire's progress.

'Turned nasty, mate,' Smokey Joe gasped. 'Split into two forks heading your way south and east. Nulla Nulla's surrounded.'

'You all right, Smokey?' Brett yelled above the roar of the engine.

'Family okay but me mob's gone. Lost a coupla good men too. On our way to Wilga. See you there.'

Brett stared grimly out of the window. He could see the great pall of smoke in the distance and the lick of bright orange where the fire was tearing through the stand of trees on the far side of Wilga. Kangaroos, wallabies, goannas and wombats were teeming out of the bush, heedless of the jeep's wheels in their desperate flight from the flames. Birds filled the air with their beating wings and frantic cries, koalas loped through the brittle grass, disorientated by the noise and the smoke, their babies clinging to their backs. It was as if every living thing was on the move.

426

Brett finally brought the jeep to a skidding halt outside Wilga homestead.

Curly Matthews the manager came to meet them. He was unshaven, his face blackened by smoke and streaked with sweat, his eyes red-rimmed.

'Got the men working the line in the far paddocks.' He took off his hat and smeared a filthy handkerchief across his brow. 'I don't know if we can hold it, Brett,' he said wearily. 'It's pretty much out of control.'

'Have you dug a trench?' He eyed the broiling cloud of smoke that seemed to be drawing closer every second.

Curly nodded. 'We got a trench, but the fire's jumping through the tree tops quicker than we can cut the bastards down. Get your men to make a start on that stand over there. If we can get it down and back-burn it, then it might slow things down. It's our last line of defence.'

Brett followed his pointing finger. Chopping down a few trees wasn't going to help much, he realised. The fire was spreading like snakes in the tinder dry grass, dragging the main body of its voracious appetite after it.

'You heard the man,' he yelled to the men clambering from the jeep. 'Go.'

He turned to grip Curly's shoulder. 'Good on yer, mate. But we'd all better get ready to move out of here fast.' Then armed with an axe, he took one of the stock horses and rode out towards the fire.

It was a great boiling tidal wave of red and orange, grey and blue. As high as the sky and roaring like a great beast in agony. The smoke was dense and he pulled a neckerchief over his mouth to stop himself from choking. If they could get the trees down on this side of the property, back-burn it and widen the trench, then maybe – if they had time – they might save Wilga.

He leaped from the horse and hobbled it. He didn't want it panicking and running straight into the path of the fire – he might need it to escape.

Brett joined the long line of men wielding an axe. He could just make out the other line working on widening the trench. He felt the satisfying bite of axe in timber and swung with greater speed and force until the tree collapsed.

427

Then on to the next. Cut. Clear. Move on. Cut. Clear. Move on.

The sweat stung his eyes. The smoke filtered through his makeshift mask and made him cough. But there was no stopping now.

They moved in a silence as grim and unrelenting as the fire until the stand of trees had been felled and cleared. It was too risky to back-burn now. The fire was too near. Then, with shovels and picks and bare hands, they helped with the trench.

Brett looked up and found Smokey Joe working beside him. Their eyes met for a telling instant, then they bent their backs and carried on digging. Words wouldn't save them or bring back the dead – only brute strength and determination.

A fork of lightning licked the dry branch of a gum tree several hundred feet away. The flame ran in a hot, hungry blue line down the white bark to the grass at its roots and within seconds the tree was engulfed. It exploded in a shower of sparks which caught and flared in the eucalyptus haze then grew taller than a man. The flames spread into the grass, and built a wall of flame that grew higher and higher as it raced towards them.

Brett and the others leaped out of the trench and beat at it with their shovels. Smoke stung their eyes and burned their throats. The heat dried the sweat as it trickled down them, scorched eyebrows and crisped the hair on their arms and chests.

'Get out of there! It's turning!'

Brett looked up and saw the fire had almost surrounded them. The horse was wild-eyed, pulling at its hobble, ears flat to its head. Smokey Joe was still pounding his shovel against the flames. 'Come on,' Brett yelled above the roar of the flames.

The old man froze, and Brett could see the blank stare of terror in his eyes. He grabbed Smokey's arm and began to run towards the horse, the flames licking at his boot heels, the heat searing his back.

Smokey Joe stumbled, then fell. He lay still, his chest heaving, his hair shrivelling in the heat.

Brett yanked him up and slung him over his shoulder. He reached the horse and released the hobble. Dumping Smokey unceremoniously across the saddle, he climbed up behind him and turned the horse's head towards the gap in the flames.

It skittered and danced and pawed the air, eyes rolling, ears flat to its head.

Brett pulled on the reins and dug in his heels. Then, reacting to his solid slap on its rump, the animal plunged headlong towards the flames.

Nearer and nearer. The fire was racing them to the finishing line.

Smaller and smaller. The gap was closing fast.

Brett felt Smokey slip in the saddle. He clutched the old man's hair with one hand, the reins with the other. With one last lunge, he drove the horse forward.

Flames reached out on both sides. Furnace heat blasted. Smoke blinded and choked. If ever there was a hell on earth – this was it.

Then they were suddenly out of the circle of fire and hands were reaching up to pull Smokey from the saddle. Brett slid off the terrified horse and led it to a bucket of water. He leaned against its heaving sides and stroked its neck until it had calmed down enough to take a drink.

His back ached and his arms felt like lead weights. He was exhausted. Reaching for a water bag, he drenched the smoke and heat from his mouth and throat, and dowsed his head. The fight wasn't over. The fire had grown and was out of control.

He looked at the others who sat in the dirt, heads lowered, every muscle showing signs of weariness. The roar of the inferno was deafening. All they could hope for now was a change in the wind. Or the arrival of rain. And it didn't look as if it would rain.


Jenny drove back along the highway towards Churinga and home. She was impatient to get there and the road seemed never-ending.

Father Ryan's revelations still haunted her, just as much as the thought of all those years in the orphanage. They had lied to her, cheated her of her rightful inheritance, abused the faith her father had put in them. If it hadn't been for Peter's determination to uncover the truth, she would never have known. She felt a hand on her arm and glanced across at Diane.

'I know how bitter you must be, Jen. I'd feel just the same.'

'Bitter?' she replied thoughtfully. 'What's the point? The nuns did what they did, and I suppose they had their own reasons.' She gave a grim smile. 'As Helen said, the church always has its hand out for something. I must have represented the goose that laid the golden egg. But that's all behind me now. I have an identity at last – and a home. And I plan to make the best of that.'

'You also have a family, Jen.' Helen said softly. 'And I know I speak for us all when I say how welcome you are.'

'Even the old man?' Jenny laughed. 'I doubt it!'

Helen's mouth twisted wryly. 'It's what he always wanted, Jen. A member of the family owning Churinga.'

'Ironic, isn't it? But he'll never get his hands on it while I'm still alive, I promise you that.'

Helen squeezed her arm. 'Good on you. Things should liven up considerably with you around. I'm glad I can call you sister.'

Jenny laughed. She hadn't really digested the full ramifications of being Jennifer McCauley, but it would be nice to have a family. Finally to belong somewhere.

'What about the house in Sydney?'

Diane was chain smoking and Jenny realised that the last few hours had been hard on her too. 'I'll probably rent it out or even sell it. I can paint here just as well as anywhere, and there's so much to commit to canvas – I reckon I'll never run out of subjects.'

Diane was silent for a moment and Jenny knew what she was thinking. 'I can still come to the city to exhibit, Diane. And I'll keep my share of the gallery.'

Her friend let out a sigh of relief. 'Thanks. There's no way I can afford to run the gallery on my own, and I don't really want Rufus taking over and interfering.'

'I don't like the look of that sky over there,' said Helen suddenly as she switched on the radio. 'Reckon we could be heading for trouble.'

They pulled over to the side of the road. The roar of the utility's engine was drowning the newscaster.

'A bush fire is sweeping across the north-western corner of New South Wales today. It is estimated there have already been six lives lost and several million dollars worth of property and stock destroyed. What began as four isolated fires has become a raging inferno due to the electric storms that have been brewing over the past few days. Coupled with the lack of rain, it is thought this could be the biggest fire in Australia's history and the emergency services of all mainland states have been called in.'

Jenny slammed the ute into gear and rammed her foot to the floor. 'Hang on, girls. We're in for a bumpy ride!'

Lightning ripped across the sky and bounced between the clouds. It cracked through the bass of the thunder as it split trees and left flames in its wake. The wind freshened, bringing small spirals racing across the earth to lift the flames and fan them to greater heights. Trees lay blackened and charred, their branches reaching skyward like hands begging for the rain. But there was to be no salvation.

Men arrived in their hundreds. From Kurrajong and Willa Willa, from Lightning Ridge, Wallaby Flats and beyond. They took turns to beat at the flames, to dig trenches and fell trees. But still the monolith crept towards Churinga. Sparks glowed as they blew in the wind. Flames touched the brittle fodder of dry grass and fed ravenously. The smoke blackened skin and reddened eyes as it rose in great, smothering plumes to meet the thunderous sky.

Wilga's remaining stock had been rounded up and herded over to the northern pastures of Churinga, but there was no telling if they would be safe there. The fire had already spread over five hundred miles and there was no sign of its letting up.

They had tried to save Wilga homestead too but no amount of water could soak the sun-bleached timbers, and Brett knew the same thing would happen at Churinga unless they'd soaked everything thoroughly. He stood with Curly and his family and watched as Wilga was consumed. Inch by inch the buildings caved in until there was only a charred chimney left to stand sentinel.

'Get in the jeep and drive to Wallaby Flats. I got enough to worry about here.' Curly hugged his kids and kissed his wife before watching the jeep disappear in the smoke.

'Jeez, I hope they'll be right,' he muttered. Then, with a

loud sniff, he turned away, picked up a shovel and joined the others.

Brett thought of Jenny and hoped she and the others were still in Broken Hill. But he had a nasty feeling that if she'd heard the news on the radio, they'd be on their way back.

He swallowed the last of a sandwich, picked up his sack and shovel and wearily headed once more towards the line of fire. The other men were small, dark shadows against the monstrous, orange glow as they beat uselessly against the flames.

Jenny drove the utility into the yard at Kurrajong and came to a screeching halt. Helen leaped out and raced into the house, Jenny and Diane followed closely behind.

'James . . . Where are you? Where is everybody?' Helen's voice was high with fear as she opened doors and ran from room to room.

Jenny shifted from one foot to another. She wanted to be on Churinga, and Helen's frantic search was making her feel more nervous by the minute. And yet she knew they couldn't just walk away and leave Helen alone.

'They've all gone to Wilga. I told them to stay here and look after their own, but they wouldn't listen. Fools!'

The words had been delivered with the speed and ferocity of a machine gun. The three women whirled round to face Ethan Squires.

He was in his wheelchair, two bright spots of hectic colour staining his cheeks. His eyes were wild and his gnarled hands gripped the arms of his chair.

'You'd better get back to your precious Churinga, girlie. It won't be there much longer.' His eyes gleamed maliciously and spittle gathered at the corners of his mouth.

'That's enough, Ethan.' Helen's voice was crisp and cold as she approached the chair and leaned over it. 'What's the damage so far? How close is the fire?'

Jenny held her breath as those hooded eyes settled on her.

'Taken Nulla Nulla and Wilga. Heading for Churinga. I wish I could see it burn. I'd give anything to go and watch.'

'I have to go, Helen. They might need me.' Jenny was already edging towards the door.

432

'Wait on. I'm coming with you,' said Helen, turning away from the old man. 'There's nothing here to keep me and James must already be out there somewhere.'

'You!'

The shotgun blast of his voice froze them. They turned.

Ethan pointed a bony finger at Jenny. 'Child of Satan. Spawn of the Devil. I know who you are – know all about you. You deserve to burn in hell along with your precious Churinga.'

Jenny heard Diane gasp, could feel her tug on her arm, but was transfixed in horror as she watched the old man pull himself from his wheelchair.

'I know you for who you really are, Jennifer McCauley. There are no secrets Churinga can hide from me. I've waited a long time for you to come back.'

His eyes were devoid of sanity but madness had lent him a terrible strength. He shuffled towards her, his outstretched hand trembling with rage. 'Now may the Devil have the pleasure of your company. Burn in hell with your mother.'

Jenny shivered as his hand clawed her arm. She took a step back – and then another, mesmerised by those crazed eyes, almost powerless before the hatred that spewed from him.

Ethan collapsed at her feet, his head hitting the wooden floor with a sickening thud. As he rolled on to his back, his lips curled into a snarl, exposing long, yellow teeth.

'You betrayed me, Mary. Stole what was mine.' Then he was still.

The silence seemed endless as they stared down at him, and Jenny wondered how Mary could have ever loved such a man. But then she supposed circumstances had made him what he'd become. If his own father hadn't been so greedy, they might have stayed together and none of them would have had to suffer the awful consequences.

'I'm so sorry, Jenny. So very sorry.' Helen stood forlornly above the pitiful remains of Ethan Squires. 'He must have known all the time. But how? Who could have told him?'

Jenny looked up, her mind working fast. 'Did Ethan ever visit Churinga during the years between Finn's leaving and my arrival?'

Helen twisted a handkerchief nervously. 'He went over a

433

couple of times in the early years,' she said thoughtfully. 'I remember James saying he didn't like the way he was poking about the place, taking things away.'

Jenny stepped around Ethan's body and grabbed her friend's hands, stilling them. 'Think, Helen. What exactly did he take?'

Her blue eyes stared back, bright with realisation. 'James said he'd taken an old trunk, but after locking it away in his study for years, he ordered it to be returned.'

'The diaries were in that trunk, Helen. That's how he knew. And I bet you a dime to a dollar he returned the trunk about the same time Peter discovered the connection between me and Churinga.'

Helen looked at her in horror. 'He meant for you to read them?' she breathed.

Jenny nodded. 'He knew Churinga would never be his once I was found. It was his final act of spite.'

'Dear God. How can anyone be so evil? But how could he have kept track of what was going on? He hasn't left Kurrajong for years.' Helen frowned, then put her hand over her mouth. 'Andrew,' she gasped. 'He had Andrew spy for him.'

'We don't know that for sure,' Jenny replied firmly. 'But it wouldn't surprise me one bit.'

She looked out of the window. The sky was dark, boiling with the storm. 'The only thing I want to do now is get back to Brett and Churinga. Are you coming too?'

Helen nodded. Without a second glance at the body on the floor, they left the house.

Daylight disappeared. The men were exhausted but still the fire raged. It was impossible to see the sky and the earth was lit by the eerie orange glow of the flames which loomed over Churinga. The men had taken the mob and the rest of the stock to the water hole beneath Tjuringa mountain. The trees were green there and the earth damp from the underground streams. It was their only hope of salvaging anything.

Fire trucks had come from miles around but water was scarce and the pumps soon ran dry. The firemen turned to beating at the flames with sacking and branches and anything else they could lay their hands on.

And still the fire roared across the paddocks and headed for Churinga homestead.

Feet trampled over the small cemetery and the vegetable garden, spades desperately cleared scrub and axes tore down trees. Water was carried in buckets from the stream and thrown over dry timber walls. Still the flames marched on.

Brett ran into the house, grabbed Ripper who was cringing in the bedroom and threw him into Diane's camper van. Then he returned to salvage what he could.

The two-way radio was ripped out and stashed in the back. This was followed by the box of paintings Jenny had obviously packed away to take back to Sydney and an armful of the women's clothes. He caught sight of the lovely dress Jenny had worn to the dance and couldn't bear the thought of it burning so added that to the pile. The diaries lay scattered around the room. After a moment's hesitation, he left them there. Fate would decree whether they survived or not.

He hurried back into the house for the last time. The silver and linen had been at Churinga for years. It was too valuable just to leave. Dumping the whole lot into the camper, he grabbed hold of Clem who was wearily leaning against the barn drinking tea.

'Drive this to Wallaby Flats and make sure it's locked up good before you leave it,' he said, handing over the keys. 'Take the pup to the pub.'

'I can't leave me mates and go swanning off to the bloody Flats, Brett.'

'You'll bloody do what I tell you,' he snarled. 'There's bound to be a lift back here soon enough and you're too tired to be of much use right now.' He slammed the door on further argument and walked away.

At least Jenny'll have something to remember Churinga by, he thought as he watched the camper disappear down the road. Because the way it looks at the moment, it's doomed.

The majority of the men had been on their feet for more than three days and nights with no more than a few hours' snatched sleep. But still they kept battling. The wind had dropped now and with it came the smallest chance of being able to turn the fire before it reached the homestead. Hope was everything. It was what kept them going.

435

Then a spark flew from a pepper tree and settled on the verandah, and within minutes that spark became flame.

'Get a line of water going,' Brett yelled as the fire took hold and began to lick at the walls.

He heard glass explode. The heat grew so intense it was almost impossible to get near enough to dowse the flames. The only way of beating the fire would be to isolate it in the clearing. The men had already dismantled the jackaroos' bungalow and a couple of the barns, now they had to do what they could to damp down the rest of the buildings before the fire reached the storage sheds and garages. The winter feed and hay, the petrol and kerosene, the gas bottles and oily machinery they stored there would only add fuel to the inferno.

Hand over hand they filled the buckets from the trickle of water left in the creek, but it was slow work and there just wasn't enough. Brett looked desperately back at the house. He glanced up and knew he had just one last chance to save Churinga from oblivion. The water tanks at the side of the house.

Quickly leaving the water chain, he gathered a few men together and explained what he wanted them to do. Then, with ropes and pulleys, they approached the homestead inferno.

It would take a brave man or a fool to do what he wanted. Brett had no doubt which one he was – why bother when it was soon to belong to Kurrajong? But he was damned if he was going to stand by and see it burned to the ground, and he wasn't going to ask the others to risk their lives.

Taking the ropes, he edged towards the nearest tank. The heat seared his face and he was driven back. He dipped a cloth in a bucket of water and draped it over his head, then took a deep breath and ran. With the rope circled around the tank, he tied it fast and made his escape.

'Pull!' he yelled. 'For Christ's sake, pull!'

He helped take the strain with the others until the great tank shifted on its pilings and crashed down on to roof of the house. Hundreds of gallons of water flooded over the smouldering wood and red-hot corrugated iron. Glass shattered and wood snapped, but the flames had been dowsed enough for him to make the run for the next tank.

Soaking the cloth once more, he wrapped it around his

head. He could hear some damn' fool bringing a ute into the yard – but he was too preoccupied with what he was doing to give it much thought.

He filled his lungs and dashed for the tank. The remains of Churinga hissed and crackled as he ran over the blazing debris. The rope burned in his hands as he circled the tank, the smoke choked him, ashes stung his eyes and singed his hair. Then a race back to the relatively cooler air, fighting for breath, putting all his weight behind the pulling of the rope.

Hundreds more gallons ran over the house and yard. Flames were quenched, earth became sodden, the dry timber of the remaining buildings soaked it up like blotting paper.

The main body of the fire was even nearer now. The distance it had travelled had done nothing to weaken it.

Another tank. More water. The earth was muddy, hands were stinging, eyes blinded, flesh seared. The smell of singed hair and hot skin mingled with acrid smoke, burning eucalyptus oil and ash. The world seemed full of the sound of animals in fear, of flames out of control and men shouting.

Jenny saw the camper in the distance. She could also see a great pall of smoke and the bright orange glow which had turned day into macabre night – and knew what they meant. She pulled the jeep to a halt and leaped out. Ripper saw her and threw himself out of the window and into her arms.

Jenny held on tightly to his squirming body. 'How bad is it, Clem? Where's Brett? Is he all right?'

'Not good, Mrs Sanders,' he replied, his soot-smeared face almost unrecognisable. 'Brett's with the others. Should be getting back meself, but he said I was to take this lot to the Flats.'

'Bugger that, Clem,' she said firmly. 'You get back to the fire if that's what you want.'

He didn't need telling twice, and as Jenny climbed back into the ute, executed a three-point turn and headed back the way he'd come.

'Tie Ripper to the seat, Diane,' she said grimly. 'Brett's in trouble and I don't want to worry about anything else.'

'So you've decided you do want him, then?' Diane yelled

above the roar of the jeep's engine. 'About bloody time.' She pulled the long silk scarf from her hair and tied Ripper to the metal bar under her seat.

'But what about kids, Jen? Don't you think you should get expert advice before you go haring off with him?' Diane yelled as she clung to the dashboard.

Jenny gripped the steering wheel. She'd had the same awful thought and already dismissed it. 'I had Ben, remember? He was a perfect baby. Why shouldn't I have other healthy children?'

'Too right,' agreed Helen. 'If there was any likelihood of anything going wrong, it would have happened with your first child. And with the incestuous link broken between Matilda and Mervyn the chances are extremely remote.'

'How come you know so much?' said Diane.

'Post grad in genetics,' Helen shouted back. 'Correspondence course I took when the kids went away to boarding school.'

Jenny slammed her foot to the floor and raced for home. She just hoped she wasn't too late.

She finally slewed the jeep to a halt by the creek and almost fell out of the door in her haste to find Brett.

'I'll stay here,' said Diane, shifting into the driver's seat. 'You'll need me to keep an eye on the ute if we have to make a run for it.'

'I'm off to find James. Good luck, Jenny,' shouted Helen over the noise of the fire and the men who fought it.

But Jenny heard none of it. Her attention was fixed on the man struggling to take a rope into the very jaws of the encroaching fire and attach it to one of the water tanks. She'd have known that figure anywhere, despite the wet shirt over his head.

What the hell did he think he was doing?

She put her fingers over her mouth and watched in terror as time and again he disappeared into the smoke and flames and brought down the tanks. She began to pray. She muttered prayers she'd thought long forgotten. Recited rosaries she'd vowed never to repeat. Pleaded with the God she'd turned her back on to keep Brett Wilson safe.

For she knew that if she lost him now, she would truly

believe Churinga was cursed and could never make her home here.

Hands helped to gather the ropes. Wet towels dowsed the smouldering sparks in his hair and clothes. His lungs felt as if they were bursting, and his skin burned, yet Brett knew he had to dredge up the very last ounce of his strength to bring down that final tank.

His sight blurred with weariness as he sucked the smoke-laden air into his lungs and began the last run. He entered the swirling, smothering world of the fire and lashed the rope firmly around the great width of the tank.

Something cold splashed on to his arm. He looked up, wondering if the tank was already unsteady on its pilings. He stepped back and a few more drops fell coldly on to his scorched face.

The rope fell from his numb fingers and he began to laugh as he backed away from the tank. It was rain. Sweet, blessed rain. And not a moment too soon.

He joined the others and stood looking up to the heavens. They opened their mouths and spread their arms to the cold, wonderful water which cooled their skin and washed away the dirt and sweat.

The flames hissed beneath the downpour and within moments the fire crept like a giant wounded beast back into the earth and was still.

Brett closed his eyes and cried.

Suddenly he was embraced by a whirlwind of arms and a torrent of kisses. He opened his eyes and looked down at the beautiful smoke-streaked face he'd thought he'd never see again. He held her tight, wanting never to let her go.

'Oh, Jen,' he whispered. 'Jen, Jen, Jen.'

'I thought you were going to die! Brett, I love you. I've always loved you. Don't leave me. Don't leave Churinga.'

He put a finger beneath her chin and smiled, his own tears mingling with the rain on his face. 'I thought you were going to marry Charlie?' He had to be sure this wasn't a dream.

'Charlie?' She laughed, throwing back her head. 'I love you, you great galah. Not old playboy Charlie.'

With the rain falling in torrents over their heads, he

tightened his hold and drew her even closer. Then he kissed her. 'I love you, Jen. I love you so much,' he murmured against her mouth.

The sound of cheering drew them apart and they emerged like sleepwalkers into the real world to find themselves surrounded by a circle of smoke-blackened faces. They grinned sheepishly as they held hands, and once the applause and well wishes were over, Jenny led Brett to the back of the smouldering house.

The cemetery was flooded, the mounds almost covered by the remains of the homestead. The picket fence was no longer white, the crosses splintered and trampled in the mud.

Brett was puzzled as he watched her pick her way over the smoking debris until she reached the largest stone memorial. He went to her side as Jenny beckoned him.

'The old Churinga is gone, Brett. The diaries, the memories, the past. I understand now why Finn put these words on Matilda's grave. But the fire has cleansed Churinga and put the ghosts to rest. Finally stopped the music. Matilda's last waltz has given us the chance to make a new beginning. One day I'll explain everything – but for now I need to know if you will be a part of that new beginning?'

'You know I will,' he whispered as he put his arm around her.

They turned as one and faced the stone to read the words Finn had so painstakingly carved into it.

*Here Lies Matilda McCauley,*
*Mother, Lover, Sister and Wife*
*May God Forgive Us*